THE MANHATTAN PUZZLE

Laurence O'Bryan has worked in marketing for many years, ten of them in London, until he was made redundant. He then returned to Dublin where he has lived since.

To find out more about Laurence find him on Twitter @LPOBryan, follow him on Facebook at http://www.facebook.com/laurence.obryan or visit his blog www.lpobryan.wordpress.com.

By the same author:

The Istanbul Puzzle
The Jerusalem Puzzle

LAURENCE O'BRYAN

The Manhattan Puzzle

AVON

This novel is entirely a work of fiction.
The names, characters and incidents portrayed in it are
the work of the author's imagination. Any resemblance to
actual persons, living or dead, events or localities is
entirely coincidental.

AVON
A division of HarperCollins*Publishers*
77–85 Fulham Palace Road,
London W6 8JB

www.harpercollins.co.uk

A Paperback Original 2013

1

First published in Great Britain by
HarperCollins*Publishers* 2013

A catalogue record for this book is
available from the British Library

ISBN-13: 978-1-84756-290-6

Set in Sabon LT Std by Palimpsest Book Production Limited,
Falkirk, Stirlingshire

Printed and bound in Great Britain by
Clays Ltd, St Ives plc

FSC™ is a non-profit international organisation established to promote
the responsible management of the world's forests. Products carrying the
FSC label are independently certified to assure consumers that they come
from forests that are managed to meet the social, economic and
ecological needs of present and future generations,
and other controlled sources.

Find out more about HarperCollins and the environment at
www.harpercollins.co.uk/green

I would like to thank HarperCollins, and all the great editors who have helped me, especially Sammia Rafique. Editing is not dead. Far from it. But I must say that all the errors that remain are my responsibility alone.

I would also like to thank all the other truly supportive staff at HarperCollins and all the great editors, designers and translators who are taking this series worldwide.

My heartfelt thanks also goes to all of my wonderful fans and writing friends in Dublin and around the world. Your encouragement and ideas have been truly inspirational. My wife and my children, and all who I have not so far thanked, are hereby acknowledged for the very real support they have provided.

And finally to all my readers, I would like to thank you for coming with me on the journey and for your belief in the power of story. Without you, writers have nothing. Contact me on Twitter with your comments: @LPOBryan.

'Men's evil manners live in brass; their virtues we write in water.'

Henry VIII, Act 4, Sc. 2, William Shakespeare

1

'Go for it. The rougher the better, girl.' The man had a black silk blindfold tied around his head. He spoke slowly, his voice thick with desire.

Xena went to the door and unlocked it.

'What's that? Getting your toys out? Wow, this is even better than you promised.'

Lord Bidoner walked into the panic room. He closed the door behind him and pressed the button to turn on the air management system. The scrubber in the roof could remove the smoke from a blazing fire and turn the output into a vapour trail.

The man, spread-eagled and handcuffed to the stainless steel bed frame, had an expectant smile on his face.

'Go on, do it,' he said.

The navy Calvin Klein silk suit hanging from the stool beside the bed gave an indication of who he was. Lord Bidoner examined the man's wallet. His bank ID card, a credit-card-sized piece of aluminium with an embedded proximity chip and his family name, Hare, embossed on it, confirmed what they already knew.

The head of global security at BXH, one of the world's

few truly global banks, was lying face-up and naked in front of him.

'Don't keep me waiting, girl.'

'I won't,' purred Xena. She stroked his leg, then his inner thigh. He quivered in anticipation.

The man's wife would surely appreciate photographs of this event, but Lord Bidoner had more pressing concerns.

He nodded at Xena.

She was dressed in a low-cut skin-tight black catsuit that fitted her thin frame perfectly. The man laid out in front of them was expecting something memorable from the woman he'd met in the champagne bar opposite Grand Central, two weeks before. Xena's story, about being an Ethiopian diplomat's daughter, and her eager smile, had captivated him.

She ran her finger down the man's stomach. It trembled under her touch.

'Don't stop, honey. Don't stop.'

With her other hand Xena clicked on the silver Turboflame blowtorch, the most expensive model in the world with its 1500C flame. She held the gently hissing blue, inch-long flame up and watched it glow brighter as her fingers moved slowly down his stomach.

'What's that?' he said.

She didn't reply.

Hare's voice was still confident when he spoke. 'Was that your sister who just came in? Is she gonna join us?'

'We have a surprise for you,' said Xena.

The man pulled on the handcuffs, which began to cut into his skin. It had taken a bit of persuasion, since this was their third meeting, for Xena to get him to go this far, but he trusted her now. And he'd made it clear that he wasn't going to put up with any crap. He'd break the bed if she didn't release him when he gave the password.

She'd smiled, hugged him and agreed.

They'd even laughed about making a written contract.

'What's the surprise?' He shook the bed, testing its resilience and the strength of the handcuffs. He'd assumed they were easily breakable toys, like a previous pair she'd shown him. But he was wrong.

And he didn't know that the bed was bolted to the reinforced slab of the panic room floor, either. Though he might have guessed that there was something wrong when it refused to move under him.

'Just a friend of mine. We have a little question for you,' said Xena.

'Yeah?' He was still curious, still expectant of further delights.

'What is the password for the security system at BXH?'

The man didn't reply verbally. He shook the bed from side to side, trying to break free. He didn't know that his only hope was if his thrashing managed to separate his hands from his wrists, and his feet from his ankles. And very few people have strength enough to do that.

Xena waved the blue flame, raised it, as if offering it up. It flickered higher.

The odour of the burning butane gas filled the room like bad perfume. The sound of the blow torch was a threatening hissing now. Xena placed the tip of the flame against the top edge of the whiskey tumbler the man had been drinking from. The glass turned blue.

'Wait until you feel this. Then you will tell me,' said Xena. Her tone had changed. It was demanding now.

'What? Fu . . .' The end of that confident word was bitten off by the piercing scream that came from deep within his throat. Xena had touched the flame against the pale skin of his shoulder.

He began thrashing. Like a fish flailing. He moved from

side to side, squirming away from the skin-blistering heat. But he couldn't move fast enough. And his legs and arms were stretched out tight.

Easy targets.

The smell in the room changed and the atmosphere with it. Pain and whimpering, sizzling and guttural roars filled the air.

The man had become a dog.

Then Xena asked him again.

'The password, please.' She spoke softly, as if they were still playing a game.

'If you give it up, I will release you. You can explain these little burns to your wife. But the ones I will inflict next will require hospital treatment. Or the services of a morgue.' She clicked the flame off, then pressed the hot tip hard and fast into the biggest blister she had inflicted, near his ankle.

'What do you say, Mr Hare?'

The man answered with a defiant, animal roar. He shook the bed under him. The last vestige of his pride in working at BXH bellowed out of him.

Xena lit the flame again. She reached forward, touched it to his chest, and ran it fast down the middle until smoke from his burning body hair filled the room with a sickly odour.

'Stop, stop!' he screamed. His body squirmed to escape the heat.

'It's #89*99,' he shouted. 'Please! Stop!'

Bidoner keyed the password into his phone and pressed send.

'I hope you're not lying,' said Xena. 'I want all this to have a happy ending.'

She squeezed his thigh with her hand, then stroked it.

Tears streamed from under his blindfold. His cheeks were red. It was good he couldn't see the weals on his body, because he would know immediately that he wouldn't be able to explain any of them to his wife.

'Please, let me go. I promise not to tell anyone. I swear, on my children's lives.'

Lord Bidoner's mobile beeped as an incoming message came in. He nodded at Xena. The code had worked.

'I believe you,' she said. 'But there is one more thing I must do for you.'

She put the Turboflame down and went to the fridge. She took out a six-inch-long serrated knife, honed with care to a perfect blade, from the freezer section.

She held it in the air, admiring its cold edge.

'Now you will find release,' she said.

The man's body went still. His toes, which had scrunched up, half straightened. The only sound was his pain-filled whimpering.

The panic room in the apartment on Fifth Avenue, overlooking the skyscrapers of Manhattan, was soundproof. It was why they used the room.

Xena flicked the blade across the man's pale skin, once, then twice, fascinated by how quickly blood gushed, how fast it flowed from a few simple cuts.

'This is for my brothers,' she said.

'Don't,' he whimpered. Fear trembled in his voice. 'I have two children, a wife.'

She growled, psyching herself up.

'*Prima quattuor invocare unum*,' she said, as she grabbed him, jerking him upwards and castrating him with one swinging motion.

She held the bloody remains up in the air.

His screams of terror and pain vibrated through the room as blood spurted two feet high. A foul smell followed and the man's words became a babbling.

Lord Bidoner held his nose. He'd seen enough. He went

out to the main room of the apartment, with its view towards the glittering Jazz-era spire of the Empire State Building.

'You did good, my dear. The first offering has been done correctly,' he said, when Xena joined him.

She was panting.

'Come here.'

He pushed her up against the inch-thick glass of the window, as Manhattan glittered behind them.

Afterwards, he handed her a balloon glass containing a large shot of Asbach 21. She sipped the brandy, then downed it in one gulp.

Then she lay down on the sleek oak coffee table that dominated the room. The canyon of lights stretching into the velvet Manhattan night reflected all the way along the length of the table and onto her ebony skin.

He reached down and stroked her shoulder. It was trembling.

'Three more before the moon rises again. That is what the book says. That is what we will do.'

She smiled up at him. Her white teeth shone as she leaned her head back and stretched.

2

A creak rang out against the muffled noise of night-time London.

'Sean?' Isabel's voice echoed. Her head was off the pillow. Was that a shadow moving? The moment of deep pleasure at sensing his return was replaced in a second by fear, as no response came.

She slid out of bed. Alek, who was now four, was in the next room. If that was Sean out there, playing some game, she was going to make him pay. Big time. She'd just finished one of the most demanding projects she had worked on during her time as an IT security consultant, and her brain had been fried to mush. She needed sleep.

She stood in the doorway.

There was no one on the landing.

She peered downstairs. The house felt deserted. The heating had been off for hours. She went into Alek's room, checked his breathing and tucked him in.

Was this going to be a replay of that night a few weeks ago when he didn't come home? The thought made her shudder. In all the time she'd known him he'd never done anything like what he'd done that night.

She remembered the creak that had woken her. What had that been about?

Had she imagined it? Her dreams had been strange recently. Images from Istanbul and Jerusalem came too often. Maybe that was what had roused her.

She went downstairs and turned on all the lights. Nothing was out of place, though there was an odd smell. A lemony tang, as if a cleaner had passed through. She stood near the front door. This was all Sean's fault. She picked up the telephone and pressed redial. The call went to voicemail, again.

She slammed the phone down.

Bastard.

Stop it. He'll be home soon.

She turned out the lights, headed back to bed, and tried to sleep. The icy wind buffeting the window didn't help. Neither did the cold space where Sean's freckled body should have been.

The matchbook-thin Bang & Olufsen docking system said it was five past three. *How many years do you get these days if you murder your husband?*

She lay there, seething, angry not only with Sean, but with the idiots at BXH too. And with whoever had decided to hold their stupid celebration the night before. It was bad enough that they demanded he work long hours, couldn't they at least let him come home?

When she woke again after a disturbed sleep, London rumbled even louder. It was ten to eight. Her first thought was that he'd come back, and had already gotten up. He usually woke before she did. He could be down in the kitchen making toast with that new poppyseed bread.

He'd stick his jaw out when she asked him what time he'd come in, then run a hand through his thick brown hair and give her that blue-eyed innocent look, his secret weapon ever since she'd met him in Istanbul.

She turned.

His side of the bed was unruffled. A prickling sensation ran over her skin.

She picked up her phone, pressed his number. He'd better have a good explanation. A very good explanation.

The call went to voicemail. She wasn't going to leave another message.

Her stomach tightened. She felt sick. Where was he?

Her life was not supposed to be like this. She was too young for all this crap. They'd gone through a lot when they'd first met, that watery tunnel in Istanbul, that hellhole in Israel, but all that was long behind them. Their life was peaceful now, family oriented.

So what about that last time he hadn't come home?

It hadn't been that long ago. Three weeks, to be precise. That had been a Thursday night too. He'd come home for breakfast, pleading for forgiveness, with that elaborate excuse on his lips. What had it been? Oh yes, a planning meeting that had gone on too long.

Did he think the bank's mega-merger finally being completed would be enough to placate her? How could a celebration dinner, drinks, explain this? He wasn't even a full-time employee there, he was a consultant, working for the Institute of Applied Research on a project that had already eaten up a year of his life.

She breathed in, told herself to calm down.

Someone would have called her if anything had happened.

He was late. That was it. That was all.

The same as last time. And she would make him pay properly this time. She listened for the soft click of the front door opening. He wasn't going to let her down. Sean didn't do things like that. They were going to Paris later that day. They were going to be soaping each other in a pink marble bath at the Franklin Roosevelt Hotel, just off the Champs-Élysées, before midnight.

That was his plan.

Everything was ready.

Since his uncle and aunt had invited them to stay in the hotel with them while they were visiting Paris, she'd been counting the days. And Sean knew it.

The trip was just what they needed. And such a great gesture from his uncle and aunt. They were the only people from Sean's family that she really got on with. They'd insisted Sean find someone to look after Alek. The Louvre and the Opera House weren't ideal places for a four-year-old, never mind one with a hyperactive streak. They deserved this weekend.

And they were booked into the hotel's honeymoon suite. Tonight they'd be sleeping in a Louis XIV four-poster under a canopy of mauve silk. It was going to happen. No one was going to take it away from her.

Not even Sean Ryan.

3

The girl's head rolled from side to side. There was no turning back now. The effects of Rohypnol wear off after a few hours.

He had work to do.

He ran his hands over her naked body. She winced as he pushed her legs apart, but didn't wake. Looking at her splayed out made him want her properly this time. But he stopped himself.

He couldn't afford for his DNA to be found.

He knelt.

The blade made a sighing noise as it cut through the air. There was a spasm of wet jerking as skin, muscle and artery were cut.

Even then she didn't wake. The blood began to flow like paint cans tipped over, and as it did the shaking in his body slowed, then stopped, as if the flames of a fever were easing.

He was glad he'd done it quickly. The next job he had to do would be messy.

4

Isabel closed her eyes, willing herself to be calm.

They were going to have a wonderful weekend. Romantically speaking, the Franklin Roosevelt Hotel was about a million miles from Fulham, from working every spare minute helping people to find endless lost or deleted files on their computers and making sure Alek was dressed and fed and not wasting his life watching too much TV. And looking after Sean too, when he came home. She listened, and willed a faint noise to be the front door opening. She waited for him to bound up the stairs, for her life to go back to normal.

But all she heard was the freezing wind battering at the window.

And now the house felt different, as if she was in it for the first time again, even though the cream Edwardian armchair was in its corner, and the white rug – the snow carpet as Sean called it – was still in front of the dressing table, a little askew, the way she liked it.

Sean's things stood out as she looked around. His books in a tottering pile under his bedside table. His watch collection in a row on top of it. His navy Macy's dressing gown hanging on the back of the door. His silver pen on the dressing table.

She went to check Alek. 'I love you,' he'd whispered sleepily, looking up at her the evening before as she'd tucked him in. Alek, named after Sean's friend who'd died in Istanbul, could make fuzzy feelings glow inside her just by smiling.

That morning he looked like a sleeping waif, his hair all over the place, his skin shining, ruddy from the warmth of his duvet.

She should have told Sean to skip the stupid merger celebrations.

She stared out at the back garden, shivering at the thought of how cold it had to be out there.

In the far corner there were remnants of the inch of snow that had fallen the day before. This winter was shaping up to be the worst in the city in years.

It reminded her of Decembers in Somerset, before her mother died. She shook her head. Those days were long gone. And anyway, they used to get proper snow then, a winter coat of it, not a thin veil like they did in London. At the bottom of the garden there was a snowdrift piled up against the six-foot-high red-brick wall at the back.

Something tightened around her, as if a ghost had hugged her.

Yesterday, as the afternoon light had been fading, she'd been out in the garden. In the corner, by the back wall, there'd been a mound of pristine whiteness. Now it all looked trampled.

Her nose twitched. That faint lemony smell was in the air again.

She glanced around the kitchen for anything else out of place.

Then she remembered the creak that had woken her during the night, the feeling that there'd been someone in the house.

She hadn't experienced anything like that in a long time.

The buzz of the landline sent her flying to the phone. She held it to her ear, ready to scream at Sean as soon as he opened his mouth.

There was no one else she could think of who'd be ringing at this time.

5

Henry Mowlam scratched his head. The lights in the Whitehall meeting room were down low and everyone was looking to the front, so no one in the group of ten senior MI5 staff attending the presentation would see him, but still he moved his hand quickly back onto the table.

Major Finch was giving the morning presentation.

'The information we have out of China is that there is something big brewing in the financial arena. New banking legislation, the biggest change since their Commercial Banking law of 1995, will negatively impact many of the richest men and women in China. The knives are out. Literally. Two middle-tier officials connected with this new law have already disappeared.'

Henry tapped the table hard with his red MI5 biro. 'What's the likely impact outside China?' he said, when Finch paused to let others speak.

'We're still assessing that. But our current best guess is a big rise in Chinese firms taking over major companies in the West, as new sources of income and places to invest their surplus cash are sought out. I expect there'll be a few hiccups.'

Henry looked down at the shiny mahogany table. This

should be fun, he thought, monitoring managers trying to impose Chinese six-days-a-week work practices.

'But the cultural impact of Chinese takeovers is not what we're really concerned about today. Our concern is that this might lead to a backlash against Chinese communities in the United Kingdom. That's why I called you to this meeting. We have reason to believe that has started.'

'Excuse me,' said Henry. 'Is the Ebony Dragon hedge fund on the list of companies being monitored?'

'No,' said Major Finch.

'You do know I submitted a report about the activities of its chairman, Lord Bidoner. Ebony Dragon has a source of funding in China now. They've been buying up British companies, even a few well known ones.'

Finch sighed. 'You are barking up the wrong tree, Henry. I know you've been researching Bidoner's link to that book that was found in Istanbul – what do they call a section of it?'

Henry looked at the faces around him. A few of them had heard what the title of a certain part of the book had been translated as. Their faces were even more expectant than the others, as if they were looking forward to a diversion.

He smiled back at them, then spoke. 'The book of dark prayers.'

Major Finch threw her eyes up to the low ceiling as a few coughs in the room disguised some of the badly suppressed sniggers.

'Yes, I read that bit, Henry. But what I don't get is why that sort of thing should be of interest to any of us. This is the twenty-first century.'

Henry waited for some more coughing to stop before replying.

'I don't believe in it, but when people start copying the crap that is in that book I think we should all keep an open mind.' He looked around. No one nodded in agreement.

'You're talking about those murders in Jerusalem. Those bodies being burnt, yes?'

Henry nodded.

'But no connection with Bidoner or his hedge fund has been proven, Henry. We monitored him for six months, didn't we?'

'Ebony Dragon were the only people who profited from what happened around that time.'

'We can't investigate everyone who makes a profit, Henry. We'd be seriously understaffed if we did. We have no proof that anything illegal went on. And Ebony Dragon is one of the largest hedge funds in the world. I expect they have fingers in a lot of pies.'

'That's what worries me,' said Henry, quietly.

Finch was already moving on to something else.

6

It wasn't Sean on the phone. It was one of his colleagues from work, George Donovan.

George was a senior security manager at BXH who took an interest in Sean's project there. He was a close-mouthed Iraqi war veteran, a borderline posttraumatic stress victim, Sean said, who'd rejoined his British army regiment when he'd heard they were heading to Afghanistan for a campaign.

She'd met him only twice. There was something weird about his stare. It felt as if he was wondering whether to kill you or not. He reminded her of Mark, her ex, who had died in Israel. He'd had a similar distant stare at times, as if he'd seen too much.

Sean had told her that George had been a hero. But why BXH needed that kind of security officer, he'd never explained.

'Good morning, Mrs Ryan.'

'Good morning, George.'

George cleared his throat. Isabel wondered was he at work, sitting in that neon-lit open-plan office on the twenty-ninth floor of BXH, the banking corporation worth the GDP of a fast-developing nation state, where he and Sean and ten thousand other Londoners worked like coal miners on twelve-hour shifts. Sean had been working late at the bank for months now, integrating the facial recognition software the Institute had developed with the bank's IT systems.

And if he was at the office already, did that mean that any minute now he was going to rush into one of those breakfast meetings Sean was always telling her about?

'Can I speak to Sean, please?' George's tone was stiff, proprietorial, as if Sean belonged to BXH, not to Isabel. Not really.

It was a tone Isabel hated. She had to tighten her hand around the phone to stop herself reacting.

'He's not here.' There was no point in lying. 'He hasn't come back yet. I thought he was with you lot last night.'

'I wouldn't know, Mrs Ryan. Sean has a meeting here at eight thirty. I'm sorry to disturb you. I thought I might catch him before he left your house.' He paused for a millisecond, to reload.

'Aren't you and Sean going away later today?' There was the tiniest note of surprise in his tone. And something else too. Did he know something Isabel didn't?

She chewed her lip. She hadn't done that in years. The pressure in her forehead was intense suddenly, as if a blood vessel had become trapped.

'We're going tonight.' She tried to make it sound as if they had plenty of time.

They had plenty of time.

George hummed. It sounded almost as if he was laughing.

Isabel wanted to explode. The pressure inside her was rising, like a wave.

'What time did you last see him?' she said, in as calm a tone as she could muster.

A dog barked in one of the other back gardens. Isabel felt the bones in her fingers pressing into the plastic of the phone.

'Maybe six yesterday evening. He was expected in here

this morning.' There was a note of anger in his voice. Was he implying Sean was late?

A prickly warmth spread over Isabel's face. She hated anyone criticising Sean.

'I thought he had a day off today?'

A tiny snort came down the line.

'What time had you been planning to leave for Paris, Mrs Ryan?'

It sounded as if George thought the trip was bound to be cancelled. The hairs on the back of Isabel's neck rose like quills.

'The train's at a minute past six. Our taxi's coming an hour before that.'

The journey from Fulham to St Pancras International station should take no more than forty minutes, even late in the afternoon, but Sean had wanted them to be early, to enjoy every second of what they'd earned, he'd said.

By five fifteen that afternoon at the latest, according to Sean's plan, they'd be in St Pancras. And after that it'd be first class all the way. It was going to be a weekend to remember. A well-deserved payback for all the evenings she'd spent alone while he was working.

'Should I tell Sean something when I see him?' she said.

'Can you tell him I'm looking for him? Thanks.' The line went dead.

Isabel tapped Sean's number into the handset and got that stupid voicemail message again. She cut the line.

She stood by the window, massaging her temples. An unsettling memory had come back to her.

Sean had said something the weekend before about a feeling he'd had that George was spying on him. Sean had reported some regulatory issue to the bank's technology security committee and ever since he'd constantly been asking him questions, Sean had said.

Isabel had told him he was getting paranoid.

But there was something about George's tone on that call that had almost been like a warning. Sean had also told her that Paul Vaughann had been taking an interest in his project recently. He'd complained that Vaughann brought out the worst in people.

Paul Vaughann III was the President and Chief Executive of the twenty-ninth-floor UK operation of BXH. Insiders called him The Shark, because of some mythical incident when he'd bitten a fellow trader's arm to get his attention. And he loved the nickname so much, Sean said, that he'd had a shark's jaws mounted behind the desk in his office.

Vaughann was also known for biting people's heads off if they criticised the bank in his presence, whether they were the bank's employees or not.

A low-flying jet on its way to Heathrow passed over the house noisily. Isabel looked up at the leaden sky.

Not far away, the traffic would be bumper to bumper on the King's Road, cars full of slowly stewing people, buses full of workers anxious to get in on time, trucks spewing diesel fumes.

Isabel closed her eyes. 'Come home, Sean.'

7

Pastor Stevson, the American pastor and tele-evangelist who had sponsored the most important archaeological dig in Jerusalem in fifty years, was coming up in the mahogany-panelled elevator of the Waldorf Astoria in New York.

He'd been sweating. His white hair and beard were sticking to his pink-mottled skin. His wife hated him looking this way, but there was nothing he could do.

He'd been out late and would have stayed out later if she hadn't called and told him she was up and praying for his safe return, and that she'd tell everyone back in Dallas if he stayed out all night.

As he strode down the blue-carpeted corridor he rehearsed his lines. His wife, whose money had sponsored his first TV station, was not someone he wanted to fight with.

But he had to put her in her place.

The first thing he noticed when he entered the suite was that someone had pulled the floor-to-ceiling blue and gold curtains back, allowing the twinkling lights of Manhattan into the room. Had she been praying at the window, as she'd told him she'd done before when she'd been suspicious about his whereabouts?

'Where the hell were you?' were the first words out of his wife's mouth.

'I was walking the streets and praying. Why are you questioning me?'

'You've been gone since dinner.' She spat the words out.

'That was no reason to call me, woman.' Pastor Stevson pointed at his wife. His finger was shaking in righteous anger.

His wife stared at him, as if he'd just pissed on the floor.

'You expect me to believe that?' she drawled.

Pastor Stevson pulled a thin prayer book out of the inside pocket of his jacket. His cream suit was crumpled, but she had no way of proving what he'd been doing. Unless that whore had had a camera. He smiled for a second. Where would she have put it?

A memory of the redhead straddling him, her breasts bouncing, came to him. He wiped a hand across his brow. He had to put such thoughts away.

He bellowed at his wife. 'How dare you question me! Ye shall be cursed. Remember Ephesians 5:22. Wives, submit to your husbands, as to the Lord!' His hand shook as he raised it high.

'I am deep in God's work and you dare question me! This is the time for belief, not listening to the tongues of the devil playing in your mind. Ye shall be cursed if you continue this.' He walked to the curtain and closed it.

'What are you doing with all the money you moved out of the church bank account?'

So that's what this is about, he thought. Okay, I'll tell her a little, just to keep her jaw busy. There can't be any harm in telling my wife now we are so near the end.

He turned to face her. 'You remember that dig in Jerusalem we financed?'

She nodded.

'Well, I've been working with a group of believers since

then. The money is invested with them. That dig in Jerusalem got closed down, but they couldn't take away what I discovered.' He pointed a shaking finger at himself. 'A wonder that changes everything.'

The pastor's wife, a thin, blonde woman, whose black dressing gown was pulled tight under her chin, waved her hand dismissively through the air. 'You told me there was a fire at that site, that the locals burnt that whole building down.'

'Samples had already been taken. I told you that too.' He put his hand towards her; it was a fist now.

'Cut to the chase, who the hell are these people and what the hell do they need all that money for?' She had a habit of asking the tricky questions.

Pastor Stevson shook his head. He sat on the long yellow flower-patterned couch. It took up the area in front of the wall-mounted TV screen. He looked at the prints of Grecian urns that sat on either side of the TV.

'What in hell's name have you gone and done? I can't believe this,' said his wife. Then she held her hand out to him. 'You are taking advantage of my family's generosity.' The oil price rise had done wonders for many families in their part of Texas in the last ten years.

It was galling for Pastor Stevson to think of all that money gushing out of the ground, just because they had farms in the right place. The Lord gave way too much to that family.

'Don't question me, Martha.'

His wife shook her head, turned away from him. She had a sour look on her face.

'We're going to bring forward the end times. His return. That's what we're working for. Our money is going to make it happen. And you have the gall to question this work?'

'Why do they need all your church's money?' she said.

She was shaking her head, slowly. Then she leaned towards the pastor, her face full of suspicion.

Pastor Stevson had his reply ready. 'I'll tell you why. Because if we don't get this right, we won't be heading to heaven. We'll all be heading for hell.'

8

Sean had warned her about getting paranoid after what they'd been through in Istanbul and Jerusalem, seeing conspiracies everywhere.

Was this just paranoia? Wasn't his work for BXH just another consulting project, even if it was a big one?

The BXH project had been going on for over a year. First there'd been a small pilot project, which the Institute, where Sean worked, had been keen on Sean managing himself, due to his knowledge of super-fast image analysis. Then there'd been a long wait for a decision on implementation, while they kept doing tests.

The whole thing should have been up and running by now, but it wasn't. Sean had complained that he was at the end of his tether with it all.

Was there anyone she could call?

She knew a few of the other wives from the Institute well enough to go to coffee mornings with them, but she'd never had a phone call from any of them complaining that their husbands were missing.

There was only one person she really trusted; Rose. Their husbands had been involved with the bank for about the same time. And she was also looking after Alek for the weekend.

Most of the wives she knew from BXH were far too competitive to show any weakness publicly. Whenever she'd met them they talked about who was going to Ascot, what they were going to wear, the private schools their children attended, or their holiday homes in the south of France or Tuscany.

Having worked in Istanbul for years, for the Foreign Office, before retiring early after an incident in Istanbul, Isabel felt like an outsider when it came to the things those people seemed to be obsessed with.

She headed for her wicker chair in the conservatory. She had an hour before her coffee date with Rose and the handover of Alek to her for the weekend. It had been a big decision to leave him with Rose. One she'd doubted ever since, if she thought about it for more than a minute.

But everything was ready. And Sean had been so definite that it would be good for them both. She deserved three nights of peace. That was what he had said.

And he was right. She pushed the shard of doubt away.

Within twenty-four hours they'd be back to normal. She'd forgive him. He'd talk about the big merger and finally finishing the project that would secure the Institute's future, their future. And that would be it.

A crunching sounded from the garden, as if someone was walking out there. She turned to the window and took a deep breath.

9

Henry Mowlam turned to the screen on his left. The hum of the office in Whitehall had hardly changed in the past few years. The only noticeable difference was that the screens they were watching at the monitoring stations were thinner and the light was yellower, more natural, it was claimed, though Henry didn't believe it.

The secure PDF on his screen was the oldest military archive file he had ever accessed. At the top there was a summary by a Royal Engineers Major. Below was a hand-written report in a thin spidery scrawl enlivened by occasional twirls and flourishes. The name at the top was Captain Charles George Gordon.

Henry scrolled down the document.

It was a personal account of the destruction of the Summer Palace of the Xianfeng Emperor of China in Beijing during the Second Opium War in October 1860.

'On the night of the 20th we were carrying out Lord Elgin's orders and came upon a remote palace building, which had not been destroyed up to that point due to its location on an island and its small size. I ordered only the porcelain to be removed and the building to be left intact, but one of

the Sergeants took it upon himself to break through a trap door and loot an underground room. He arrived back while we were loading up the boats. He was carrying a green jade statue, about the size of an owl. I confiscated it in the name of Barkers & Son, Bankers, whose kin had been tortured and murdered by the Chinese, and whose shipment of opium had been lost on the Pearl River six months before.'

Henry closed the PDF. Barkers & Son were one of the early manifestations of the BXH banking conglomerate. Henry switched to his right-hand screen and studied the report on Lord Bidoner that had recently been emailed to him.

So this was where Bidoner was going to invest the ill-gotten loot he'd escaped with after the Jerusalem incident. It couldn't be proven that it was an attempt to provoke a war and then profit from the surge in certain shares of companies, but that didn't mean it wasn't true.

Henry still seethed at the thought of how much money Bidoner had made. He read the report again. It stated that Lord Bidoner had already built up a shareholding in BXH that should have been notified to the authorities, but hadn't. And now he was doing more buying through nominee accounts.

What was he up to?

BXH was definitely in trouble, on the blocks for an immediate takeover. If that didn't happen, the bank could very well be taken over by the US Government. And if *that* happened Bidoner would lose his investment.

Was there something going on that he didn't see?

He read the email from Lord Bidoner to the CEO of BXH, which they had intercepted. It requested an inventory of the bank's artworks. It also stated that Lord Bidoner had an artistic interest in a jade statue that the bank was rumoured to have in its possession since the time of the Second Opium War.

He turned to look at the report from Captain Charles George Gordon. Was Bidoner looking for the statue mentioned in this report? It certainly looked like it.

But why?

10

Isabel went to the back door and looked out, her face close to the window. She could feel the cold leaking through the glass. She moved away. The noise could have been a neighbour's cat, hunting for mice. Or it could have been an early rising burglar. She checked the back door was locked, rattled the handle. Hopefully whatever it was would go away.

A memory of the thugs who had chased her and Sean from the hotel in Istanbul came back to her.

She put the back door key on the top of the mahogany dresser. The doorbell rang. It was one of those old-fashioned bells that emits a buzz for as long as the person outside wants it to. Whoever was pressing it clearly wanted an answer quickly.

She was at the door in seconds.

Had Sean lost his key?

Through the stained glass front door window she could see a bulky shape. It was Sean! He'd lost his keys. Her heart thumped like an overexcited schoolgirl's. She swung the door open and froze, her body temperature cooling fast.

It wasn't Sean. It was a young man with streaky blonde

hair and purple skin eruptions, a before specimen from a magazine ad for acne treatment.

As he stretched his hand out to her she felt stupid at having opened the door so quickly. She could easily have checked in the security viewer. She stepped back and got ready to close the door, fast.

Mr Streaky Blonde's suit was light grey. It had thin lapels and it looked way too tight, bulging in all the wrong places.

'James Kilfeather, from Gold and Ferry in the City.' He smiled at her, like a salesman who'd just seen his next bonus appearing in front of him.

The look on her face must have taken him by surprise. He stepped back, his expression changing from friendly to troubled in a second.

'Is Mr Ryan here?' He glanced over her shoulder.

Had Sean made an appointment he hadn't told her about?

'No, he's not. I'll tell him you were looking for him.' She tried to sound friendly, but all she wanted was for him to go away.

That was when she saw the clipboard. It was one of those big blue plastic ones with a shiny silver clip to keep the papers down. Under the clip there was a sheet with printed boxes, as if he was about to fill something in. He was holding it as if it was his *raison d'être*.

'Did Mr Ryan tell you I was coming to do the valuation?'

She stared at him.

'Valuation?' The word stuck in her throat, as if it were a piece of bread too big to swallow. She could feel herself getting angry, the muscles in her neck tightening.

'Mr Ryan rang our office on Wednesday. He was very specific. He asked us to value this property. Are you Mrs Ryan?' Streaky Blonde was getting peeved, as if it was her fault Sean wasn't there.

Why would Sean need the house valued?

She felt light-headed. This had to be a practical joke.

'You're mistaken. We're not selling up. I'll get Sean to call you, sort all this out when he gets back.'

She smiled thinly, closing the door on his reddening face.

She watched his shadow through the stained glass, her pulse drumming. Would he go away? A second later he was gone.

What the hell was Sean up to?

That was when she noticed the silver front door key.

It wasn't hers, she was sure of it. All her keys were on her key ring with the enamel apple she'd picked up on their last trip to New York, on a visit to BXH's head office, which even the wives had been invited to.

Was it Sean's key? She moved it near the pile of mail that had arrived for Sean the day before. Then she pulled her phone from her jeans pocket.

She tapped in his number. Number unavailable. This was getting too weird. She stood in the hall. The house seemed very quiet.

'Alek,' she called out. Anxiety exploded inside her. She rushed up the stairs. As she got to the top she saw Alek's bedroom door was closed.

She pushed it open, fast. Alek was on the bed, moving a toy soldier up a pillow mountain. His amber locks looked adorable. She slumped against the wall and closed her eyes. Her heart was drumming rapidly. What the hell was happening to her? She wasn't normally this paranoid.

'Come on, Alek, let's get ready. We're going.' Alek didn't budge.

'Remember,' she said. 'You're going for a sleepover. And Rose is going to take you to that new movie.'

She felt a tug of guilt looking at his upturned face, but when he moved off the bed like a boy possessed, the guilt subsided. The thought of a new movie beat just about anything in Alek's mind.

'Pick one toy to bring with you,' she said, as she left the room. Alek's hands were full already.

Sean's weekend Samsonite bag was in a corner of the bedroom. It was empty. She'd already packed hers with most of what she'd need for the weekend.

She threw some of his things into his bag: socks, two shirts, his leather jacket. She was determined to keep to the plan. He wasn't going to let her down. They had plenty of time before the taxi came.

Just as long as Mr Vaughann didn't insist he stay at work. And she would conveniently forget about that message George had given her until they were safely on the train. Sean deserved a break too.

They'd hardly had any holidays in two years. Not like some of them at the bank. One of the few financial downturn-induced changes at BXH, as far as Isabel could make out, was that some of the senior managers had been forced to call off their weekday golf outings.

A cruel punishment indeed.

The only other change Isabel could see was all the extra hours Sean had been putting in.

It was time to go. At least without Alek hanging off of her, she'd be able to focus on finding Sean, and getting away to Paris in time.

She stopped, and put her hand to her forehead. Was she crazy thinking their trip would still happen?

11

The dining table in Lord Bidoner's Fifth Avenue apartment was set for breakfast. The silver coffee pot in the centre of the table was letting out a curl of steam.

Lord Bidoner was dressed in a black kimono, as was Xena, though hers went only to her thigh. He poured coffee into a thin gold-edged cup, as Xena went to answer the doorbell.

The two men who entered, the head of trading and the head of risk at the New York securities division of the Ebony Dragon hedge fund, were both Harvard educated and experienced in the animal world of Wall Street.

'Come in, the coffee and pastries are both warm,' said Bidoner.

The two men took coffee and stood near the picture window. They were both quiet and watchful. It wasn't often that they were summoned to meet the chairman of the fund they worked for at his apartment. It had only happened once before for each of them, when they were being recruited.

'Sit, gentlemen,' said Lord Bidoner. He stood with his back to the wall of glass and its million-dollar view. The sun still hadn't risen, but the buildings around them were starting to come to life.

The two men sat on the edge of the leather sofa, a few feet apart. Xena stood at the far end. Her long legs glistened, but neither man glanced at her.

'As I told you when I approved your salaries, there will be times when each of you will be asked to do unusual things. This is one of those times.'

Neither man responded.

'You know our fund has larger goals than simply making a profit.'

The head of trading, who wore a black suit and a blue knotted silk tie, nodded curtly. The other man stared at Lord Bidoner, then spoke.

'Isn't profit what our shareholders want?'

'And we will make a profit from all this,' said Lord Bidoner. He walked closer to the two men. 'A serious profit. And we will need it. There are scum out there who threaten us all. There is a change coming and you can be part of it.'

The head of risk, who had spoken, pressed his lips together and nodded.

'Soon, gentlemen, we will know who will be the new slaves and who will be free in this world. You may think I overstate it, but when you see people lining up everywhere outside banks that have stolen their money, you will know I wasn't lying.' Lord Bidoner pointed at the two men, first one then the other.

'Many things must be destroyed before they can be reborn. And you will have a role in this, if you follow my instructions to the letter. With no deviation. Is that clear?'

The head of risk spoke. 'What exactly do you want us to do?'

'You will spend every dime we have on BXH's shares and options. And then you will start selling it all at a loss, until the price dives, because there is so much of BXH on sale.'

'We could be ruined in a day, sir,' said the head of risk.

'That's not your problem, gentlemen. Those are your instructions.'

The two men looked at each other. Both were pale under their perma-tans.

'Are you sure you want to do this, sir? This is a major gamble,' said the head of risk.

Lord Bidoner walked to where Xena was standing and whispered something in her ear. She went out of the room.

'Gentlemen, consider this,' said Lord Bidoner, coming up to the two men. 'My friend is very strict when it comes to relationships. She was raised differently from us. An eye for an eye is what she believes in.' He leaned towards the men. 'It was said in her village that she wore a cloak of darkness after what happened to her family.'

He stepped aside to let her pass him. She was carrying a newspaper.

'Would you like to see what happened to one of the other bankers I worked with, gentlemen? It was such a shock I kept the article.'

The two men just stared at him. Then the head of risk nodded.

Xena dropped the paper on the glass table. The newspaper was the *Times of India*. The main article was accompanied by a picture of a stretcher being carried out of an office building. People were milling around and whoever was on the metal stretcher was clearly dead, as they were in a fully zipped up body bag.

The headline read – CASTRATED BANKER DIES.

'This was a few years ago, but it was a sad day for the man's family, I can tell you. To die in such a way is dishonourable in India. It implies so much. But I am sure it was a lot more painful for him.' Lord Bidoner picked up the newspaper and passed it back to Xena. She left the room with it.

'This man didn't believe my warnings. I hope that doesn't happen with you two.'

The two men shook their heads.

'I want you to understand where I'm coming from. There will be no turning back on my directive and there will be no discussion of what happened in this room after you leave here. Is that clear?'

The head of risk nodded first.

'Yes, sir. You don't have to worry. We will carry out your instructions to the letter.'

They walked slowly to the door and exited without saying another word. Lord Bidoner was already on his phone, as the front door of the apartment closed behind them.

Red, he typed into the email. Then he sent it.

12

Rose Suchard was sitting at a back table in the otherwise almost empty In Italy restaurant at the bottom of their street when Isabel and Alek got there.

In Italy was one of those new places with all white wooden tables and chairs. On the long side wall there was a giant map of a futuristic subway system made up of multicoloured dots. The restaurant attracted a young crowd who enjoyed the real Italian coffee, great pasta dishes and the atmosphere. Sean and Isabel went there regularly. It was one of the reasons she loved the area.

A waiter was flirting with Rose when they arrived.

Carlo, his name badge said, turned and smiled at Isabel as she sat down.

'And for you, signora?' he asked, as his smile said, you also look fantastic. The black wool sweater and midnight blue jeans she'd put on was her basic outfit these days. It was nice to be complimented, but she really didn't need it.

'A late breakfast, maybe?'

But Isabel wasn't hungry. She ordered a latte and an orange juice for Alek. He was wiggling on the chair to her right. She took off his jacket.

Once he was settled she turned to Rose.

'Sean didn't come home last night,' she whispered, leaning close to her, so Alek wouldn't hear.

'The bastard,' Rose hissed back. 'Are you okay?'

'Not really, I still don't know where he is.' She put her hand to her forehead. Rose tutted.

'If I'm arrested for killing him, don't be surprised.' She looked out the window, hoping to see his car going by.

'I'll stand by you,' said Rose. 'Did you see the news?' She leaned even closer to Isabel. Alek was caught up with galloping an armoured knight across a corner of the table.

'What news?'

'About BXH,' she whispered. She had an are-you-still-with-us look on her face.

She was scaring Isabel now. 'You know I've sworn off TV in the morning.'

All the endless bad TV news was like an infection. She'd decided to keep it all out until the evening each day, when Sean brought enough of it home for both of them.

'They were going on about the merger,' said Rose. 'Apparently BXH's share price should be going up, but it's not, it's collapsing. You know what Terry said?' Her voice dropped to a whisper.

Isabel shook her head, slowly.

'He said if the merger doesn't happen, BXH will collapse in on itself, like a black hole or something. They've been hiding . . .' She leaned towards Isabel. Her voice went even lower.

'Something big, he reckons.' She glanced around, as if they were in a conspiracy movie.

'I don't like the sound of that.'

'Me neither.' Rose looked genuinely worried.

'Sean said if the merger fell through, BXH would still be okay,' she said.

'Sure, but where is he?'

She opened her mouth, looked at Alek, closed it again. She felt like cursing Sean and BXH, but she couldn't, not in front of Alek.

'You know . . .' said Rose. She looked sad. Her mouth opened. Her eyes were brimming. 'It's . . .'

Rose was crying. Big tears were running down her nose. Sympathy flared inside Isabel. Her problems suddenly seemed minor. Rose was usually so upbeat. When the western world had been about to melt down, she'd invited them around for a party.

'We're going . . . we're going to lose our home,' said Rose.

'No way.' Isabel glanced at Alek. He hadn't noticed anything.

'What happened?' she said.

'Terry's overtime's been cut. They're cutting loads in IT. We borrowed so much to get this house. We're going to lose it all. I just know it.'

Isabel squeezed her arm. Rose smiled at her and straightened herself up. It was the smile of someone determined not to let anyone else down.

'Maybe it'll be for the better,' she said. 'We don't need such a big house.' She sniffed and tried to compose herself. 'Terry took out another loan. He didn't even tell me.' There was a wounded, shocked look in her eyes.

'That's terrible,' said Isabel.

The waiter arrived. He made an elaborate show of placing their drinks in front of them. He was far too solicitous. Had he seen Rose crying?

'You know what else?' said Rose, after he'd gone.

She arched a neatly plucked brow, then started talking about how Terry had been acting odd recently. Isabel encouraged Rose to tell her more. After a few minutes she leaned towards Alek. 'Are you looking forward to playing with Aunty Rosie?' Alek nodded. She gave his hand a squeeze.

That was her signal.

'I gotta go,' she said, She'd hardly touched her coffee.

'Make sure he tells you where he was,' said Rose.

'He'll have some amazing explanation,' she said. 'Just like the last time.'

She gave Rose her long-suffering-wife smile.

'Did I tell you Alek likes to sleep with the lights on?' she said.

'Three times,' said Rose. 'Go on. Have a good time. Making up is always the best part.'

Rose was definitely the most reliable friend she had. Alek would be in good hands.

'Go on,' said Rose. 'Call me if there's a problem.'

She pecked Alek on the cheek. He looked so cute. His little green weekend bag was under the table. She slid it near Rose. 'That's his things. You have my number, don't you?' Rose nodded.

Isabel took the bill.

'This is on me.' It was the least she could do.

A blast of bitter wind greeted her as she left the restaurant. She wanted to run all the way back to the house. She could picture Sean waiting there, standing in the hall, smiling, all apologetic.

A last-minute hitch to the merger could easily have stopped Sean from coming home. The merger was supposed to be a coup for BXH; the first time a Chinese state bank had ever taken a large stake in a major American bank, but God only knew what last-minute hitches might occur or what information was needed on Sean's software initiative, facial recognition for all customers.

Sean had said the project would still go ahead, despite the takeover but she had got the distinct impression that he was worried about something, though he hadn't elaborated about it. He'd been so preoccupied during the last few weeks that they'd hardly spoken more than a few words.

Even yesterday morning, when he'd called to tell her he'd be back late, he'd been strangely distant.

'Be home, please,' she mumbled, as the reality of what was happening hit her. She stared at the house as she neared it, looking for any sign that he might be back.

There wasn't.

13

The policeman fixed the blue and white tape stretching from side to side of the alley. The two jumpsuited forensic officers who'd just gone under hadn't bothered to secure it properly after they'd passed; typical.

They were probably too excited about the corpse to think about mundane matters.

It wasn't often you found a murder victim with these sorts of injuries in Soho. He was glad he didn't have to stand near the body any more. How anyone could do such a thing to a beautiful woman was beyond all understanding.

Maybe now, at last, they'd move the body. It was attracting far too much attention. The journalists and the TV crew were a gawping entourage.

'Sorry sir, this area is restricted,' he said.

A tall man with close-cropped dark hair and a weary expression pulled an ID card he'd seen only once before out of his pocket. It was in a brown leather wallet. It had the crown insignia and the words SECURITY SERVICES MI5 beneath it.

'May I take your name for the crime scene log, sir?' said the policeman.

'Henry Mowlam,' said the man, as he lifted the blue tape and passed underneath.

Henry went up the stairs slowly. They were narrow, nicotine coloured. He passed the policeman guarding the entrance to the room. This one had a better look at his card, which was a good thing, and then he let him through.

The room where the girl had been murdered was splattered in blood. There were trails of it on the walls and on the ceiling too. Henry stood in the centre of the room and turned slowly.

Then he went close to the splatter lines. Were they triangles?

He shook his head. 'It's just a coincidence,' he whispered to himself.

Ever since he'd figured out that the square and arrow symbol in that old book could also be a representation of a skull, he'd been seeing them everywhere.

He been warned about how certain 'cases' could get under one's skin at his last annual evaluation and they'd both known what the lady from human resources had meant.

But that didn't mean he was going to heed the warning. There was no way he could just let all this go.

There was a lot more than a takeover and a murder going on here. He could feel it deep down inside him. He'd seen evil before, seen its effects, but he'd never seen it like this, part ancient, part modern. It was like a layered puzzle.

And Henry had a theory about it.

14

Their house, with its blood-red brick frontage, and olive-green eaves and sash windows, looked, she often thought, like something from an Edwardian fairy tale, when London stood at the centre of an Empire that stretched around the globe.

Living there was a fairy tale too. She hadn't expected such happiness, and at times she felt uneasy about how quickly they'd achieved all this. She'd sold her apartment for a small profit. Sean had sold his house for a bigger one. A bargain had come on the market. And she'd deserved it.

Her first marriage, to Mark, who had worked beside her at the British Consulate in Istanbul had been a disaster. They'd lived in a dull Foreign Office apartment in the city and he used to go missing for weeks. The final insult had happened when he'd abandoned her in a house in northern Iraq that was under fire.

He was supposed to be her security escort.

Meeting Sean hadn't seemed like such a big deal when it happened – he was in Istanbul to identify a friend's body – but after they'd escaped those waterlogged tunnels under Hagia Sophia together, she'd wanted to be with him. The feeling was strong, unexpected, but he'd been what she'd needed.

She trusted Sean totally now. He wouldn't let her down, like Mark had. He wasn't like that. After Mark had died in Jerusalem, and Sean had rescued her from a hellhole cave in the Judean Hills, where she'd been held against her will for stepping across the wrong person's path, their connection had become stronger, cemented.

She couldn't imagine anything happening that could break it.

As she looked at her front door, her stomach was churning. She closed her eyes and said a prayer that he would be inside the house.

She remembered the day they'd moved in. They'd arrived together by taxi. And they'd found a window in the attic to stare out of. They'd both gazed over the slate roofs of London to the big wheel of the London Eye and the jumble of glittering buildings all around it. It had been a wonderful summer's evening. The wind had been as light as a baby's breath. They'd made love for hours.

Stay calm.

There were a lot of things she had to do. She had to finish packing, find her black jacket, get some cash out, check the timer switches on the lights, check their passports, tickets, and make sure all the windows in the house were closed.

She looked at her watch. It was eleven forty-five. He had to be back by now. Isabel put her key in the lock. She closed the door behind her quickly to keep the heat in.

'Sean,' she shouted.

There was no reply. Had she missed him? His scarf was hanging at the bottom of the stairs. Had it been there when she went out?

She took it and headed upstairs, sniffing at it. Would she feel heat coming off it, if he'd just put it down?

She called out again as she reached the top of the stairs. Alek's room was on this floor, as was their bedroom and the main bathroom. You had to go up again, to the top floor, to reach their shared office room. The doorbell rang. A short ring. She gripped the banisters and headed down fast, half afraid she might fall in her eagerness. Even before she got to the bottom though, she could see that it wasn't him, and the thumping slowed to be replaced by a jolt of recognition as she opened the door. It was Sabrina, their Neapolitan cleaning lady. Isabel opened the door wide. Sabrina was overweight. She had to stand aside to let her in.

'Ciao, Mrs Ryan,' she said. She wore her trademark big smile, but it disappeared quickly when she saw the look on Isabel's face.

'What happened, eh?'

Isabel tried to smile. She didn't think it worked.

'I'm waiting for Sean. We're supposed to be going to Paris in a few hours. But he didn't come back last night.' The words came out in a rush.

'Men, huh? They're all the same. He'll come back, Mrs Ryan.' She waved her hands in the air. 'He's not going to miss a weekend in Paris with you.' She flicked her hands through the air again, motioning towards Isabel, in an almost jealous gesture. Then she headed for the kitchen. It would be a few hours before she'd finish the ironing and cleaning. Isabel was halfway up the stairs. 'I'll be down in a while,' she said, as Sabrina's back disappeared.

She'd wasted enough time. Sean had a laptop in their office. His electronic calendar was on it. If anything ruled his life, that thing did. If there were meetings he'd been due to attend today that might explain where he was.

His life was dominated by meetings. Trying to break in on one of them would be like trying to break into the Sistine Chapel when they were picking a new pope. But at least she'd know where he was.

She felt like an intruder as she opened Sean's laptop.

But she didn't care. The air in their home office was often musty. Now it felt stuffy. She wondered if Sean still used the same password he'd had a few years before, when they'd both used the same machine.

To her relief he did.

She was in.

She opened Outlook. He had two meetings in it for this morning. One was with Paul Vaughann at eight thirty. Another one, re: merger/Mr Li, was at nine thirty. That was it. It had to be. She relaxed a little. He'd gone straight to the office after staying somewhere last night. He'd probably arrived soon after she'd spoken to George. That would explain it all. He was in that meeting right now, looking at his watch, wondering how he could get out, call her. She launched his web browser. The last page he'd visited was the *Wall Street Journal*.

She swallowed hard, as if a frog was going down, when she saw the main headline on the site: BXH UNDER INVESTIGATION

She read the story, her face tingling as the words scrolled in front of her.

The merger with the Chinese bank had not been completed. A UK Fraud Squad investigation was under way. The bank was claiming short sellers were spreading rumours about the company. The next paragraph talked about the layoffs that would happen at BXH if the merger didn't go ahead. She took a deep breath. Rose was right. Talk about reality sneaking up behind you. Sean had been telling her for a long time that there was nothing to worry about, that the contract with BXH would save the Institute.

Was it all a lie?

She looked out of the window, down at the street. A car horn beeped. A siren echoed distantly. That stupid bank. She banged the window frame with her fist.

Their train tickets were lying on the nearby bookcase. She picked them up and checked the date, before putting them in her back pocket. Whatever happened, they were still going to Paris. To hell with all the rest. She took up the phone handset from beside the laptop. The first thing she should do was check in with BXH. She tapped in his direct dial number.

But it wasn't Sean who answered, it was George Donovan.

Damn.

He announced his name as if he was on parade.

'Hi, George,' she said. There was silence. 'It's Isabel. Is Sean around?' If Sean wasn't answering his phone, he could be in that meeting.

'Hello, Mrs Ryan. Hold on a moment. I'll get him.' His tone was as flat as an unruffled page. The line went quiet.

A burst of relief tingled through her. He was there. He was going to come to the phone. At last!

15

Xena closed the door of the apartment. Pastor Stevson walked slowly into the main room overlooking Fifth Avenue.

He poured himself a coffee, then sat on the black leather sofa.

'I didn't get much sleep, Lord Bidoner, but I'm here.'

'Thank you for coming. We need to move things forward.'

'You told me to get ready, sir. I've done that. The money has been rounded up and the laboratory is up and running. I've even told my wife that His return is near.'

'Have you told anyone else?' said Bidoner.

'No, no. I did as we agreed. She knows nothing about how His coming will be achieved.'

'Tell no one else. I told you this already,' said Lord Bidoner. 'He will return, but we must keep every detail secret. No more talking.' He pointed at Pastor Stevson.

'You ain't got nothing to fear on that count.'

'There are many who will try to stop us.'

'The devil's workers are all around.'

'Your tests are finished, you said?' Lord Bidoner stood up and began pacing.

'You bet, they can clone from any good cell sample now.'

'Good. They should be congratulated.'

'It's all working, like you said. This doc did some research for another IVF clinic, he didn't even put it on their website.' He shrugged. 'It's amazing. The whole process is simpler than I thought.'

Lord Bidoner smiled. 'But he has no idea of our real plans?'

'No idea at all. He still thinks I'm some crackpot millionaire who wants to clone a dead relative. He's happy to get his payoff and then disappear. And he's all ready. He's tested injecting a whole range of DNA cells into defective human embryos at least a dozen times. Each live embryo has been a hundred per cent clone of the DNA sample. He hasn't had one single failure.'

Lord Bidoner smiled. The process of producing full clones had been done with mice for years. It was illegal with human embryos, but once the embryo was planted in a womb no one would know the difference between what they had done and standard IVF treatment.

'All we need now is that DNA sample,' said Stevson. He leaned forward. 'You're sure we can find it?'

'Yes. We had the carbon dating repeated on the page with the symbol on it. It came back again as the period around Christ's death. The symbol will verify the DNA, when we find it.' He sat down.

'Most people assume that such a quest is a romantic fantasy. They have no idea that there is truth at the heart of it.'

'That book resurfacing now, out of the blue, when we can do something with it, has gotta be divine intervention,' said Pastor Stevson.

'I agree.' Lord Bidoner smiled. 'It is an intervention.' He was staring out of the window. There were flakes of snow driving up against it now. It was a surreal view.

Pastor Stevson smiled. 'You know, I always liked that story about Joseph of Arimathea catching Christ's blood in a cup.'

He smiled. 'But I really never thought I'd be involved in a search for it.' He sighed, shook his head, as if remembering something.

'You are sure DNA survives from dried blood that old?'

'Human DNA can survive thousands of years. That's been proven, again and again. DNA cells from long-dried blood have been extracted many times.'

'And you're near to getting into the site?'

'Very near. I've managed to persuade someone to give us some useful security codes. We have access.'

'You're sure it's the right site?'

'It couldn't be anything else.'

The pastor shook his head. 'Like I told you, it's divine intervention.'

He leaned forward, put his hands out as if he was appealing to the heavens.

'We have been chosen to open the Seventh Seal.' He closed his eyes, went forward until he was kneeling on the thick white carpet.

Lord Bidoner had his hands together too.

Pastor Stevson whispered, 'And the vials of his wrath will be poured upon the earth.'

Lord Bidoner stared out at the twinkling lights of the city. The skyscrapers looked like shards of sparkling crystal as the snow flurries gathered in intensity.

'Have you made the transfer into the fund?' he asked, after a minute had passed.

Pastor Stevson opened his eyes, then rose to his feet. His legs were unsteady under him. 'That was a lot of dough you needed, but it's done. A hundred million went into your fund this afternoon.'

'The price of heaven is not cheap,' said Lord Bidoner. 'If there was another way I would have chosen it. Every penny I have is tied up in this. I can assure you of that.'

Xena came into the room. She placed a phone on the oak coffee table. It was vibrating. She was wearing only a gossamer-thin black shift, which came down to her thighs. Her thin body was visible through it.

The pastor stared at her.

'I must take this,' said Lord Bidoner. 'I want you and my friend to pray together.' He put the phone to his ear and walked to the other end of the long room near the double-height window. The glass shone as if it were a mirror. Outside the twinkling lights of other skyscrapers filled the air.

He listened for a few minutes. Then he spoke, forcefully.

'You will make him cooperate. Do whatever it takes,' he said.

He closed the line and put his hand on the window glass.

'The last one is near,' he whispered.

Then he turned and went after Xena and the pastor. She had left the door of the panic room open just a half an inch. Through the crack he could see her helping the pastor take his shirt off. He stood in the darkness of the hall and watched until they were both naked.

She ran her hands all over the pastor's pudgy white body.

Few could resist the way Xena prayed. And this pastor certainly wouldn't have needed much persuasion about the earthy spirituality of her ancient beliefs.

He had no idea what he was letting himself in for.

16

Isabel heard heels tapping across a floor. Then another voice came on the line. A woman's voice. A voice she didn't recognise.

'Sorry, Mrs Ryan, Sean isn't here. George asked me to tell you.'

Her balloon popped.

Anger threatened like a sudden storm.

'But George said he was there two seconds ago. He went to get him.'

There was a long pause.

'Sorry, Mrs Ryan, George was mistaken.' She sounded like a doorman telling some loser she couldn't get in to their club.

'Please, can you check again? Sean is supposed to be in a meeting there now.'

There was a pause. This one was longer than the last. Isabel wanted to shout at the woman.

'I'm sorry, Mrs Ryan, I have to go. Your husband is not here.'

'Can I speak to George?' She wasn't going to get any sense out of this woman.

She replied instantly. 'Sorry, Mrs Ryan, George is out for lunch. Was there anything else?'

'But I just spoke to him!'

'He's gone out now.'

The conversation was coming to a quick halt. But there was one other thing she had to find out.

'Was Sean in at all today?'

'I don't know, Mrs Ryan.' She sounded irritated.

'Okay.' Isabel cut the call.

The activity light on Sean's laptop was going mad. The Wi-Fi light was blinking. They had night-time only updates set on their machines. There shouldn't be any Wi-Fi access going on that wasn't user initiated.

She checked what processes were active. There was one taking up 90 per cent of CPU time. She killed the process. What the hell was going on? They had the best antivirus software in the world.

She checked to see what data streams had been active. It took her a while. The result caused a chill to pass through her. Someone had, in the last few minutes, taken a copy of a document from a folder called TAKEOVER.

She opened the document. It was a three-page executive summary of technical and data protection issues relevant to the Institute's facial recognition project, to be resolved in the event of a takeover of BXH by a non-EU or -US entity.

She felt like a spy, thought about closing the document, but there was the possibility that it had something to do with Sean's disappearance.

The second page was a list of EU and US data protection regulations that would need to be complied with in the event of a takeover. The third page contained a list of the bank's officers who were to be tasked with ensuring compliance with these laws.

The final paragraph made an icy chill move up her spine. '*There are significant data protection risks to the proposed merger. The identification and tracking of criminals, suspects, politicians, law enforcement and government officials will be greatly enhanced with widespread identity-validated facial recognition. Laws created to prevent privacy breeches can be circumvented, as previously described (BHZC124566/8.odm). There are significant state security implications to the project in its current form.'*

She looked at the date of the document. It had last been saved the previous morning before Sean had gone to work. She checked his email sent box. He'd emailed it to a long list of BXH staff, minutes after it had been saved. The next thing he'd done was to come down and have breakfast with her.

She tried to remember what he'd been like. He'd seemed distracted, that was for sure. She looked at her watch. It was twelve fifteen. The second hand was moving fast, as if it was trying to tell her something.

Had George really seen Sean at BXH? Why hadn't he told her Sean wasn't there himself? Was Sean dealing with whatever had made him make that warning? She balled her fist, pushed it against her lips. It was a nervous habit she used to do in uni. She moved her hand away. She wasn't going back to those days.

She should go to the bank, ask to see him. She closed her eyes. There was something depressingly familiar about all this. Rose had told her about one of the BXH wives who had arrived at the bank's offices one day the previous summer and had demanded to know if her husband was in the building, after being told by an assistant that he wasn't there. Apparently he'd stood her up.

The security manager at BXH's reception had relented under the woman's you'll-have-to-arrest-me-if-you-want-me-to-leave glare and had told her that her husband was in the building and that he would personally find him. Isabel had been shocked at the story at the time, and glad that Sean wasn't the type of person who just disappeared.

And now she was going to the bank on a similar mission.

She opened her eyes. Okay, let's get it over with. At least she could get there quickly. Sean always bragged about how it only took twenty minutes on the underground from Sloane Square to get into work.

She ran down the stairs. She could be there and back by two thirty, maybe earlier, if she went straight away.

She knew exactly where his office was in the BXH building too. She'd been to a reception that the bank had given six months earlier. Sean had pointed down a wide, fawn-carpeted corridor to the door behind which he worked. The atmosphere had been hushed in the whole building, as if they had giant machines sucking away noise in every corner. Should she text him, she wondered, as she picked up her leather shoulder bag, tell him she was coming?

No.

She smiled. He hadn't bothered finding a phone to let her know what had happened to him. He deserved her turning up at his office unannounced.

No doubt he'd have some merger-related excuse; the project was collapsing or whatever. And maybe she would forgive him, eventually, but he was going to find out how pissed off she was, right down to the soles of his shiny black Loake shoes.

Sabrina simply smiled at her when she'd told her where she was going.

Outside, the wind was even icier. She glanced at Rose's house as she passed. It looked dead, except for a light on upstairs. Had she taken Alek to the movie? She didn't have time to find out.

At Canary Wharf station the metallic grey escalators were crowded. The steel and glass canopy above seemed to be holding up the gunmetal clouds as she came up to street level.

She could sense people getting ready for the weekend, for

their Friday night out. No matter how many offices were gutted by redundancies, there was always an appetite for a good time in London. If anything, she'd heard it had increased in the past year, as people threw caution to the four winds.

This was BXH's world.

As she crossed the road on Bank Street, past the gleaming towers of fund managers and little-known banks, she shivered as the ice-sharpened wind cut into every exposed piece of skin. *What does this say about our marriage if I have to go to his office to find him?*

As she came up to the BXH building she noticed the airplane-wing shape of a black Mercedes S-Class standing at the curb. A trickle of white smoke was slipping from its exhaust.

Paul Vaughann had an S-Class. As she passed the vehicle she gave it a quick glance.

There was someone in the back. Her snow-blonde hair was hard to miss. It was Vaughann's wife, Suzanne. She was staring at her.

She didn't nod, or shown any sign of recognition. Was she surprised? No. They'd met only once. That time she'd had the demeanour of an ice sculpture too.

She was probably waiting for her husband to come out of the BXH building. With the bonuses he'd notched up in the last few years there wouldn't be any change in their lifestyle, whatever happened about the merger.

She felt underdressed as she entered the marble and glass canyon-walled reception area of BXH, but she didn't care.

The place had been designed to look like the home of money. Intimidated was how you felt in other, lesser institutions. Here the feeling was of total awe. There was a hush in the air, broken only by the click of heels, a big shiny gold logo filled the far wall, and the smell of money, of leather and sweet marble polish, was hard to ignore.

She waited in line, like a supplicant, at one of the queues in front of the reception desk. There was a group of five, mainly Chinese, businesspeople in front of her.

They were muttering among themselves. They looked sleekly prosperous in their well-cut suits and shiny hair. The security guards on each side of the reception desk overseeing the glass turnstiles, which were the real access points to the building, looked like heavyweight boxers.

Behind the reception desk there were four model-type receptionists, all wearing black uniforms and with TV-advert hair. They must have spent half their spare time keeping themselves glossy.

It was her turn.

The girl behind the desk smiled, her pencil-line eyebrows raised, as if she too was surprised to see Isabel standing there in her fashionably torn jeans and slightly distressed suede jacket, but she was far too polite to say.

'Can you ask my husband, Sean Ryan, to come down, please?'

Isabel returned the girl's smile with equal insincerity. She had emphasised the word husband. She knew that for many of these receptionists the pinnacle of achievement would be for them to marry one of the bankers who slipped past their desks every day with few sideways glances.

'Certainly, Mrs Ryan. Please wait over there.' The receptionist pointed at a cluster of black leather sofas to her right. They weren't in the best position in the foyer, the Chinese were occupying that, but it wasn't the plumber's entrance either.

She went to her allotted place, anxiety burrowing through her gut, as if it was trying to break out.

'Please be here,' she whispered to herself.

She watched the elevators. If Sean were to appear, a worried smile on his face, she'd be tempted to hug him, but she might just hit him instead. Hard too. He deserved it. Every time one of the elevator doors opened her nerves jangled. And every time it wasn't Sean, her heart contracted as if an angry hand was squeezing it. She saw a few faces she knew from the reception they'd been to, announcing Sean's project was going live. None of them gave her a second glance.

Then the buzzer the receptionist had given her, a thick credit-card-shaped thing, was making a noise in her hand.

She stood. A woman she didn't know was talking to the receptionist.

She was waving at her. Isabel hurried towards her.

'I'm sorry, Mrs Ryan, your husband isn't here. We've checked.' Her smile was sweet, like a goodbye kiss.

17

Henry Mowlam closed the document he'd been looking at. He stretched. The files he'd extracted from Sean Ryan's laptop were of less interest than he'd hoped. The description of what had happened to Sean and Isabel in Jerusalem he'd checked before.

The implications of the facial recognition project he was already aware of. The matter had been discussed at length within his unit and beyond. The project raised lots of red flags. The ability of a bank, and by implication a state's security, revenue and police departments, to know who had what amounts lodged where throughout the world, gave unprecedented powers of oversight to any who had access to that information.

By matching databases of who was controlling individual bank accounts you could uncover undeclared income, suspicious money flows and match accounts in alternative names for people with multiple passports and identities. High definition security cameras that could identify individuals at half a mile meant opportunities for hiding wealth or ill-gotten gains were disappearing.

Facial recognition data, matched with global bank account

statements would give foreign powers access to information on the wealth of individuals, regulators, businessmen and even politicians, as they arrived in that country.

Such data would provide endless opportunities for coercion of the unexplainably rich and the embarrassingly poor.

But they hadn't reached that point yet. Thankfully. The software was still only being piloted in a few locations at BXH.

What concerned Henry more now was the fact that he didn't know where Sean Ryan was.

The man in charge of the most sensitive information technology project in the United Kingdom, possibly in the western world, had disappeared into thin air.

He didn't like it. And it wasn't his only worry about Sean Ryan. The number of unanswered questions swirling around him and BXH was growing at an alarming rate.

He felt like a theatregoer watching actors pushing hard into the stage curtain while they moved around unseen behind it. There was something going on and he was only glimpsing part of it.

What he knew for sure was that there was a connection between the murder in Soho and Mr Ryan. The connection was looser than it might be, but it was real. The book Sean Ryan had found in Istanbul contained pages sewn in about obscene prayer practices from the early days of Christianity. It listed prayers that required real blood being poured and drunk, fire rituals, the castration of offenders and the murder of heretics and apostates, including cutting patches of skin from victims.

The most gruesome ritual involved murdering four people in twenty-four hours, each in a more sadistic way.

The purpose of that ritual was given in a Latin phrase above the small line-drawn images of how each murder should be carried out.

The phrase was: *Quattuor Invocare Unum*.

It had been translated as *Four to Invoke the One*. Henry shook his head. Whoever the sick bastard was who'd killed that poor girl, at least he hadn't started the ritual where four people were going to die. He never wanted to see someone being murdered the way it was shown in those drawings.

Because they were the cruellest things he'd seen in a long time.

18

Isabel held the edge of the desk. She was getting the runaround. Something was going on that she wasn't being told about. That's what it felt like, even if she couldn't prove it.

Yet.

'Is the security manager available?' she said, as calmly as she could, addressing the receptionist.

The woman looked at her, her mouth slightly open. Then her expression changed. Her mask of smiling professionalism slipped back on.

'Certainly, Mrs Ryan. If you'd like to wait over there, I'll see if she's available.'

Isabel sat on the front edge of one of the sofas, examining everyone who passed by. Was it still too early to call the police? Would BXH be a bit more accommodating if she had a police officer with her or if she told them they were on their way?

She looked at her watch. It was still only eight or nine hours since he should have been home, not twenty-four. She took a slow breath, then counted to ten. The world around her was continuing in real time; prosperous-looking people were going out for their lunch break. Though many of them were grim-faced, others were smiling, as if they had nothing to worry about and the stories all over the media about BXH were just lies.

The buzzer in her hand went off again. She turned. Standing beside the receptionist was a small, wide-shouldered, cropped-haired woman. There was going to be no friendly smiles with this lady.

'Are you the security manager?' were Isabel's first words.

'Your husband is not here, Mrs Ryan.' Her tone was as definite as a punch in the ribs. 'His car is in the car park all right. It's been here since last night. The rules of this building are quite clear. No employee is allowed to leave a vehicle overnight. When you see your husband, will you ask him to remove it?' She looked at Isabel as if she had a contagious disease.

'Can I speak to George Donovan?'

'You'll have to call him later. He's out.'

'A lot of good that'll do.'

The woman recoiled, as if Isabel had slapped her.

'It's all I can suggest, Mrs Ryan.'

She thanked the woman for her help, and crossed the foyer, pulling her coat tight around her as she left the building.

The black Mercedes was still standing, purring at the curb.

Then it came to her. Maybe the wonderful Mrs Vaughann might know something about what had happened last night. Her husband had probably been with Sean.

She headed for the car and tapped on the window, hard. Mrs Vaughann stared at her, eyes wide, as if Isabel was a beggar. She knocked again, harder this time.

The window slid open less than an inch.

'Mrs Vaughann, we met last summer. I'm Isabel Ryan. My husband works with Paul.'

'Isabel,' Mrs Vaughann shouted, as if she'd found a decades-lost friend. The door clicked open.

Mrs Vaughann leaned forward. She looked like someone waiting desperately for something, the way an alcoholic looks while waiting for a bar to open. Her eyebrows were raised. Her skin was pale. Her cheeks hollow. Her brow was all scrunched up.

Isabel stepped inside, then pulled the door closed behind her. It made a perfect reassuring clunk. The driver was in front behind a wall of thick glass. He didn't even turn his head as Isabel got in.

'I have to tell you,' said Mrs Vaughann. 'I almost didn't open the window.' She sounded amazed at herself that she had.

'Thanks. It's horrible out there.' Isabel shivered. 'There's something I want to ask you. You always have your finger on the pulse.' This was the woman most of the other BXH wives wanted to be.

Mrs Vaughann smiled, like a Siamese cat enjoying being stroked. 'Please, call me Suzi.' She put her hand on Isabel's arm. Her skin looked translucent, as if she was made of expensive porcelain.

'You poor thing. You're wet.' She handed Isabel a tissue.

'I'm okay.' Isabel rubbed her hands together.

Mrs Vaughann leaned back, looked at her appraisingly. She made an exasperated noise.

'You know, I'm glad you came over. I do hate sitting here. You know they've gone too far this time.' She sounded angry.

'Who's gone too far?'

Mrs Vaughann picked up a copy of the *Evening Standard* lying on the floor near her feet. It was folded open at an inside page. She pushed it towards Isabel as if it had a bad smell. Her hand was gripping the paper so hard her knuckles were white. Then she uncurled them, as if she didn't want Isabel to see how anxious she was.

'A few BXH people were at some horrible place last night.'

Near the top of the page there was a picture of police tape cordoning off the front of what looked like a crummy restaurant. On a canopy above the door was part of a word – Magnol. Isabel's pulse was beating on both sides of her forehead.

The headline above the picture read: 'Lap Dancer Murdered.'

A prickling sensation ran up her neck. 'BXH people went there?'

Mrs Vaughann looked at her as if Isabel was a slow learner. 'They were there when that poor girl was murdered.'

Sean couldn't have anything to do with this, could he? He'd been working late last night.

Please, God, make it so that he isn't involved in this.

'What is it you wanted to ask me, Isabel?'

She swallowed. 'Sean's missing.' Her voice cracked. 'I wanted to find out if you knew where they were last night.'

Mrs Vaughann's eyebrow arched. 'Since when is he missing?' She sounded almost happy at the news.

'He should have come back at two, maybe three this morning. He hasn't turned up.'

Mrs Vaughann sucked air in through her pursed lips. 'Paul didn't come back either,' she said quickly. 'We're in the same boat, my dear.'

She put a hand on Isabel's thigh. It was a sisterly gesture, she knew, but Isabel was tempted to say her husband wasn't like Mr Vaughann. Sean had told her that Vaughann liked to be friends with lots of women in the bank. Friends with benefits was the rumour.

Sean wasn't like that.

'You should know,' said Mrs Vaughann, 'that if I find out there's another woman involved or if he's got anything to do with what happened to that dancer, I'll cut his equipment off myself. He won't be a big swinging dick if I do that.' She sounded like she meant it.

Mrs Vaughann pressed her hand to her pale forehead. She looked the picture of a wronged corporate wife in her Jimmy Choo shoes and steel-grey Agnès B dress. She'd probably just come back from one of her charity coffee mornings, which she was famous for.

'What about your husband? Do you have any idea why he . . . ?' Mrs Vaughann's voice trailed off. Her pencil eyebrows were raised even more now.

Isabel imagined what she was going to say next. Was Sean cheating on her? She'd been pushing the thought away all morning. But she couldn't do that forever.

Her standard reply to any girlfriend, who suggested he might stray, was to say that he never stayed out late. But she couldn't even say that now. She plucked at her sleeve, as if there were fluff there. There wasn't.

'I don't know what to say.' She knew she sounded uncertain.

Mrs Vaughann looked at her and smiled. Her teeth were perfect. Most of the wives of the bank's top executives had tight-lipped superior expressions. Most of them still had a personal masseuse, trainer and a holistic therapist pampering them every day or two. They usually tried to hide how superior they felt to the rest of humanity, but not very successfully.

Smugness oozed from them like the rotting smell from a carcass. But Mrs Vaughann was different. Her smile was genuine.

'All men are bastards,' she said.

'I trust Sean,' said Isabel. But there was a hollowness in her tone, as if she didn't believe what she was saying. Her mouth was dry too.

She shook her head, glared out the window at some people leaving the bank.

'I'm sure you're right about Sean,' said Mrs Vaughann. 'It's probably just bad timing, him going missing.'

Isabel turned to her. There was something sad about the way Mrs Vaughann looked, all taut, like a wire about to snap. Suddenly she felt sorry for her.

'Have you talked to Paul about all this?' She pointed at the *Evening Standard*.

If staff from the bank, senior staff, had been in that sleazy club when a dancer was murdered that was definitely bad news for the bank. Their reputation would be in the gutter. But did Isabel care? Sean mightn't have even been there. He certainly wouldn't have done anything stupid there.

'No, I haven't. Not yet. But I'm not leaving here until I do.'

Isabel stretched towards the door handle. Outside, hail was ticking and slithering against the window. Great, even the weather was conspiring against her.

'I have to go.'

Mrs Vaughann squeezed her arm, held it.

Then she coughed, and bent forward. As she did Isabel caught a glimpse of her neck, and saw rows of wrinkles. She looked older than Isabel had imagined. There are some things even Botox and plastic surgery can't hide.

'Prepare yourself, Isabel. The media will be all over us because of this takeover.'

Her eyebrows rose. They looked to be in the wrong place now. Her eyes were fixed on Isabel, as if she was working out if she could trust her. Her lips were pressed tight. Mrs Vaughann looked out of the windows on both sides, as if she thought someone might be listening to them.

'Your husband is leading the facial recognition project, isn't he?'

'Yes. Is there a problem with it?'

Mrs Vaughann's eyes narrowed. 'There's a problem with everything at the moment, Isabel. I just hope your husband is able to cope with the stress.'

She looked worried.

'I have to go.' Isabel opened the door. The urge to leave was getting stronger by the second.

She had to find Sean. And she wasn't going to do that listening to Mrs Vaughann. She stepped out of the car and didn't look back.

The hail was coming down like a million icy arrows. She raced for the entrance to the underground.

19

Adar got out of the taxi. He headed for the coffee shop overlooking Bank Street. He could see the front and side entrance to BXH from one of the window seats.

He put his backpack on the floor and sat in the empty chair opposite the older grey-suited man who was talking softly into his phone. He eyed Adar with surprise and suspicion. A minute later he stood and left the coffee shop.

Perhaps it was the way he'd stared at him, unblinkingly, or perhaps it was the hood that covered his head, which he kept pulled down to the level of his eyebrows.

The only time he'd taken it off had been when he was walking through immigration at the City Airport corporate terminal twenty-four hours before. Immigration officials like to be able to see who they're letting into the UK and for people to smile.

He accommodated them.

The Bombardier Global 5000 he had arrived on would be ready to fly back to La Guardia on Long Island, in New York State, in a few hours. It was the fastest private long-range jet available. The leasing company they had hired it from had allowed Lord Bidoner to provide his own crew.

Adar's flight record was well beyond the number of hours needed to pilot long distance with only passengers, and La Guardia was used to the odd arrangements of the sporting and corporate elite, heading for their Gold Coast Long Island mansions. He put his day old pay-as-you-go phone down in front of him and downloaded the email app. He looked at the saved message in the draft folder.

Red, it read.

He added the word 'green' to the message, then saved it. That was enough. Lord Bidoner would be able to see that he was about to proceed.

He downloaded the Instagram app, and logged in as the agreed identity. His next message would be a picture of a London black cab. That would mean he had completed his next task and was on his way back with the package. He glanced at the entrance to BXH as he put the phone away.

He didn't want to miss him. He had a message for George Donovan. All he had to do was work out how to deliver it.

20

This was all getting ridiculous, Sean wouldn't have gone to a strip club – he was not that kind of man. But it would explain the late nights. The thought of Sean visiting that club left an ache in Isabel's chest. The weekend in Paris didn't matter now. He'd been the best thing in her life since they'd come back from Istanbul. She could almost feel his arms around her when she thought about him.

As the cab came up the street she saw a police car outside their next door neighbour's house. A dark Ford was double-parked outside their house. She got out of the cab by the police car, and peered in. What was she expecting, Sean to be in handcuffs in the back?

He wasn't. She fumbled for her keys. The black paint on their front door glistened. The glass was opaque. She could see a shape moving on the other side. She heard someone behind her, turned.

It was one of the neighbours. She was wearing a bobble hat. She glanced at Isabel, then looked away as she passed, as if she suspected that the police car had something to do with her. Isabel didn't care. She turned back to the door. She wanted her old life back. Now.

She took out her keys. Her hand was trembling. The mist on her breath filled the air as she turned the front door key.

Before she even got a chance to take it out, someone on the other side yanked the door open, almost catching her fingers. A burly, hard-eyed policewoman was looking at her as if she were a criminal.

Isabel felt weak. Blood was rushing the wrong way inside her. Her knees had stopped working.

The police were in her house.

'What's going on? Where's my husband?' Her words came out in a rush.

'Are you Isabel Ryan?' the policewoman said. She'd have been able to find a place on a Soviet-era ice hockey team, she was that big.

'Yes?'

The policewoman looked at her. For a heart-twisting moment Isabel thought she was going to say that Sean was dead.

Then another man, in plain clothes, said something Isabel didn't catch, and the policewoman stepped aside.

'I'm Inspector Kirby,' said the man. His accent was from the north of England. He was tall and had a sickle-like jaw. He was standing at the bottom of their stairs, as if he'd just come down.

What was going on?

'Don't be alarmed, Mrs Ryan. Your cleaner let us in. We have a search warrant.' He patted his breast pocket.

She didn't want to see any search warrant. She had nothing to hide.

'Is Sean okay?' she said quickly.

'We thought you might be able to help us with that, Mrs Ryan.'

The weakness in her legs came rushing back. She put a

hand out, steadied herself against the wall. The policewoman reached towards her. She shrugged her away, straightened herself, and focused on the inspector.

'Why the hell are you in my house?' She knew she sounded angry, but she didn't care.

'We're investigating some serious matters, Mrs Ryan.' His voice had a passive quality, but his eyes were as hard as granite.

'Under our search warrant powers we're permitted to remove all the computer equipment in your home, and any papers or any other items related in any way to the matters under investigation. All these powers have been granted under regulations contained in the Financial Services and Markets Act 2000.'

It sounded like a set of words that he was well practiced in delivering.

'Your cleaner showed us your husband's office.'

'Sorry, Mrs Ryan. There was nothing I could do,' called out a weak voice from down the corridor. Sabrina's head poked up over Inspector Kirby's shoulder.

'It's all right, Sabrina. It's to do with the bank.' She closed her eyes for a moment. She had to focus. She couldn't care about them being here.

'You're trying to find my husband?' She rubbed her forehead. It was slick with sweat.

'Yes,' was Inspector Kirby's curt reply. His tone made it clear he thought she should be the one answering questions.

'I have to go, Mrs Ryan.' Sabrina pushed past the inspector, gave Isabel a weak smile, and patted her arm as she went by.

Sabrina opened the door and then went out.

A gust of freezing wind swept in. The policewoman followed Sabrina outside, pulling the door closed behind her. 'We need to ask you some questions, Mrs Ryan. Where can we do that?' Inspector Kirby looked like someone who'd seen everything the world could throw in front of a policeman.

'You probably know the house as well as I do by now, Inspector. Where would you suggest?'

'The kitchen.'

She led the way. The walls seemed to be closing in as she went down the corridor, as if the house was suddenly smaller than it had been, as if it wasn't hers any more.

'You have a nice house,' said the inspector. His tone was cool, official, but there was a hint of something else in it, as if he was questioning how they could afford such a big place.

She entered the kitchen and stared at Alek's baby drawings on the wall, which Sean had framed so beautifully and simply, in black wood with a thick white border. A lump formed fast in her throat.

Had he done something stupid?

Why would the police be here if he was innocent?

Her fingers felt icy. She hadn't noticed the cold when she was outside, adrenaline must have been warming her up, but now she was back in the house, and with the police here, they felt frozen.

There was a picture of her on a cork notice board on the kitchen wall, from the time before Alek had been born. She looked pale, smiling tentatively. Sean had been so concerned about her back then. She sat in the green wicker chair at the end of the kitchen table. It was a giant well-worn table, the type they had in the kitchens of big old English country houses. And now a policeman was sitting at it with her. She gripped the edge of the table with both hands. She must have looked stupid, or mad. But she didn't care. Inspector Kirby sat, leaning over his notebook. She forced herself to breathe. They hadn't told her he had done anything wrong. Not yet.

21

The pastor was spread-eagled on the steel bed. There was a gag in his mouth. He was naked. His eyes were wide open. He'd been hours in that position.

Xena had persuaded him once again to allow her to put handcuffs on him, but now he was definitely regretting it. She hadn't been in the room for a long time. And she hadn't left him like this the first time they had done it. Lord Bidoner had told him she was a bonus for him then, but he was starting not to like it.

If this was some technique of hers, it wasn't doing anything for him.

What time was it, he wondered. Martha would be going mad. He hadn't told her where he was going or what he was doing.

As if he could.

He tried to break the handcuffs again, pulled at them hard, but they were too strong.

That thought worried him. And his heart started beating faster again. He should have taken his medication before he came out. All this excitement would not be good for him.

He thought about shouting for Lord Bidoner, but he decided to wait a little longer. She had to come back soon to release him. He had things to do in New York.

He shivered. Maybe he shouldn't have told Lord Bidoner that he had discussed anything they were doing with his family. Hadn't he heard him rant after he found out what had happened in Jerusalem?

He listened.

The door to the room opened. In walked Xena. Pastor Stevson began grunting. He couldn't speak properly, because of the gag, but it was clear he was appealing to be let free.

And then his eyes widened some more. She was naked. And the snake tattoo around her thigh rippled as she walked towards him. This was getting interesting again.

What was she going to do?

She leaned towards him, rested her hand on his big white belly.

'*Secunda quattuor invocare unum*,' she whispered.

That was when he felt something cold and sharp touch his belly.

22

'What's all this about, Inspector?' She tried to sound collected. The hesitation in her voice didn't help though.

Inspector Kirby was holding a silver pen as if it were a baton, and he was about to conduct an orchestra.

'We don't want to alarm you, Mrs Ryan, but we need to speak to your husband, urgently.'

'That makes two of us, at least.'

He smiled.

'Has he done something wrong?' She dreaded the answer, shifted her body back a little, as if it was a blow she was expecting.

The inspector shrugged, noncommittally.

'I don't know, Mrs Ryan. We believe he has information that could help us with our enquiries.'

She let out her breath.

'What enquiries?'

'I work for the City of London Financial Crime Unit. We're investigating activities at BXH.'

'What activities?'

'I am not at liberty to discuss that. Let's just say our

investigations, since the eurozone crisis, now cover the management and the supervision of all financial institutions.'

'What the hell does that mean?'

'I'm not here to defend or describe our investigations, Mrs Ryan. But we do have the power to carry them out. The public expects robust supervision and that is what we provide.'

It sounded like a pat answer he'd learned by heart. She licked her lips. They were dry, rough. At least he hadn't said they were investigating him for murder.

'Can you tell me the last time you saw your husband, and the last time you spoke to him, please?'

'I saw him yesterday morning before he left for work. We haven't spoken since. He sent me a text message telling me he was going to come home late last night. But he never turned up.'

'And you've tried his mobile phone?'

'Lots. It must be switched off or the battery's dead.'

'Is that unusual for him?'

'Yes, totally.'

'Did your husband discuss his work with you, tell you anything about what's going on at BXH?'

Had other men's wives, who he'd interviewed, told him everything they knew, just because he'd asked them so politely?

'No.' She shook her head, took her hands from the edge of the table, rubbed them across its waxy surface, taking comfort from the reassuring smoothness.

The inspector had an I'm-glad-I'm-not-you expression on his face.

'Why are there so many police officers in my home?'

'We need to do a proper search, Mrs Ryan.' He shrugged, as if none of it was his doing.

She felt a blast of icy wind coming from the corridor.

He turned, looked over his shoulder. Then he stood.

'Wait here, please.'

She did as she was told.

She heard voices, the sound of people creaking the floorboards upstairs. She stood, then sat down again. A part of her wanted to fight them, ask them all to leave, shout at them. But she knew it wouldn't do any good. She rubbed her hands together, trying to warm them.

The policewoman came into the kitchen. She dominated the room, smiling at Isabel as she sat down. It was her turn to ask the questions.

She started by questioning Isabel about her relationship with Sean, whether he had gone missing before. Isabel told her what had happened a few weeks ago. The policewoman took notes. Then she asked Isabel whether Sean told her much about his work.

'No, he doesn't talk about anything to do with BXH. I told your colleague.' She leaned forward. 'Why aren't you concerned about his safety? He's missing. Anything could have happened to him.'

The policewoman's expression was not sympathetic.

'We are concerned about your husband, Mrs Ryan. A missing persons alert has been issued. If we find out what has happened to him you will be notified.'

'What do you do when someone's reported missing?'

'We check out all the likely places, hospitals, police cells, the river police, the security people at his work.'

'The river police?'

The policewoman looked at her, assessing her, it seemed. 'In case he committed suicide.' Her expression softened a little.

She swallowed hard. Suicide. She held the edge of the table tight, her fingers white with the effort.

'Are you all right, Mrs Ryan?'

Isabel nodded.

The policewoman went on, leaning towards her. 'Did you and Mr Ryan have any marital problems?' She emphasised the word, marital.

'No.' Isabel looked her in the eye.

'How does your husband normally react to stress?' She reminded Isabel of a cat playing with its food.

'Nothing gets to Sean. He just keeps rolling, bouncing off things. That's how he puts it.' She sat up straighter, the memory of him saying that playing through her mind.

The policewoman smiled at Isabel, as if she didn't believe her.

'We were supposed to be meeting Sean's uncle and aunt tomorrow. They're on holiday in Paris.' A pang of guilt ran through her. Sean's uncle had been diagnosed with Huntington's a few years before. The last thing he needed was for his dead brother's son, who he'd promised to look out for, to disappear and for the police to be investigating him.

How was she going to tell them?

'Did your husband organise this holiday?' The policewoman's eyebrows were up.

'No, I did.'

'Was there any particular reason for the timing? Isn't BXH pretty busy right now?'

'We're going to meet Sean's nearest relatives. This is the time when they come over to Europe. And we need a break. I deserve it. Sean deserves it. He's been working very hard.' Isabel gave her a paper-thin smile.

'Have you any reason to believe your husband might be with another woman?' The policewoman leaned forward. Her eyelids were drooping.

'No.'

She made a note in her notebook, then glanced at Isabel. She wasn't smiling now.

'I've never even suspected him of anything like that.'

'We're just trying to understand where he might be.'

There was a stubborn look on the policewoman's face, as if she wasn't at all convinced that Sean wasn't with a mistress somewhere, enjoying himself.

'We found passports upstairs, but not your husband's, Mrs Ryan. Does he keep his somewhere else?'

'I thought they were all upstairs.' Had Sean taken his with him? Her hands felt cold again. She spotted the red apples and Conference pears she'd bought the day before to snack on. The thought of eating made her stomach tighten.

'What did you study in college, Mrs Ryan?'

She didn't answer for a few moments. It suddenly struck her that she might be a suspect too; that her background made it possible that there was more going on here.

She'd become an IT security consultant because she wanted to do something that took advantage of her security experience while she was with the Foreign Office.

'Biology,' she said. When she went to the University of London, she'd imagined biological science would be a great course to get dates on. As it turned out, most of the other students were either too painfully shy to talk to a girl, or they acted like superior nerds.

The policewoman sniffed. 'I see.' There was a pause while she wrote something down. 'And have you worked for BXH at any time?'

'No,' she replied. 'I worked at the Foreign Office until a few years ago. But you will be aware that I'm not allowed to talk about my work there.' They had to know about the Official Secrets Act. They would have signed it themselves.

From the curious look on the policewoman's face, Isabel got the impression she thought Isabel was hiding something.

'My husband is working on a project for BXH. That's all.'

The policewoman gave her a nod.

'Did your husband keep anything from his office anywhere else in the house, aside from in that room upstairs?'

'No.' She shook her head.

That was when she noticed all the drawers in the kitchen cabinet, one of those old ones with shelves for showing plates and jugs, were a little pulled out. Had the police been through every corner of their house already?

'When will you be finished here?' Isabel waved at the house above them.

The policewoman countered with, 'Do you mind showing me where your husband kept whatever he did bring home?'

As they went upstairs she saw a plainclothes officer exiting the front of the house carrying one of those bright blue plastic storage boxes.

When they got upstairs Inspector Kirby was pulling out books from Sean's bookcase in the office, flicking through them one at a time, putting them back haphazardly. Sean would have gone crazy if he'd seen him.

'This is the only place Sean kept anything from work. If he did bring anything home it would be in this room. And that laptop is mine.' She pointed at her shiny black Toshiba. It was in a pile with Sean's laptop and some papers near the door.

'I'm afraid we'll have to take that one too.' The inspector's tone could have sliced steel. He looked at the policewoman. They were communicating in some unspoken language.

She should have been raging, fuming at them, but she wasn't. Every file on her laptop was stored on the internet, in a cloud. None of what they were doing mattered. The only thing that mattered was getting Sean back.

She stood there, watching him as he took out and looked through the last of the books on the bottom row of Sean's bookcase. After he was finished he stood and surveyed the room.

The plainclothes officer she'd seen carrying the other blue box came into the room. He had an empty box in his hand now.

'Just one more, Tom,' he said. He bent down and put the laptops into the box. He dropped them in, as if they were far more rugged than you'd imagine they would be.

'Be careful,' said Isabel.

'Thank you for your cooperation, Mrs Ryan. We're finished, for now.'

'You're going?' The weight on her chest diminished.

'Yes, Mrs Ryan. We'll let you know if we find out where your husband is, and please, don't forget, call us if he contacts you or you hear any news about his whereabouts. We wouldn't want to disturb you again. We do take into account the impact our investigations have on families. We try to be as reasonable as we can.'

To Isabel that sounded like a threat.

He took out his card, handed it to her.

When they were all gone she sat on the stairs, trembling. She felt exposed, vulnerable. They'd poked into every corner of the house, of their lives.

Her watch said 4:20 p.m. She held her head. She felt as if she'd aged ten years in the last few hours.

23

The dirty white van with the ACE PLUMBING sticker on its side shook a little as the police car went by. The two men inside didn't react. They were in the back of the van and could see the front door of the house the police had come from and the entrance to the lane that ran around the houses without moving an inch. But they couldn't be seen. The black one-way filter on the back windows of the van made sure of that.

Each of the men had two plastic bottles. One to drink from. A second to piss into. It could be a long night. A lot of people stay at home, weeping, when their lives fall apart. Others head for relatives or friends. Some ramble the streets or visit people they blame for what's happened to them.

Their instructions from Henry Mowlam had been clear. Report on the movements of the target, photograph everyone she meets. Watch out, in particular, for anyone else taking an interest in Isabel Ryan or her house. It was unusual for Henry to request live surveillance, but when he did there was always a good reason.

As the larger of the two men moved in his seat, he reached down and adjusted the holster strapped above his ankle. It was unlikely he'd have to use the weapon, but he always carried it. You never knew what way a job like this could go. There had already been one recent murder in London related to the woman they were watching and further incidents in the past.

He pulled his trouser leg down, hiding the gun.

'Did you hear what happened to that dancer who was murdered' he said, softly. Then he leaned towards his companion.

'Whoever did that was pure fucking evil. This ain't no ordinary murderer we're tracking. Just make sure you stay awake on your watch, mate. I don't want no pieces of my skin getting cut off.'

24

Had the police got what they wanted, Isabel wondered? Did Sean have anything she didn't know about on his laptop?

She pulled her phone out of her pocket. The button on the side, which set it to ring silently, had been moved. It did that of its own accord occasionally, just to annoy her.

Had he called?

She checked.

No. No one had.

In front of her, on the hall floor, jutting out from under the crimson curtain that hung down on one side of their front door, was a small pile of letters. She picked them up, more out of habit than anything else. Her hand was trembling. She pressed it to her lips, forced the trembling away.

She went to the kitchen and opened the letters. There was an early Christmas card from Rose, a letter from the gas company, a request for immediate funds from Save the Children, and a bill from their mobile phone company. She was about to put them all in the dresser, in the usual place, when something struck her.

A few months before, when they'd been planning to switch phone companies, she'd gone through one of these phone bills. She'd wondered whether they needed all that detail, all those pages. Shouldn't they have stopped getting this paper by now? Hadn't she asked for an online-only bill years ago?

But maybe this was exactly what she needed, details of who Sean had been calling recently. If, and this was definitely one of her total nightmare scenarios, he was seeing someone else, if that was the explanation for all this, there had to be a chance that someone else's number was in this bill.

Her hand hesitated as she looked at the pages. She didn't like prying.

Would it be better that he had been with someone else, than that he was involved in some fraud at his office or something worse? She closed her eyes for a moment, rubbed at her forehead. It wasn't a choice she wanted to make.

She examined the bill. She felt compelled to look, to check the numbers. She examined each page. Some of the numbers she recognised. Their home number, her mobile number, his office number. Then there was a sprinkling of other numbers, some the same, many different.

This was totally impossible. How could she ever figure this out? There was no way she was going to be able to find out anything except by ringing these numbers, and if she did ring them, what was she going to say? Are you and my husband having an affair? Is he hiding out with you?

Yes, that was going to work.

And then she noticed something.

Right at the end, there was a series of calls to the same number. Sean had made ten calls in one day to the number, five the next. Then the calls had stopped. That was two weeks ago.

Who had he been calling ten times?

Why had he stopped?

Her breathing quickened. She could imagine some woman answering the phone, laughing, then cutting the line, if she called the number, asked if Sean was there. Would she hear his voice in the background? Would the woman say something about Sean? Was Sean's real life somewhere else? She stood, gripped the back of a wooden chair, held it tight with both hands. It was clear what she had to do.

Bzzzzzz.

The front doorbell. Was it Sean? Hope switched on like a floodlight in her brain. Then she heard a strange voice, and the floodlight switched off again.

'Taxi.'

It was the taxi she'd ordered to take them to the station.

She pulled the door open fast. What the driver thought she had no idea, but she expected the £20 note she gave him helped.

As she tapped in the number Sean had been calling into her phone, she caught a glimpse of herself, hunched over, in the mirror in the hall. She looked haunted.

Bzzz. Bzzz.

An urge to end the call gripped her, as if she was a teenager ringing a boy for the first time. She pressed the phone tighter to her ear.

'Hello.' A jolt of recognition passed through her. It was George's voice. This was his mobile number. As the cogs in her brain turned she opened her mouth, closed it again. Nothing came out. Then a panicky feeling hit her.

'George, sorry to bother you.'

Her brain had worked out what to do.

'Who's that?' She heard noises in the background, laughing, the chink of glasses. He was in a bar or at a party.

'It's Isabel, George. I was wondering if I could ask you something.'

'Isabel?' He didn't sound pleased.

'Did you see Sean today?'

'No.' It sounded as if he wanted to get her off the line.

'George, I need your help.' She spoke quickly. 'Sean's missing. I don't know if he's in trouble or what's going on. When did you see him last? Please.' She tried to sound firm, but polite.

'Sorry, I can't help. Why don't you try the office or,' he paused, 'the police.'

'George.' She was begging now. 'Your number, this number I just rang, it's all over Sean's phone bill. He called you lots of times, every day last month. Then the calls just stopped. What happened, George? What's going on?'

He didn't rush to reply.

She heard a girl shout. 'Georgie, over here!' Then there was a click. For one taken-aback moment she thought he'd put the phone down.

'Mrs Ryan. I can't help you.' His tone was serious. 'But I'll tell you this. I warned your husband. Maybe he should have listened. Now I have to go. There's nothing else I can tell you.'

The line went dead.

She put the phone to her forehead, pressed it into her skin, thought about what had just happened. Then she pressed the redial number. He wasn't going to get away that easy. His line rang only once. Then he answered it. She spoke before he could say anything.

'What did you warn him about, George?'

She could hear him breathing.

'I don't have to talk to you. Your husband isn't in our team any more.'

Something went zinging through her. If Sean wasn't in the team any more, had the contract been pulled already? Was that what was going on?

'George. I'm going mad, please.' It felt as if a lifeline was being pulled away. It was obvious he knew more than he was saying. 'I spoke to the police already. They were at our house. They're looking for him, George. I can't . . .' She gulped, harder this time.

'He'll turn up.' He wasn't going to help.

'I know something's wrong, George. If you don't tell me what's been going on, I swear to God whatever happens will be your fault. Just let me come and talk to you, please. For a few minutes.'

'Seriously? You want to come to North London?' He snorted, as if he thought she'd be out of her depth up there.

'I know North London. Where are you?' She looked at her watch. It was 4:42 p.m. She could leave a note in the hall, the way she'd done many times before. If Sean came back he'd call her. Inside though, she had a feeling he wasn't going to come back in the next few hours. Something had happened. Something to do with the bank.

'I'm in the White Rose in Maida Vale. Do you know where that is?' He was delighting in the idea that she'd have no idea where he was.

But he was wrong. A flashback of the life she'd lived in her first year at college, before she'd met Sean, hit her brain like a YouTube video. She knew the White Rose well.

It was a big old Victorian pub filled with goths and new-agers the last time she was there. It was one of those places she never wanted to see again.

'I'll be there in half an hour.'

'You'd better be, 'cause I won't be hanging around for long.' The line went dead.

25

Henry Mowlam peered at his screen. Major Finch was standing behind him.

'Did the pathologist have an opinion as to why the skin was removed?' he said. He hadn't read the whole of the five-page report on his screen, just the summary, which took up half of the first page.

'No. She says she won't guess,' said Finch. She leaned down. He could smell her shower gel or perhaps it was her skin cream. It was a sweet honey smell.

'So you think it's more than a coincidence that someone is cutting the skin off a murder victim, when that report on the Istanbul manuscript talks about the uses of human skin?'

Henry turned to face her. She hadn't previously taken much interest in the Istanbul manuscript, but it was clear now that she'd at least read the latest report on it.

'There used to be all sorts of weird sects who thought using human skin to write on would give more power to whatever they wrote,' he said. He stretched his arms out.

'In ancient times whole books were made from human skin.'

'Yeuuch,' said Major Finch.

'One of the groups who did this stuff recently was a Christian cult from the US. The authorities there were worried they were heading for a mass suicide. They thought the end times were near.'

'I hope we're not dealing with anything like that here.'

'People have used bodies for religious purposes for a long time,' he said.

He put his hands behind his head. 'I did a bit of research on this after I read the report. Some cult in Germany in the Victorian era used the skin of murdered virgins, hung up and preserved like calfskin parchment, in some sick protective prayer.'

'Lovely.'

'It was also done in the Nazi era.'

'But you still haven't found out why Sean Ryan is missing,' said Finch.

'No,' said Henry.

Finch sighed. 'If he murdered that girl we'll have to go back over what happened in Istanbul and Jerusalem, you do know that, don't you?'

Henry nodded. It wouldn't be the first time he'd had to change his mind about someone by 180°.

It was one of the hazards of his profession. He shook his head.

'Are you all right, Henry?' said Major Finch.

'Yeah, I'm fine. I just can't get out of my mind the four ways you're supposed to murder people in one of those horrible prayers.'

'I saw it. It is sick, all right. How the hell could any of that be related to Christianity?'

'An eye for an eye and a tooth for a tooth. I reckon that's where it all comes from.'

'It's worse than that.'

26

It took Isabel thirty-five minutes to reach the White Rose. She was lucky too. The Fulham Road was busy heading back into town, and the taxi driver dropped her at Westbourne Park station. As she crossed Elgin Avenue, anxiety gripped her as a chill wind played at the back of her neck. Memories of her life before Sean, before she'd joined the Foreign Office, jostled for attention.

With them came a tingle of fear.

She didn't want to remember that time. She didn't want to remember feeling so alone. She wanted to be with Sean heading for the Eurostar train to Paris. She looked at her watch.

The train would be pulling away slowly right now, full of lovers and excited Christmas shoppers all warm and cosy, heading for the pleasures of Paris in December.

She wrapped her arms tight around herself. She wasn't going to think about that. She turned to the wind. The cold was almost a drug, numbing her. A blast of freezing wind made her lower her chin as she walked on, fast.

From the outside she could see the White Rose was buzzing. Its high windows shone bright yellow through elaborate stained glass. There was a subliminal pulsing coming from the place, as if it were alive. She pushed the door open. Her phone rang. She pulled it from the pocket of her jacket, stepping back outside to answer it.

'I can't wait, Isabel. I'm sure you don't need me to find your husband.'

'I'm here, George,' she shouted.

The line went dead.

She opened the pub door. She couldn't see him through the mass of shoulder-to-shoulder bodies that filled the pub.

Bastard.

He'd brought her all this way.

She saw the door on the far side. She went back out, then around the building. He was sauntering up the street on his own, head down against the wind. He must have left the bar only a minute before.

She ran after him as fast as she could. Her cheeks were burning from the cold, her soles pounding on the hard concrete.

There was a hundred yards between them. Faster. Run faster. Her chest heaved. Air ripped from her throat. She couldn't let him disappear into one of the five-storey red-brick mansions that lined the street. And as she pounded up behind him he turned. He was drunk. His red tie pulled to one side. His hair was awry. His cheeks flushed. The collar of his black suit was turned up against the freezing wind that swept angrily down the street. She pulled her suede jacket around her neck with one hand as she stopped in front of him. She had to bend forward to ease her breathing.

'Hello, Mrs Ryan. I thought you'd got lost.' There was an exasperating, condescending tone to his voice. Then he grinned at her, as if she was a date he'd been trying to avoid.

His teeth were irregular. Two of them were at odd angles to the others. And there was a gap between them on one side.

George was the type of man she could never like. He reminded her of the idiots she'd met who only wanted to use women.

His accent grated too. It was Scottish, but mixed with a North London burr that seemed put on. Sean had told her George had served in Iraq, on two tours, as well as in Afghanistan. He also said George never spoke about any of it. Not one word.

'You could have waited for me.' She was still puffing. Her breath was filling the air between them with funnels of steam.

'Mrs Ryan, I told you everything I could. It's very simple.' He rolled the *very* out for a long time.

'When did you last see him, George?'

'I answered that question already.' He swayed. An Indian couple passing stared at him. They walked around him as if he were infected with a contagious strain of flu.

'Why won't you help me, George? I thought you and Sean got on.' She wanted to shout at him, kick him, do something to break through his stubborn resistance. He could help her if he wanted to. She just knew it.

'Listen up, Mrs Ryan. Sean and I worked together, that's it, alright. An' if he got himself into trouble, it was 'is doing. I told you, I warned 'im.'

'What trouble is he in?'

He shook his head slowly from side to side, as if he was dealing with a child.

'I can't tell you a thing about BXH. You know that. You best look for your answers somewhere else.' He turned and walked up the street.

She watched his back. His jacket was creased in a criss-cross pattern, as if he'd slept in it. He was swaying too, as if he was on the prow of a yacht in a storm. Would she get anything useful out of him in this state?

When he'd gone no more than fifty feet he put his hand

out and reached for the roof of a red BMW, one of those recent models with a low profile. He started fumbling in his pocket. Was he going to drive?

She walked up behind him. 'George, you can't drive, no way.'

'What's it to you?' He'd found his keys, was fumbling with them as he tried to locate the button to open the car doors.

She reached for them. She didn't know why. God knows, considering what happened later, she should have left him to his downfall.

'Let me do it.'

He looked at her, cross-eyed, and gave them up. She pressed the right button.

'Where are you going?'

'I'm not stupid, Mrs Ryan. I live one minute from here. I could drive there with my eyes closed.'

'That's something I don't want to see.' She sighed. 'Let me drive. If it's that near, it won't take long.'

'No, you go wait for your husband. Leave me alone. And good luck to you.'

She felt for her phone. It was still in the front pocket of her jeans.

'George, you are in no state to drive. Just tell me if you've any idea where Sean is on the way. Don't argue.' She pushed him towards the other side of his car. If this was what it took to find out something useful from him, so be it.

She walked after him, pushed him. 'Let's go, you idiot.'

He swayed, went around the car, stumbled, and got in the passenger side.

She was inside already.

'Is this a BXH car?'

He nodded.

'You are a total idiot, George. You know that, don't you? Now which way?'

He grunted and pointed. She pulled out, and headed down the road. The car had good heating, thank God. Her hands gripped the wheel.

Why was he so drunk?

'Is it something to do with BXH, George, Sean disappearing?'

He grunted louder.

'Come on, George.' She tried to sound lighthearted. 'You must have some idea. Just point me in a direction. I'm not asking you to spill any of BXH's dirty little secrets.'

'Let it go, Mrs Ryan. Run on home.' His tone was even more forceful now, as if being alone together in the car gave him the right to raise his voice.

'Don't tell me what to do.'

'My, my, you are upset. What are you so worried about anyhow? That you've lost your wee meal ticket?'

'Are you always this obnoxious, or is it just when you're drunk?'

'Naw. I'm usually worse.'

They passed two turns. At the next traffic lights he told her to turn right. This was a bit more than a few blocks away. They passed a row of shops, a restaurant. That was when she saw the police checkpoint. It was too late to turn around. Just what she needed. She tried to smile.

They were next.

George was silent.

The policeman put his hand up to stop them.

27

Lord Bidoner stepped out of the cab outside the UBSC building on Park Avenue. It was midday. The wind cutting through Manhattan was icy, but the snow had stopped. Xena, dressed in a dark pinstriped suit, similar to his own, got out behind him.

The black steel and shiny glass skyscraper, reaching so high you had to swing your head back uncomfortably to see its upper floors, glistened with lights. The foyer had a ten-foot-tall UBSC logo in gold behind a long cream reception desk. There were sleek-looking men everywhere. The reception was manned by two of them.

Lord Bidoner walked inside the building and took out his phone. He dialled a number.

'Jurgen, we are here. Thank you for the invitations.'

He slipped his phone back into his pocket. A minute later a young man with a pale and earnest look approached them. He was carrying a gold envelope.

'Lord Bidoner?' he said. His accent was middle European.

'Yes.'

The young man bowed and handed him the envelope. He clicked his heels as Bidoner took it and passed it to Xena.

'The venue is next door, my Lord.'

Lord Bidoner didn't bother replying. They walked outside into the freezing air. A few minutes later they were in a long conference room with white linen-covered tables and a small podium at the far end. It was on the fourth floor of the next door building, an art deco masterpiece of Manhattan.

A heavy glass chandelier dominated the room. Each table had a carafe of water and a trio of dark suited financiers. Most of them were men. They were listening intently, their devotion to their craft visible in their faces.

Lord Bidoner looked around. There were twenty-five of them listening to one of UBSC's vice president's speaking excitedly about currency trading opportunities. He turned to Xena.

'We must leave here in an hour, when this talk ends.'

Xena stood, then slipped out of the room. She went to the elevator and pressed the button for the twelfth floor.

As she strode down the blue carpeted corridor she touched her wig of straight black hair and held her hand to her forehead as she passed the security camera.

Then she pulled the room pass from her jacket pocket. The pastor had been careless keeping his room card and pass together, but he probably didn't expect to die that day.

But instead of using the pass when she reached the room, she simply knocked on the door. She had placed a white napkin on her arm and was holding it to her side. You would have been forgiven for thinking she was a waitress.

'Who is it?' came a feeble reply.

'Room service.' Xena's tone was bright. If there was someone in the room with the pastor's wife she could apologise and return some other time.

But when Martha opened the door Xena knew immediately that she was most likely alone. The pastor's wife had on a black dressing gown and there was the remains of a meal on a tray on the coffee table in front of the wall-mounted TV.

It was only a few hours since the pastor had met his fate, so his wife would be a little concerned, but not panicking. Not yet.

'I didn't call for room service,' said Martha.

'We like to collect things quickly,' said Xena. She moved past Martha and crossed to the coffee table. She couldn't see into the bathroom, as the door was closed.

'I will just check your bathroom,' she said, softly.

The pastor's wife looked taken aback. It wasn't normal for room service to check the bathroom in a guest's room.

There was no one in the bathroom.

Xena removed the knife from the thin sheath that sat on the inside of her thigh. She also put on the black medical gloves she'd extracted from her pants pocket. She held the knife behind her back as she came out of the bathroom.

The pastor's wife was sitting on the bed near the phone. There was a quizzical, but relaxed look on her face.

That changed and her hand went out with a surprising swiftness when Xena spoke.

'Do not scream and I may let you live. If you scream I will kill you.'

A startled half cry came out of Martha's mouth. It wouldn't have been loud enough for anyone to take notice of. In any case, she would have had to scream at the top of her voice for an extended period for anyone to take fright for her in the rooms around them.

'Turn over. Lie down,' said Xena.

The pastor's wife's face had gone bone white. She had thin lips and flaky skin.

But she did as she was told. She probably assumed she was being robbed and that her wallet and valuables would be gone with Xena in the next few minutes.

She certainly didn't expect the weight of Xena on her back.

Xena pulled the woman's arms from her side and pinned them painfully, bending them backwards and up by her shoulders. Then she put the knife between her teeth.

She looked around quickly, checking no one was watching.

'*Tertium quattuor invocare unum*,' she whispered.

Then she pressed Martha's head hard into the pillow on which it was lying. Muffled shouts filled the room. Then terrified grunts echoed as the woman's air supply ran out and her heart raced.

Perhaps, if she'd been ten years younger she might have been able to shift Xena from on top of her, but she wasn't.

And now it seemed the room was listening as Xena slid the knife under Martha's throat and yanked it sideways.

There was a loud gurgling and the old woman's body shook as blood soaked into the bed.

The muffled gurgling lasted about two minutes. Longer than she'd expected. At one point the woman's kicking and thrashing almost unseated her, but she had done this before. She knew what to expect.

When the shuddering had finally stopped she released Martha's head. Then she listened. Far in the distance she could hear a TV. And beyond that the hum of the city.

She stood. She'd felt a wetness on the bed under her knees. The woman had pissed herself.

Xena took the knife from between her teeth and pushed it hard into the woman's side. People can play dead for a while, but if a knife is used on you it is almost impossible not to flinch.

Martha didn't flinch.

Xena stood. She let her own breathing subside. She had to finish the job quickly. The real room service people could come at any moment.

She took the long silver specimen case out of the inside pocket of her suit.

She put it on the bedside table, and turned Martha over. Her mouth and eyes were wide open. Blood was pouring from her neck. Xena put her gloved hand into Martha's mouth and gripped her slippery tongue. It was swollen from her asphyxiation, but it came forward enough when Xena pulled it, hard.

Xena sliced at it, about halfway along. The knife was sharp. Blood pumped out of the raw pink stump. It filled the dead woman's mouth and began drooling out.

Xena already had the tongue in the container and had slipped it back into her jacket pocket.

After washing and wiping everything she had touched, she headed for the fire exit stairs.

Two floors down she went back into the corridor and called the elevator. She got out a further three floors down.

She had no wig on when she arrived back at the room where Lord Bidoner was waiting. She simply looked into the room and headed for the street. Lord Bidoner followed her a few minutes later. They took separate taxis to Central Park and mingled with the tourists at the obelisk.

As they travelled back downtown together Lord Bidoner asked her, 'Do you have it?'

Xena simply tapped her jacket pocket in reply.

28

The young policeman in his fluorescent yellow jacket looked at the tax disc on the windscreen, stared at Isabel for a few seconds, then let them through with a nod. Her knuckles were white on the steering wheel.

'That was your driving they pulled us over for,' said George. 'That's the last time I take a ride with you.' He laughed to himself, turned in his seat, and stared out the back window.

She could smell the alcohol on his breath.

She'd be lucky, she knew, to get anything useful out of him. He directed her to a parking space on a narrow street with five and six-storey red-brick mansions on each side. The empty space was well past the building he pointed out, where his apartment was, but that was his problem.

'Women drivers, you're useless,' he said.

She'd had enough of his crap.

'What kind of a sick bastard are you?' She didn't wait for him to respond. 'You work with Sean, but you don't give a damn what happens to him. Well, I hope you get what's coming to you. You don't deserve to be a part of the human race.'

He stepped back, examined her.

'You think you did me a favour?' His tone was taunting. 'Those cops back there weren't looking for drunks, darling. They were looking for drug dealers, pimps with sub-machine guns. You haven't been to Kilburn in a while, have you? I bet you didn't even notice the armoured vest that cop was wearing.'

She stared at him. The wind whistled around them. Above, great cloth-of-coal clouds were moving fast. Any second the hail was going to start again.

'You think you deserve help because you look sweet? Well, stand in line, honey.'

With that he turned, walked away.

She couldn't resist it.

She went after him.

'This is your last chance to be a decent human being, George. The City of London police were at my house earlier. You better tell me what's going on, or I'm going to call them, tell them that you're up to your neck in whatever it is they're investigating. And the first journalist who camps on my door, when all this gets out, is going to get your address and your phone number and every detail about how many calls Sean made to you.' Her finger was shaking as she jabbed it towards him.

'My, my, you are a fiery one, aren't you?'

'What's happening at BXH, George?'

'Don't you watch any TV?'

'As little as possible.'

'Shame. You're missing a lot of good programs.'

'What's happening with the merger, George? Is it under threat?'

He smiled, then his eyelids drooped.

'Why is BXH's share price crashing?' She leaned forward.

'It's all about the money, honey.'

'That's it? What about Sean? He isn't involved in anything underhand. He's as straight as they come. You know that.'

'The straight and narrow runs right through people sometimes. Like an arrow.'

'What do you mean by that?'

'Just what I said.'

He was definitely hiding something.

'That club that murdered girl was from, George, what's it called?'

He looked at her blankly.

'You know the place I'm talking about. Mrs Vaughann told me some of them went there last night. The name is probably in the *Evening Standard*. It's not a state secret.'

George hesitated. When he spoke, his tone was more sympathetic.

'Magnolia.'

'What kind of a club is the Magnolia, George?'

'It's a sleazy rip-off lap-dancing club. The kind that serves food and champagne at £500 a bottle. It's for banker dummies who've got too much money, who get sucked into doing stupid things to prove how important they are.'

'When do they open?'

His eyes glistened. 'I don't know. You're not planning on going there, are you?' He guffawed.

She was going to find out what had happened.

'What did you mean the straight and narrow runs through people, George?'

'I'd have to kill you if I told you the answer to that.'

29

Lord Bidoner closed the small laboratory fridge. It clunked shut. He walked to the glass window of the apartment. Far below on Fifth Avenue, the traffic was bumper to bumper. It had started snowing again. Flakes of snow blew against the glass, then flew away. A few inches from his face the world was icy and blustery. Where he stood it was warm and hushed. He smiled to himself.

Then he turned back and contemplated the laptop screen at the far end of the room. On it was a slowly revolving gold-on-gold depiction of the square and arrow symbol that had consumed his life for the past four years. Ever since he had learned it had been in the manuscript that contained a record of Jesus' trial, that it had been referred to in the trial document explicitly, he had wanted nothing more than the symbol's secret to be revealed and the dark prayers it had contained to be invoked.

Because the symbol did hold a secret. A secret that would help them find the most important DNA sample in history.

The images of the manuscript they had obtained from Dr Hunter's home, before it had been torched, had made that indisputable. Dr Hunter, who had been tasked with translating the manuscript that had been found by the ever stupid and interfering Sean and Isabel Ryan, had probably never even realised that copies had been taken.

He walked towards the painting above the fireplace. It was blazing with a perfect fake fire. This was a good moment. The recent news about Sean Ryan had been positive. The man's stupidity, his real character, would be obvious to all soon. Lord Bidoner had kept his enemy close and the situation was resolving itself. He couldn't have asked for a better outcome.

It is strange the way things work out, he thought. Just when his search for what lay behind the symbol reached its fruition, the problem of the man who had discovered it would be resolved.

He deserved some good fortune, after all he had done, all he had invested in this project.

A light knock on the front door of the apartment broke his thoughts. He walked across the soft grey carpet and stood near the door.

'Who is it?' he asked.

'Jim Green,' came a voice. Green, the head of trading at Ebony Dragon was early, but that probably just showed his eagerness. He reached for the button that would unlock the door.

30

'I told you this place wouldn't be open so early,' said George, as they walked back along the lane that led from Jermyn Street to the row of five-storey white stuccoed Edwardian houses tucked away behind a department store. The Magnolia club appeared to take up the basement levels of two houses, at least.

'They probably open at eight. We could come back then.' It sounded as if he was trying to cheer her up.

There'd been a light on above the door of the club, but no one had answered when they'd knocked.

'It's only half an hour.'

They'd taken a taxi. He'd refused to tell Isabel any more, not another word about what he knew, but he'd insisted on coming with her to the club.

It seemed almost as if he felt guilty. She didn't argue with him. She wasn't going to say it, but having him with her had some upsides. Not the least of which was that she would have more time to work on him, especially if he kept drinking.

The wind was hurtling up Jermyn Street. It felt as if they were in a wind tunnel in the arctic.

'Let's go for a drink,' said George. His shoulders were hunched against the chill. 'I know a good place on the other side of Piccadilly.'

She expected he knew a lot of good places on the other side of Piccadilly. He leaned towards her.

'You don't have a clue what Sean was into, do you?' He had a smug I-know-a-lot-of-things-you-don't look on his face. What the hell gave him the right to be so condescending? She felt like slapping him. But instead she jabbed her knuckles into his upper arm, hard.

'Let's get you a drink. Then you can tell me what he was into.'

He gave her a wink. She looked away.

As they waited for the pedestrian lights to change at the bottom of Regent Street, she felt a jostling behind them. A lot of people were waiting at the crossing. Traffic was speeding past dangerously, only inches away. Suddenly, the crowd around them was moving, swaying, as if someone was pushing through it. She was about to turn around.

Then it happened.

A red Routemaster double-decker was looming in front of her, like a red elephant charging by. George grunted loudly. He staggered forward. A rush of adrenaline pumped through her. Her mouth opened.

She reached out.

Time slowed.

She felt the rough fibres of his coat slide past her fingers. A lump crammed her throat, stopping her breathing. The front corner of the bus hit him with a stomach-twisting thud.

George spun.

It felt as if a ghost had fallen through her.

And then, all at once, there was the deafening noise of braking, a high-pitched scream, a man's shout. Then other vehicles were braking too.

George bounced off the bus like a doll being thrown. His arms and body flew in front of her, in a surreal kaleidoscope.

She leaned forward. She didn't know why. It was exactly the wrong thing to do.

Someone grabbed her shoulder. The bus stopped right in front of her, a shiny, creaking red machine, steam pouring from its engine, people screaming inside, faces pressed up against the window grotesquely, like meat in a sausage machine.

She looked down and to her right.

George was lying, crumpled, in the three foot gap between the railings and the bus.

With an impolite shove of her elbow she pushed past a gaping onlooker, and headed for George.

She heard a whistle behind her, a car horn beeping, a voice from somewhere demanding, 'Don't move him, love.'

There was a despairing pounding in her ears.

She knelt beside George, bending close to see if his eyes were open, with a stink of diesel in her nose and mouth, almost making her gag. His eyes were closed.

There was blood down the right side of his face, dripping thickly. Thoughts of Sean flowed through her. Was that why she was crying like this or was it because she'd brought George here, that it was her fault that this had happened to him?

'Don't die, George,' she whispered. She heard the wail of an ambulance. Behind her an authoritative voice said, in a Cockney accent just like Michael Caine's: 'Stand back, please, love. Stand back.'

She stroked George's arm lightly, and said a prayer. A shiver ran through her. What the hell was happening? First Sean. Now this.

Was this how someone who'd fought for his country was going to die, in oily dust, while Friday-night revellers passed by, annoyed that their night out had been interrupted for a few seconds?

'Move away please, miss,' a voice said.

She felt a pressure on her back. She looked around. Her forehead was pounding. A man in a yellow emergency vest pushed past her, roughly.

She took a step back, heard a cough, looked up.

The bus driver was leaning out of the door of his cab, holding a hand to his mouth 'Move back more please, miss,' the policeman said, more firmly this time.

She straightened up, stepped back some more.

A second man in a yellow jacket pushed past her. She was stuck to the spot, staring. They were manoeuvring George onto a folding stretcher with thin steel bars. There was a contraption, a thick white brace, around his neck.

She couldn't believe what had happened. There was something so weird about it all. Was George just unlucky? She looked around. Or had someone pushed him? Or did he fall because he was drunk? She went back over everything, trying to remember.

The cold was making her hands and face numb. The icy feeling was seeping up her arms. It felt as if her body was someone else's, as if she didn't have to be concerned about it getting cold.

She went to the back of the ambulance waiting nearby with its lights flashing, filling the air with a sickening blue radiance. She still didn't know if George was alive or dead.

The idea that he might be dead already or that he was dying right now, hammered into her brain.

'Were you with him, love?' one of the ambulance men asked her, as the other one closed the back door. Her last sight of George had been of a white face, a plastic oxygen mask and a bright green blanket lying over him haphazardly.

She nodded. 'Can I come with you?' Over his shoulder she noticed the policemen bent over a notebook, writing.

'Are you a relative of his?'

She shook her head.

'You can follow us, love. We're taking him to University College Hospital. Do you know where it is?'

She nodded. Euston Road wasn't far.

'You didn't get hit, love, did you?' There was concern in his eyes.

She shook her head.

'Is he going to be okay?'

'He's alive. That's all I can say. How do you know 'im?'

'He's a friend. I was with him.' The pounding in her forehead was easing.

'What's his name, love?'

She gave him George's name. He wrote it down. She told him where George lived, though she couldn't remember the house number. He raised his eyebrows. They weren't that close, was the unspoken implication.

And he was right.

And then they were gone and a policeman with a pointy helmet and a bulky black and yellow jacket, was beside her.

He was asking her questions. She answered them all, gave him her name and address, then told him what had happened. Then he closed his notebook. 'You've had a terrible shock,' he said, with a sympathetic smile. 'You should go home. We'll be in touch.' Then he was gone.

And she didn't want to go home.

31

The door closed with a click behind Jim Green. He passed into the main room of the apartment. The early afternoon noises from Fifth Avenue, the honking of car horns and the occasional shout for a taxi, were unheard up here on the twenty-fifth floor.

'How can I help you?' said Lord Bidoner.

Jim Green looked around. He seemed relieved that they were alone. He held his hand out.

'I'm worried, sir.'

'That's what I pay you for, Mr Green. To be worried. To lose sleep. To make me money.' Bidoner's tone was angry. 'But indulge me, tell me what's going on. I am sure you wouldn't come back here unless you had a very good reason.'

Jim Green was sweating. 'My colleague is holding back some of our reserves, sir. And he expects me to agree to this.' There was a slight tremor in his voice. He clearly wanted to betray his colleague, but the reality of it all was getting to him.

That was the moment Xena choose to walk back into the room. She was carrying a knife. She laid it down on the coffee table, then sat near it. She didn't speak, but watched Jim Green's every move.

Lord Bidoner stood in front of him, invading his personal space. 'Are you truly ready to crush your enemies, Mr Green?'

'Sure.' He said it as if they were talking about playing a round of golf.

'Are you committed, Green?'

Green nodded.

Lord Bidoner took his phone from his pocket, opened an encrypted file storage app and flicked through some files. He stopped at one and turned the phone to Jim Green.

The video that played was of a little girl running with a pink satchel on her back. She ran into the arms of a woman, her mother no doubt. There were other children behind them. She was clearly just after leaving school.

Little voices squealing in delight came from the phone.

'Where the hell did you get this?' Green's voice had risen. He half reared in his seat. His face was ashen.

Bidoner put his phone back in his pocket.

'I just want you to understand that we expect one hundred per cent commitment. Your wife and daughter are lovely. You were trying for a child for a long time, I'm told. Is that true?'

Green nodded and sat back down. His expression hardened.

'I know what I have to do, sir. And I will do it. You will have no trouble about my commitment.'

'Good.' Bidoner took a step back. As Green stood, Bidoner said, 'Do you remember the oath you took when you joined us?'

'Yes, I do. I swore to carry out whatever instructions given without question.'

'Good. Because, God forgives, but we don't.' He paused to let his words sink in. 'And we will be even more powerful soon. Xena, show our friend to the door.'

As Green opened the door Xena came up beside him.

She looked him in the eye, then rubbed at the front of his trousers. She had a smile on her face. It turned to an exaggerated scowl as she took her hand away.

'Don't worry. My friend just likes to size people up. And don't forget, keep me informed of everything your colleague gets up to.'

'Yes, sir.'

'And remember, there is no room for failure, Mr Green.'

32

The busy corner of Regent Street and Piccadilly Circus was returning to normal. Isabel was standing exactly where they'd been standing waiting to cross the road, but George was on his way to hospital, perhaps dead already, and she was on her own, feeling hollow.

After a few minutes of being jostled by passers-by, she turned and headed back towards the club, just for something to do. There was no way she was going drinking now.

As she waited to cross Piccadilly, heading for the lane leading to Jermyn Street, she stood well back from the edge of the road, and looked around to see if anyone suspicious was near her. Then she turned back towards Piccadilly Circus. There was a long queue at the cash machine outside the BXH branch. There must have been thirty people waiting. God only knew what they were saying about BXH on the news. When a bank gets into trouble, anything can happen. She passed the queue quickly.

Should she go to the hospital, to see if George was okay? She looked at her watch. It was only twenty minutes since they'd taken him in.

She thought about calling Rose, but decided not to. She

might ask her to pick up Alek if she heard she wasn't going away. That was the last thing she needed. Looking for Sean with Alek beside her would be impossible.

She decided to ring Sean's aunt and uncle. She had to tell them they weren't coming. What exactly was she was going to say?

Sean's aunt, Karen, was kind, but there was a toughness to her, a wiry strength. That's the way her generation was. Everyone was supposed to stand on their own two feet, as far as Karen was concerned. Sean's uncle, Frank, was different. He was warmer, friendlier. But he had Huntington's. And he didn't need her ringing up, panicking, telling him everything that his favourite nephew might or might not have done.

As she rang Karen's number, disappointment rose inside her. Not for her, but for them. They'd been looking forward to seeing her and Sean. She felt guilty now, as if it was her fault they weren't on their way to Paris.

'Karen here.'

The urge to put the phone down, to avoid telling her bad news, was strong.

'Hi, it's Isabel.'

There was a pause.

'Where are you, honey?' Her tone was happy, but a note of worry could be heard at its edge. A worry she was supposed to dispel with her reply.

Her mouth was dry, hard, as if she'd sucked on blotting paper.

'I'm in London, Karen. I'm sorry. Sean's gone missing.' Better to come straight out with it.

There was a sharp intake of breath. 'Missing?' Karen's tone made her concern clear.

'He didn't come home last night.' Her voice sounded stronger than she felt.

'Have you tried his office?' Karen spoke fast.

'I've been to BXH. He's not there.'

'Did you guys have a fight?'

'No, no. It's not that.' Isabel straightened her back and looked over her shoulder. A young boy with cropped hair was staring at her. A shudder ran through her.

'Have you called the hospitals, the police?'

She licked her lips. She couldn't tell her about the police being at their house. 'The police know he's missing. I'm sure I'd have had a call by now if he was in a hospital.'

'Well, that's a relief, isn't it?' There was something distant about her tone, as if she was thinking about something else.

'What's going on with the big merger? There was tons about BXH on the TV before we left. Frank thinks it's just what they need.'

'I don't know what's going on with the merger, Karen. All I know is Sean was supposed to be out celebrating last night.'

'Celebrating?' Karen sniffed. It felt like a criticism. 'Does he often disappear after a night out?'

'No,' said Isabel, firmly.

'Do any of his colleagues know where he is?'

Karen was trying to help her, by telling her to contact people, but her condescending tone made her advice hard to take. It wasn't the first time Isabel had heard it.

'I have to go now, Karen.' She didn't want to go into any more detail.

'Call us. As soon as you find out where he is. And if there's anything we can do, let us know.'

'I will. I promise. I'll call you.' She cut the line. She needed answers.

33

Henry Mowlam put the glass of Chardonnay on the small wooden table in front of Major Finch. She was pressed up against the corner of a red banquet. They were an hour out of the office and two drinks down already.

The Chandos pub, near Trafalgar Square, was just far enough away from the control room in Whitehall where they'd spent the day, to not have to worry about every second person recognising them.

Their corner table was surrounded by a mass of humanity enjoying a night out. The noise level of conversation was a wall of sound that almost certainly ensured their own conversation could not be listened to.

'Have you decided?' he said. He turned and stared into Major Finch's eyes. They were blue, large and, if he thought about them too much, very attractive.

Major Finch smoothed the hem of her knee-length black Mark's & Spencer skirt. Her right leg was crossed over her left.

She let her head fall back to the banquet and closed her eyes.

'You don't give up, do you, Henry?'

He put his pint of Old Brewery bitter down and glanced at the party of twenty-something Italian tourists at the next table. Not one of them was looking their way.

'Do you blame me?' He took another sip of his pint. Their Friday-night-after-work-drinks were one of the few pleasures in his life, since his wife had divorced him.

'I can't be the only level seven officer you know, Henry.'

'No, but you're the only one I know well, and who probably knows the answer to my question off the top of her head.'

Major Finch turned to look at him. 'I suppose you think because I've had a few drinks you can have what you want?' She smiled.

'I was hoping.' He shrugged, picked up his pint again. He'd been pushing his luck with Finch since soon after his divorce papers came through.

'You can't have any more resources for watching Isabel Ryan, Henry. And I'm not changing my mind just because you bought me a drink.'

'Even after what's just happened?'

'Yes. We're going beyond what we should be doing anyhow. It was supposed to be an observation operation, not a personal protection one.'

Henry sighed, looked away.

Finch leaned towards him until her mouth was near his ear. She breathed heavily as she spoke. 'I'll give you this much, Henry. That symbol you keep asking about is upsetting people in the Met, the Home Office, MI5 and GCHQ. That's a bit of a record.' She leaned back.

He let the edge of a smile linger for only a second on his lips. He was obviously going to have to tease what he wanted out of her.

'Why? You have to tell me why.'

Their eyes locked. The rest of the pub was just noise now.

'Certain people don't like ritual murders on their patch. Your speculation about that poor girl's murder has stirred things up.'

'I don't like coincidences,' said Henry.

'Do you think we're going to get more deaths like that?'

'My crystal ball needs a good clean, but if I was a guessing man I'd say there's a real possibility. People used to die that way during the inquisition, when they tortured people, pulled their tongues out and other stuff you wouldn't believe. There were inquisitors in Constantinople too, when the Catholics ran the place. We have no idea what they believed they had to do to save the city.'

'It's what whoever murdered that girl believes that worries me.'

'That symbol at the back of the book is the key to it all, I reckon.'

'So what would you think that symbol was, if you saw it on the street?' Her head shook as she finished the sentence. Her hair was loose now and her white top was open an inch more than it should have been.

He shrugged. 'It'd be a signpost. Go straight ahead, if it was pointing up. Go right or left, if it was pointing either way.'

'Exactly.' She looked all knowing. It was probably an act.

'That doesn't tell me anything.' He downed the rest of his pint. Would she be on for another, he wondered.

'Henry, Henry, Henry, it's all staring you in the face. The bloody symbol is a signpost. It's pointing somewhere.'

'Great, you are a proper genius. I'll get on to the Nobel committee first thing tomorrow.' He snorted. 'So where does it point, Miss Genius?'

She sighed. 'I'll tell you this, and no more. The symbol in the book does not point directly north.'

'So where does it point? Has anyone figured that out?'

'Not exactly, but a few people think they're getting close.'

'The colours, those two-headed eagles, they're clues, right?'

'That's the theory.'

'So what the hell is this place they point towards? Some treasure trove?' That would be interesting, he thought. A Byzantine treasure trove could be worth a hell of a lot.

'This is the part you're not going to believe.' Her grin widened.

'Try me.'

She finished her wine and put the glass down.

'I will.' She leaned towards him again.

'Are you ready?' She nodded towards the door.

Henry smiled. This time he didn't try to wipe out his smile. It would have been too difficult.

34

Isabel walked up Regent Street. She couldn't feel her fingers any more, or her feet. Was she in shock? She wanted to be home with Sean and Alek, sitting at their kitchen table, with Alek's favourite apple pie in front of them; the warmth of the kitchen all around. She could almost smell it.

She pulled her phone out, and rang Rose's number. There was no answer. Her fingers jabbed at the phone. She called Rose's mobile.

It was turned off.

She looked at her watch. Had Rose taken Alek to the cinema, as she'd promised? That had to be what was going on. She took a deep breath. If there was one thing she had to do, it was to stay calm. Rose was the most reliable person ever as far as children were concerned.

She'd never let her down.

She breathed deep, closed her eyes. The last thing she needed was to crack up. A group of people passed her. One boy bumped into her. She looked around, startled. Was there any possibility someone was after her? She looked in a shop window, watched people pass in the mirror of the glass, examined everyone who was hanging around. She couldn't see anyone suspicious. An ACE PLUMBING van was pulled up on the far side of the street, but there was no one visible in it.

No one was watching her.

What should she do?

If only she could go back twenty-four hours, find Sean, persuade him not to go to that club.

She let her breath out. She should start visiting hospitals. Wasn't that what people did if someone didn't come home; look for them? Maybe he'd lost his wallet, his ID, his memory? But where should she start?

University College Hospital, on the Euston Road, of course.

That was where they'd taken George. And if anything had happened to Sean in the West End last night, that was where he'd have been taken too.

She looked down at herself. Would she even be allowed in the hospital at this hour? She was bedraggled-looking, her jeans were wet, clinging to her calves, but she didn't care. She hailed the first black cab with its light on.

'Is it accident and emergency you're looking for, love?' The driver pulled up at the front of the hospital.

The tower block of the hospital, there must have been fifteen or sixteen floors to it, was lit up like a corporate headquarters.

'Here's fine.'

She paid him, then went inside the main entrance. The hospital was still busy, despite the time. She went to the bright yellow-fronted reception desk. Two women wearing white shirts with an NHS logo in blue on their left breast were sitting behind the desk dealing with a queue of people.

'I need to find out if someone's been admitted,' she asked the smiling woman behind the reception desk when she finally turned to her.

‘What’s the name?’ There was a computer in front of her. The reception area had an airy, bright and antiseptic feel.

‘Sean Ryan.’

The woman looked at her screen, tapped at her keyboard.

‘Sorry, love, we have no one here by that name.’

She breathed in. Then she blurted out.

‘If someone were found . . .’ The words were stuck in her throat. ‘Dead or without any identification, what do you do?’

‘Come back in the morning, love. Someone will help you then. All I can tell you is the names of the people who are registered.’

She remembered George.

‘Has a George Donovan been admitted?’

She looked at Isabel over her thick black glasses. ‘Hold on.’ She tapped at her keyboard again.

‘He’s in the acute admissions unit. Are you a relative?’

She blinked, nodded. Would it work?

‘I’m his sister.’ In a metaphorical sense, of course, but she didn’t say that.

‘Go to the first floor, that way.’ The woman pointed behind her, to where a staircase led upwards.

As Isabel went up, she checked her wallet. Would they ask for ID? She felt like a criminal. Maybe she could tell them her maiden name was Donovan. She’d just keep it simple, find out if he was okay. Then she could go home. She walked along a bright clean corridor. A big arrow sign pointed her to turn left.

As she pushed the door of the unit open a male nurse brushed past her. Then she was in a small reception area with new-looking black leather chairs. A man in a blue collarless shirt was peering at her from behind a counter straight ahead.

‘Can I help you?’ he said. His tone had a note of anxiety. It was late, of course. Visiting times were probably long over.

'I'm looking for George Donovan.' She put her elbows on the high, shiny plastic-coated surface of the reception counter.

'Do you have ID?'

She showed him her driving license. He looked at the picture, then at her, as if he was wondering if she was using someone else's. Thank God driving licenses don't show your maiden name.

'Thanks, we have to check everyone these days,' he said, apologetically. 'Go on through. He's in a cubicle at the far end. One of the nurses will direct you.'

She passed through a double door into a busy corridor. A man with a pale bare chest was on a trolley. A nurse was leaning over him. Other patients were staring at her from high beds. There was an irritating whirr from the ceiling. A pungent antiseptic smell filled the air. The unit was Friday-night busy.

She kept walking. Eyes stared at her hungrily, as if she might have some special news for them. There was equipment everywhere, humming, blinking. The smell of antiseptic was stronger now. A notice told her to clean her hands. She stopped to squeeze some antiseptic gel on to them. As she did a plump black nurse came towards her.

'Are you here for George Donovan?'

She nodded. 'Is he all right? I was with him when he got hit.'

'He has internal bleeding, a fractured skull. Would you like to see him?'

Isabel nodded.

The nurse took her to a door on the right and opened it.

'He's sedated. It's better if we don't disturb him. You can't stay long. A few minutes, that's it.'

George was lying under a white sheet, surrounded be a semicircle of medical equipment. A low hum filled the air. He had a couple of drips connected to him. His head was bandaged with white gauze. Isabel felt something rise up inside her. She'd been walking around with this guy only a few hours before. He'd been trying to help her. The welling almost burst to the surface. She pushed it down. *Stop.*

'A colleague from his work was here earlier. A nice woman.'

'Which colleague?' she said.

'I didn't get her name.' She sounded irritated that Isabel was asking her questions.

'What was she like?'

The nurse looked at her oddly, her head turned sideways. Isabel didn't care what she thought.

'Sorry, I can't help you. Lots of people go through this place every hour.' Her expression hardened, as if she didn't like where the conversation was going.

It was time to change the subject. 'Will George be okay?'

'I can't say. We'll know more tomorrow.' She was looking at Isabel's crumpled clothes now.

'I'm sorry. You will have to go.' She stared into Isabel's eyes. Was there a suspicious gleam there, or was she imagining it?

'Okay.'

Isabel headed back towards the reception area. She had to sit down. She flopped onto one of the leather chairs. She needed a few seconds of peace. And she needed to call Rose.

Rose's line buzzed at least ten times before she answered. Isabel was about to cut the call off, race to her house, start banging on the door to find out where Alek was, when Rose's voice came on the line. She sounded odd.

35

Xena rubbed a little olive oil on the henna square on her forearm.

'We have stayed here too long,' she said.

'Once the final sacrifice is over, and we have what we want, we will go,' said Lord Bidoner.

Xena stretched her arm towards him, showing him the tattoo.

'The lines are straight?' she asked.

'Perfect' he said.

'My grandmother taught me. She was from Tigray. Her clan were the kings of Aksum. She taught me well.'

The laptop screen on the coffee table in Lord Bidoner's apartment flickered. He took his eyes off her and returned to looking at the screen. There were six boxes on it showing line graphs. Each of them was heading downwards.

The initials 'BXH' were under each graph along with the name of the class of security and the stock market where the shares were listed.

The names included the London Stock Exchange, the Hong Kong Stock Exchange, Euronext Paris, the Frankfurt Stock Exchange, and the New York and Vienna Stock Exchanges.

'Everything is good?' said Xena.

He turned to her and stroked her bare arm.

'Better than good. The BXH share price fell straight through the floor. They are calling it the greatest banking rout since Lehman's.'

He switched tabs on his browser. The *Financial Times* had a leading article about BXH's shares being in free fall all around the world.

'And no one knows what you have done,' said Xena. She stroked his leg, rubbing her hand hard into his thigh.

Lord Bidoner turned to her. The skin on his forehead was flaky and his grey hair was receding, but his blue eyes were fixed on her and a smile was emerging on his lips.

'Is the room ready for its next visitor?'

Xena nodded.

'You will enjoy this one,' he said.

She shrugged. 'I only do what was done to me or my family. I take no great pleasure in it. Not like some.' Her eyes flickered away from his face, as if she was remembering something.

Lord Bidoner stared at her. It was hard to find someone as committed as Xena.

In many ways they were mirrors of each other. She'd suffered a botched circumcision and her family, two brothers and her mother, had been tortured to death in the Eritrean–Ethiopian War.

She'd been taken in by an orphanage run by nuns, but they had beaten her remorselessly for the tiniest infraction.

Most girls who suffered like that either cut themselves off from human contact, or harmed themselves in one way or another, but she had taken the pain and had forged it into a willingness to do what others were unable to.

Which was exactly what he had done.

His mother had died in the liberation of Vienna in 1945.

She had been raped and brutalised by partisans working with the Soviets until she'd died. His grandmother had taken him in. He'd been a few months old. The old woman had been good to him, but when he got older she'd disciplined him harshly, beating him for any display of emotion.

Both he and Xena had been brought up on stories of what had been taken from them. With force.

And both of them had felt the blows of frustrated tormentors.

Until they had fought back.

'The next one will be more interesting than the others,' he said.

She stuck her tongue out at him.

36

'Hello?'

'Rose, it's me. Just wondering how Alek is.'

There was a long pause. Isabel pressed the phone tight to her ear.

'Alek's great. He's sleeping right now.' She sounded distant. She was probably tired, possibly sleeping, like she should be.

'I tried you earlier. Did you go to that movie?'

'No. We were all watching DVDs.'

'Great. Thanks again for looking after him. See you Monday night.'

'See you.' The line went dead. The call had only lasted a minute, but at least it had answered one big worry.

Seconds later her phone buzzed.

It wasn't a call. It was that faint noise a phone makes when it's trying to attract your attention. She'd missed a call. She looked at the incoming call list. Someone had called her five minutes ago. The number was a US number. She pressed call-back.

'Hello? Did you just ring this number?'

'Isabel, it's Karen.'

'Hi Karen.' She tried to sound as normal as possible. The number was Karen's mobile.

'I was on the internet,' she said. Then she paused, as if there was more she had to say, but she really didn't want to say it.

'And?' Isabel could feel something ominous coming.

'Sean's picture is on the front page of the *Daily Mail* website.' Karen's words came out fast. 'They say he's wanted by the police. There's a search warrant being issued. I can't believe it.'

For a long moment Isabel didn't register what she was saying. Then, like a shutter falling, she understood and her whole body tightened, every muscle. A slick of sweat broke out on her forehead. Then a warm flush passed through her, starting on her arms and ending up on her cheeks. She didn't care about the embarrassment of him being on some newspaper's site. What worried her was the fact that the police were hunting him. She'd almost fooled herself into thinking they just wanted to speak to him.

And she'd fooled herself that all this wasn't actually too serious.

She straightened her back, swallowing the lump that was forming in her throat. She wasn't going to crack up.

She wasn't.

'I can't imagine why he's on that site.'

'But they're looking for him, Isabel.'

A weird tremor started in her leg. She pressed her foot to the floor, steadying her calf muscles.

'Isabel,' said Karen.

'Yes?' Images of Sean were flashing through her mind. She saw him surrounded by police, being taken away.

'I'm so sorry.' She sounded upset, as if she was crying.

She heard the sound of a TV in the background.

'Everything's going to be okay, Karen.' Her voice was hard,

confident, but there was a tremor in her hand holding the phone.

'Frank . . .' Karen started the sentence, then stopped. Then she started again.

Isabel could feel distress coming over the line.

'Frank thinks Sean going missing is connected to what's happening at BXH. There's a lot of strange talk he's been hearing.'

'What do you mean?'

'That's all he knows. Just be careful, Isabel.'

'I will.'

Karen coughed. 'I thought he might call us, but he didn't.'

She looked up. There was a nurse standing over her, the same nurse who'd shown her to George's room.

'Thanks for calling, Karen.'

She closed the line.

'I'm glad I caught you,' said the nurse. 'Mr Donovan asked if his visitor was still around.'

Her mouth opened.

'Yeah, right, okay.' She felt stupid. The nurse nodded, as if prattling visitors was a normal occurrence. Isabel stood up and followed her.

When they reached George his eyes were closed.

'He was conscious a minute ago,' said the nurse. 'He might wake up again soon. Can you hold on?'

Isabel nodded. The nurse turned and left the room.

She stood by his bed, wondering whether she should say something, try to wake him. She coughed.

His eyelids flickered. One of the pieces of electronic equipment he was connected to beeped. She waited some more. A minute passed.

Then two.

She felt the tension of the last twenty-four hours like a weight pressing into her. The good news was that George was breathing. He was injured, but he hadn't died because of her.

She paced up and down, slowly.

He looked like someone who was lucky to still be alive. There were tufts of hair springing out from under a white gauze bandage that was wrapped around the top part of his head. There was a purple bruise on the side of his face, extending under the bandage, and a wire cage, under a thin sheet, protected his lower body.

A machine beeped.

How long should she wait?

She bent towards him. 'You're going to be okay, George.'

His eyelids flickered.

'Yeah.' His voice sounded as if it was coming from a deep well.

'I don't want to disturb you, George. I'm sorry about what happened. I better go. I just wanted to check you were okay.' She leaned down, put her hand out, squeezed his arm.

George grunted, moved, shifting his shoulders a little, as if he wanted to sit up. Some of the wires connected to him swayed.

'George, don't.'

'Isabel.' His voice was clear.

She bent close. His breath smelt stale, still alcohol-tinged.

He raised himself a little. The wires shifted again. Then his head dropped back down onto the thin blue pillow.

He let out a groan, as if he'd used up all his energy.

'Did you see them?'

'Who?' What was he saying?

He shook his head, slowly, as if trying to clear it. Then he stared into her eyes.

'I. Was. Pushed.' Each word came out separately.

'My God! Did you tell the police? I didn't see anyone push

you.' She felt cold, as if the temperature in the room had just dropped.

He shook his head, slowly.

'Why would anyone push you? It could have been an accident.'

A shout echoed from the corridor. His attention drifted to the door. She looked over her shoulder.

'You don't know, do you?' His voice was clearer again.

'Know what?'

His eyelids fluttered. 'About BXH.'

She could barely hear him.

'They've got a ton of secrets, Isabel. You know they used to be the biggest opium trader's bank, don't you?'

'That was all a long time ago.' She shook her head. Had the accident affected him mentally?

He licked his lips. His tongue was big, purple, dry looking. 'You're not listening.' His voice drifted away. His eyes closed again.

'Go home,' he said. 'Wait for him. You don't know what you're getting into.' He groaned softly. 'Remember that girl who was murdered six months ago,' he said. 'The journalist.'

'Who? What journalist?'

'Sean didn't tell you?'

She shook her head. 'Should he have?'

'She was investigating BXH.'

'Investigating what about BXH?'

'Lots of stuff, Isabel. Lots of stuff.' He leaned forward an inch. His hand came up.

'He's in New York.'

'What?' A rush of anger threatened to explode inside her. Had he known this all along?

He stared at her.

'Why didn't you tell me?' She hissed her question.

He looked away. 'They went to New York on the company

jet this morning. Sean was with them. I'm sorry.' His voice trailed away.

She wanted to scream. She bent down to him. 'But the police came to the house looking for him! Did they not go to the bank, find out where he'd gone?' There was a noise from outside, an alarm beeping loudly.

'The police came to BXH at four in the afternoon. The plane had already landed in New York. Look, I honestly thought he would call you.' He leaned towards her. His eyes were appealing to her.

'I was going to tell you, later.'

She didn't believe him.

'What's he doing in New York?'

'There's a press conference tomorrow at the bank in Manhattan. They're announcing something big.'

She banged her fist into her forehead, closed her eyes. How could he be such a bastard? She was following his footsteps, checking hospitals, clubs, and he was relaxing in Manhattan!

'There's something else,' said George, softly.

'What?'

He let out a sigh. 'If they find out I told you this, I'll be fired, and sued. Please, don't tell them.' His eyes looked haunted.

'I won't. I promise.'

'They're clearing Sean's office out tonight.' It sounded as if he was shocked too.

'Tonight?'

'They're boxing his stuff up. Remember the whistle blower last year? They did it to him too.'

She did remember this time. An older banker, some guy coming up to his retirement, had gone to the UK Financial Regulator and then to the newspapers. He'd claimed the bank had been skimming investor's funds, cooking the books like a five-star chef. He'd been fired immediately. Then it went around that the guy had been passed over for promotion, that he wanted revenge. It was hard to know what to believe. That was what Sean had said.

Isabel turned her head.

The nurse had come bustling into the room.

'You'll have to leave,' she said. 'He's too weak for long visits.' She stood there, holding the door open, clearly expecting Isabel to go.

She did, but not before squeezing George's hand. She'd been right. He knew a lot more than he'd been letting on. Outside, the streets were busy. She felt disconnected from reality, as if she'd been taken to a different planet, one she recognised, but didn't feel part of.

She'd made a decision. She was going to New York.

37

The basement room in Soho was almost bare. It was the type of place people could hide or be kept in against their will for long periods.

Rose and Alek were lying on a giant dirty mattress. Nearby was a one litre blue plastic bottle of water and the wrappers from four cheap sandwiches.

There was a man outside the locked steel door. Rose knew that because he had come into the room quickly and had told her to answer the phone, say everything was okay, when Isabel had rung. He'd also forced her to send her husband a text to say she'd met an old girlfriend and would be home late.

Alek was sleeping in her arms. It was uncomfortable, but it was the least she could do. She felt responsible. If she hadn't taken Alek for a walk that afternoon she mightn't have been bundled into that van by those two psycho bastards.

The shock of what had happened had almost given her a heart attack. She'd wheezed for twenty minutes, but now her mind was cold.

She'd heard a telephone call being made from the sealed front of the van. From the little she'd heard he was reporting their capture to someone. The not knowing why this was happening was one of the most worrying things. Was it because of Sean and Isabel? Was it something random? No explanation had been provided.

Her brain sifted through memories of movies about people who'd been kidnapped. Anything was possible now. She knew that. She'd experienced how rough they'd been. She'd felt their grip on her arms, vice-like, as they'd bundled them down here. There was no pity in their eyes. She tried to sleep. But then the door opened. Alek didn't wake, he just stirred. And the man who'd opened it was different from the one behind him, who'd kept guard.

This one was tall, well over six foot, and built like a soldier. There was an air of menace coming from him.

He bent down to Rose. 'You are staying here. The boy is coming with us. You will be released in forty-eight hours. The police will track your phone by then, maybe even sooner. Make no trouble while we take the boy and you will still be alive when they find you. Now give him this to drink.'

He handed Rose a small water bottle with an inch of clear liquid at the bottom.

She shook her head, slowly, her eyes widening.

'It will not kill him. It will simply keep him sleepy.'

He opened his jacket. Under his arm there was a knife in a sheath.

'If you prefer, I will cut your throat and finish with you.' His eyes were the hardest she had ever seen. They were balls of glass.

She took the bottle with a shaking hand.

'Don't make a mistake. I would hate to frighten him with the sight of your blood.'

She nudged Alek until he woke. He looked up, startled, at the big man beside Rose.

Eventually she got him to drink the liquid. A minute later

his head went to his chest. The man snapped his fingers. The other man came into the room. He picked the boy up.

Rose stared at him, but said nothing.

That was when she noticed the passports in the man's trouser pocket. Just the corner of them was visible, but they couldn't be mistaken for anything else.

38

When Isabel arrived at Heathrow Airport Terminal 5 early the following morning, it was hard to be positive about Sean. His face, it looked like his ID picture from the bank, was on the front of most of the newspapers in the first shop she went into.

She almost had a seizure when she saw the picture. She froze, mid-step. She'd known he was being covered in the media, but she'd never imagined this, his face wherever she went.

She grabbed a paper, paid for it, and left the shop, though she'd wanted to get a magazine to distract herself. That idea had simply fled. It felt as if the world was turning on her. She decided not to read the story until she was on the plane. She headed for check-in.

At the desk there were less braying City types than the last time they'd travelled to the States. They'd been in first class that time. The bank had paid for it all. She was glad now she'd gone with him. It meant she knew exactly where the bank's headquarters was in midtown Manhattan, and where their big press conference room was on the fiftieth floor, near the top of their building.

She'd been in it.

She swayed as she checked in. She'd only had about four hours sleep. Though she reckoned she'd been fortunate to sleep at all, her mind had been racing so much.

After checking in, she headed for the gate. She ate half a croissant and drank two-thirds of a medicinal cappuccino on the way, but she had no appetite. She'd been given a window seat and as soon as she settled in she took out the paper with Sean's picture on the cover.

She had to read the article twice, the second time with less thumping in her chest, before she was sure it didn't say anything she didn't know already. She was doubly glad she'd been given the window seat when she saw one of Sean's colleagues from BXH striding down the aisle towards her from first class.

She looked out the window. He went by. Thankfully, he didn't recognise her. She couldn't remember his name, but the sight of him reminded her of the pampered life every senior person at BXH wallowed in, as if it was their divine right. It didn't matter that almost all the other banks in the world were cutting back, both on bonuses and salaries. The top tier at BXH always believed their own propaganda.

They were Masters of the Universe, or wannabe Masters, able to conjure up money out of thin air and at will. One thought alone kept her optimistic. Sean was in New York. And what a surprise he'd get when he saw her. In her more positive moments, as the plane flew on, she was sure that it was all a big mix-up.

He'd come back to London with her on the next flight to clear his name. In a few days all this and BXH's troubles would be a memory.

They could sue all those stupid newspapers for using his picture, and for implying his guilt. That would be good. Very good.

Her positivity didn't last.

She was barely able to sit still on the plane for more than a few minutes, thinking about it all. Thankfully, getting through JFK went quicker than the last time she'd been through. She grabbed a yellow cab at the rank outside the terminal. As she travelled into Manhattan through the Saturday afternoon traffic she tried to remember what Sean had been wearing the last time she saw him, so she could fix a picture of him in her mind and decide which part of him she wanted to tear a strip off first.

Soon after the taxi pulled up at the Grand Hyatt New York.

She'd booked a two night deal when she'd booked the flight. It was 3:20 p.m. local time now and New York was freezing, but busy. There wasn't any snow falling, but pale clouds were threatening, and the temperature was touching zero.

When she stepped out of the cab, an arctic wind sliced into her.

The reception at the Grand Hyatt was enormous, on two wide levels, with elevators leading up to the main reception, and banks of lifts sucking guests up to their rooms in the seemingly endless floors above. All she wanted to do was dump her stuff, have a large coffee to stop her body slowing down, and head up Lexington Avenue to 45th Street, three blocks away, where BXH had its headquarters.

From her room, on the fifteenth floor, she could see down 42nd Street. She felt hungry. Then suddenly starving. She went to the lobby restaurant to eat. She dosed herself with a double espresso, a Manhattan burger and double fries. It was the type of comfort food she'd eaten when she was in university.

Her plan was to go to the BXH press conference, and come out of the crowd and confront him. If he was there, that was. And if he wasn't, quiz his colleagues until they told her where he might be. If he hadn't been arrested already, of course.

She clattered her knife and fork onto the square green plate. She was ready.

It was after four in the afternoon when the taxi pulled up outside the bank. She was tired and it was too cold to walk, even if it was only a few blocks. And the way the wind was racing down Lexington, as if a pack of Alaskan wolves was running behind it, made her glad she hadn't been foolish enough to try.

The BXH building sat on a gigantic neoclassical base of grey granite. The row of columns on its third floor made it look like an ancient temple or mausoleum. And up above that, almost in the clouds, it had a crown of similar pink pillars. It was taller than most of the skyscrapers around it and gloomier-looking, all grey and with smaller windows than the more modern buildings nearby.

The Grand Central Post Office, with its grey pillars and neoclassical doorways, looked miniscule beside it. Sean had told her all about the BXH building's history when they'd visited it the last time. How it had opened with a big party in early 1928. A good year for parties in New York, by all accounts.

As the taxi let her off she looked up, bending her head back almost until it hurt, as she tried to see the top of the BXH building. Three blocks away the iconic art deco Chrysler building with its seventy-seven floors was the only taller building nearby. The BXH building, the Chrysler Building, and the other lesser skyscrapers stretching away into the distance, gave Lexington Avenue the feel of a concrete canyon.

She pushed through the high glass doors. They had shiny brass rivets around their edges and brass fretwork panels.

The entrance lobby had a deeply coffered ceiling like the

inside of an egg box, tiers of pink marble columns, and faux-ancient brass and glass torches spewing light high up on its walls.

The comparison with BXH's ultra-modern headquarters in London was striking. The New York building was the kind of place cigar-chomping old-school financial barons operated from when New York was the capital of the world. The building in London was about the future of finance, all minimalist and anonymous. It was a building that could have been moved to Shanghai or Delhi or wherever the next wave of growth was going to come from.

Her footsteps echoed as she crossed the giant black and white tiles of the hall. Everything was shiny, reflecting the yellow light blazing from the torches high above. On the far side of the lobby, an out-of-place-looking row of half-height thick glass turnstiles separated the public area of the lobby from a row of elevators beyond. A shiny ebony reception desk dominated the lobby. Behind it two guards, one black, one white, both giants, waited.

They stared at her with far-off expressions as she came towards them. Her tight dark denims and zipped-up black suede jacket were out of place here, she knew, but she smiled at them anyway as she came forward and tossed her hair off her face.

'Can we help you, ma'am?' His belly was a whale's. His white shirt bulged over it. His epaulettes were gold braid. His smile back at her was real though.

'Hi, what time is the press conference?'

'Which press conference, ma'am?' His colleague was looking at her warily, leaning back, as if wondering if he'd seen her someplace before.

'The BXH merger press conference.'

'That's at seven, ma'am. You want me to reserve you a seat?'

Could it be this easy?

'Sure.' She gave him a bigger smile.

'May I see your press ID, ma'am?'

Her smile faded.

'Aaah.' She patted her pockets as if she was checking for it. She couldn't tell them the truth. The last thing she wanted was for Sean to find out she was here and not show up.

'I'll bring it with me at seven.'

'You do that, ma'am. This is strictly a press only event.' He had a half-suppressed smile on his face. There was going to be no easy way to get by this guy.

'See you later,' she said.

They didn't reply.

She turned away, then turned back again. 'Can anyone from the press get in?'

'No, ma'am,' said the other guard. He had a voice like gravel being stirred. 'You gotta be on the list to get in, ma'am.'

39

Li clicked the Skype encoder software button. It would be thirty seconds before the link with Beijing would be active. He wiped a breadcrumb from the faux-Louis XVI dining table and looked around the room.

The Carlyle was the grandest of the five-star hotels in Manhattan. The suite he was in, the Churchill, was the best in the 1960s-era building that dominated Madison Avenue, but still he wasn't happy. It wasn't the suite. Its marble bath, original artwork and connecting deep-pile carpeted rooms were perfectly acceptable. The summons he had received by text was what was troubling him.

The Mandarin character text message had been explicit in its brevity.

CALL AT ONCE

Only the identity of the originator caused him distress. The man who had sent it would normally never resort to sending text messages. The General Secretary of the Financial Reform Committee of the Chinese Communist Party was not a man to be kept waiting.

The Skype screen was replaced by a small video link. It switched from black to showing an image of an ultra-modern apartment on Liangmaqiao Road, in the high class Chaoyang District of Beijing. Li knew the apartment. He had received a personal vetting there.

'I am here,' said Li, softly.

The image still showed the wall with the original Rothko print and the edge of the sliding glass door to the balcony, but now it showed a flame too. A lit black candle, six inches tall and wide, had been placed on the desk in front of the laptop camera.

Li breathed in quickly. The message was clear.

'When the candle is finished,' began the General Secretary's voice. His tone was as hard as the triple glazed doors that led to his balcony, overlooking the Bird's Nest Olympic stadium. 'A decision will be made as to how to finish the matter of our involvement with this project.'

Li waited. When nothing else had been said after two minutes, and he thought he could almost hear the sound of the water feature on the balcony, he spoke.

'I am clearing the stones,' he said. 'The benefits of this undertaking are worth your patience, General Secretary. What we find will transform our situation.'

A hiss sounded from the Beijing apartment.

'No more promises!' The voice was angry. 'One hundred and fifty-five years have passed. We are happy to wait a little longer.'

Li didn't reply this time. He was trying to work out what had angered a man who he had thought he could count on. The reference to the burning of the Summer Palace in Beijing, during the Opium Wars, was an unnecessary reminder of the importance of his mission, but the fact that it had been mentioned at all surely meant that pressure had been placed on his friend.

Perhaps the exceptionally large transfers to the branch in London had raised questions beyond the group he had already paid off. That had been his biggest gamble so far. But he'd had no choice. Lord Bidoner had insisted the money be transferred to his hedge fund.

'Do not look for me again, until the item is in your hands,' said the voice.

The last image Li saw was the flame burning. Then the screen went blank. He let out his breath.

Then, frustration etched into his face, he smashed his hand down on the table.

The table rattled.

He didn't have much time. The black long-lasting candle would burn out in twenty-four hours. If he didn't have what was needed by then he would soon after be a dead man waiting.

He closed the lid of the laptop, then raised a fist to his lips. A long-forgotten memory had come back to him. He could almost smell the blood still, and feel the man's trembling as the blade had sliced into flesh. That had been ten years ago.

Was his turn coming?

He smashed his hand down again.

That could not happen. He would do whatever it took to ensure that.

40

Back on the street outside the bank Isabel walked to another smaller entrance to the BXH building around the corner on Lexington. It looked as if it was kept permanently locked.

There was also a car park entrance, a lowered red steel shutter with a ramp going down, which presumably meant some of the staff could drive into the bank. She remembered something Sean had told her about the town cars that ferried BXH's top managers to and from Wall Street. This must be where they came in and out, straight onto Lexington. Then a fast ride downtown.

She headed for a diner, Luigi's, which was open across the street. Inside was like being in a movie about New York. There were plastic chairs, plastic menus and a selection of food that could add inches to your waist in one sitting.

She ordered a donut and coffee, looked at her watch. It was ten to five.

The guy who served her was well over six feet. He had slicked-back black hair. He gave her a big smile from behind the counter. Above his head a yellow fan twirled.

She found a table near the window.

Was there any way she could get into the press conference? Did she know any journalists? Who was that editor she met a few years back?

The only problem was, the *Birmingham Weekly* probably didn't cover financial events in New York City. She looked around. This really was old New York, the kind of place Sean's aunt and uncle would have loved.

Sean's uncle. That was it. He'd been with a big bank. He might know some of the journalists on the list. Maybe they could help her. It had to be worth a shot.

She pulled her phone out of her pocket. What time was it in Paris? Ten in the evening? She held the phone tight. As Karen's number rang she leaned sideways so she could see the entrance to the bank's parking garage. When would people start arriving? An hour before the press conference? Or were they all already in there?

She looked up towards the upper floors of the BXH building. A quarter of the building, from the part she could see, was lit up. Did that mean there were lots of people up there working? She had no idea. It could be just what the place looked like every Saturday afternoon in winter.

'Isabel,' said Karen's voice. 'I'm glad you rang. I tried calling you at home. I thought your phone was busted. What's happening? Did you find Sean?'

Emotion came welling up inside her. For a moment Isabel couldn't speak. She held the phone away from her, pressed her knuckles to her lips.

Fight it. Don't let it get to you.

'No.' She cleared her throat. 'But I know where he is.'

'You haven't seen him?'

'No.'

'That's terrible. I can't believe he hasn't contacted you.' She spoke fast. There was an accusation in her tone too, as if she was getting ready to defend Sean.

'Can I speak to Frank?'

She heard a sigh, a rustling.

Frank came on the line.

'Are you okay, honey?' were his first words. How typical. How decent. She used to think Sean was so like him.

'I can't believe what's going on, Frank.'

'Where are you?'

'I'm in New York, near BXH's headquarters. I was told Sean is here. He's going to be at some BXH press conference in a couple of hours.'

'For the merger announcement? And he hasn't called you, told you what's happening?'

'No. He's avoiding me. He came here and he didn't even tell me. I can't believe he'd do that.' She wouldn't have said that to Karen, but Frank was so open she knew he'd take it all the right way.

'Jesus H. Christ.'

She didn't reply. She didn't want to tell him the police were looking for his nephew. She didn't want to shatter him completely.

'My God, Isabel. Is there anything I can do? Anything at all?' She could hear his breathing, slightly laboured.

'Maybe it's all a misunderstanding, Frank. There is one thing you could do though.'

'Sure, whatever. I told Sean he was working too hard.'

She rubbed her hand along the edge of the plastic covered table.

'Do you still know people in the financial press here in New York? Anyone who might be on the invite list to this press conference? I want to get into it, Frank. I have to see him.'

She heard a sudden intake of breath. Then silence.

'I'm not going to cause a scene. I just want to surprise him. Sit at the back, find out what's been keeping him away from his family.' Her voice broke a little at the end, shook, then rose a notch.

'Jeez, I don't know, honey. Sean might . . .' He stopped.

'Please, Frank. I came to New York to see him. If I don't get into that press conference, find out why he's avoiding me, I'm going to go totally crazy.' She could hear her voice rising all the way through that speech, but she couldn't stop it. She almost shouted the word crazy at him.

She glanced around to see if anyone was looking at her. The guy behind the counter was staring, wide-eyed. A woman two tables up had turned around and was giving her the are-you-a-wacko look.

'I'll see what I can come up with. Should I give them this number?'

'Yeah. Get them to call me straight away. The press conference is in a couple of hours.' Hope soared inside her.

'Okay, honey. You take care now.' The line went dead.

She put the phone on the table by her coffee cup and stared at it, willing it to ring soon.

What should she do if Frank didn't know anyone? Should she go to the NYPD, get them to investigate, look for Sean? Was she deluding herself that she could find him?

What a stupid mess.

Her phone rang!

'Hello.' Hope spiked inside her again.

'Hi, Isabel, this is Jenny from down the road. Just ringing to see if you're okay?'

Tiredness hit her, as if her blood sugar level had just dropped. Jenny and Isabel had been close the year before, but they hadn't seen much of each other recently. She wasn't sure why.

'Jenny, hi. Listen, everything's fine. Can I call you back? It's just I'm waiting for a call. I'll get back to you. I promise.' There was an awkward silence.

'Okay, Isabel.' She sounded offended. The line went dead. Crap. But there was no way she wanted to be on a call if someone else tried her line. There'd be time for patching things up with Jenny later.

She took a sip of coffee. At least there was one thing she could be sure of. Alek was safe.

41

Above the Atlantic, the Bombardier Global 5000 was following the edge of night. Behind was Europe, darkness and the twinkling of stars. Ahead was a snow storm and the late afternoon skies of Long Island, and the continent behind it.

The cloud beneath them was a rolling blanket with occasional gaps, where you could see down through cascading layers of deeper, roiling grey.

Above, the constellations shone. The seven stars of the plough stood out to the north and directly above, the Milky Way was like a path of glittering marble.

Adar had agreed to a long route, when the controller at Shanwick had offered it to him. It would mean them taking the most northerly U trans-Atlantic track, which would bring them well inland, over Newfoundland, but that suited him.

He was flying at 42,000 feet and below the Bombardier's maximum speed now, at Mach 0.7. An altered, slower flight plan had been agreed minutes before his departure. He had to ensure he arrived at La Guardia when his favourite senior immigration officer was on duty.

The man would check all passports diligently and run

them through the Department of Homeland Security IT systems, to ensure they weren't on any watch list, but he was happy to do it with no more than a two minute visit to the cabin of the Bombardier to ensure there were no stowaways or obvious contraband, though he would check the hold properly. But Adar had nothing to fear there.

The boy would be sleeping again, and groggy, by the time they landed in a few hours.

He turned and looked into the long thin cabin. His colleague was sitting with the boy in the leather seats facing the TV screen. A Spiderman movie was playing. The boy had been told, when he woke, that he was being taken to meet his father. Then he'd been given sweets and a drink. It was a lot of effort to ensure they got the boy into the States without difficulty, but Adar did as he was told.

When Lord Bidoner wanted something done he always had a good reason. And if a few people had to die on the way, then that was just collateral damage.

Adar had known when he was recruited that murder was one of the tasks he would be asked to carry out, but after four years working as a mercenary in Chechnya, killing whoever got in his way, the idea was not unpleasant. He had shot families, children as young as this boy in front of their parents, to make them talk. Whatever was necessary.

And he had become good at it.

And now there was no turning back. No squeamishness could enter his mind. Because if he ever hesitated, his own life would be forfeit.

That had been what he signed up for. And the money in his family bank account in Lebanon, which would make a life and death difference to many of his relatives, was compensation enough for what had to be done.

And Lord Bidoner had promised a large bonus after this job was complete. Which meant that no matter what he wanted, how many people he wanted dead, it would all happen.

He thought about the boy in the cabin behind him again. He shook his head.

Maybe after this he could retire. He would, at last, have enough money for that villa in the hills overlooking Tripoli.

He looked down.

A red light on the console was flashing. Another weather warning had been picked up. He looked at the green-hued radar screen with its slowly moving lights and sweeping arm. The storm was heading inland, south of Manhattan.

Just as long as it didn't turn north in the next few hours everything would be fine. The boy had an appointment for the coming evening. And his boss would not be happy if he missed it.

Lord Bidoner did not accept failure. Not even once. Adar touched the throttle, eased it forward a notch. Then he looked back into the cabin.

He'd heard the boy talking.

His soft voice was so like his own son's that a memory had come back to him. When he'd visited his wife that last time the boy had been in another room playing with her sister's children.

He felt a shudder rise up. He gripped the throttle. Whatever they were planning for this boy, it would not be pleasant.

He rubbed his hand across his brow. It was throbbing.

With a bit of luck he would not be there when they did it. And the sooner this contract was over the better.

42

'More coffee, ma'am?' The guy from behind the counter with the slicked-back hair was standing beside her.

'Yes, thanks.'

He filled her cup. She glanced towards the window.

'You work for the bank, ma'am?'

She shook her head. 'No, I'm going there later.'

'That makes two of you,' he said. He was about to walk away when she said, 'I'm sorry?'

'Yeah, that guy over there's waiting to go to something at BXH too.' He pointed at a young guy wearing a black ski jacket with fur lining on its hood, sitting near the window. He had steel glasses, a regulation army haircut and a sullen air coming off his hunched up shoulders.

'And he's been here a lot longer than you, ma'am.'

The waiter whistled as he walked away.

The guy in the ski jacket looked around fast, as if he'd sensed someone was talking about him. Then he went back to staring out of the window.

Maybe if Frank couldn't get her into the press conference, she'd have to do whatever it took, including chatting up strange men.

She stood and walked over to ski jacket man. There was a prickle of sweat on her brow, but she didn't care.

'Hi, you going to the press conference too?' She stood by his table and gave him a tentative smile. Then she flicked her gaze towards the empty chair opposite him.

He looked at her, as if she'd just told him the room was full of zombies. His eyes were wide, his cheeks pink.

'Who told ya that?' His voice was loud, high pitched. People nearby glanced at them.

This guy wasn't going to help her.

'The waiter,' she said.

'That guy? He don't know nothin'.' He spat out the word nothin', then looked around the room.

'My mistake.' She turned, walked back to where she'd been sitting.

To hell with him, a super-heated hell.

She sat, pushed her hair back from her forehead, and closed her eyes.

'You okay?'

She opened her eyes, fast. Ski jacket man was sitting in the chair opposite her.

'Yeah.' She leaned forward. His eyes sneaked down towards her breasts. Predictable. Then they snapped up again.

She gifted him a smile. 'I'm Isabel, what's your name?'

'Timmy, Timmy Wilson. You going to the press conference, Isabel?'

She nodded.

'You don't look like regular MSM.'

'MSM?'

'Mainstream media, you know, regular journalists.'

'I'm not. Where are you from, Timmy?' She leaned forward, as if she was really interested in his answer.

'Alabama. Huntsville. I got a zoomin blog. We got readers

in every state. I flew in just for this press conference.' He looked pleased with himself.

'Why?'

He put his elbows on the table. 'You tell me why you're going, first,' he said. 'Seeing as how you came over to me.'

He looked like someone who'd have a lot of trouble getting dates. His skin was a flaky, floury white. He was probably spending too much time online, on sites his mother disapproved of.

'I just want to find out what's going on at BXH,' she said. Would that be enough? Was she going to have to make up some other story?

There was a long pause. He was daring her to stay quiet. She began debating what to say next. Then he spoke.

'That makes two of us.'

'So what do you want to find out?'

'You know those BXH guys are foreclosing businesses all over the place, don't you?'

She nodded. He went on. It sounded as if he was getting on to his number one topic.

'Someone has to look into what those guys have been up to. That's why I came up. Every newspaper in this whole country just prints out the goddamn big-bank press releases without even editing their spelling.' He snorted, then continued.

'They're what I call robot journalists. You know, you slip a press release in one end, and a newspaper article comes out the other, with only one change, the words – press release – have been removed from the top of it all.' He beamed.

'Robot journalists, that's good.'

'You know what else?' He leaned forward.

She shook her head.

'Have you seen their goddamned logo?'

She blinked. BXH's logo?

'It's one of those alchemy symbols.'

'What?'

'Yeah, I saw them in this old puzzle book. I reckon they're all into black magic over there.' He glanced towards the window, then over his other shoulder, as if some devil worshippers might be listening in.

'Wow, that's amazing,' she said. 'You got a pass to go to their press conference?'

He gave her a toothy grin. His teeth were nicotine stained. He looked better when he didn't smile. She held his stare.

'Maybe, how about you? Why don't'cha tell us your story? You're English, right?' His eyes sneaked to her breasts again. They stayed there a microsecond longer this time.

'I'm interested in what's going on at BXH, that's all. My dad got foreclosed by them in London,' she lied.

One of his eyebrows twitched. 'Yeah, they been doing that a lot. You know they took a trillion federal bailout dollars just to pay their fat bonuses.' He looked over his shoulder again.

What the hell had he got to be paranoid about? Did he think the bank's goons were out looking for bloggers?

'What time are you going over there?' She didn't bother telling him it was a hundred billion dollars they'd got, not a trillion.

'Starts at seven, so I heard.'

'How did you get your name on the press list?'

He shook his head. His eyebrows came down. 'Why you wanna know?'

'Forget it. Are you on your own, Timmy?'

He clamped his mouth shut.

'Jeez, you are paranoid. I'm not wired you know.' She opened her jacket wide and turned in her seat, so he could see the back of her jeans.

'I didn't think you were.' His voice was softer again. He gave her a lopsided grin.

She wanted to run out of the place.

'You know, Timmy, I was hoping someone like you would come along, get me into that press conference. To tell you the truth, that's why I came over to talk to you.'

His cheeks reddened. 'I could meet you afterwards. Tell you what happened.'

'I want to see these guys for myself.'

He leaned towards her. Their faces were inches apart. She caught the smell of stale French fries and tobacco from his breath.

'You wanna see the whites of their eyes. Find out if they're all lizards, right?' He bared his teeth. It was a lovely sight.

'I been watching for black helicopters.' He pointed at the sky.

'Did you see any?'

'Not yet,' he said. 'But I reckon it won't be long before I do.'

He was warming up. He probably didn't get too many females showing an interest in him.

'So what about the merger? What's that all about?' she said.

'That ain't no merger. That's a takeover. Them goddamned Chinese want a big slice of the USA. BXH are gonna sell us all out to a bunch of commies. You know, half the big businesses in this country are gonna end up owned by that goddamned Chinese communist party, if we ain't careful.' He said the word – communist – as if he was spitting out gristle. He shook his head.

She smiled at him.

'So you could get me in? We could go there together?'

He looked sad now, as if he thought he might be missing

out on something by saying no to her. 'I only got one press pass,' he said.

Then he grinned, showing his lovely teeth again. 'But I'll meet you after, if you want. You know, we can get together at my hotel. I can tell you what they're really like. I got a bottle of Jim Beam in my room.' He winked at her.

That was her limit. 'I gotta go. I gotta find someone who can get me in.'

She stood, zipped up her jacket. If he knew how to get her in, this was his chance to reveal it.

'Take it easy,' she said.

43

Henry Mowlam looked at the text message. It was Saturday evening in London and he'd been planning an early night. His apartment in Kentish Town was small, but it was clean.

There were others on duty who could deal with whatever happened over the weekend. But the text that had arrived had sent him looking for his jacket.

George Donovan had been a senior security manager at BXH UK until yesterday. Then he'd been hit by a bus in Piccadilly Circus. Afterwards, he'd had a couple of visitors in hospital and then, within hours of being admitted, he'd been found dead.

He'd been asphyxiated.

Confirming that that was the reason for his death had delayed the incident being reported to him. Henry had an alert out for all BXH-related activity. This latest development had to be viewed with suspicion.

There was no way the murder of a senior BXH security staff member at this moment was a casual thing, an accident. It had been professionally done and it implied there was a war on for control of this bank.

A half-dozen government departments and quangos would want to have a say in how this was handled.

Major Finch was right. They needed to talk.

The second bit of news concerned him perhaps more than the first.

Isabel Ryan had travelled to New York. Henry had requested FBI cooperation on keeping tabs on her. At the very least her mobile needed to be located every five minutes and her calls intercepted. In addition, the local FBI office in Manhattan, where she had booked a room, should be notified and the feed from the security cameras in her hotel made available to him.

The reply, from the FBI office, had been less than satisfactory. The request would be reviewed, within twenty-four hours.

He felt a familiar frustration rising inside him. There was something going down in Manhattan and he had no idea what it was, but he had a bad feeling.

Could Major Finch pull rank and get the Yanks to cooperate? It would be a nightmare of recriminations if something happened in Manhattan because they simply didn't respond fast enough.

44

Isabel was half-hoping he'd come after her, offer to try to get her in. She stood near the door for a moment, looked at her phone. No calls. She went out into the street. Timmy waved at her as she passed the window, as if they were friends. She didn't wave back.

Asshole.

She decided to walk around the BXH building, to see if she could see anyone else waiting to go to the press conference. It was a long shot, but better than just going back to her hotel.

A seagull swooped in front of her on huge wings. It made a cackling noise as it picked up some scrap, as if warning her off its territory. She crossed the street and walked alongside the old Grand Central Post Office building, heading up towards 45th. The BXH building loomed above her like a presence, something from an old movie with Fred Astaire, set in the thirties when the elite arrived at restaurants in tuxedos, while ordinary people in rags watched from across the street.

A bum was coming towards her. He was wearing what looked like ten coats, all too big for him. He had newspapers wrapped around his feet, or maybe around his shoes. She couldn't exactly see which.

Instinctively, she moved away from the wall of the bank. He looked harmless, but she'd heard too many warnings every time she came to Manhattan. A bus swayed past. The bum veered towards her. What the hell was he playing at? Spook the lady?

'Spare a dollar?'

He was still a few paces away. Then he stepped into her path. She saw his eyes. They were bloodshot, purple-rimmed. His hands came up, as if he was going to reach out, grab her.

She sidestepped back towards the bank building. She'd be past him in a second.

His right hand reached out. She could smell sweat and some sour fragrance, urine.

His hand brushed her arm as she lengthened her stride.

She was past him.

He grunted, loudly. She glanced back. He'd fallen down onto his side, and was holding his head.

'I'm gonna sue you, lady. That was a goddamned assault,' he shouted. He shook a grubby fist at her.

She kept walking. This was one of those tricks they use to get you to stop. There was a rushing in her veins. Her stride lengthened again as if someone was pushing at her back. His shouts were diminishing far too slowly. Was he going to come after her? A taxi beeped its horn, then slowed as it came towards her. She put her hand up.

'The Grand Hyatt.' It was time to get out of here. She could come back later.

She settled back in the seat. The heat in the cab was stifling. Seconds later sweat was prickling out all over her forehead, then down her back. They'd stopped at a traffic lights. She looked back. The bum was still on the ground. He was pointing towards her, as if she was a criminal getting away. That was some act he had.

'How you doin?' said the driver.

'You got some crazies in this city,' she said.

'He ain't nothin',' said the driver. 'Wait'll you see the mob that's gonna turn up back there in a couple'a hours. The kooks are gonna be out tonight.'

'A mob?'

'Don't you read the papers, lady?' He looked at her in the rear-view mirror. His eyes were huge, as if he was forcing them open out of tiredness.

'Not today.'

'You know that BXH bank back there, where I picked you up, they got a lot of people's savings in those vaults, and now they say some commies are gonna come and take it all over. Now that ain't right. No sir-ee.'

'There's gonna be a demonstration?'

'Yeah, damn right there is. They're gonna rename BXH, the First Commie Bank of the USA. We ain't got that in New York yet.' He waved a hand in front of him.

He kept talking until she got out.

In the hotel she headed for the elevators. She needed a shower. She needed to get clean. She needed to think. After that she could work out what to do next. It didn't look like she had too many choices. As the elevator doors started to close a British couple stepped in. She could tell where they were from the moment they opened their mouths.

'Which floor, darling?'

'Twenty-two,' he said. He put his arm around the woman, hugged her.

Envy rose fast inside her. She and Sean should have been in that amazing hotel in Paris right now, heading for their room arm in arm, just like these two. She had to look away.

Why hadn't he contacted her?

She let the water in the shower run over her for ages. The hot water felt good sluicing over her skin. She let it wash away her tiredness. She should go back to the bank, try to get into the press conference, whatever happened. She'd put on her black trousers and her black silk shirt and tie her hair back this time. It was her stand-back-I'm-coming look, Sean used to say.

As she squeezed shampoo on her hair, she heard a faint trill. Was that her phone? She half slipped on the floor of the bathroom, knocking her knee against the door as she scrambled out, naked, wet, looking for it.

It was taking too long to find it.

She was sure the phone would have stopped trilling by the time she picked it up.

But it hadn't.

'Hi,' she said, when she finally got it to her ear.

She held her breath as she waited to hear who was on the other end or if the caller had gone. It might be Sean. The next few seconds were empty of sound, a vacuum dying to be filled.

'Isabel, hi. I'm Laura Jenkins. My old buddy Frank tells me you need some help.'

Thank God for Frank. Thank God for a friendly voice.

'Hi, Laura.'

'Where are you, girl?'

'I'm at the Hyatt, at Grand Central.' Cooling water was dripping from her. Shampoo was congealing in her hair. She didn't care.

'Wicked, great little hotel. You wanna go to this press conference, yeah?'

'Sure.'

'Well, I'm gonna be up there at BXH in five minutes I reckon. And I'm allowed to bring a photographer. So if you can get up there in five, maybe ten, I'll be in the lobby waiting for ya.'

'I thought it was starting at seven?' What was she supposed to do, race out of her room naked?

'Yeah, me too. But then I got an email saying they're gonna start early. They wanna try and have it over by seven. So if there is a big demo firing up they'll miss all the action.'

'They're scared of a demonstration?'

'Yeah, sure. BXH is attracting nut jobs like flies on a dead dog. That's what happens when there's a smell, ain't it? See ya. Gotta go.'

The line went dead.

She was sure there was still shampoo in her hair as the yellow cab dropped her off at BXH. This time there were people in the lobby. Outside the building there were people too, all muffled up, most of them directly across the street from the main entrance on 45th, hanging out, it looked like. Except it was too cold for hanging out. A few of them stared at her as she headed for the entrance to the bank.

Some well-heeled types were queuing at the reception desk. MSM journalists no doubt. How would she recognise Laura?

She needn't have worried. A tall woman, whose black hair fell in a curtain to the small of her back, came striding towards her. She was wearing tight black trousers and a long black jacket with a Mandarin collar and purple buttons.

'I knew it was you. Frank told me all about your big hazel eyes.'

She held her hand out. Isabel shook it. Her grip lasted less than a second. Then she passed her a camera bag, as if they'd shook hands just so she'd be able to slip it to her.

'You do know how to press a shutter button?' she said.

Isabel nodded.

'Okay, that's the induction training over. Let's get up there. I wouldn't want the dicks from the *Wall Street Journal* to get all the best seats.' She nodded towards the four corporate types in pinstripe suits, both the men and the women, who'd already passed security and were waiting at the elevators.

As the guards viewed Laura's press pass and invitation, they only glanced at Isabel. There wasn't even a flicker of recognition that they'd seen her earlier. They ticked twice on a list, then let them through. It felt as if she was crashing an upmarket private party. Was that it? Was she in? It certainly looked like it. And it felt good.

She was going to surprise Sean's ass. Maybe she'd blow him a kiss. Maybe she'd throw a goddamned shoe at him.

They went up alone in the elevator, an elegant pink marble box with a silver handrail, heading up to the fiftieth floor. She'd thought that they'd have time to talk for a few minutes before going into the press conference. But everything was moving very fast.

'What do you think of the merger?' she asked, leaning towards Laura.

Laura put a finger to her lips, shook her head violently, as if Isabel had offered to moon the security men.

The lobby on the fiftieth floor was like the one downstairs, only smaller. It too had a black reception desk, torch style lights and a pink marble floor.

In front of glossy black doors on the far side of the lobby a couple of tables with badges on them had been set up. In front of the tables there was a short queue, consisting of the *Wall Street Journal* people they'd seen downstairs and a few others who must have come up before them.

There were two security guards behind the table and a rope cutting off access to a set of doors. One of the guards was a slim black guy. The other one was a big white guy with a shiny bald head. The black guy was tapping at a handheld device, slowly and deliberately, as everyone waited in front of him.

Laura held her arm as they joined the queue.

'Your husband's disappeared. That's so bad,' she whispered.

'He's probably going to be here. That's why I want to get in.'

'You do know over a million people are reported missing in America every year?' She peered at Isabel as if she was a slow student, and she was her teacher.

Isabel shook her head. 'A million people?'

'Yeah, most of the ones who don't come home after twenty-four hours have psychiatric problems or addiction problems or both. That covers ninety-five per cent of everyone who's still missing after the first day. Amazing, huh?' She looked at Isabel with a condescending expression.

'Sean doesn't have psychiatric or addiction problems.' Isabel shook her head. 'But maybe he will have after I talk to him.'

Laura looked her up and down, as if appraising her for a date for a friend.

'Were you two getting on, you know what I mean?'

Isabel nodded, but not too vigorously. She was asking the right questions. To get a high heel stabbed into her toe.

Laura put her mouth close to Isabel's ear. 'I'll do the talking when we get up to the front.'

The people ahead of them had moved on.

They were at the table.

'Name?'

'Laura Jenkins from the *State Street Times*.' Laura pointed to her. 'This is my photographer.'

The guard looked at Isabel as if she might be a terrorist Laura was trying to smuggle in.

'I gotta check the photographer.' He tapped at his screen. 'We ain't got her ID on our system.'

'You got ID on you?' he said to Isabel.

She gave him her passport. He looked at it, raised his eyebrows, perhaps because it was British, but said nothing. He tapped at his screen again. Then he held the passport open in front of his device for a few seconds before giving it back to her.

He started tapping again.

Isabel's temples were throbbing. A sinking sensation was pulling at her. She was imagining she was going to be sent back down. And she'd come so close. She looked around.

Maybe Sean was here. One of the corporate types behind them, a brown haired six-foot athletic guy smiled at her.

She turned away, pulled her jacket zip up. She looked at the guard holding the hand-sized screen.

'You can go ahead, ma'am,' he said to her.

Laura tugged at her arm. 'Let's go.'

She stared at the guard, suddenly remembering something. 'Where are the rest rooms?'

He pointed at the opposite corner of the hall. Then his gaze moved to the people behind them.

'Jeez, you'd think this was Fort Knox we were trying to get into,' said Laura, as they walked away.

'I gotta go. I'll find you in there.' Isabel nodded towards the doors the other people had gone through.

'You okay?' A look of concern flitted across Laura's face.

'Sure. No problem. See you in there.'

The toilets were almost all marble too. Even the taps were marble. And there were chunky iron radiators painted pink along one wall. The air in the room was stifling hot. She needed to think.

She went into one of the cubicles. Everything was building up inside her, tiredness, anxiety and the anger that had driven her here from London.

She massaged her forehead slowly in small circles. She thought about what she should say to him if she did see him. Could she accept this kind of shit from him, from anyone?

And if Sean didn't show, maybe she should get the high and mighty Mr Vaughann to answer a few questions, tell her what had happened on Thursday night, and exactly where

Sean was when he'd last seen him. She held her breath. The throbbing in her forehead was easing.

She heard the door to the lobby swing, the tap-tap-tap of high heels on the marble floor.

The tapping stopped. Then it started again.

Someone was pacing up and down. She heard a voice.

'Are you sure the National Guard's outside?'

It sounded like Mrs Vaughann's voice.

She heard the door to the lobby creaking. She opened her cubicle door just in time to see a straight back, a snow-blonde head of hair and a pair of pink high heels, Manolos they looked like, exiting the toilet.

It was Mrs Vaughann.

What was she doing here?

45

The leather sofa in Lord Bidoner's apartment extended all the way along the back wall of the main room. It was deep enough and long enough that a couple could sleep there, easily.

Xena was stretched out on it, naked, except for a belt made of brass rings positioned high on her hips. She stretched her long, thin arms out, as if their recent exertions had pleased her.

She looked sated, though Lord Bidoner knew that that was probably an act. He turned his back on her as he did up his shirt buttons and stared out at the flurries of snow smashing against the glass windows. The slight swaying of the building told him the snowstorm was intensifying outside. It had turned north, but with luck their guest would touch down before it reached La Guardia.

He could make out the lights of the building opposite but almost nothing distinct could be seen because of the snow-flakes now.

'I still can't work out why Arap called you a traitor when you met him outside Jerusalem.' He turned to stare at her. She looked even thinner naked.

She turned on her side snaking her long leg along the edge

of the sofa. She knew he was watching her. The blue tattoo of a snake that coiled around her thigh, where a garter might have been, seemed to move as she did, under the soft light from the giant lamps that sat on marble-topped tables at each end of the sofa.

'Did you tell him about the report on the Summer Palace in Beijing?' she said, softly.

He turned, as he tucked his pale blue shirt into his black trousers. 'No, and I didn't send him the report about Nuremberg either.' He sat near her, stroking her ankle. There were scars there, but her skin was shiny, her foot long and athletic.

'I know you want to get going,' he said. 'But we cannot make our next move until our visitor arrives.'

He stroked her calf. 'You have confirmed with the lab that they are ready for the DNA sample?'

'Yes,' she said. 'The doctor is waiting for me to arrive.'

'He doesn't know the pastor by name?'

'No, just who he worked for.'

Lord Bidoner stood.

'We are near the end.'

There was a soft clicking noise from his phone.

She picked it up from the floor, stood and handed it to him.

Then she started stretching, as if she was on her way to a run.

He spoke as he watched her.

'Do not injure him,' he said.

He closed the line.

'Your friend is not being cooperative.'

'He will do anything I want when I bring the fire to him. No one ever resists it,' she said. She kept stretching.

'You are right. And you enjoy doing that, don't you?'

She looked at him and smiled.

46

The carpet in the press conference room was an opulent wall-to-wall Persian with swirling fronds in forty shades of red and brown. The room looked even more over-the-top than Isabel had remembered it. The far end had a raised area, with a row of chairs behind a long table with a red and gold front. It looked like an altar. There were ten lines of straight-backed blood-red chairs with gold piping around their edges in front of the altar. There was nobody sitting behind it.

One wall of the room was a giant window. Drifts of snowflakes swirled outside, tumbling against the glass. It was coming down thicker now. She hesitated near the door. Mrs Vaughann was at the front of the room sitting down. Maybe she shouldn't attract her attention until Sean came in or it became clear he wasn't coming. She might warn him. She didn't want Sean to run away if he heard she was here.

But she wasn't going to hide either.

Maybe she'd just wave at Mrs Vaughann if she recognised her. If it upset anyone that she'd come, what the hell did she care? They hadn't bothered telling her he'd flown to New

York. And she had made it clear to a lot of people at the bank that she was looking for him.

She spotted Laura. She was sitting on her own two rows back from the pack of corporate journalists. She was talking into her phone, using it as a dictation machine it looked like. She grinned at Isabel as she sat beside her, then put her phone down.

'You okay, honey?'

'Yeah.'

'Did you see who's here?' said Laura. She jabbed a finger towards the front row, towards Mrs Vaughann. Isabel took a deep breath and looked to the front. Was Mrs Vaughann better known than she'd thought?

'You know Mrs Vaughann?'

Laura looked at her as if she was a dummy. 'You can bet your boots on that. She's just about the biggest charity supporter in New York City. Her picture is forever in the papers. There's not many publicly acceptable Fifth Avenue philanthropists left after the last few years. She has big connections in the Treasury Department in Washington too. Some people say that's how her husband got his job.'

She noticed Laura's skin. It was flawless.

Isabel leaned towards her, spoke softly. 'I overheard her on the phone saying something about the National Guard being outside. Do you think they're expecting trouble?'

'Honey, there was a riot in this city last weekend. Didn't you hear about it?'

She shook her head.

An older man with thick white hair sat down beside Mrs Vaughann. The two of them began talking animatedly.

'My God, is it hot in here, or is it just me?'

'It's hot.' Laura opened her jacket to reveal a purple skin-tight jumper underneath.

Isabel looked at her watch. It was six thirty. She glanced

around. Any moment now she might see Sean. It felt as if something in her muscles, her arms, her neck, was wound up tight, like a spring aching to loosen itself.

Stay calm.

She turned her head, scanning the room. Timmy was sitting two rows behind her. He grinned at her. She blanked him. A blast of corporate music blared out. Two big, sixty-inch LCD screens on tripods to their left and right burst into life. She'd hardly noticed them up until this.

Then they were watching one of those flashy corporate videos. It had drum and base music, and helicopter views of Manhattan, London and Shanghai at night. Glass towers gleamed like stacks of crystals. Images of bridges, hospitals, wind farms, ultra-fast trains fled by. This was the world that high finance was building.

Then the images changed. Pictures of families, churches, temples, replaced the towers. The face of the bank's CEO, Fred Pilman, came into view with a halo of other faces around him. Fred looked good, square jawed, determined. He wore his light Bahamas' tan as if he was proud that BXH still had its own corporate jet waiting to take its titans anywhere they wanted, and to points south whenever they needed a break in the sun.

'Welcome to BXH. America's international bank for the twenty-first century,' Fred's voice boomed from the speakers.

'Soon to be owned by China,' whispered Laura in her ear.

Isabel's hands were in fists in her lap. She turned again, glanced all the way around. Any moment now the doors at the back of the room would open and she would see Sean.

Then the video screen went blank. It looked as if something had gone wrong. This wasn't like BXH. They waited. They waited some more. Then a slamming noise echoed through the room.

And, as if they were all connected by wires, everyone in

the room turned their heads towards the door they'd come in through.

Striding towards them was a giant of a man. He must have been twenty stone, at least. He was well over six feet tall too. In his arms, folded over his stomach, he was carrying a thick yellow pad. His black suit was rumpled, as if he'd been working in it forever. His skin was as white as dough and had a similar consistency.

He was one of those creatures who live in the bowels of some offices, who don't get out to see the sun much. As he strode towards the top of the room, he was clearly enjoying every step, he didn't look to the left or right. By the time he'd reached the table and had sat at a seat in the centre, a buzz of voices, like a hive coming to life, had sprung up from the rows of journalists.

'My name is Adam Bruckhaus Jr,' he said loudly, over the noise. Did this guy even need a microphone?

The noise level went down a notch.

'I represent Hardman, Weiss and Bruckhaus.' His accent was old-style gravelly New York. He sounded like the kind of guy who ate petitioners, three at a time, on the steps of the courthouse for breakfast.

The buzz in the room went up another ten notches. It sounded as if the hive was under attack.

Laura nudged her, hard.

'Holy cow!' she said.

It took only a few more words from Adam for Isabel to work out what Laura meant.

'I am the lead insolvency consultant for our firm.' His brow furrowed, as if he was trying to show everyone how difficult his position was. He placed his hands slowly on the table, spacing them wide in front of him. It looked as if he had, by that gesture, taken possession of it, and everything else in the building beneath him.

'I have the unfortunate duty to announce that BXH will be filing a Chapter 11 bankruptcy petition before midnight tonight.' He looked at his watch. 'A little over five hours from now. All of BXH's retail and business clients will, you'll be glad to know, receive their deposits back under the appropriate Federal deposit guarantee schemes.'

'Mr Bruckhaus,' 'Mr Bruckhaus,' 'Mr Bruckhaus,' voices called out.

'I will not be taking any questions at this time.'

'What about the merger?'

'What about a Federal bailout? They did it for AIG?'

Mr Bruckhaus stood, pushed his chair back, and headed for the door. A posse of journalists followed him. Others gathered in small groups, gesticulating. Isabel just stared.

Laura stamped her foot.

'I bet some of their top staff are bringing forward their bonuses right at this stinking moment. They won't be the ones to lose out. The regular staff will. Thousands of families won't be sleeping tonight. Did you see Mrs Vaughann?'

She hadn't. She looked around. She was nowhere to be seen.

'She followed Mr Shithaus out.' Laura shook her head.

'Bruckhaus,' Isabel corrected.

'Whatever.' Laura shook her head and squeezed her eyes shut.

'Now BXH can get sold off in a stupid fire sale. And God only knows what that'll mean for this city. This is a total fucking wipeout. Have they any idea how many people, how many small businesses BXH supports in this town?'

'Don't forget London,' said Isabel. 'There are 10,000 BXH employees in the London office.' She thought about the offices in Canary Wharf, all the people she knew at the bank.

And what about herself? Did this explain why Sean hadn't come home, because BXH was about to go out of business with a very large bang? She felt light, as if air had filled every cell of her body.

'Why the hell are they announcing this now?' Laura looked pale, bemused.

Isabel shrugged. The skin on her face felt tight.

'God only knows what's happened to Sean.'

Laura looked at her sympathetically. Suddenly, Isabel remembered that their main bank account was at BXH. This was crazy. She remembered Sean fretting about it. He'd promised her he'd do something about it. But he'd never told her he had.

If BXH went bankrupt would her ATM cards still work? She could almost understand why Sean might be afraid to come home.

But where was he?

'What a mess,' she said.

'A lot of people are gonna get fucked if they pull the plug on BXH. Someone's gonna step in, honey. They have to. There's gotta be frantic rescue efforts going on down there.' She pointed at the floors below them.

And then she walked, as if in a trance, towards the doors.

Isabel followed. She looked back, as they exited, for a final glimpse of the room. There were only a few people left, tapping at their phones or deep in animated conversations. There were no security guards trying to move them on either. It looked as if a party had ended abruptly. There was a crowd of people standing around the elevators. One door was painted gold. All the other elevators had silver doors. One of the guards who'd checked them into the press conference – what a joke all that security seemed now – was standing near the elevators, presumably to make sure they all left the building the right way and didn't take souvenirs.

Then the gold elevator door opened.

It was packed full of men in black suits. They looked as

if they'd been squashed into it like salary men on a Tokyo subway train at rush hour.

The guard stepped forward, blocking anyone from approaching the elevator. As the doors closed Isabel felt something reach inside her chest and brush her heart.

Sean was in the elevator!

47

The large white clock in the monitoring room in Whitehall in central London showed the time as 12:08 a.m. Henry Mowlam was at his desk. Only half of the twenty desks in the room were occupied.

He'd always loved the excitement of being called in to monitor late night operations, but what he didn't enjoy was the often cruel realities that people had to face when terrorists or rogue elements began implementing their self-serving plans.

This was the third time he had monitored a situation involving Isabel and Sean Ryan. He felt a personal involvement now, which was definitely not a good thing, given the reality of what Isabel, in particular, might be facing.

He closed the emergency notification system on his main computer screen. The message he had just sent would wake officials in the Bank of England, the Cabinet Office and the Treasury. A conference call would be held in twenty minutes.

The officials he'd notified were all middle-ranking grades, but each of them had the authority to institute emergency procedures in their area of responsibility.

The emergency measures that would be required to ensure

BXH's UK arm was able to open on Monday would be the main item for discussion. Henry would represent the Security Services on the call.

He probably wouldn't mention the disappearance of Rose Suchard or the fact that the Ryan's son was also missing. But he would mention the murder that was connected with BXH and he would inform them that it was one of the connected incidents he was investigating. The involvement of Sean Ryan with the murder had still not been proven a hundred per cent, but his subsequent disappearance and the disappearance of his son gave cause for real concern. The case against Sean Ryan was strong and almost irrefutable now.

Whether any of that had anything to do with BXH's announcement was another matter entirely. However, the murder, and the subsequent headlines, certainly hadn't helped their image.

He looked at his second screen, the one on the left of his desk, and scrolled through his secure email system. There was still no message from the Manhattan FBI officer he had been put in touch with. The man was likely to be busy, they always seemed to be in the FBI office in the downtown Federal Plaza building, but he would be letting his UK colleagues down badly if he failed to respond to this request.

Henry had mentioned the possibility of the woman becoming a serious crime target, but he hadn't passed on the full details of how the dancer, connected to Isabel Ryan through her husband, had died. He'd saved that information for when the agent made contact.

Perhaps that had been a mistake.

He reached over, attached the preliminary autopsy report for the dancer to an email to the agent and sent it, with the following text:

Please respond to surveillance request 786/425/MTY. The attached file gives my reasons for heightened concern, as the surveillance target – Isabel Ryan – is married to a prime suspect in this murder case.

Please go directly to Page 7, where a summary of the victims' injuries, including a ritual-like removal of skin from the torso, and the number of deep stab wounds suffered, give evidence to the pattern of behaviour the perpetrator is capable of.

We believe this prime suspect is now in your area of operations. Extreme caution and an armed response is advised in this case.

Please respond ASAP.

I hope the Yanks catch Sean Ryan, he thought, as the message sent icon flashed up. They don't have a lot of sympathy for murderers. They often, and quite justifiably, put bullet holes in them.

48

Isabel only saw Sean side on. But it was definitely him. Her mouth opened. The elevator doors were closing, just as the word, 'Sean' left her throat.

And then her chest was being compressed. Her vision was focusing tightly on the doors, tunnelling everything peripheral away. A rushing filled her ears.

It was like being caught in a car crash. Everything was moving in sticky-motion. And she was reacting way too slowly.

'Sean,' she roared. The doors slid closed as Sean's name echoed off the walls.

Everyone in the lobby turned and looked at her. The studied professional atmosphere shattered, as if a chandelier had fallen.

Someone laughed. Then everyone went quiet. But only for a second. Then a hubbub of voices rolled over her as the noise of thirty or so people talking excitedly rose up to a pitch. They had all turned to look at her, but just for long enough to take in that she'd stopped screaming and that she wasn't a threat.

'Are you okay?' a black-suited woman said.

Isabel couldn't speak. She was transfixed by the image of Sean in the elevator. Her brain was focused on one thing; trying to work out what to do next. She looked at the old-fashioned circular dial above the elevator door. The elevator was going down fast. Could she follow him? She looked at the other elevators. None of them were near their floor. And people were waiting at each set of doors.

A security guard was beside her now, eyeing her up and down suspiciously.

'Can you call that elevator back?' she said quickly. 'There's someone in it I have to see.'

'Sorry, ma'am. No can do.'

Laura was beside her.

'You can't or you won't?' said Laura.

He looked at her, his expression as hard as a frozen statue's.

'You should leave quietly, lady. You're making a disturbance.'

'My husband's was in that elevator.' Her words tumbled against each other. 'He's been missing for two days. That's why I screamed. Can you speak to someone, intercept him, tell him that I'm here, please.'

He paused for only half a second before responding. 'Sorry, I can't do that either. Why don't you call him on his cell?' He sounded suspicious.

Isabel let out a groan. It came all the way from the bottom of her soul.

The security guard must have figured out she was for real, because after glancing up at the indicator above the elevator, he said, 'Look, that elevator just went down to the executive parking. He's likely to be driving straight out of there. Don't you know where he's staying?'

'Can't you take me down there?' Vital seconds were being wasted. She was rocking back and forth. There was something pushing at her to get going, to go after Sean. But none of the other elevators had come to their floor yet.

'I gotta stay here.' He glanced towards the people hanging around. One or two of them were listening to their conversation.

He bent towards her. 'But if you go to the side of the building you might catch him coming out of the car park,' he said. 'It takes a heck of a long time to get a car outta here.' He paused. 'Just don't say I told you.'

'Thanks,' she said. 'How many exits are there from the car park?'

'There's only one, ma'am, but you better get there quick, just in case.'

One of the other elevators made a soft ping.

She barged into the crowd assembled around the elevator door, elbowed people hard, pushed quickly into tiny gaps. She could feel warm bodies under her hands, shiny cottons.

'Hey, don't push,' someone shouted.

The doors shut, almost catching her shoulders.

She hadn't even had time to say goodbye to Laura. She turned her head, tried to glimpse her, but Laura was still at the back of the crowd.

She wriggled forward. She'd taken up a space in the elevator that didn't really exist. She'd created it by pushing someone in the back.

Some people were grumbling, loudly, at what she'd done. She didn't care.

When she reached the street it was snowing thickly.

The view from the windows upstairs hadn't been a mistake. And it felt a lot colder too. The snow was compacting as it hit the concrete under her feet, making it slippy and uneven.

She had to get to the car park exit. If she was there when Sean came out, he'd see her, he'd stop the car.

He'd have to.

As long as she got there in time she had a chance.

She looked at her watch. How long had it been since she'd seen him? Two maybe three minutes, that was all.

He could have been working up there all day on something to do with BXH's bankruptcy. Maybe he had to do a project report to make sure the Institute's project survived.

Her breath was coming fast. Clouds of mist clung to the air around her as she ran to the corner of the building. She slipped and heard a shrill noise behind her, a screech. But she didn't look back. She turned onto Lexington. The wall of the bank was on her right. She used it to steady herself. The car park exit was just ahead. Two hundred feet away.

Not far. She ran on, slipped again.

She could see light streaming from the exit through cracks in the steel shutters.

There was snow on the bottom of the shutters. Two inches of it at least. It was one of the places the snow was sticking most. There, and on the ledges of the building, around the edges of the high stone blocks that made up its walls. She stopped three feet from the shutter and stamped her feet.

The cold was eating at her toes.

But there was good news. The build-up of snow meant the shutter probably hadn't gone up in the last few minutes. That meant Sean was still inside.

She'd made it in time.

But was there anywhere else he could have gone? Could he have gone back up again, maybe to the CEO's suite with its panoramic views of Manhattan, which he'd told her about? If the elevator had gone down to the car park, that had to mean he was planning on leaving the building.

Didn't it?

She slapped her arms against her sides, over and over. She used to pray when she was seven, to believe it all. But she hadn't asked for God's help in years. She wasn't even sure if she believed in him any more. But she'd thanked him enough times for good fortune, hadn't she? So maybe she did. In her own way.

So Isabel prayed for good fortune, the shutter opening, Sean seeing her. It was the kind of good luck she hadn't needed in a long time.

She looked up. A thick snow-globe cascade of white was falling from the sky, making her feel small.

Please, make me suffer in another way. Bring him back. Now.

She felt a presence and turned her head.

Standing behind her, only feet away, was the bum from a few hours before.

He was shuffling towards her.

'What are you doin' back here?' His voice was a sinister growl.

What was he going to do?

'It's a free country.' A familiar rotting smell filled her nostrils.

He straightened. Something rustled.

'Yeah, right.'

He spat towards the wall of the bank, pushed his hands deeper into the pockets of his matted, torn coat. There was thick snow in his hair, something brown and slimy on his cheek.

'Tell me about it.'

He moved between her and the car park exit.

'You sure are a sweet thing.' He leered.

A rattling sound interrupted him, the noise of chains, as if a drawbridge was being raised. Then the steel shutters clanked and rose slowly upwards. Thank God! The bum turned his head to stare.

The shutter was only three quarters of the way up when a black town car slid its sleek nose out of the ramp behind, like an animal checking the weather.

'Hey,' she screamed.

The bum laughed.

'You are dreamin', lady. Those magicians can't hear you.' His face was twitching, one eye more open than the other.

She turned to face the car as it stopped, waiting to slip onto Lexington. She rushed forward.

There were dark shapes in the back. Two men.

'Sean!' she screamed. She waved frantically. A rush of adrenaline shot through her making her tremble. He couldn't miss her.

She reached towards the car.

It was him!

But he was staring straight ahead. And her legs were weak, like stacks of crumbling papers.

He looked worried.

Her fingers were a half inch from the window when the car jerked forward, turning into the street. She could feel the air being disturbed in its wake, warm, as if an animal had passed. And she'd almost touched its shiny coat.

And in that next second all her hopes were lost. She deflated like a burst party balloon.

Stupid. So totally stupid. Why hadn't she thrown something at the car?

And now it was gone.

And the whole thing had taken no more than a few seconds. Sure, the good news was Sean was alive and in New York. But there was something very wrong. Something terribly wrong.

The steel shutter clanked down. The light behind it went out. She was a foot away from the bum. She stepped towards the kerb and looked around quickly for a taxi. She'd memorised the license plate of the car Sean had been in. Maybe she could follow him. If only she could get a cab quickly enough.

But there were none coming down Lexington. Why was it always this way? Too many when you didn't need one, never even one when you did?

The bum shuffled closer.

She stood her ground.

'Go away.' She glared at him. She didn't care that he was bigger than her, smellier.

The car Sean was in had almost disappeared into the gauze of falling snow.

'Are you okay?' It was Laura's voice. She was standing beside her. Isabel was glad to see her.

'Is he bothering you?'

'Not any more.'

The bum was backing up.

She was still trembling. Partly from the cold. Partly from the shock of seeing Sean and not speaking to him. There was something awful going on.

And it wasn't a story on the news or a movie. This was her life. And now she felt isolated, cut off.

'It's too cold to hang around. Come on, let's get a cab at 45th.' Laura linked her arm through Isabel's. They walked.

'You could have waited for me, honey.'

'Sorry.' Her mouth was dry, her lips cracked and hard. Snow brushed at her face, ice prickling at her cheeks.

'Your husband was in that car, wasn't he?'

She nodded. She'd been rude to Laura, she knew, and she was lucky she'd come after her.

A yellow cab with its light on was rolling towards them. Laura put her hand up. The cab pulled up with a screech, as if its brakes weren't working properly. A wave of slush surged towards their feet. They both jumped out of its way.

Isabel got in first.

'Where you going, my ladies?' The driver was wearing a turban.

She thought about asking him to follow the car Sean was in, but she could hardly see cars a block away with the falling snow. Driving around looking for him when his car had disappeared would be a totally stupid idea. She rubbed her forehead. She'd been so close to him. So close.

Goddamn it, she had to focus on the good news. He was alive. He was here in New York. She'd seen him.

'Just drive, buddy. Down to 37th,' said Laura.

He pulled out. There was hardly any traffic. They passed the intersection where Sean's car had turned. There was no sign of it. Then they were at the turn for her hotel. Should she get out, go back to her room?

As they waited at the corner of 42nd she realised she wasn't going to get out. She didn't want to be alone. Not now.

'Did you get the license plate?'

For a sinking moment she thought the number had gone from her mind. She could see the car, feel its heat, but she couldn't see its plate. Then it came back to her – AFC 35P450. That was it.

'Yeah, I did. But what the hell good will that do?'

'Maybe we can find it.'

'You mean track it?'

Laura nodded.

'Do they have an app for that?'

'I know someone who might.'

She looked out the back window. What about the police? Should she get them involved? But she could hardly report him missing. Because he wasn't. She'd just seen him.

What would she say at the station? My husband hasn't called me? I have a feeling something's wrong, even though he looked healthy an hour ago, if a bit downbeat? They'd refer her to the psych ward.

'Where are we heading?'

Laura put a finger to her lips and looked out the back window.

'What did that nut job back there want?' she said.

'God only knows.'

'Did he threaten you?'

'Not really. He said no one in that car could hear me.'

'Wow, a genius.'

'I saw him before. He was in the same place this afternoon. We had a run in then too. He . . .' She didn't finish her sentence. She couldn't get Sean's face out of her mind.

Laura whispered in her ear. 'Maybe he's stalking the bank. There's been a lot of that in the last few months. Some people are out for revenge after losing everything. You gotta be careful, Isabel. Nut jobs can go postal here any time.'

Something had struck her.

Might they say she was stalking the bank too?

With a cold hand she brushed away the last few snowflakes that hadn't melted on her jacket. Her breathing was almost back to normal now.

'Stop.' Laura roared at the driver.

He pulled over with a screech. They were opposite a brownstone building. It soared into the sky like a fortress and took up a whole block.

'Where are we?'

'My brother's got a place here. He'll help you.'

'Are you sure?'

'He's a sucker for a pretty face.'

Greg's apartment was just about the smallest Isabel had ever seen. It was one room, if you didn't count the toilet. Which they probably did, as the toilet had a shower right beside it. But you couldn't have dried yourself there. Your elbows would hit the walls every time you raised them.

But the view from the window in the corridor outside was incredible. Lexington Avenue looked like a canyon in an apocalyptic movie, with cliffs of skyscrapers leading to a vanishing point. Pearl-like strings of headlights were moving slowly down it and snow was falling from orange-tinged clouds as if it was a nuclear winter.

'Is this weather in for the weekend?' Isabel asked, after Greg had brought them inside, and they were sitting on his shiny brown leather sofa.

Everything about the room was well ordered. There were shelves on each wall and a red cherry-wood office table sat in a corner. On it there were piles of magazines, jars of pens, black Russian dolls in a row, a 19 inch flat-screen Apple monitor, and loads of software manuals for Photoshop and Flash and other programs.

'You bet. It's gonna be a couple of feet deep, at least, by Monday,' said Greg. 'That's what the weather sites are saying. If you can believe 'em.'

Greg was six feet tall. He had short unruly black hair, and a cynicism similar to Laura's. But that was where the similarities ended.

Greg was a neo-goth or something like that. He had long black smudges of eye make-up and wore a tight black T-shirt with an elaborate winged skull in cracked silver on its front.

She had to take her jacket off quickly. He kept his apartment at an amazingly high temperature. Or was the whole block like this?

There was only one window in his room too. She went to it, touched the frosted glass. The cold from outside seeped into her fingers. Had Sean gone to a hotel? She checked her phone. No calls. She pressed his number again. Number not available. Each time he didn't pick up was like a cut to her soul.

Laura and Greg were talking behind her.

'Can I open this, get some fresh air?' said Isabel.

'Sure, but don't open it far. This room flash-freezes in a second,' said Greg.

The window had one of those handles that allows you to open it at the side, or the top. She opened it at the side, just a couple of inches.

The view was of the inside of an air shaft. The building had a fifty-foot wide, red-brick-lined shaft at its centre, with windows facing each other across the void. They went up in a checkerboard pattern out of sight, and down as far the eye could see.

Snow was falling in the shaft, like sifted flour.

They were on the tenth floor. Almost all the windows facing into the shaft had frosted glass, which meant you couldn't see what the other inhabitants were up to, but you could see their lights, their curtains, books and boxes piled up against windows and, in one case, an odd pink shape pressed up against the window glass, as if a dead body was being stored there.

She closed the window. Greg was making a pot of coffee on a hot plate.

'What are you doing in New York?' he said.

'Looking for my husband.'

'You lost him?' He had a smile on his face, as if he enjoyed hard-luck stories.

'Something like that.'

'When did you last see him?'

'Thirty minutes ago.'

'And he's missing already?' He raised his eyebrows.

'I didn't speak to him. I saw him in a car. He didn't look right.'

He leaned forward. 'He's cheating you, yeah?'

'No, it's not that.' She shook her head. 'He's working on a project at BXH. There's something totally weird going on there. I saw him, but I can't contact him. His phone is off.'

'BXH? You know they've been handing out ten-million-dollar bonuses this week?' His eyes gleamed.

'My husband is not on that list.'

'Not many are,' he said.

She was sitting on a comfortable steel and black leather chair near the window. 'You know that they're about to declare bankruptcy?'

'They'll be taken over before that happens,' he said. He stretched his legs, pushed them up against a black bookcase with a large LCD TV sitting on top of it. It was switched on, tuned to some MTV channel with a rock band playing silently.

'What project is he working on for BXH?'

Isabel hesitated, but only for a second. It wouldn't help her to try to protect BXH. 'He's working on software project that allows them to use facial recognition for all clients and staff. He's based in their London office.'

'Neat. That's where all the trouble started.'

'Trouble?'

'Yeah, it's all over the net. It's even got its own Twitter hashtag now. Some strip club dancer was murdered in London. BXH's CEO was in the club the night it happened, some Vaughann guy. He's under suspicion, so they all say. *The New York Times* reckons that's why the Chinese pulled out.' He shook his head. 'Not much fun if you're a BXH serf.'

'Vaughann's under suspicion?' She felt a selfish wave of relief. If Paul Vaughann was under suspicion, that meant things had moved on. Sean might be in the clear.

'Take a look for yourself.' Greg took an iPad from the table and passed it to her.

The front page of *The New York Times* was on the screen.

The main story was about Mr Vaughann. The article related how BXH in London had held a premature celebration two nights before in a club and that a dancer had been found dead later, and that the UK CEO, Paul Vaughann, had used the bank's jet to travel to New York, though the British authorities had wanted to interview him.

She read the story twice. There was no mention of Sean.

'That ain't all,' said Greg. 'The *Wall Street Journal*'s got a story about BXH being Lehman Brothers all over again. They say the Fed isn't going to bail them out. But I reckon they're wrong. BXH has got trillions in derivatives under management. If they blow up, the whole financial system will collapse. It's scary stuff. It'll be worse than the Lehman's crisis. Way worse.'

'They won't let BXH go down,' said Isabel. 'Someone will sort it out. Don't they rescue banks all the time?'

'Not as big as this one, with all the international offices they got. The Feds don't like rescuing outside the jurisdiction. And who would take them over now? That's the sixty-four-trillion dollar question.'

'BXH wants to stay in private hands,' she said.

'Is that what your husband thinks?' His eyes were wide, bug-like.

She didn't answer.

'Did you try texting him?' said Laura.

'A dozen times.'

'What was that license plate?'

'AFC something.' Crap, it was gone!

'35P450,' she said. 'Thank God.'

'What license plate is that?' said Greg.

'The car her husband disappeared in,' said Laura.

'So that's what you're here for. Why didn't you tell me you wanted to use me? Not that I'd mind.' He gave Isabel the tiniest smile.

Then he stood, went to the table, and pulled a skinny leather office chair out. Its back was supported by what looked like an aluminium human spine. He sat on the chair. Then he launched a browser on his big screen.

'Most times I can get the license plate holder's address, but I can't guarantee anything else.'

'You can get more, sometimes?'

'Sometimes. No guarantee. Like I said. Give me five.'

She checked her watch. It was 7:25 p.m. She had to ring Rose again, see if Alek was okay.

'I gotta make a call,' she said. She took her phone out of her pocket and called Rose's number. She felt a twist of guilt at being so far from Alek. But this time the fluttering in her chest was stronger, like the beating of bat wings. Everything was spooking her now.

Not available, was the message that came back from Rose's line. She breathed deep, held it down. Don't get paranoid, she said to herself.

He's okay with Rose. To believe anything else would be stupid.

49

'Keep him quiet,' said Adar. They were in a white GMC Savana with windowless panel sides and an interior in the rear section, which had two seats on one side and space for equipment on the other.

The boy, Alek, had been sleeping when they'd landed and they'd got out of La Guardia after a thirty-minute wait for a proper customs inspection of their hold. Two US Customs and Border Protection officers had given them the all clear only after using sniffer dogs.

The Department of Homeland Security officer hadn't been as friendly as in the past, and there had been one difficult moment, when Adar had thought he was going to question the boy. The officer had leaned down to him and touched the boy's shoulder, until the boy woke and looked up at him.

But he must have been simply checking the boy's eye colour, as he didn't speak to him.

After that he'd checked all their passports again. The boy's family name matched Adar's. He'd said he was his son when he'd met the officer as he was mounting the steps of the plane.

The officer also used a mobile scanner, probably to check the boy wasn't on a runaway or wanted list. And he wasn't.

Getting the passport right in London had been what had delayed them flying back. But Adar always made sure that that part of a job was done properly.

And now they were on their way in to the city. They'd be passing through the Midtown Tunnel into Manhattan Island in the next few minutes. The traffic around them was light, but there was still a steady stream of cars on each of the three lanes heading in, despite the snow.

Alek let out a cry again. He'd been restless since he'd woken and even after stopping at a burger joint near La Guardia and getting a kids' meal for him, he still hadn't settled down. The plastic toy he'd got didn't keep him occupied for long.

Adar was glad he had stayed with him in the truck while his colleague went in and got the takeaway. He didn't like attracting attention unless it was necessary. He was also glad that he'd be handing him over to Lord Bidoner soon.

Dealing with children on a job always made him nervous.

The entrance to the Midtown Tunnel loomed. The noise of the cars around them changed as rolling tyres echoed from the concrete roof.

Twenty minutes later they were pulling into the underground car park on Fifth Avenue, where he was supposed to do the handover. He headed down to the lowest level. It was almost empty.

When he saw it was Xena waiting for him, whom he'd met with Lord Bidoner when he'd been interviewed by him, he knew the boy was in real trouble. He'd heard Bidoner talking about some guys in Amsterdam she had tortured and burnt to death, just for talking out of turn.

He got out of the GMC and didn't even speak to Xena. She went to the back door of the van and opened it.

'Come on. Come and meet your Daddy,' she said.

The boy jumped out of his seat and was out of the back door in a second. How easy it is to fool children, Adar thought.

The boy looked around, confused.

'Let's go, Alek. I'll take you to meet your dad.'

She put her hand out to him. Alek took it. Adar shook his head. Too easy. What a shock he's going to get.

She was even smiling. And she didn't look back as she headed to a blue Ford Focus. It had blackened windows. It looked like a rental. And there was someone in the back, and though Adar couldn't see, he knew who it was.

Then he glimpsed Lord Bidoner's silver hair as the boy got in.

Adar reached for the door of the van.

That was when his phone vibrated. He had an incoming message. *You are needed at BXH.*

He'd guessed there would be more work to do in Manhattan, and he was right. He didn't mind, though he was hoping he wouldn't be involved in whatever they were planning for the boy.

The boy increasingly reminded him of his own son. And the last people he'd ever want his son to end up with were Lord Bidoner and his friend.

50

'When are you going back to London?' said Laura.

'I've a ticket booked for late tomorrow night. I have to pick up my son, Alek. He's only four and a half. My friend is looking after him. I promised her I'd be back on Monday.' Isabel felt a lump in her throat.

Why did she feel so paranoid about Rose and Alek?

Then she remembered something. Next Saturday they were all supposed to be going to Hamleys on Regent Street, to sort out Alek's Christmas presents. How could they do that if Sean wasn't with them?

'Result,' said Greg, loudly.

'What?' She stood behind him. She had to put her worries about Alek aside. He was in safe, if slightly erratic, hands.

There was an official-looking site with a list of names and addresses on the screen in front of Greg.

'That car is registered to some Jersey City limo service,' he said.

'Great,' said Laura.

Greg rubbed his hands on his jeans, then held his knees. 'You're lucky I found anything, sis.'

'Chill, Greg.' Laura put a hand on his arm. He shrugged it off.

She leaned towards Isabel, whispered loudly. 'If he didn't spend so much time on his stupid blogs he might get out, meet people, find a real girlfriend.'

'I get out,' he snapped. 'And my blogs ain't stupid.'

'Yeah, you see daylight once a week. When you visit that loser's goth bar in the Village. Why you go there I have no idea. It's such a throwback. You need a real girlfriend, Greg.'

'Right, and you sound more like mom every day. Anyhow, the world's heading for a climate shock, so I don't think this is the right time to be settling down with anyone.'

'You are so totally brainwashed,' said Laura.

'What do you think?' They both looked at Isabel.

'I just want to find my husband.'

He turned away. 'Don't say you weren't warned when this snowstorm becomes an ice storm,' he said.

'Thanks a lot, Mr Cheerful,' said Laura.

'No charge.'

Isabel wasn't up to listening to any more banter. She looked up. Creaks were emanating from the building around them, as if the plumbing was struggling.

'You do know all this stuff with the BXH merger being cancelled and them going out of business,' said Greg, in a more serious tone, 'smells as rotten as a pile of fish heads.' He peered at his screen.

'A big scandal just as someone is about to do a takeover could easily be a scam, a diversion. I bet the merger can't go through for some other reason. They probably have a black hole in their balance sheet. And one of their competitors is complaining. It wouldn't be the first time a New York bank has been brought down so that others could prosper. In 1907 some of the biggest banks in the state went bust, but it worked out well for the others. They took the bad ones over.'

'Isabel doesn't want history lessons, Greg.'

There were a lot of things hidden from people. That wasn't big news to Isabel. What Isabel needed to know was what Sean's role in all this was.

'I don't believe in conspiracy theories,' she said.

'Me neither. I like to see evidence,' said Laura.

'Evidence?' said Greg. 'Did you ever read the history of BXH? You know it was founded by a slave trader, who became a mayor 'cause he was so good at it. And when bankrolling slave ships dried up, they started bankrolling opium shipments to China. I could go on.'

'Please, stop with the ancient history,' said Isabel.

Despite herself, she yawned. She'd got very little sleep on the plane, and it was way after midnight by her body clock.

Greg was tapping away at his keyboard. 'I'll see if I can do something on this one,' he said.

She closed her eyes and rested her head against the padded leather arm of the sofa. She needed to sleep, if only for a minute.

She woke with Greg pushing at her shoulder.

'Wake up, I found something.'

She blinked. Her eyelids felt horribly sticky. He went back to his Apple. Laura was looking at her.

'You okay, honey? I told him we should let you sleep longer. But the dork wanted to wake you up straight away.' She tapped the top of Greg's head.

He rubbed at it. 'Hey, quit it.'

Isabel's head felt as if it had been in an oven. Her body felt equally bad, bloated, lethargic. Her eyes didn't even want to focus.

'You got any coffee, any painkillers?'

'Just made a pot, and there's some Tylenol in the cabinet back there.' Greg waved in the direction of the toilet.

She found the tablets, washed her face, and got herself a mug of coffee. She still didn't feel right, but at least her eyes were focusing as she stood beside Greg peering at the screen in front of them.

'What did you find?'

He turned to her. There was a pleased look on his face. 'You know this stuff ain't available to any internet junkie who can Google?'

'Tell her, Greg. Cut the BS,' said Laura.

'Okay, I know a website that tracks vehicles coming and going through the Lincoln Tunnel and a couple of bridges.'

'Yeah?'

'I put your license plate in it, and guess what?'

'What?'

'Tell her, Greg.'

'That plate passed through the Lincoln Tunnel twice in the past two hours.'

'Twice!'

'Yeah. At 18:58 it went through heading for Jersey. And fifteen minutes ago it came back!'

'Going back to BXH, I'd say,' said Laura. She sounded excited.

'Can you track the car in Manhattan?'

'I'll have a look.'

Isabel leaned towards him. 'Please, Greg. I need to find my husband.'

The phone on his desk started warbling. Greg picked it up before he answered her. It was the first time in her life she saw someone go from pale to bone white in two seconds.

'Thanks, Steve,' was all he said.

He reached forward, grabbed his mouse, clicked at a skull icon on his screen, and as the screen went blank he spoke quickly, looking up at them, his eyes wide, frightened looking.

'We gotta go. Some fucking idiots are on the way up.

Come on.' He was almost shouting. And there was a note of desperation in his voice.

He leaped out of his chair. The air in the room felt suddenly heavy.

'Stevie says they're the kinda guys who shoot first, then ask who you are.' He grabbed keys, a wallet, and put an iPad under his arm.

Isabel was putting her jacket on. Her hands didn't want to go through the sleeve holes.

Was this to do with her?

Laura had her coat on. Isabel went to the door and listened. She couldn't hear anything outside. All she could hear was her own breathing, her heart pounding.

'Could this be a mistake?' she said.

'No way. Steve's an ace doorman.'

He was beside her now, talking fast, peering through the spy hole.

'He got a call asking who lives in 1180, that's me, and a minute later some guys burst through the front door, then pushed some poor old girl out of the way. Then they try his door. He didn't answer it. He's got a half-inch steel plate on it. If he says we got seconds. We got seconds.' He opened the door. 'He'll call the cops, sure, but they could get here in an hour.'

The skin all over Isabel's back and on her arms was tingling. She wanted to get going. She knew how important a few seconds could be.

The elevators were to the left, around a corner, so at least whoever it was wouldn't see them as soon as they got out at their floor.

They were all in the corridor. The door to Greg's room closed with a thunk.

A distant hum echoed.

'Let's go' said Greg. He nudged her, then took off in the opposite direction to the elevators. She followed.

There was a bad smell in the corridor, stale food, backed up plumbing or something worse.

Were they overreacting?

She kept running.

The corridor went right. Her heart was thudding from the exertion as she turned the corner. They were on the opposite side of the building to the elevators now. If they kept going they'd come all the way around. Where were they heading?

Greg stopped, rapped on a door.

Laura and Isabel reached him as it opened. As it did they heard a loud cracking noise, like something being broken, behind them. A muscle in her neck started to jump.

The door in front of them had only opened an inch. Out of the crack came lilting Chinese music, and the sweet smell of roses, as if a door into a garden had opened.

What the hell are we doing here, thought Isabel.

'Lai ho, Greg,' a reed-like voice said.

'Hi Bao. Can we come in?'

Isabel saw a big dark brown eye examining her. Then she heard running in the corridor behind them. It was coming their way. There was a momentary hesitation, then the door in front of them opened wide.

They stepped inside. It was wonderful to get out of that corridor. Bao was a slim Chinese girl, three quarters of her height, with an innocent smile and a wave of black hair that went down almost to her waist. She bowed as Isabel passed her. Then Greg closed the door, gently, and put his ear to it.

'What you doing, Greg?' Bao looked worried. One of her hands was in the air, a finger pointing to the ceiling, as if she was directing traffic or about to scream at them and tell them to disappear. She was wearing a white silk kimono

'Don't kick us out, Bao. Someone's looking for us, and they're not cool people.' He shook his head and moved away from the door.

Her apartment was all white, and almost twice as wide as Greg's, but it had the same single window facing into the inner shaft of the building. Against one wall there was a white trolley, the kind of the thing you'd use if you were a masseuse. Above it there were certificates in Chinese.

They could have said she'd done well in her flute lessons, for all Isabel knew. A low table stood in a corner. On the table there were the remains of a simple meal, a white cup and a bowl with a few grains of rice still in it.

Bao touched Greg's face, brushed her hand over his cheek.

'Greg, you know you always welcome here.' She put her head to one side, letting her hair swish in front of her.

Greg watched her.

'Thanks, Bao. You're the best.'

'No,' she shook her head. 'What trouble you in this time, Greg?'

'Something different,' he said.

He walked to the window. You couldn't make out much through the frosted glass, except patches of light and darkness.

Isabel's breathing was returning to normal, but a muscle in her neck was twitching. She held her palm over it. What the hell had she gotten herself into?

Was all this connected?

Greg opened the window halfway.

Most of the windows to the right, where Greg's apartment was, had lights on behind them. Only one of them was out.

Greg had turned the light out in his apartment as they were leaving.

'Which one is yours?' said Laura, softly.

Greg's lips started moving. He was counting.

'Fourth one from the far end.'

'The light's just turned on in your apartment,' said Laura.

51

Lord Bidoner held Alek's hand as they went up in the express elevator.

'Are you hungry?' he said, leaning down to Alek.

The boy nodded. He looked pensive, unsure. His eyes were red rimmed, as if he'd been crying.

'We have some food for you.'

'When do I see my Daddy?' came a little voice.

'Soon, very soon. But you must be a good boy, like we warned you.'

'I am.'

Xena went into the apartment first. She took Alek's hand in hers and led him to the panic room.

'You will have a room all to yourself until your Dad arrives,' said Xena, as they went inside.

Alek looked at the stark white room and the big steel bed and his chin went down.

'I want to go home.' There were tears rolling down his cheeks.

Xena bent down to him. 'This will be over soon,' she said. 'Very soon.' She handed him a teddy bear. It was brown and still in its wrapping from the shop.

He hugged it. The plastic wrapping scrunched.

His tears didn't stop. He sat on the floor, looked around, then closed his eyes and rocked back and forth. Xena watched him for a minute. She bent down and stroked his head. His whimpering became quieter.

Then she left him alone and locked the door of the panic room so he couldn't get out.

Lord Bidoner was on the phone in the main room of the apartment.

'Mr Pilman,' he said. 'Can you confirm to Mr Vaughann and your security staff that I have permission as a possible buyer for BXH, to visit the the bank and tour the building?'

The voice at the other end came across clearly.

'I will certainly do that, Lord Bidoner. I don't think you'll find any hidden value here, though you are welcome, as the preferred bidder at this time, to inspect the premises. I will inform Mr Vaughann and our security section that they are to cooperate with you. Though I have to tell you our head of security has gone missing and he had access to places in the building that even I have never seen.'

'I'm sorry to hear he's disappeared. I hope he comes back soon.'

Bidoner smiled. It was all going exactly as he'd planned. His Ebony Dragon hedge fund was holding a significant shareholding in BXH, they were a suitable buyer for the bank, and now he had access to even the most secret parts of the BXH building.

And they would succeed in their takeover, now that they had Li's money behind them. The collapse of the shares had helped, as had the cancellation of the original takeover bid. BXH was far too vulnerable now to resist a white knight in the form of a well-known hedge fund.

He smiled to himself as he looked out at the snow being

blown against the window of his apartment. Everything was falling into place. All his planning was paying off. The moment they'd been waiting for was near. Very near.

All they had to do now was make the final sacrifice.

52

The muscle in Isabel's neck started twitching faster.

Whoever had turned the light on over there was looking for them, for her maybe.

A dark shape filled the window of Greg's room. She could hear Greg breathing fast beside her. There was someone very big over there.

She licked her lips. They were rough, dry.

Bao pushed the window closed, fast.

'So sorry, I forgot, I'm expecting a customer, Greg. Will you need to stay here long?' She wanted to get rid of them.

Could she blame her?

'Who do you think's over there?' said Isabel.

She held her fist to her forehead. Her skin felt cold. She took a deep breath, willing herself to calm down. For starters, whoever was over there had no idea that they were here.

'I don't think it's one of my Twitter buddies,' said Greg.

'You got buddies?' said Laura.

'He got good buddies,' said Bao. She put a hand on his shoulder.

'Do you think they're looking for me?' said Isabel. Everyone looked at her.

Greg shrugged. 'Your guess is as good as mine. The only thing I've been doing recently is researching BXH, and their stupid merger plans and then looking up that number plate for you.'

'Why don't we call the police?' she said.

'The last time someone in this building called a cop, they were dead and cold before the cop arrive,' said Bao. She put her hand to her chest, as if she was holding something close to her.

'I told you to be careful, Greg,' she continued. Then she turned to Laura and Isabel.

'The Chinese bank that was going to buy BXH eats journalists for breakfast, whole. I knew them from Hong Kong. Greg should be hiding what he's doing. He must be very careful. I need my good customers to stay alive.' She shook a white finger at him.

Then she retied her white kimono. It was one of those short ones that only come down to her knee. She gave them a brief glimpse of her thighs as she did so. They were thin, pale.

Laura and Bao were staring at her.

'You okay?' said Bao.

'She lost her husband,' said Laura.

'I know what that's like,' said Bao. 'There is always a piece missing inside you after something like that.' She smiled, but it was fleeting. Then she glanced at a thin gold watch on her wrist, frowned, and shook her head fast.

'So sorry' she said. 'No time to listen to any story.'

Isabel's pulse was quickening.

'We'll go,' said Greg. He had his iPad open and was tapping at the screen.

'So sorry everybody. In two minutes there'll be a knock on this door. My customers need to relax, even when it's snowing.' Bao smiled, but it didn't reach her eyes.

This wasn't someone who would let you impact on her money making. Not for one minute.

'Why don't you go down the fire stairs?' said Bao.

'Did they fix the lights?' said Greg.

'Sure. I use it sometimes. It's good exercise.'

'Okay,' he said. He tapped at his iPad. Bao was standing near the door staring at him.

She couldn't have made it any clearer that she wanted them to leave. Isabel went to the door and put her eye to the spy hole. There was nothing but blackness. Was it broken?

'I can't see anything,' she said.

A growl sounded from the other side of the door. It was low and was followed by a snuffling at the bottom of the door, as if a dog was trying to get in.

'Your customer brings a dog, right?' said Greg to Bao.

'No.' She motioned them away from the door. Then she pointed at the window.

'There is a ladder. Go that way.'

Isabel opened the window wide. There was a proper metal ladder running past the window to the right. It had a wire cage around it to stop you falling and was secured by iron studs pushed into the wall. 'It's a long way to go down.'

There was a barking now and a banging from the front door.

The banging stopped. It felt as if someone was listening.

'When you get two floors down you knock on the window,' whispered Bao. 'My girlfriend down there.'

Greg blinked. Whatever he was about to say was interrupted by more, faster banging on Bao's door. This wasn't polite banging. This was a banging intended to test it for weaknesses.

'You go first,' Isabel said to Laura.

'I can't,' said Laura.

'You have to,' Bao hissed.

Laura looked from Greg to Isabel. She gripped Greg's arm.

'You can do it,' he said. 'You always went first when we were young.'

She gave a fake smile, reached towards the handrail and pulled herself onto the ladder. Isabel and Greg watched her go down a few steps.

Then Greg went after her.

'Are you coming with us?' said Isabel.

'I'm not staying here,' said Bao.

Isabel looked over the edge of the window. It felt as if she was falling, her skin pulling back along her body. Vertigo sucked at her. She looked up the shaft, to steady herself, then grabbed the rough, cold handrail. She said a prayer under her breath and swung her body into the cage.

Being ten floors up, even in a wire cage, was like being near the top of a cliff.

She could feel the icy air moving into the cracks of her clothes, sliding inside, touching her skin. There was an odd smell in the shaft, as if there was something bad down below. A loud mechanical hum filled the air.

She heard another crack, as if the door of Bao's apartment was about to give way. She forced herself to go down the ladder, counting each step to distract herself. The thought of falling, banging against the wire, the ladder coming away from the wall, filled her mind until she could almost see it happening.

The ladder was held away from the wall about three inches by metal spikes. It meant she could move down smoothly. But it was also bad, as it felt as if she was descending into thin air. And every time she looked down she had to grip the ladder so tight she was afraid it would disintegrate.

So she looked at the wall, the bricks passing, and kept going.

She heard a noise below, and when she looked down she

could see Greg's head. He had the beginnings of a bald patch in the centre. He was leaning out of a window.

Snow was settling on her shoulders. Flakes landed on her nose. She kept going. She was thinking about Alek waiting for her now.

She felt the emptiness around her, the space and air extending down and up. One slip and this wouldn't be fun any more.

Then she felt a hand on her legs. She moved down, grabbed the top of the window opening and went in completely.

There was an older Chinese woman in the room. This apartment was all red. The woman was dressed in a long white kimono. She bowed to Isabel as she came in.

'Thank you,' said Isabel.

Bao, who'd been coming down only a foot above Isabel, came in behind her and closed the window. Then she pulled across a red curtain. You couldn't even see the window any more.

'No one can tell where we went,' said Bao. 'I will go up later, after my number one customer comes. Nobody frightens him.'

'We should go,' said Laura. Greg was outside in the corridor looking one way then the other.

The older Chinese woman bowed again as Isabel went past her. Isabel bowed back.

As she closed the door Greg was waving impatiently at her and Laura from a doorway up the corridor.

Isabel's every muscle tensed as she looked first one way then the other. Had they done it? Had they escaped? And who the hell was that following them with the dog?

Echoes of what she'd been through in Istanbul and Jerusalem came back to her. Was all this connected?

She needed to think, but first of all she needed to get out of this place.

'Come on, we gotta fucking go!' hissed Greg.

She walked fast towards the door he was waiting fifty feet down the corridor.

When the door closed behind them she breathed properly for the first time in minutes. Then they were heading down a cold concrete stairway. All she could hear now were groans from the pipes and the bee-like hum of the fluorescent lighting. The air was freezing in the stairs, way colder than in the corridor up above. And their breath was visible as if they were smoking. She touched the metal handrail only once. It was icy and reminded her of the ladder.

They'd gone down about halfway now. She felt better, relieved to be moving. It seemed they'd left their pursuers behind.

'I hate running down stairs,' said Laura.

'I ordered a taxi on my phone while we were waiting for you,' shouted Greg. 'It's on its way down Lexington. It'll be below in one minute. That's what the app says.'

'I hope it comes,' shouted Laura.

Then she heard a bang from up above. Anxiety exploded through her. She took the next set of stairs in two jumps. Laura was ahead of her, going faster now too.

Greg was even further down.

Then she heard a shout from up above.

'Get 'em boy!' And then barking and a scrambling noise. She started to run.

53

Henry Mowlam was sitting at a wooden meeting-room table in a spartan room on the sixth floor of their office building in Whitehall. The view from the narrow window was of offices and a stretch of the River Thames, with the upper part of the illuminated Millennium Wheel visible behind them. The wheel glistened.

Finch was in the small modern kitchen, next to the meeting room making them coffee. They'd left the observation room, underground, a few minutes before.

'This is explosive stuff,' said Henry, as he stacked the files he'd been leafing through together.

'I know,' said Finch, poking her head through the doorway, then disappearing again.

Henry had spent the last ten minutes speed reading what was in the files. When Finch set the mug down in front of him he had his questions ready. 'Why do the Chinese want this facial recognition software so badly?' he said.

'For automated population control, and for the elimination of genetic aberrations, which lead to dissent. That's the best guess of the geniuses in the research agency.'

Henry shook his head. 'All that from a face?'

Finch nodded. 'It's about tracking people. Once they have this working they'll be able to pick up relatives of high-risk individuals at choke points, like bus stops and train stations, and revoke their city residence permits.'

'You think this is connected to what's going on in Germany?' he said. He glanced at the file he'd been looking through detailing the funding sources for the nationalist party that had come from nowhere to dominate the headlines during the recent parliamentary elections in Germany.

'Yes, the money for their first six months came from this hedge fund Lord Bidoner is involved with. It's not the sort of the thing that would put anyone behind bars, but it's worrying.'

'You do know we still haven't got FBI approval on tracking Isabel Ryan.'

'It's being escalated, Henry.' She picked up the files and put them under her arm.

'We better go back downstairs,' she said. 'I just wanted you to see these.' She smiled at him as she passed.

'I appreciate it,' were his last words, before he closed the door.

As they walked down the corridor to the elevator he walked close to her. Their arms touched. He could feel her body heat. He closed his eyes. This was not the time to get distracted. He had to stay focused.

They had some decisions to make soon. Very soon.

The BXH conference call had shown their lack of reliable information on what had been going on at BXH. But what concerned him more was the fact that every member of the Ryan family was now missing.

54

Greg hit the exit door running. It swung wide, banging hard against the outside wall. The noise it made was like a clang from a kettle drum.

It had stopped snowing.

The door had a brass sheet on it, covering it completely inside and out. Once it must have been luxurious, in a sixties sort of way. Now it was dented, scuffed.

There was snow and slush under their feet. Isabel's shoes were holding up well, so far, but they weren't snow shoes. Her fingers and cheeks tingled. It felt as if she was being assaulted by the cold.

A yellow cab was waiting at the end of the alley. She went after Greg and Laura, slipping, sliding, towards it. She knew at that moment what the phrase having your heart in your mouth meant. Her throat felt as if it was almost blocked.

It was so good to get inside the cab. It felt safe.

'Let's go uptown to my place,' said Laura, as the cab moved off. She was settling back as if nothing had happened.

'Is Bao okay?' said Greg. He leaned over Laura and looked Isabel straight in the eyes.

'She's fine, I think,' said Isabel.

'Who the hell was that?' He grabbed her knee.

'I don't know.'

The words caught in Isabel's throat.

Goddamn it. Goddamn them all.

'Look,' said Laura. Isabel turned and looked out of the back window of the cab.

A man had come out of the alley they'd just come from. He was bald and wearing a long buttoned-up navy coat. He had a large Alsatian on a lead. He looked like a security guard from a high-class gated estate. He stared at their cab, as if he was memorising it.

'I suggest we don't go back there for a while,' said Laura. 'I don't want to meet that guy. You don't want to either.' She nudged Greg.

Isabel had a weight inside her. It grew as the cab speeded up and she could see through the back window that he was just standing there not following them. Everything that had happened in Istanbul and Jerusalem had come back to her. She'd been kidnapped by a man just like this.

'Bastard,' shouted Greg. He waved a fist briefly, then banged it into his chest.

'Leave us alone,' he shouted.

The taxi slowed down. Laura shouted at the driver. 'Keep going.'

U2 were belting out 'One' on the cab radio. She looked out of the window. She was almost hallucinating. The snow, the lights of the other cars, their combined heavy breathing, all added to the sensation that this was the cab ride from hell. Then the car bounced through a pothole and the music got louder. They passed 42nd Street. She definitely didn't want to go back to her hotel.

Maybe she could go back there later. Much later.

And breathe. This isn't about you. Go to BXH in the morning. Tell them you want to see your husband. There's no way they can deny that he's here in New York. You saw him, for God's sake.

Her heart slowed.

At least she knew the routine in the bank on busy weekends. People would go in there at eight on a Sunday morning if necessary, so Sean had said. And as they were heading into Chapter 11 that was definitely what was going to happen tomorrow.

She stared out of the back window. There were cabs and trucks and a snowplough behind them.

'Who was that fucking idiot?' said Greg. 'A friend of yours?' He sounded angry. She didn't blame him.

'Do you think that guy was from BXH?'

Isabel shrugged. 'I don't know. Could be.'

'They're up to their necks in dumb contracts,' said Greg. Someone's going to end up holding one hell of a giant bag of worthless paper if they go south.'

'It won't be that big a disaster,' she said.

'What? No way, their balance sheet has more holes than a Swiss cheese. The shock wave from BXH defaulting will go around the world and flatten tons and tons of people. Millions I reckon.'

'But they won't default.'

'That's not what the market thinks. Their share price is close to zero. All their depositors will start queuing for their money back soon. Maybe from tonight.' He turned his head to watch someone at an ATM.

'They'll need a loaves and fishes moment to survive what's coming.' He sniffed. 'I hope they don't get it.'

'The Fed'll step in,' said Laura. 'Pump hundreds of billions in.'

'There's a bunch of senators who are against any more big bailouts,' said Greg. 'This is gonna give them a real fright. They might just stand up to Wall Street this time.'

He closed his eyes, bent his head down.

They were heading up Third Avenue. They'd reached 59th Street already. Towers of glass and concrete were all around.

Isabel's phone warbled.

A text had come in. A tiny ember of hope glowed inside her. Could it be Sean? Her cold hand pulled her phone out.

It was Sean!

He'd sent a message!

It was short.

But it was good news.

He wanted to see her.

She tried to call him back immediately. She held her breath as she waited to be connected. Any second now she'd be speaking to him.

A woman's voice came on the line.

'The number you are calling is not available at this time. Please try again later.'

Goddamn it!

But why was he texting her?

Someone must have seen her. Was that why his limousine had come back into the city? Would there be some simple explanation as to why he hadn't called her? Doubtful. And was it even him? She just didn't know.

So what should she do about Greg and Laura? She remembered how Sean used to tell her to keep things quiet. Not to involve too many people. He was good at all that. He never ever panicked. And his smile was good too, of course, the way it flashed across his face, warming her inside.

She felt a familiar longing, a deep desire to see him.

'Pull over,' she shouted.

'Jeez Louise,' said Laura, as the cab swung.

'I have to go,' she said.

'What's up?' said Laura,

'I have to do something.'

She couldn't bring them with her. Sean would flip right over in a second. And they didn't deserve getting caught up in anything else. She and Sean attracted trouble.

'I'm sorry about your apartment.' She reached over and gripped Greg's arm.

'Me too,' he said. 'Are you gonna be okay?'

'Yeah. I'll call Laura tomorrow. I promise. If your place is trashed and the police need me to make a statement I'll be there. I'm not going to disappear. I just need to do something.'

'Be real careful,' he said. 'This is all too fucking crazy.'

'Thanks,' she said.

'So that's it?' said Laura.

'I'll call you. I promise. I'm sorry. I mean it.' She gripped Laura's hand.

Greg was looking at her, his eyes wide.

'Was that your husband texting you?'

She looked at him blankly, as if she hadn't understood what he'd just said. She couldn't tell him what she was doing. She'd probably said too much already. She felt lightheaded. The shock of hearing from Sean was building like a wave inside her. She wanted out of the cab.

'I'll be okay,' she said. 'There are a lot of cabs out.'

And it was true. There was a string of them with their lights on coming up Third Avenue behind them.

The cab driver turned to her. Wondering who was going to pay the fare, probably.

'Can I put in some money?' she said.

'Don't insult us,' said Laura.

As she opened the door, she said, 'I'll call you.' She was still pointing a finger at them as the cab pulled away.

She stood there with her hand up. A cab pulled over. She got in and gave the driver directions.

She closed her eyes and gripped the edge of the seat. Was Sean waiting for her? Or was she being stupid? A memory came to her of him calling her name, 'Isabel'.

She shivered. Let this be the end of all this stupid searching. One way or the other.

'Here you go,' said the driver. 'This is as far as I can take you.' He turned to her. He had a thin scar down one side of his face. They'd reached the intersection of 45th and Lexington.

It was even colder outside now. The slush by the side of the road was icing up, crunching loudly under her shoes as she got out.

Lexington was quite busy with traffic, but 45th Street had been cordoned off with blue and white striped police barriers across the road. Cars were being diverted.

There were three police trucks in a row on one side of the street, officers in thick coats talking to each other, and an ambulance further on. And a crowd milling around in the middle of 45th, in front of the entrance to the bank, as if they were waiting for something to happen or for someone to show up.

Most people were wrapped in scarves and wore heavy, padded overcoats. It was a middle-class, middle-aged mob.

There must have been a few hundred people hanging around, stamping their feet, talking to each other. Some had flasks with them. Others had banners with things like 'SAVE OUR JOBS' written on them. Some were jabbing their banners in the air.

At the entrance to the bank there were three police officers in uniform, and the same number of security guards in black puffy jackets with white badges on their arms. It didn't look like they were letting anyone in. Her heart sank deep down inside her. This was not what she'd expected.

Across the street from the bank entrance the arc lights of

TV news camera crews were lined up above the crowd like a row of glaring vultures.

BXH going down had clearly become a major news event. How the hell was she going to get into the bank?

She took her phone out, stood beside a street light, and tried his number again. Nothing. Still nothing. And this time it didn't even connect. Was this it? Was someone playing nasty games with her? Her heart contracted, as if someone had reached in and squeezed it.

55

Alek banged on the door again. No one came. The room felt cold. He was hungry. He hated the people who'd brought him here. They had lied. His Daddy wasn't waiting for him. He was tired. And so cold.

He headed for the bed. There was a blanket on top of it. He pulled it over himself and curled up in a ball. He trembled as the tears rolled down his cheek.

He wanted to go home.

He wanted so much to go home. And he needed a drink. And he was hungry.

He heard the door opening. He turned to look.

Someone was coming in.

Was it Daddy?

No, it wasn't.

He closed his eyes and screamed.

56

The guy next to her had a shiny bald patch. He looked like a bank teller from Fifth Avenue. He had a black Crombie coat on, which went down to just below his knees.

He was smiling grimly. When he spoke his accent was French, with an American twang.

'You will get cold in that thin jacket.' His smile had been replaced by a worried look.

'I'm not hanging around. Who are all these people?'

He looked at her for a moment, as if wondering why she was asking. 'I work for BXH. Most of these people do too. Not you?'

She shook her head.

He leaned close to her, whispered. 'Are you a customer?'

She nodded.

'There's a BXH ATM around the corner. Some of us are taking our money out. I heard BXH cash cards will be rejected by the ATMs from tomorrow.' He wiped his brow. 'But that's just a rumour. I'm sure it's not true.'

'Someone will take BXH over.'

'Maybe. The retail part, but who knows about the rest of us. They have been very naughty at the top here, you know.'

A vein was thumping in his forehead.

'They have been gambling with all our futures.' He leaned close. 'And they have lost.' His eyes glowed with an alarming intensity. He made an exasperated noise.

'It's all too crazy for me,' she said. It was hard to take in what he was saying. A disturbing memory from a dream, of red eyes in the darkness, had come to her.

'I'll tell you what's crazy, young lady. I've been working here for twenty-three years and all my savings are in BXH, and my retirement fund is stuffed with BXH stock. If they've thrown it all away, what will I do?' He rubbed a hand across his forehead.

'They'll be rescued,' she said.

He shook his head. He raised his eyes to the building looming like a castle above them. Lights were blazing from various floors. 'You know some senior people are in there. Protecting their asses, I'd say.'

What would he say if she told him her husband might be in there, that he'd just sent her a message?

'I'm sorry. I have to go.'

She pushed through the crowd. The security guards in front of the entrance were turning people away with shaking heads. Her hopes were low as she elbowed her way to the front.

A security guard, six foot of hard muscle and menace, glared at her. He looked like the kind of guy who would shoot you if you made any sudden movements.

'My husband's inside. Can I go in, please?' she said.

His eyes were dead. He stared at her for a long moment.

'This building is closed.' His accent was hard, as if he ate rusty beer cans for breakfast.

'I have to get in. My husband told me to come. He's in there.' Her voice had despair and frustration in it.

'No way, lady.' He was looking over her head, as if he had finished with her.

What was she going to do?

She turned away, heading back towards the intersection with Lexington.

She read the message Sean had sent her again.

COME BACK TO THE BANK. WHAT ARE YOU DOING IN NY?

It wasn't a lot to base your hopes on. But it was enough. Did he know all these people were outside?

HOW DO I GET IN? THERE'S A MOB OUTSIDE she texted to his number. A young guy beside her was groaning loudly as she sent the message, as if he was sick.

'Does anyone know what's going on?' shouted the young guy, turning to the people around him.

'We're getting stiffed,' someone shouted back.

She walked on. What should she do if Sean didn't answer? Would he come out looking for her? Should she wait?

She heard a siren. Then flashing blue lights were reflecting all around.

Her phone buzzed.

Thank God. Thank God. He'd replied.

COME TO THE CAR PARK ENTRANCE ON LEXINGTON.

Almost every part of her filled with hope now, as if she'd been warmed by his message. She could leave all this mayhem behind. If it was him, of course. There had to be a possibility someone was using his phone or his number. She had to be careful.

She threaded her way through a group heading up Lexington. The crowd outside the bank's front entrance was going to get a whole lot bigger soon, by the looks of things. She reached the car park entrance as a police cruiser passed, driving slowly. The officers inside were staring out, looking left and right, as if they were looking for recently escaped criminals.

She looked away.

Then, crossing Lexington, coming towards her, who should she see, but her friendly bum from the last time she was here.

Her heart bumped against her rib cage. She took a quick breath. She was nearer the car park entrance, and he was still a hundred yards beyond it, maybe she could avoid him.

Please gate, open.

Before he gets here.

57

The onyx-black GMC Yukon 4x4 with darkened windows and brand new plates parked with its engine running near the corner of Lexington and 44th had three occupants inside. The man who had spoken, Mr Li, his accent a lilting mix of Hong Kong and Shanghai dialects, tapped the shoulder of the man in the front passenger seat, a younger Chinese man. He repeated what he had said in English.

'Is she near?' He was clearly agitated.

The younger man stared at the small silver tablet on his knees. The blinking red dot in the centre of the screen was still showing on the map as being a few hundred yards from them, but it had stopped.

'She's on the sidewalk, up there.' The younger man turned and pointed across the street, past the snowplough.

'Move forward,' barked the older man.

The driver did as he was asked. All the occupants, the driver, the young man beside him and the older man looked out through the darkened glass of the front window. Now they could see the back of the bum they'd watched earlier. He was near the Lexington Avenue car park entrance of BXH.

'准备好. Once she goes inside go and get him,' said the older man. 'I want to talk to him. Tell him I have some money for him, and his friends too, if he can round a few up.'

The younger Chinese man, an American citizen, in the front, felt for his weapon. He had a black Norinco NP24 pistol in a holster under his armpit. He checked his jacket was loose enough to reach the gun quickly.

The NP24 was his favourite. Manufactured in high numbers over many years in Chinese state munitions factories, it was the weapon of choice for many overseas divisions of the PLA, elite Chinese police units and senior members of Chinese tongs in New York City.

The younger man held the smooth pistol grip with his right hand as he pulled the door handle with his left. He knew the older man in the back of the Yukon would not get out, nor would the driver.

And he knew he was expendable.

They would drive off if there was any trouble.

But he knew his duty.

58

The car park shutter vibrated. Someone was listening to her prayers.

With a loud clanking the red steel leaves went up. There was someone standing behind them. She could see their shoes. They were black, highly polished. For a moment she thought it might be Sean.

Then the shutter came up some more and she saw it was only one of the security guards. He was wearing a black puffy jacket. As she stepped towards him he ducked his head down under the slow moving shutter and looked at her.

'Name?' he asked. His gaze flickered around suspiciously, as if he thought she might have accomplices hiding nearby who were about to pounce on him.

'Isabel Ryan.'

'Come in, Mrs Ryan.'

She could have hugged him.

'And you.' He pointed a black leather-gloved hand at the bum, who was still walking towards them, and about ten feet away now.

'You've been told not to hang around here,' he said. Then

he put his hand on his belt, as if he was going to draw his gun.

'Are you okay?' said the guard, glancing at her. As the shutter finished its journey above their heads with a thud he straightened himself to his full height. Behind him a warm yellow light flowed out.

He looked uncomfortable, on the edge of his territory, as if he didn't like leaving the building. When he looked down at her he smiled, but she felt zero warmth coming from him, and the smile vanished as quickly as it had come.

'Is my husband here?' She looked behind him.

'Follow me. I gotta escort you to the elevator, ma'am. That's all.'

As the shutter clanked down behind them they walked down a short ramp. It took them from the winter city above into a seasonless basement checker-boarded with square red-brick pillars. It was cold in the basement, but not freezing, which was surprising given the height of the roof. On the walls there were circular patterns in the brick, darker reds against lighter ones.

There was a smell of petrol. And there were four black late-model Lincoln town cars parked to one side, like the one Sean had been in earlier.

In the middle of the basement there was a large circular steel plate set into the painted concrete floor. It could have been a turning circle, or a circular elevator allowing vehicles to be taken down to lower parking levels.

The whole area looked as if it would be humming with activity during the week. Was this where BXH's armoured cars were prepared after being loaded with cash boxes from some underground vault?

As the guard followed a bright yellow path painted onto the floor, her hopes retreated.

What the hell was going on? Where was Sean?

The elevator doors were ornate like the ones upstairs, decorated with brass mouldings. She hoped one of them would open as they approached and Sean would appear.

But he didn't.

What looked like the executive elevator, with a golden door, was at the centre of the bank of elevators, as it was up above in the building. The guard pressed the button beside the elevator on the left, the nearest one to them.

'Where are we going?' she asked. 'Where's my husband?'

'I have instructions to take you below, ma'am,' was his reply. Then he continued staring straight ahead.

The door opened with a ping.

'This way,' he said.

She hesitated, then went in. He followed her. None of this felt right. Inside, the elevator was panelled in shiny mahogany.

She could feel the guard's presence. He was a giant. For a moment she wished she'd kept up her karate classes after leaving the Foreign Office. She'd thrown plenty of big bruisers, but she felt very rusty.

'Did you see the snow outside?' she said.

He didn't reply. Being friendly was clearly a wasted effort with this guy.

'What's below?' She'd been feeling so elated, keen to see Sean, she hadn't thought about where they might be going.

He didn't reply.

The elevator jerked, rattled, and went on down. She'd read about the basement levels in the BXH building the last time she was here with Sean. They made a big deal about them in one of their brochures. Sean had pointed it out to her.

A million cubic feet of earth had been excavated to construct the seven underground floors of the building. Apparently that made it the deepest basement in New York when it was constructed in the late 1920s, though this fact was largely unknown, claimed the brochure.

Even the New York Federal Reserve Bank, built near Wall Street, further down Manhattan Island six years before in a grand Italian palazzo style, which previously had the lowest vaults, had only five basement levels.

She looked up at the floor indicator above the door. It had seven levels marked with a B. They were descending through them.

Why were they going down so far?

As they neared the bottom the elevator slowed, then rattled again. It felt old, from a different generation. Its doors pinged loudly as they opened. There was another guard waiting for them outside.

This guy was even bigger than her talkative friend. He looked like a Kazakh wrestler. His face was all hard angles and tight lips. He had a charmless uninterested expression too, which probably would have taken a jackhammer to loosen. He eyed her from head to toe, then he spoke.

'This way,' he said. She followed him down a dark red-brick-lined corridor. It was wide enough for six people to walk abreast and had shiny steel doors at regular intervals. The decoration down here wasn't as elaborate as up above, and the roof was lower, but you could see the whole place had been designed by the same team.

'Wait in here,' said the guard. He opened a door near the end of the corridor and motioned her in. She went inside.

She could feel the weight of the floors above them. Maybe it was the red ceiling in the long room, or maybe it was the steel girders that ran from side to side every few feet above her head. Whatever it was, she didn't like it. Not one bit.

'Okay, where's my husband?' She raised her voice.

She didn't want to be too aggressive, but she wasn't going to accept waiting indefinitely down here in this creepy basement, without any idea of what was going on.

'Wait here,' was the guard's eloquent reply.

Then he closed the door. She heard it being locked. What the hell?

They couldn't lock her in!

She banged on the door immediately, pulling at the handle.

'Open this door. Come on. You can't lock me up,' she shouted.

She banged again.

There was no reply. She kept going. After about two minutes, with her anger rising, she heard a scraping noise. She stepped back. The door opened.

'I am very sorry, Mrs Ryan. That guard shouldn't have locked this door. I'm afraid some of them take their duties far too seriously.' The man who'd opened the door extended a hand to her.

She didn't take it.

'You can't do this.' She pointed at him. 'You can't lock people up in a room. That's kidnapping. Where is my husband?'

'As I said, I am sorry, Mrs Ryan. It was a mistake.'

He looked like a relic from the last century. He had slicked back silver-grey hair, and was wearing a tight fitting black suit, crisp white shirt and a thin red tie. He walked past her into the room. He looked like someone who hadn't changed his style since the days when secretaries sat on their bosses' knees.

'Come in, gentlemen,' he said, over his shoulder.

Two men came in after him. They looked like upmarket plain-clothes policemen.

She followed the grey-haired man to the centre of the room. 'Where is my husband?' she said, loudly.

'That's why we're here, Mrs Ryan.' He pointed at a large LCD screen on a narrow table at the far end of the room. In front of it there were four rows of blue plastic chairs. It looked as if the room was normally used for training purposes.

'Take a seat, Mrs Ryan.' He was clearly used to telling people what to do.

She stood in front of him, put her index finger to his chest and pressed it hard into his white shirt. An indentation formed.

'Tell me where my husband is. Right now!'

He simply stepped back, pointing at the seats.

'Please, Mrs Ryan. I will explain everything.' The other two men sat down. Both of them held themselves rigidly, as if they assumed they were being watched. She felt a chill and looked around. On the nearest wall there were two smoked glass cases high up, by the roof. Each of them about three inches square. They could easily have held security cameras.

'Take a seat, Mrs Ryan.' Grey hair sounded very sure of himself.

She sat, though she didn't want to. She had a cramp in her stomach. What the hell was all this about?

'I apologise for bringing you here under these circumstances. But I think you'll agree, when you see what I'm about to show you, that we're a hundred per cent justified in doing this.' Grey hair reached inside his jacket and pulled out a shiny USB storage device.

He waved it in the air as if it was a trophy, then he walked towards the LCD screen. He plugged the device into the side of the TV, then pressed a button on the top.

It sprang to life, flickering briefly. A menu screen appeared. Then the screen flickered again.

A voice was coming from somewhere behind the camera. The camera was facing a red-brick wall, just like the ones around her.

'This termination interview is taking place Saturday 11 December, at BXH's headquarters, Lexington Avenue, New York.' The voice paused. His accent was steel-hard mid-Atlantic.

Sweat sprung out on Isabel's forehead.

'This recording is time and date stamped,' he continued. 'My name is Paul Vaughann. I am the UK CEO of BXH. This contract termination interview is with a Mr Sean Ryan.'

Goosebumps formed on her arms. Why was she being shown this? A hand appeared. It moved the camera. Someone was turning it. Red-brick walls flashed by. The room was like this one, only smaller.

Sean's face appeared.

She could feel the blood draining from her face. It was the first time she'd seen him properly in days. His skin was pale, his eyes bulging. He did not look good. She bent forward to see him better.

She wanted to shout at him, but she didn't.

He was sitting on the other side of a table. He looked up at the camera. She said 'Sean,' under her breath. The two men sitting in front of her turned and gave her an inquisitive stare.

Then Sean started talking and they looked away.

She wished she wasn't seeing this. But she couldn't stop watching it. Her hands felt cold. Her skin felt too tight for her body.

'Please state your name, relationship with BXH and the particular circumstances of this interview, Mr Ryan.' If this was taken earlier, she could have been outside, a few hundred feet away, while this was all happening. No wonder he'd looked weird, preoccupied, when she'd seen him.

She sucked in her breath. She hadn't even realised she'd been holding it.

'My name is Sean Ryan. I'm the head of a software project at BXH's London office. I work on contract for BXH.' He coughed.

She wrapped her arms tight around herself. It looked as if he didn't want to say more.

'Please state the circumstances of this interview, Mr Ryan.'

Sean looked up. His gaze moved, as if he was looking at different people behind the camera. He did not look happy. His eyes were dead.

There was a taste of dust in her mouth. Her face felt hot.

'Okay,' he said. 'I'll say it.'

He looked at the camera, spoke slowly. 'I murdered a dancer I met in a club in London the other night.' He sounded defiant.

She blinked. There was pressure building inside her.

It took long seconds for the words to register. Then a whooshing followed in her ears as the meaning became clear. The air felt heavy, hard to breathe. Something was stabbing into her, as if a pin had been rammed into her head. She put her palm to her forehead. It felt as if her whole head might explode. This couldn't be happening.

This was a nightmare. It had to be a nightmare. Or a lie.

59

The only sound in the panic room was from Alek crying. Xena was standing over him.

'Soon all this will be over, little boy,' she said. She leaned towards him.

'You will be as free as a bird.' She straightened, then went to the long wooden table on the right of the bed.

It was where she kept the handcuffs. Not one of the pairs was small enough to hold the boy, but the black silk cords would be.

She turned as she heard a noise.

Lord Bidoner had joined them.

'All is ready?' he said. He turned the dimmer switch. The lights in the room faded.

The boy was whimpering. He was curled up under the blanket in the centre of the bed. He had his eyes closed. He opened them for a second. When he saw what Xena was holding he squeezed them shut again. His whimpering became louder. It was mixed with half-stifled sobs now.

'I am ready,' she said.

'*Quarto quattuor invocare unum*,' said Lord Bidoner. He spoke softly, then bowed his head.

Xena was standing on the far side of the bed. She reached towards Alek and pulled the blanket away from him. He was shivering.

60

Sean's voice echoed in the room. 'I . . . ' His eyes were wide. He looked manic, not at all like the Sean Isabel knew so well.

She stood up, knocking the chair in front of her forward.

'Where is he? I don't believe any of this crap.' She waved her hand at the screen. Her voice was loud. But she didn't care.

'You can't show this to people. You've no right to show this to anyone. What the hell's going on? Who the hell are you?' She glared at the two men in front of her. The muscles in her arms and legs were vibrating as if she'd run a marathon.

Grey hair didn't say a word. He pressed a button on the remote. Sean's face stopped moving. His mouth was wide open. You could have cut the atmosphere in the room into toxic chunks.

The thinner of the two men sitting in front of her said, 'My name's Gus Reilly, Mrs Ryan. I'm Assistant DA in the Financial Crimes Unit at the New York District Attorney's office.' He shifted a little in his chair.

'I'm here to investigate the circumstances of the collapsed

merger between BXH and another party. We received a referral from the SEC regarding suspicious activity at BXH's London office. Your husband is one of the individuals we're investigating. I have every right to view this material under a subpoena issued this afternoon by US District Court Judge, Bernard M. Stanton.' He reached into his jacket, pulled a sheaf of papers out and held them in the air.

A numbness was spreading through her veins like poison.

'Do you know were my husband is?'

Mr Reilly turned back to face the screen. Her mind flickered from one possibility to the next. Was there a chance Sean was guilty? The answer had to be no. So what the hell was going on? She felt a constricting pain in her chest. It was getting tighter by the second.

The other man turned to her. He had a long nose and short black hair.

'My name's Dick Owen, Mrs Ryan. I'm Assistant Director, Trading Markets Division, at the Securities and Exchange Commission's New York office. We've been investigating BXH for eighteen months now. Earlier today we asked the DA's office to get involved in this case.' He had a snooty expression.

Her mind was churning this information, as if her brain had been frozen and was slowly thawing.

'I received a federal warrant this afternoon to enter this building and seize any evidence related to the commission of any criminal acts contrary to SEC regulations.'

He was reciting something.

'I think it's best if we play the recording in full before we discuss anything else,' said grey hair.

She didn't want him to play any more of the recording.

She'd heard too much already.

'Unless you'd like not to be present. If you find all this too difficult.'

'I'll stay,' she said, as firmly as she could. 'But I want to know where my husband is.'

'We don't know where he is, Mrs Ryan, honestly.' He had a concerned look on his face, which she didn't like. 'I think you should see this recording. I think you need to see it, for your own sake. For your safety most of all. That's what I'm concerned about.'

She gripped the edge of the chair in front of her. Was he implying Sean might be a danger to her?

Had one of these people texted her, not Sean? The message hadn't mentioned him by name.

This was all way too crazy.

Her knuckles were white against the blue of the chair in front of her. She gripped tighter. The safe world she lived in, her reality until forty hours ago, was disappearing.

'I'll watch it, but don't expect me to believe one word.'

'I understand your reaction is to deny what's in front of you,' said grey hair. 'It is only natural. All I ask is that you have an open mind to everything you see.' Then he turned and pressed at the remote control in his hand.

'I . . .' said Sean. The recording continued. He looked pained.

'I'm sorry,' he said. 'I lost control. I couldn't stop myself.'

A wave of tears threatened as she heard the genuine sorrow in his voice. She pushed her arms into her sides and held herself tight. She could feel her ribs.

On the screen Sean looked down, as if he didn't know what else to say. This was so unlike him.

'Are you aware of clause 47 of our contract with the Institute you work for, Mr Ryan, allowing BXH to terminate the contract with immediate effect, without compensation, should any contract personnel commit an act of serious criminality?' The voice droned from the recording.

Sean nodded.

What would she say to Alek?

He was expecting his daddy to come home, make a big fuss of him, lift him high in the air.

The screen went black.

Gus Reilly turned and reached towards her, holding out a slim cream-coloured business card. She took it. Her hand was shaking. The emblem of the New York County District Attorney's office, an eagle and a circle, was embossed on it in pale blue.

'I'm sorry, this must be a shock, Mrs Ryan, but our investigation of BXH is ongoing. If you know anything about any illegalities in connection with BXH, either here or in London, you have a legal obligation to inform us. And I don't say that lightly.'

She put the card in the back pocket of her jeans.

'Don't believe what you've just seen, Mr Reilly,' she said, loudly. 'I certainly won't, until I hear him admit all this myself. Anyone can doctor a video recording these days.'

Grey hair shook his head slowly, as if he felt sorry for her.

She'd had enough. She stood, pushed a chair out of her way and walked fast towards the exit. She wanted out of the place. She couldn't stay in this ugly room one second longer.

To hell with them all.

As she neared the door she heard fast footsteps behind her, grey hair speaking.

'Please, Mrs Ryan, Mr Vaughann would like to see you.' His emphasis on the word Vaughann made it clear that the illustrious Mr Vaughann did not expect to be turned down.

She stopped. It didn't take much to imagine the self-serving crap that BXH's UK CEO was going to throw at her.

She didn't want to hear it.

And then a memory came back to her. Last Christmas Sean had taken the blame after she'd scratched their next door neighbour's shiny new Lexus. She'd been reversing late on Christmas Eve and had misjudged the size of the space outside their house in the dark. Sean had gone around first thing Christmas morning. He'd told them he'd done it.

He did it because she'd had a run-in with their wonderful Scottish neighbours months before. He'd been trying to protect her, he'd said.

Could he be doing the same thing now? But why, and for who?

She had to meet Vaughann.

Grey hair was talking. She'd missed what he'd said. He had a pop-eyed expression on his face, as if he was about to burst. It was the way she felt.

'He is waiting for us,' he said, quickly, as if he was repeating himself.

'Fine,' she said.

When they reached the end of the corridor, almost at the elevator, grey hair knocked on a shiny bottle-green painted steel door. He waited for a reply, his head leaning a little sideways, as if he was a hunting dog waiting to be whistled at.

Standing there was like being in school again thinking up excuses outside the principal's office.

She tried to calm her anger. Someone was trying to make her believe Sean was guilty of something despicable, make a lot of people believe it. But she wasn't buying it.

'Why don't we just go in?' she said.

Grey hair looked surprised.

'We have to wait,' he whispered.

'You could have just told me what Sean said. You didn't have to show me that video.'

He knocked on the door again, then turned to her. 'Mrs Ryan, BXH has only your best interests at heart, honestly. You are the spouse of someone who may well be a danger to others. We take our duty of care seriously. We understand most people instinctively deny a partner's wrongdoing. That's why it was important for you to see with your own eyes what your husband has admitted to, not for us to relay such news to you or interpret his words.'

'Yeah, BXH really cares,' she said. She closed her eyes. She didn't like being told she was in denial.

'Yes, Mrs Ryan, it does.'

She pressed her lips together.

The door opened. She was looking at the sombre face of Mr Vaughann.

'Mrs Ryan.' Vaughann sighed. 'I expect you're having trouble taking all this in.'

61

Four to Invoke the One. Henry shook his head. If someone was trying to re-enact this ancient ritual they hadn't much time left to finish the job. The moon would rise soon in London and in about four hours in New York, where Sean Ryan was.

Henry was still in the monitoring room in Whitehall. It was almost one thirty in the morning now. His FBI contact had finally responded.

Surveillance of Isabel Ryan was being initiated. Her current whereabouts were known. She was in the BXH building on Lexington Avenue.

He'd looked up the BXH building. It was an art deco rival to the nearby Chrysler skyscraper. The majority of its floors were still in use as BXH offices. It also had some urban myths connected to it. One stated that a dozen men had died on a single day during its construction, when an underground fall-in had occurred. Apparently the building had been declared as cursed by a construction workers' union soon after.

But none of that had kept him in the office this late. What worried him was the discovery of a woman who had been mutilated in her hotel room not far away, in the Waldorf Astoria. That was very concerning.

The woman had had her tongue removed. And it was missing. The FBI officer had passed on the details after he had read how the dancer had died in London and had spotted that there was a possibility that her murder was part of some blood soaked serial-killing spree.

And the fact they still hadn't located Alek Ryan, Isabel and Sean Ryan's little boy, had given him nightmares. Because the final death in the ritual in the book was that of a young child.

The act of crushing heretics or non-believers was praised by some in ancient Byzantium, he had read, as proof of an unshakeable faith. And rituals involving such acts could be used to bless a major enterprise, such as the beginning of a siege defence or the commencement of a war.

Twenty-first-century sensibilities made most people squeamish about such things, but when fighting for survival meant fighting against people who wanted to take over your city and put everyone you knew to the sword, such rituals would have been acceptable.

He understood the connection between the recent murders now, and he had read how horrific the other deaths in the manuscript were. Now he had to make sure the FBI had everything they needed, that he had done everything he could to prevent such an evil twisting of faith ever being played out again.

The Metropolitan Police had set up road blocks in the Fulham area of London, looking for witnesses who might have seen a boy being moved around, but so far they had come up with nothing substantial.

Henry was also checking if the boy had been taken out of the country, perhaps by the woman who'd been minding him.

Sean Ryan was in Manhattan somewhere, BXH had confirmed that. Perhaps he'd arranged for his son to be taken there too.

He went to his UK flights arrivals and departures passenger identification software again. He keyed in the search terms. A boy travelling to the Eastern seaboard of the US in the last forty-eight hours, probably listed as three to five years of age.

Two hundred and twenty-six children were now listed as having travelled to the US in the period from UK airports. He looked through the photo IDs of them all.

Twenty-six new images had been added from the last departing scheduled flight, which had taken off, late, ninety minutes before.

It took seconds to scroll through them all. But none of the children bore any resemblance to the ID picture he had on his screen of Alek Ryan. Then something came to him.

What about private planes or private charters?

He opened another tab on his browser, then pressed his fist to his forehead.

He was tired, and his migraine was back, but he had to keep going.

No one deserved to die the way that book described, especially not a child.

It was the sickest thing he had ever read.

62

'Isabel, I'm so sorry about all this.' Vaughann's sympathetic smile might have been put in place with staples, it looked that phony.

'You must have had a terrible shock. Please, come on in. You know we can find you support services, counselling, if you need it.' He stepped back.

'I won't need it,' she said. 'What I'd like to know is where my husband is.'

Vaughann stepped further back. 'I'm sorry, I simply don't know,' he said. 'But come in. We will try to help you.'

She went into the room. Grey hair disappeared. This room was similar to the other one down the corridor. It had the same red-brick walls, painted floor and sixties-style fluorescent lighting.

'I saw Mrs Vaughann,' she said. 'Did she find you?'

'Yes, she did. Thank you for asking.'

The floor here was less scuffed, and the room was a good deal smaller, more of a meeting room. In fact, this looked like the room in Sean's video, where he'd done that interview.

She could feel Vaughann staring at her.

In the centre of the room there were old-fashioned

heavy wooden tables facing each other in a rectangle. Plastic chairs were pushed in neatly around the tables.

There was a row of iron eyelets protruding from above the wall at the far end of the room. God only knew what they had been used for in the past.

'Please sit down, Isabel,' said Mr Vaughann. His tone was pleasant, but cool. The kind of tone you might take with contractors that were embarrassingly far beneath you.

If Sean ever spoke to her like that she would know exactly who he was copying it from. And it would be grounds for divorce.

She sat on a chair at the corner of the rectangle of tables.

'My husband was in this building earlier with you,' she said, as he made his way around the tables to the far side.

'That's true,' he said. 'But I have no idea where he is now.' If he sounded any smoother, he'd have slipped off himself.

Could she believe anything that came out of his mouth?

'Why am I down here?' she said.

'This is where our staff watched the second Obama inauguration,' he said. He gestured, as if he was giving her a guided tour.

She looked around. 'That was a big celebration at BXH?'

'We had balloons up. We gave everyone an hour off. If they wanted to watch it at their desks they could have. We have a lot of responsibilities.'

Would this be a good time to ask him about his corporate jet and his art collection? Sean had told her about the rare Byzantine tapestries that lined the walls of Mr Vaughann's office in London.

'I'm here for one reason, Mr Vaughann: to find my husband.'

'I do understand.' He smiled, like a vulture watching over its prey.

There was a noise behind her. She glanced around expecting to see her grey-haired friend hopping from foot to foot.

What she saw instead were people trouping into the room. First, Dick Owen clutching a black leather folder. Then there was a policewoman with a badge hanging from the belt of her black pantsuit. She had a pained expression on her wide crumpled face, as if she was unhappy. Or maybe that was the way NYPD officers look at ten on a Saturday night, when they should be at home. Another thin, owlish-looking man in a blue suit followed her in.

Isabel stared at them.

'These people want to see you, Mrs Ryan. That there is Mike Brock,' said Vaughann, pointing at the last man who came in. 'He's the nearest thing we've got to a criminal lawyer. I thought it would be in your interest to have him here.'

'Why?'

Vaughann ignored her question. 'You know Mr Owen from the SEC already, I believe,' he said.

Owen waved at her, then headed for a seat on the other side of the rectangle of tables. The policewoman was standing nearby. Isabel could feel herself being examined.

'This is Detective Tess Grainger, Isabel. She's with the NYPD. She wants to ask you some questions. I agreed to let her meet you here only because of the highly unusual circumstances. I do think you should have your own attorney present, but in the meantime, Mike will make sure everything is done correctly.'

The lawyer smiled at her. The guy was good at making it look like he cared.

She looked up at Detective Grainger. There was a sheen of sweat on the detective's forehead. Isabel got a feeling that she was about to pull handcuffs out and arrest her.

'How you doing, Mrs Ryan?' said Detective Grainger.

'I'm not good,' said Isabel. Detective Grainger leaned down.

'I've got some urgent questions we need answers to, like an hour ago. But you don't have to do this with these people here. We can do it all somewhere else, if you want. Down at the station, maybe?'

Isabel waited. She looked from face to face.

'I've got nothing to hide.' She emphasised each word. 'Ask me anything you want, I mean it. Anything. I don't care who's here.'

'Okay,' said Grainger, a little tentatively, as if she was working out the best way to play this. She looked at Vaughann, then back at Isabel.

'But I'll want to see you on your own some other time, down at the station, Mrs Ryan,' she said. There was a protective note to her comment, Isabel noted.

'You don't have to agree to answer any questions you don't want to,' said Mike, the criminal lawyer.

'He's right,' said Vaughann. Then he leaned over the table towards her. 'Your husband was one of our most trusted contractors, you know. I do have some idea about what you're feeling. So remember, you really don't have to say anything, if you don't want to.'

She looked at Vaughann. 'You know what gets me, Mr Vaughann?'

He shrugged.

It was time to tell him a few things.

'You don't understand what BXH's culture does to people. BXH has stolen my husband, as far as I'm concerned. He put everything into working for you, and this is where we end up.' She waved dismissively at her surroundings.

Vaughann's eyebrows went up. A vein in his forehead was throbbing.

Isabel leaned forward. 'You were at that club in London too. The one that poor murdered dancer worked in. What were you doing there, setting an example?'

'Your husband has confessed,' said Vaughann, softly. 'I understand why you're angry, but I don't think you can blame me for what happened. Not at all.' He looked around for support.

Was she the only person who could see the truth?

'You don't get it, do you? I don't believe that Sean's guilty. And I won't believe it, until I hear it from his own mouth as he stands in front of me.'

He shook his head, as if he was dealing with a stubborn child.

'Maybe, if your husband was here, Mrs Ryan,' said Detective Grainger. She was sitting on the chair next to Isabel now. She turned it a little more towards her, scraping it horribly on the floor. Her accent sounded like bins rolling.

She had short straight blonde hair. It sat in an unruly bundle on her head halfway over her eyes, making her push at it now and again.

'Do you know where he is?' said Grainger.

'No, do you?' Her mouth was painfully dry, her lips hard from the cold, the tension. The pounding in her head was low-key.

'We were really hoping you might be able to help us with that.' The detective stared at her. Did she think Isabel was hiding something?

'I'll ask you a straight question now, Mrs Ryan. Do you have any plans to meet your husband?'

'Are you crazy? I'm looking for him! He told me to come here.' She raised a hand, pressed it to her forehead. This was making her mad.

'When did you last see him?' Grainger took a small leather-bound notebook from an inside pocket of her jacket.

'Earlier tonight. I think it was half past six.' Isabel closed her eyes. He'd been so close, only feet away. Why hadn't he seen her?

'Where was that?'

'He was in a town car exiting the BXH car park up above. He didn't see me.'

'And you haven't seen him since?' Her eyes were unnaturally open, as if she rarely believed anything anyone told her, and Isabel wasn't going to be an exception.

'No, I haven't. Have you checked hotels? BXH usually books him into one.'

'We have, ma'am.' Her smile could have cut glass.

Isabel looked around. The SEC man, Dick Owen, looked tired. He was sitting beside Vaughann. He had his fingers steepled together. His red tie was a little off centre.

Detective Grainger pushed her chair away from the table. She put her notebook on her knee. Vaughann whispered something into Dick Owen's ear. The SEC guy raised his eyebrows, stared at her. Then he spoke.

'You came to New York to find your husband, is that right, Mrs Ryan?'

All eyes were on her. It sounded as if she was being investigated now.

'Yes.'

'You are aware that the woman who died in London was a drug addict and a prostitute?' said Owen.

'What the hell has that got to do with anything?' said Isabel. She pointed at Vaughann. 'You know Sean isn't into drugs or anything like that. What the hell is going on here, a character assassination?'

'We're just trying to get to the truth,' said Vaughann.

63

The GMC Yukon pulled up in the alley on the far side of 45th Street from BXH's entrance. As the man in the back got out, a policeman looked down the alley. Then he looked away. There was nothing to see, just a nondescript businessman on his way into a nondescript office.

The reception area of the firm Li had come to visit was on the twenty-sixth floor. It had a high ceiling and a sculpture of a bear raised up on its hind legs ready to attack.

When Li reached the twenty-sixth floor there was no one behind the reception desk, but there were still lights on. He passed the plastic card he'd been given over the blue-lit panel at the side of the glass door. There was a click.

The toughened glass slid open. As he walked inside a man appeared from a corner of the reception area. He appeared to have been waiting for Li.

'Welcome,' said the American. Then he bowed.

'Everything is ready,' he said, motioning towards a door.

Li put his hand up. 'I do not want to visit the trading floor, even if it is empty. Just tell me one thing before we talk. What is the prediction for US banking sector shares on Monday?'

‘They’ll dive to their lowest ever. I guarantee it,’ said the American. He grinned.

It didn’t seem to worry him that the future of his country was being gambled over. Only one thing concerned such men, Li knew. What they can walk away with from the table.

64

Detective Grainger put her hands up. 'Hold on. I don't want any more questioning of Mrs Ryan in my presence until I advise her of her rights.'

Isabel sat up straight. Was she serious? She hadn't done anything wrong.

She rubbed a hand across her forehead.

'You all right with that, Mrs Ryan?'

She nodded, though she didn't feel all right.

Then Grainger began. 'Okay, Mrs Ryan. You have the right to remain silent. But anything you say can and will be used against you in a court of law. You have the right to an attorney. If you cannot afford an attorney, one will be provided for you. Do you understand the rights I have just read to you?'

Isabel nodded. The air in the room had cooled by ten degrees.

'This is crazy. What the hell are you reading me my rights for?' she said.

'This is all just-in-case stuff, Mrs Ryan,' Grainger gestured, waving her hand through the air, as if reading Isabel her rights was not a big deal.

But it was a big deal.

Did she think this conversation was going to go sour? Did she really want to do all this down the station?

Grainger lowered her voice. Her tone was conspiratorial, even though the others at the table could hear her as well.

'My friend over there from the SEC might start asking you questions, and I don't want you incriminating yourself, and then some fancy lawyer telling us later on you hadn't even been read your rights.'

'Am I under suspicion?' It felt as if steel bands had been placed around her chest and they were being tightened, slowly. These people were supposed to be helping her, not questioning her.

Detective Grainger leaned back, looked up at the ceiling as if she was looking for holes or inspiration.

'Look, you gotta understand. We're investigating some real serious matters here. There's been some brutal murders. And now we've a suspect who's disappeared. And you're related to that suspect. We've also got a number of alleged serious financial crimes, which are under investigation. Now, the way I see things, suspicion falls everywhere. You got that? I mean everywhere.' She looked across the room at Vaughann, then at Owen, then at Mike the lawyer.

Isabel liked that.

She also liked the fact that Grainger's jacket had bobbles of pink wool down one arm, as if it had been pressed up against someone in a pink sweater just before she came out.

She looked like someone who stood up to bullies, and who wouldn't take a dime to do anything crooked. Ever. She probably annoyed the other officers in her precinct for that. The male ones that is.

'Are you sure you don't want to go down to the station, get some privacy?'

'Yes, I'm sure.'

Detective Grainger reached forward, took one of the small

bottles of Aquafina from the middle of the table and handed it to her.

'You want some water?' she said.

Isabel took one of the white paper cups beside the water bottles and poured herself a glass. She drank it quickly.

Mr Vaughann glanced at his watch. It was a gold Rolex. Sean had told her how he'd been in a meeting once in the bank where everyone in the room had been wearing a Rolex, except himself. He'd refused to stop wearing the Hamilton his dad gave him.

It was one of the reasons she loved him. He didn't care about impressing people.

She felt a longing to see him. It pulled at her like a tide.

'Are you sure you're okay, Mrs Ryan?' said Detective Grainger.

'I want to know why my husband is missing.'

'I can assure you, whatever his reasons are, they won't be anything to do with BXH,' said Vaughann. His tone made it clear that any contrary notion was preposterous.

'You weren't listening,' she said. 'Whatever happens to Sean I put at your door, at this stupid casino's door.' She waved at the walls.

She turned to the SEC guy. 'Why don't you just take over this bank, clean it all out? You could do that, couldn't you?'

'First of all, Mrs Ryan, that's not our role. The FDIC do that kind of thing,' said Dick Owen. 'Second, do you know how many banks they've taken over this year already?'

She shrugged. Whatever the number, what difference did it make?

'Does that matter?'

'We're looking for alternatives, Mrs Ryan.'

'You mean between now and when they file for Chapter 11, before midnight tonight?' It all sounded very last minute.

There was a pause. Owen and Vaughann looked at each other.

'What the hell are you doing down here talking to me?' she said. 'Shouldn't you be upstairs saving BXH's ass?'

Detective Grainger smiled, just a little, before looking at the floor.

'We thought you might know where your husband is,' said Vaughann.

Isabel felt a strange sensation. She'd realised something.

'You're not telling me everything. I can feel it.'

Vaughann looked at Dick Owen. The look on his face confirmed it.

She wouldn't have believed it was possible, if someone had told her this was all going to happen a few days ago. She'd have said they were dreaming or mad.

'Let's establish a few facts,' said Detective Grainger.

Isabel wanted to get out of the room. This was all a distraction from her finding Sean. A distraction that seemed to be suiting Vaughann and Owen. Why would that be?

'Did your husband visit strip clubs regularly?'

Isabel's cheeks flushed. It was bad enough he'd gone to one of those clubs. Now she was being asked about it as if it was somehow her fault, and in front of a room full of men.

Her grip on the paper cup tightened. One side bent in. She stopped squeezing just in time before the water dripped over the edge.

'He went a couple of times, a long time ago.' That was what he'd told her. But was it the truth? She drank some water. A little spilled down her chin.

'Why don't you ask him what he was doing there?' Isabel pointed at Vaughann.

He put his hands up, as if she'd pointed a gun at him. 'I can assure you it wasn't my idea to visit that club. I didn't even know what kind of place it was until I got inside. I exited the place immediately. As quickly as I could actually, under the circumstances. I already told the Detective all this.'

She turned to Detective Grainger. 'Are you looking for my husband?' She dreaded the answer.

'We have an APB out for him, Mrs Ryan. We're watching the airports, the bus stations, the train stations. The usual stuff.'

'Great.' But it wasn't. It was proof that her nightmare had just entered another level. They were hunting him down like they would a terrorist suspect.

'Have you any idea,' said Detective Grainger, leaning towards her, 'why your husband would confess to something he didn't do?' She put her head to the side, as if she was sceptical about the confession too.

'No. But I do know he's not guilty.' She pushed her chin forward. Someone had to stand up for him.

Vaughann guffawed quietly.

'You gotta think straight now, Mrs Ryan,' said Grainger, softly.

Isabel looked away. There had to be an explanation for all this. She rapped the table between her and Vaughann. 'What about you? Were you with that poor dancer the other night?'

Vaughann leaned back in his chair.

'I told you. I went straight back to the bank soon after I got to that club,' he said confidently. 'My driver can testify to that. As can about twenty people who were in the bank working on the merger when I got there. And I stayed in the building all night.'

She was clutching at wisps.

She shuddered. Could the man she loved really have met with a prostitute and killed her? She thought about Alek.

Thank God he didn't have to see this. She got an urge to call him, to speak to him. It wouldn't be long before it was Sunday morning in London. She closed her eyes. Thank God for one thing. At least Alek was safe.

'Mrs Ryan, I know you're under stress. It's a terrible thing your husband has admitted to, and I understand it's hard to believe,' said Grainger.

Isabel's hand on the table was trembling. She put it in her lap, gripped it with her other hand and pressed them both into her stomach. She kept her eyes closed.

'Have you been told that your husband bailed out of a moving vehicle?' said Detective Grainger.

She shook her head. A part of her didn't want to hear any more bad news, didn't want to see any more bad news.

'Someone should have told you.' She put a finger on Isabel's knee and pressed it down hard, as if she was trying to get through to her.

'You may need some protection.'

Isabel's eyes opened.

'What happened?' she said. She sat up straighter.

'As your husband was being driven to the 17th precinct station house earlier this evening, Mrs Ryan, he jumped out of the car taking him there. He'd agreed to be driven there following that recording you saw.'

'Why would Sean come to New York, if he was going to confess?' she said, opening her eyes. 'He could have done that in London.'

Detective Grainger looked at Vaughann, then back at her.

'You should tell her what's happened, Mr Vaughann.' Grainger had a stiff look on her face, as if she had plenty of thoughts about all this, but wasn't going to reveal any of them.

Vaughann coughed, then began talking. 'I confronted your husband about all the speculation in the English media earlier. It was at that point Sean agreed to make the statement.' He paused, as if he thought he had done something commendable.

'This follows our protocols precisely.' He looked like someone for whom that mattered a lot.

'Serious incidents involving the bank's reputation have to be reported to the authorities immediately.' He shook his head, as if disappointed at the timing of all this.

'You decided to terminate the Institute's contract without hearing Sean's side of the story?' Isabel said.

He stared at her. 'We spoke to your husband, Mrs Ryan. You saw the interview.' He sniffed.

'I'd say he wanted your husband on tape in case he was arrested, isn't that right, Mr Vaughann?' said Detective Grainger. 'You were covering your backsides.'

'Detective, this is also about business. I made it clear at all times that the Institute's contract had to be terminated if he admitted a criminal offence.' He was staring at Grainger. 'I did tell you this already.' His tone was firm.

'After he made his admission there was nothing else I could do, no matter what my personal feelings were.'

'Yeah, you did the right thing,' said Isabel. 'You always do the right thing.'

'Yes, we do. Your husband has been acting odd for a while,' he went on. 'But this is not about me or about BXH. I had no choice in this. Sean volunteered his replies. You'll have to ask him why. We've exceeded our obligations. You wouldn't even have seen his confession if we hadn't done it this way.' He sounded pleased with the way it had all worked out.

'Your husband has no further contractual relationship with BXH. He assaulted one of my colleagues when they were stopped at a red light. Then he got out of the town car and ran up Lexington, against the traffic. It's all verifiable. He was probably on two or three different security cameras when he ran for it. It was like something from a movie, so I'm told.'

She took a huge breath. Air poured into her. None of this sounded like Sean. It felt as if they were talking about someone else, some stupid criminal. What the hell could have driven him to do all this?

She looked up. Everyone in the room was staring at her. She saw pity and distaste in their eyes.

65

Henry Mowlam put the phone to his ear and listened. The office was quiet around him.

'Henry, there's been a development.' Finch's tone was at its most officious, which meant there were people around her.

'What's happened?'

'We've discovered your stupid symbol on the plan of the underground levels of the BXH building in New York. Apparently it's on the original plans from 1923. They show the deepest level of the building with a vault marked with a square and arrow.'

'That's it?' He tried not to sound too exasperated. He wasn't sure if he succeeded. 'No, Henry, that's not it. Isabel Ryan is in imminent danger. I need you to make contact with her and warn her about her husband. She knows you, so she's more likely to believe you. Her husband has confessed to that dancer's murder. The NYPD will treat him as armed and dangerous from this point on. It looks like you were right.'

Henry put the phone down. He took no pleasure in being

right. What he wanted to do now was make sure Isabel Ryan and Alek Ryan got out of this situation in one piece.

He dialled Isabel Ryan's mobile number.

The call diverted to voicemail.

66

Isabel looked down at the table. She wasn't going to give in. And there was the question of timing. Detective Grainger had said the vehicle Sean had been in had been on its way uptown. But if it had been, how had it gone through the Lincoln Tunnel only a few minutes later?

She closed her eyes and imagined herself standing looking at the screen in Greg's tiny apartment. What time had the screen said it had gone through the tunnel?

Then she remembered Greg saying, '18:58,' and pointing.

'Mr Vaughann,' she said.

He raised his eyebrows.

'How come that town car Sean was in went through Lincoln Tunnel just minutes after I saw it outside the building here? If they were heading to a police station they wouldn't have been able to get to the Lincoln Tunnel in a few minutes.'

'I don't have to explain anything,' said Vaughann. He paused. 'But I will. Your husband jumped from the car only three blocks from here. They had plenty of time to get to the Lincoln Tunnel.' Three blocks? Had he seen her?

'Why didn't they go straight to the precinct, report what had happened?'

'We got a call reporting what had occurred, Mrs Ryan. That's good enough for us,' said Grainger.

Everyone was still looking at her. They were all totally convinced of Sean's guilt. She was the last juror in the room holding out for an innocent verdict on some guilty bum, preventing him from being convicted.

There was a knock at the door. A policewoman, in full uniform this time, poked her head inside the room.

'Can I see you, Detective Grainger?' she drawled.

Grainger rose to her feet and exited the room.

They sat in a silence broken only by distant groans from the pipes and the hum of the fluorescent lighting. Dick Owen turned to Vaughann, leaned close to him and whispered.

She closed her eyes. Would she have to accept Sean's guilt?

Grainger came back into the room.

'Your husband has been seen, Mrs Ryan.'

Isabel rose to her feet. Her legs felt jellylike, as if she'd been in a hospital bed for six months. For a moment everything went black. She swayed and sat down again.

'Are you okay?' said Grainger

'Where is he?' she said. She shook her head to clear it.

'He was seen on a security camera in this building,' said Grainger.

'What?' exploded Vaughann.

The hairs on the back of Isabel's neck stood up like porcupine quills.

'They don't know how he got in, but he was spotted in your underground car park, Mr Vaughann,' said Grainger, calmly. It sounded as if she was blaming him. An alarm bell rang out in the hallway. The noise filled the room with a klaxon-like sound. More bells joined in, including one directly above them on the roof. The noise ran through her, making her bones vibrate.

Then, they all stopped as quickly as they'd started.

‘I have to go,’ said Vaughann. He stood up.

Dick Owen did too. ‘I should check on my people,’ he said. He stabbed a finger at the ceiling. His face was pale.

‘We need to talk a bit more, Mrs Ryan,’ said Detective Grainger.

Her head was throbbing. Why hadn’t he given himself up to the police?

She looked at her watch; her Gucci with the interchangeable rims. Sean had bought it for her in Macy’s for her birthday last year.

How far away that time seemed now.

‘You’re going to have to be real careful from this point, Mrs Ryan,’ said Grainger, softly. She pointed a finger at her.

‘You don’t think my husband’s dangerous, do you?’

‘He could be. You have to be open to it.’ Grainger crossed her legs. Her scuffed black shoes looked as if they hadn’t been polished in a long time.

Isabel shrugged.

Grainger put her face closer to hers.

‘BXH’s security manager here in New York is missing. Nobody has any idea where he is. We’re searching for him. And we’ve had some other incidents I’m concerned about. I don’t want any more victims.’

‘But if he did murder someone, why has he come back? That would be crazy,’ said Isabel. She was trying not to sound too anxious. She wasn’t succeeding.

‘Your husband could have come back for the purpose of revenge, Mrs Ryan. We can’t discount that. Revenge is behind a lot of the craziness I see. Your husband may blame BXH or some individual here for what’s happened to him. He might have a weapon now too. We have to plan for every scenario.’

‘I don’t believe that.’ She massaged her forehead.

‘I had to tell this poor woman last week that her husband had killed himself. I also had to tell her he’d killed a co-worker in their broking firm. God only knows why.' Her expression wavered for a moment. A look of weariness appeared.

'Revenge is a powerful thing.'

'What if Sean's innocent?' said Isabel.

'Listen, your husband would have come to us if he was innocent.'

'This is so not Sean.' Her hands were gripping each other.

Grainger was looking pensive, as if she was working out how to tell her bad news.

'Mrs Ryan, your husband is considered dangerous at this point. He's a wanted man; a suspect in a murder case.'

'Sean's as straight as they come. He's the most honest man I've ever met, Detective. You have to believe me. Please.'

'This is not about you,' said Grainger. She sounded sympathetic. 'You gotta trust me. It is real hard to believe it when someone you know well goes off the rails.'

'I hate this stupid bank.' Isabel looked around. 'You know someone invited me here by text this evening. What the hell was that about?'

Grainger shrugged. Her pained expression made it clear she thought Isabel was still trying to hold back reality.

'Are you married, Detective?'

Grainger nodded. 'That's how I know how difficult this is for you,' she said. Then she leaned towards Isabel. 'You staying near here, Mrs Ryan?'

Isabel told her which hotel she was in.

'You should go there right now.'

'Okay.' She wanted out of the room. 'Did you see a bathroom near here?'

Grainger grunted, motioned her to follow, then pointed to the elevators.

'See that guard?' She waved to him. He was standing beside the elevator doors. He was a short guy with blonde hair. He waved back, nonchalantly.

'I'm gonna ask him to escort you out of the building.' She put a hand on Isabel's arm 'Please, stay in your hotel until we call you, understood?'

Isabel nodded.

'When are you due to fly back to London?'

'Ten tomorrow night.'

'If you get any more text messages or any calls from your husband, call me as soon as you get them. Don't go off and meet him. That's real important, Mrs Ryan.' She slipped a card out of the back of her notebook and handed it to Isabel.

'You got all that?'

Isabel nodded.

The toilet had white tiles on every wall. She washed her face, letting the water drip into the square old-fashioned porcelain basin. She looked at herself in the mirror. Her skin was chalky, her hair sticking out at odd angles. The dark patches under her eyes were spreading.

Was she right to believe in Sean or was she being stupid?

She remembered a long walk they took in Hyde Park the previous summer, how they'd talked about everything. How she was sure she knew him better than anyone else on the planet.

Had it all been a lie?

She bent over the basin, a wave of emotion engulfing her. Stop! You're going to make yourself crazy.

She straightened. She looked like a ghost. She needed to sleep. She knew that rationally, but she also felt as if she'd passed the lowest ebb of her tiredness. A notice beside the mirror caught her eye. It looked as if it had been put up in the seventies.

It was about the fire exit.

The FIRE EXIT, at the end of the corridor on each floor, should be used only in the case of emergency. For those in the basement levels, please remember that you must walk upwards to exit the building.

And she knew in that second that she wasn't going to go back to her hotel. She wasn't going to stop looking for Sean just because someone had told her to. What could they do to her anyway? Charge her with trying to find her husband?

She pushed her hair behind her ears. It looked better that way. Sean always said that. She took off her jacket, tied it around her waist. She didn't feel cold, though that was probably because of the giant hot water pipes running along one wall.

Then someone knocked on the door of the toilet. There was a muffled shout.

'You in there?'

She stood still. She didn't answer. Seconds ticked by, dripping slow like the water from one of the taps.

Whoever it was didn't knock again.

She waited, looking at herself in the mirror. Her black silk shirt was surprisingly un-creased. If you didn't look too closely she could be mistaken for someone in the bank's IT Department. One of the less formal staffers.

Maybe, if she timed it right, as the guard was looking the other way, and if she was quiet, she could slip down to the fire exit and go up through the building.

The door to the corridor opened without a sound. Her breath was coming fast. Maybe that guard was walking back to the elevators. She had to look.

She put her head beyond the door.

There was no one in the corridor or at the elevators. She spun around. There were two doors between her and the red-brick wall at the end of the corridor. She walked fast. The first door was locked. She put her hand on the second door. It had a fire exit sign on it. It opened soundlessly.

Through the door there was a concrete stairwell. The stairs were dusty, abandoned-looking, framed by dull green iron hand rails that spiralled into the air. She looked up. The air was musty, yellowy. It was far colder than in the corridor too. She put on her jacket and started moving up the stairs, fast.

A distant muffled bang echoed from somewhere up above. At each level there was a door. The first two doors were locked. She got the impression that there was nothing behind these doors but concrete. Her hands were shaking with the cold now. Adrenaline had kept it from her mind for the first few flights of stairs, but now she couldn't avoid it.

It wasn't until the third floor up, about halfway to street level, she guessed, that she found a door that would open.

It creaked loudly. Her heart thumped hard as she pushed it.

67

Li headed for the elevator.

As the glass doors of the reception area closed behind him he heard the exhalation of breath from the American. The man probably expected to make the biggest killing of his life in the next few days. He probably also thought he was about to get one over on a stupid Chinese billionaire, even though two of Li's men had been in the man's offices for the past few days

Li smiled and pressed the blue back-lit basement button. Greed, that self-inflicted slavery, was the best motivator. It kept people tied to the wheel when most rational players had long ago departed. He rubbed a hand through his hair. There were other things to worry about now.

What was it the Americans called them, flies in the ointments? What a strange expression.

He thought about what his driver had just told him, and about the call he'd received from inside BXH. Li knew well the benefits of having people on the inside. He would have been dust a long time ago if he didn't. One call could be enough, he knew, to make the difference between him being caught red-handed or smiling in innocence, like the time the ICAC raided his office in Hong Kong.

This time he would not take any chances. The final words he'd said to the driver had made that clear.

'I want it all over with tonight. Tell that to Lord Bidoner.'

68

When she opened the door, the light from the fluorescent tube above Isabel's head spread out like a wave along the corridor in front of her. It had wooden and frosted glass partitions on each side. They extended into the darkness. She reached around the wall by the door and found a light switch.

When she turned it on a row of ancient frosted-glass circular light fittings lit up all along a panelled corridor to an elevator far in the distance. She walked towards the elevator. Was she crazy, trespassing like this? Halfway along the corridor there was a door in the partition on either side. She opened one. The entire space inside the room was taken up with brown metal filing cabinets. Each had a number, and each row of filing cabinets had a long yellow metal sign hanging above it, with more numbers on it.

It was like looking at the forgotten archives of a long-lost empire. She got a spooky tingling feeling all over. She went across the corridor. The other room was the same. But there was an area at the end of this room separated by frosty glass from the filing cabinets.

Presumably this was where anyone wanting to access files

would come, back in the old days, when they were still being used. How long ago was that?

A mahogany table at the top of the room had the word 'Supervisor' painted elaborately on it in yellow curly writing on a chunky piece of wood, as if someone might turn up at any moment to take up the post.

She said the word – Sean – but her voice simply echoed. He wasn't down here. She was just being stupid. She made her way back to the fire-exit stairs.

She was almost at the next floor walking up when she heard a noise from down below. She stopped.

There was someone coming.

Whoever it was, was still near the bottom, but was definitely coming up fast. The pressure inside her chest increased. She ran lightly up the next flight of stairs. She didn't want to be found, hauled away, thrown out of the building.

Thankfully, the door on the next floor opened. The pool of light from the stairs lit up a concrete open area stretching away in front of her. It looked as if everything had been stripped out of this space. She found a bare light switch and turned the lights on.

There was a line of large sarcophagus-like food freezers along one wall at the far end, near a single elevator door. There must have been ten freezers. This was probably where they kept the food for the CEO's executive dining suite or whatever dining facilities they had up above.

She ran across the concrete floor, her shoes slapping loudly. She almost stumbled at one point as her toe hit a ridge in the concrete, but she recovered. The noise of her feet echoed horribly around her. Would someone hear the commotion?

It was like being a runaway with dogs at her heels. Her breath was coming in gasps. She was swearing to herself.

The only light now, with the door to the stairs closed

behind her, was from the string of yellow bulbs running down the centre of the room, where the corridor should have been.

The brick-lined walls on either side were half in shadow. It appeared as if she was running across a concrete-floored plain, the type of thing you might see in a computer game.

She focused on the freezers. They were all a foot or two away from the wall on the right, as if whoever had put them there had wanted a gap behind them for some reason.

The nearest freezer was bigger than the others. It was one of those oversized ones you see in restaurant-based reality-TV programs. You could have kept a small European car in it. The others were half its size. From what she could see, as she ran up to them, they all had big locks on them, silvery steel locks the size of your fist. There wouldn't be any hiding in any of these freezers, even if she wanted to. She ran on, heading for the elevator.

The door was dented, but it had to work, didn't it? How else would anyone get down here to access these freezers? And then she saw a dark stain, which spread out onto the concrete from under the last freezer. It must be leaking, she thought.

As she came nearer, she saw the stain was dark red. It almost looked like blood. It was shiny too, as if it had a skin on it. And it seemed to be expanding.

She expected to smell something bad, but aside from a tinny smell, there was no other odour at all.

A giant cockroach scurried out of her path. It must have been three inches long. She slowed. The elevator was a few feet away.

She hit the call button. The light came on behind it. There was a distant rattling. Every muscle in her body relaxed. She would get away.

Then she saw them: two shoes visible behind the last freezer, sticking out. And she recognised the shoes. And she knew immediately that the stain ebbing out from under the freezer didn't mean that it was broken.

She walked towards it.

And she was floating.

Her mind was saying – *No, please, no.*

And then there was a noise. A door banging.

'Hey, stop right there.'

A man had come through the door from the stairwell at the far end of the basement. He was bald and wearing a buttoned navy-blue coat. It was the guy from Greg's apartment block. The guy who'd come after them.

A shiver of recognition passed down her body.

'Stop.'

Time slowed. She stared at him.

The man was running towards her, moving purposefully, head down. But still she had to look at what was behind the freezer.

There was a hammering in her brain, as if there was a crazed carpenter banging at her skull from the inside. She had to move to avoid the expanding pool of blood at the front of the freezer.

Iciness gripped at her chest. And then heat rushed through her body.

Detective Grainger was lying behind the freezer, oddly snug in the gap, her hands tight at her side. She was peaceful-looking, except for the gaping wound at her neck. It was seeping blood from a glistening slash.

And crawling over the detective's face were cockroaches.

Bile rose in her throat. She swallowed hard.

Could this be an accident?

Stop being stupid.

The elevator pinged loudly.

She took one last look. The gold wedding ring on Detective Grainger's hand sparkled.

She walked fast towards the open elevator. The warm flush that had passed over her was gone. All her muscles were trembling now. She was a drum that had been struck hard. Too hard.

She glanced over her shoulder. The man was near. His shouting echoed, almost unintelligibly. He had something in his hand. Something black.

It was either a taser, or a gun.

She stepped into the elevator. She had enough time.

Just.

She pressed the button.

Nothing happened. She didn't panic. Calm had taken over. Some calculating auto-pilot that knew just what to do. And all she had to do was stand there.

'STOP. Get out of that elevator.'

She could hear his feet slapping on the concrete. He was almost on her.

As the bald guy reached towards her his face contorted, all bulging blue veins and white eyes, as the doors closed with an uncaring glide.

Bang!

There was an explosion as he hit the metal. The doors buckled a little. They opened half an inch. A shadow loomed. She stepped back, her breath catching in her throat.

Then she was going up. And the banging was coming from below. And then it stopped. He'd probably got the doors open.

But she was gone.

She shivered violently. A torrent of anxiety was passing through her.

She bent down, could smell a lemony polish. She looked around. The inside of the elevator was a gleaming panelled-wood refuge. She leaned against the wall, crouching. It felt as if she'd just missed being hit by a truck.

She looked at the button she'd pressed. It was a middle button. Another one of the buttons had the words 'Post Room' beside it. Another, at the top, had the letter P beside it. Was that the penthouse?

She pressed the P, and straightened herself up. She had to look normal in case anyone else got in.

It wasn't going to be easy. An image of Detective Grainger's slumped body was still in her mind. A physical wave of revulsion passed through her. She shook, as if she was ill. She had to report this to Grainger's colleagues.

Who could have done this? She gripped her arms around herself.

And what about that bald guy? Was he involved in the murder? Then she imagined him contacting other people, getting them to intercept the elevator. But at least they wouldn't know which floor she was getting out on until the elevator stopped.

The elevator kept going up. She willed herself to calm down. Maybe he hadn't alerted anyone. But who the hell was he?

She was leaning against the back wall, staring at the doors, waiting for them to stop and for someone to be standing there. A disturbing flashback of Detective Grainger kept playing in her mind. Over and over.

She'd have to call the detective's colleagues, tell them what had happened, do something about her lying there. It wasn't right. All those cockroaches. Another wave of nausea ran through her. Poor woman. Just doing her job. She closed her eyes.

Would Sean get blamed for this too?

If the NYPD had been looking for him with their guns holstered, they'd certainly hold them in their hands after they heard about what had happened to one of their own.

The elevator stopped.

The doors opened, rattling at one point as if they were bent. She held her breath. She was looking into a dark corridor. Reflected lights from another building twinkled through a window at the far end.

Her mobile beeped. She pulled it out.

There was a voice message waiting for her.

69

The office in Whitehall was almost empty. Only four other staff members were monitoring news sites and video feeds.

Henry Mowlam and Major Finch were watching a security camera feed from the exterior of the BXH building in New York. It was three forty-five in the morning London time and ten forty-five in the evening in New York. The crowd outside BXH was getting bigger. And people were still arriving, which, given the weather, was a small miracle.

Then the camera view changed and Lexington Avenue appeared.

'You did leave a voice message for her, didn't you?' said Finch.

'I told her to contact me urgently. I couldn't have made it any clearer that we needed to speak to her,' said Henry.

'Good.'

'Why haven't we got internal access to the BXH building cameras?' said Henry.

'Ask the Prime Minister, Henry,' said Finch.

'I will, the next time I see him.'

'You keep an eye on things while I brief the others.' Finch gathered up the print-out they'd been arguing about and headed for the conference room, where two senior Bank of England executives were waiting, their heads close together, exchanging whispers.

Henry didn't mind that they were involved. It would relieve some pressure to know that the UK financial authorities were monitoring what was happening to BXH. Tens of thousands of UK employees would be directly impacted if anything happened to the bank. Henry didn't want to have to worry about that. He had other things to concern himself with.

The plan of the lowest level of the BXH building, and its likely significance as a location marker for a tomb of some type was what he'd been arguing with Finch about. He had convinced her not to tell anyone his pet theory yet, and he was glad of that victory.

Now he had to work out what they would do when Sean Ryan was captured, because he surely would be. The murder case was increasingly looking closed against him following his confession.

Whatever happened, it was likely that the US media would find out about the murdered dancer in London having a part of her skin cut off. That meant the internet would be alive with Satanist banker stories by Monday. The NYPD were notoriously leaky.

The question he had to think about now was which part of this nightmare had any significance for his ongoing investigation; the threat to the UK financial sector, the threat of a psycho murderer on the loose, or the fact that he'd located a square and arrow symbol tomb site, which it appeared Lord Bidoner was about to take control of.

And was there really something of significance in this symbol?

He turned to his screen. And where was Isabel Ryan? Why wasn't her phone on, and why hadn't she picked up her messages?

70

A UK number was calling her again, it couldn't be Sean as he was in America.

Whoever had called her would have to wait.

She gripped her forehead. The elevator doors pinged closed. It started moving up again. It felt as if the walls were closing in on her. She jabbed at her phone, called Sean.

Answer, please, answer.

A dizziness filled her.

If ever you're going to listen to me again, God, let it be now.

A message – the number you called is unavailable – was read out by an incongruously optimistic-sounding female voice. She slid down the wall. What the hell was going on?

She pushed herself back to her feet. She wasn't going to disintegrate. Not now. Not ever.

The light in the ceiling dimmed for a second. Then it came back, as if the building power had been cut off.

The elevator jerked, but kept going up.

She felt in her back pocket for the card Gus Reilly had given her. She should call him.

The elevator stopped. The door pinged open.

She was looking into a corridor with oak-panelled walls and polished side tables. This had to be the penthouse level. The depth of the shine on the wooden floor alone said that.

Then the heat hit her. The elevator had been cold. But this floor was heated enough to walk around in just your socks. She stood still, the skin on her face prickling, sure that some guard would appear at any moment.

Gold-framed Currier & Ives prints of old New York hung on the walls of the corridor. Yellow fake-looking marble pillars protruded from each side. A small crystal chandelier hung from the ceiling halfway along.

If he was in the building this was definitely where Sean would be. She could feel it. And the best thing was that there was no one waiting for her. No one in the corridor. She'd gotten away.

She stepped forward. The elevator pinged closed behind her. Then it hummed away. For a moment, as silence descended, she felt as if she was the only person in the building.

She waited and listened, trying to work out what to do. There was a deep rumbling from somewhere far below. She thought about Detective Grainger again. She had to call someone when she was finished up here. It shouldn't take long to check one floor.

She stepped forward. After the concrete floor below, the polished wooden floor felt like glass under her shoes. Her head was buzzing with the implications of what she'd just been through. Seeing Grainger's body had rattled her deeply. She had to be careful now. Very careful. Her heel squeaked on the floor. She stopped. There were two doors in the corridor, near where it opened into what she could already see was a high-ceilinged lobby.

She started walking again. Her pulse was throbbing in her

neck. As she came near the end of the corridor she heard a buzz of conversation. She stopped.

She'd heard a whirr.

She turned to her right and looked through a doorway. A two-foot-high stack of paper was feeding itself into a large shredding machine beside an office table. The machine was vibrating, quietly. A stream of shredded paper was falling into a giant white box, almost soundlessly.

She moved closer and looked into the room, trying to be quiet. There was no one in it. The stack of papers was sitting in a box on the floor and a feeder was whirring every few seconds, sucking in sheets one at a time. She was about to go when she noticed what was on the sheets. It was something familiar.

She went nearer the shredder.

Each of the sheets had a line drawing of the square and arrow symbol on it. And each of them had notes on it, as if someone had being trying to work out what the symbol meant and had printed out copies.

She stared at the sheets. Sean had been right. There was a connection between BXH and the book they had found in Istanbul. But what was it? What could connect a bank to a little known two-thousand-year-old symbol?

Then she heard something else.

It was a faint voice.

And it pulled her forward like a fish on a hook.

It was Sean's voice.

Oblivious to the throbbing in her chest, and feeling a sudden sense of vulnerability, she stepped out of the room through a door at the far end. She was in a double-height tomb-like lobby. A black marble staircase curved upwards in the centre. On the far side there was a large doorway. It was partly open. Sean's voice was coming from it.

'I did it. I killed her. Are you happy?' he said, loudly.

A sucking emptiness pulled at her. She was listening to her husband confessing to murder.

She pressed her hand into the pit of her stomach and headed towards his voice, a moth moving towards its destruction.

The double doors were in front of her. She could get through them without touching them.

She moved into the room, her sense of vulnerability overridden by her need to see Sean. The space was bigger than a tennis court. It had three high windows overlooking the twinkling lights of Manhattan. At the far end of the room the crackle of logs burning emanated from a giant fireplace.

Two people were standing in front of the fire, staring off and down to their right as if there was someone sitting there, out of sight. She walked towards them, moving almost silently, hoping to see Sean, yet afraid of what his words meant.

Mr Vaughann was one of the men. Fred Pilman, BXH's US Chief Executive, was the other.

She'd only seen him once before. But he wasn't the type of person you'd easily forget. He had silver hair, a square jaw and silver-rimmed glasses.

She kept walking. For a long moment she felt invisible.

Until Mr Pilman saw her. He raised an eyebrow, and touched Mr Vaughann's arm. Vaughann looked towards her, did a double take, and swayed backwards. He looked like someone who'd spied his worst enemy.

Her eyes scanned left and right as she went up the room. She had to walk around some ornate high-backed chairs.

Sean had to be sitting on one of those chairs, half-turned away from her. The pounding in her throat had reached her ears.

And then she saw what they were looking at.

71

Henry reached for his phone. It was time to call Isabel again. He looked up at the big white plastic clock on the end wall of the situation monitoring room. One more minute and he'd call her.

That would mean he'd be calling her exactly every fifteen minutes. You didn't want to frighten someone by calling every few minutes and it was best to have a pattern you could stick to. And report on.

He looked at his screen. The information about the movement of funds into the Ebony Dragon hedge fund was giving him real cause for concern. The original Chinese suitor for BXH was a bank controlled by a Mr Li. But that takeover had been cancelled.

But now Li's funds were being made available to the Ebony Dragon hedge fund, which was the preferred bidder to take over BXH. It would look like a Western fund was taking over the bank, but much of the money was still going to be Chinese.

It would be quite a coup, if Lord Bidoner pulled it off.

He pressed the call button on the phone. He waited.

Then, at last, her phone began ringing.

72

They were watching Sean on a small LCD TV. It was sitting on a low table near the wall on her right. On the screen Sean was holding his head, looking down. She felt a sharp tug of disappointment, followed by a warm rush of relief. This was just the same confession she'd already seen. It was a different bit of it, but it was still a recording, which could be doctored.

Her phone warbled. She pulled it from her pocket and switched it to vibrate. Someone in the UK was calling her again.

'How did you get up here?' said Pilman. His voice was weedy, but firm.

'Where's Sean?' she replied, her words tumbling out, as she put her phone back in her pocket.

'And what the hell's going on here?' She looked at the TV. It was silent now.

'You can't just walk in here,' said Vaughann, loudly. His tone was superior, gold-plated confidence. He pointed a remote control at the TV. It went blank.

Then he turned to her.

'This is a private floor.' He looked past her, as if he expected to see a guard behind her. 'I know your husband being missing is traumatic, but you are trespassing up here.'

‘I’m looking for Sean.’

‘Well, you can see he’s not here. Now you must go.’ Vaughann sounded angry.

That was good.

‘You have no idea where he is?’ She said it calmly, though every cell in her body felt raw.

‘That’s correct, Mrs Ryan. You need to look for him somewhere else.’

She jabbed a finger at Vaughann. It was shaking. ‘If Sean did anything wrong, I’m damn sure it was because of BXH. There’s something very odd going on here. Or maybe you’re shredding all those documents for no reason.’

Vaughann shook his head. ‘We shred all unnecessary documents every week, Mrs Ryan. It doesn’t mean anything.’

She raised her eyebrow. ‘Yeah, right.’

‘You must leave,’ he said. He waved at her, dismissing her. Then he sneered.

‘Go away. You are trespassing.’ His voice was raised. She was a piece of dirt he wanted removed.

He stepped towards her, put a hand on her upper arm, gripped her and pushed to get her to go.

Something flipped inside her. Anger rose. She couldn’t control it. She spun, rage slipping loose from its reins and hit his cheek, hard, in a backhanded gesture.

He cried out in a high-pitched moan.

The blow had reverberated into the bones of her hand and wrist. There was a horrible moment of sudden regret when she thought he was going to push her back or maybe even hit her. But she stood her ground.

And he stepped back, even though he was a lot taller than her. One hand went to his cheek. The smell of his aftershave was in her nostrils.

‘You deserved that,’ she said. She was shaking.

She pointed at him. ‘Don’t touch me again. Ever.’

Vaughann was rubbing his face. His eyes had narrowed. He stared at her with undisguised malevolence.

Pilman came towards them. His hands were high in the air, as if he wanted a truce.

'Mrs Ryan, we just want you to leave. Mr Vaughann will not touch you again.' He put a hand on Vaughann's shoulder, pushed him gently to the side.

Then he smiled at her, as if he was trying to sell her something.

She was trembling.

'I am sorry that he touched you. My colleague is under a lot of pressure.' His eyes flickered over her shoulder.

She glanced behind her. Standing by the door was a security guard. She could feel the blood moving out of her face, a weakness in her knees. But at least it wasn't the bald guy she'd seen earlier.

'You can leave this to us,' said Pilman, loudly. Her turned to her. 'We know Mrs Ryan.'

Vaughann looked pissed off. His facial muscles bulged, as if he was physically restraining himself.

The trembling inside her slowed. She gave Vaughann a crooked smile. The guard turned on his heel and left the room.

'Detective Grainger is dead,' she said.

'We heard the news a few minutes ago,' Pilman replied 'It's been a terrible shock. Absolutely awful. Apparently every free NYPD officer in midtown has been called to this building. We've never had anything like it. We haven't had a serious criminal investigation here for twenty years. This building is going to be swarming with officers soon, all looking for your husband, Mrs Ryan. That's what all this is about.' He stared at her.

She got the impression he was almost blaming her for it all.

'Sean isn't a murderer,' she said. Her voice came out high-pitched.

'Yeah, right,' said Vaughann. He had straightened his expression. He looked unruffled now, though she was sure he wouldn't easily forget what she'd done. But she was still glad she'd slapped him.

'You're not going to frame him.' She was trying not to shout, but her head was buzzing. She took a deep breath, making a conscious effort to slow her breathing.

'Some people just snap, Mrs Ryan. You have to accept that. His confession is damning,' said Pilman. He sounded concerned at her refusal to face facts.

Vaughann was staring at her. You could have bottled his contempt, sold it as an anti-personnel device.

'Someone came running at me down there. He looked very strange.'

Vaughann looked as if he doubted everything she said.

'You must explain everything that's happened to you to the police, Mrs Ryan. We'll see to it that Sean gets a good lawyer here, though we don't have to,' said Pilman.

Isabel saw a silver pot of coffee on a warmer with some gold-rimmed cups and saucers on a mahogany table near the window. She walked towards it. Her legs felt shaky. She had to get some caffeine into her. She didn't ask for permission, she just poured herself a cup.

They were whispering to each other when she turned around.

'Sean knew a lot about BXH, didn't he?' She gripped the cup firmly. The coffee was lukewarm, but good, damn good. She drank almost the whole cup in one gulp.

Then she walked over to where they were standing, in front of the low table.

'Why are you watching Sean's confession?'

'We're still getting used to having an employee confess to murder,' said Vaughann.

She put her empty cup down. Behind the coffee table, there

was a door with square panels of sparkling leaded glass. The glass was tinged yellow, like the ornately patterned wallpaper, which covered the walls with intertwined flowers. The door looked as if it might lead out to a balcony. Should she be looking around, doing what she'd come up here to do?

'You have a balcony?' she said.

'Your husband isn't out there,' said Vaughann.

'Why don't you show Mrs Ryan our terrace,' said Pilman. He clearly thought he was dealing with a slow child.

Vaughann took a brass key from a hook behind the yellow brocade curtain at the side of the door and unlocked the balcony. A wild blast of icy air and snow rushed into the room as he pushed the door open.

She stepped back, acutely aware of her vulnerability again. Freezing air poured in. The balcony was small, stone floored, but big enough maybe for a coffee table and a few chairs in the summer.

It was a place of demons in winter. She could see gargoyles along the high outside edge of the balcony. The freezing wind had a lot of snowflakes in it too. And there was something rattling out there. She didn't want to go out. She'd seen enough.

Vaughann smiled and locked the door. She glanced around. She was wasting her time.

'I'd have imagined a woman like you would know when to cut her losses,' said Pilman.

'I'm full of surprises.' She was standing by the marble table now. One of her knees was pressing into it. It felt cold through her trousers, despite the heat in the room.

'Your support for your husband is truly touching, really it is,' said Pilman.

He sat on an armchair covered in patterned cream silk. Every piece of furniture in the room looked as if it could have been in a museum or an art gallery.

'Don't you think it's time you got some sleep?' said Pilman. 'You look shattered.'

Vaughann's eyes bulged. He looked to be getting angrier. Was she keeping them from something? Good.

'You have no idea what's going on tonight, do you?' said Vaughann. 'You are incredibly lucky we have given you so much time, Mrs Ryan. I wouldn't be as understanding as Mr Pilman. You should know that he took a call from the President of the United States this evening. Millions of people will be affected by what is happening to BXH. So, I am afraid you will have to leave. We have things to do. Important things.'

'I hope you told the President about the billions you've wasted.'

Vaughann took a step towards her.

Pilman put his hands up. 'Please, both of you. I want this to end amicably.' He paused, gave her that dead salesman's smile again.

'I'm sure BXH will be willing to compensate you for your distress.' He gave her a lips-pressed-together smile. 'I'll get our legal team to draft something up.'

It sounded as if she was being asked to drink poison. She'd probably be bound by some secrecy clause until well after she died.

There was a chill deep in her stomach. Her anger rested with it, twisting at her gut. She could hear the wind pressing against the windows. It sounded as if something was scratching at the glass.

'I don't want compensation. I'm not one of your underlings.'

Pilman sat on the nearest sofa. He leaned back, making himself comfortable. It looked as if he'd resigned himself to her taking her time before leaving.

An elaborate gold clock on the mantelpiece chimed. It was two feet high and had little gold figures and an ivory face.

'I'll call Gus Reilly,' said Vaughann. 'I expect he wants to talk to you.'

That was the moment her phone rang again. She answered it this time. There had to be a good reason for someone to keep calling her in the middle of the night.

She walked towards the window and turned her back on Vaughann and Pilman.

A minute later she had to sit down on a high-backed seat. A rush of emotion threatened to overwhelm her. She held the arms of the chair tight. She knew Henry Mowlam from when he'd visited them in London, but she'd never expected to be called by him in the middle of the night with such news.

Such shocking news. She pressed the phone to her ear as if it was her lifeline.

73

Henry Mowlam held the phone tight to his ear. He had just told Isabel Ryan that her son, Alek, was missing.

He hated such moments. He had only informed two other people that their loved ones had disappeared, but each time it had been unnerving and very unpleasant.

'Mrs Ryan, there is more I need to tell you. Are you sitting down?'

'Just tell me,' she replied.

She was tougher than he expected. Her Foreign Office training kicking in, no doubt.

'You are in danger. We advise that you come back to the UK as soon as possible.'

'How am I in danger?'

'You know your husband has confessed to a murder, yes?' said Henry.

There was a hesitation, then she said, 'Yes, and I don't believe it.'

'There is more going on that I can't tell you, Mrs Ryan. All I can say is that there's a connection between BXH and what happened to you in Jerusalem and Istanbul.'

'What connection?' she said, quickly.

'Your husband may have been involved in what happened in each of those cities.'

He couldn't tell her about finding the square and arrow symbol in the BXH building. He didn't want her any more involved than she already was. The screen in front of him was showing the current coordinates of the mobile phone he was calling, overlaid on a map of Manhattan.

She was in the BXH building.

The last thing he wanted her to do was start digging around looking for where her husband might be hiding. But he had to make her realise she was in danger.

There was a pause. 'I'll try to get back on an earlier flight. Please, do absolutely everything you can to find Alek.' Her voice cracked. 'Everything.'

'We are looking everywhere, Mrs Ryan. We won't let up until we do find him. You can be sure of that. Call me as soon as you touch down in England.'

'I will.' The line went dead.

He closed his eyes. Hopefully he had intervened in time and had told her enough, but not too much.

74

She gripped her arms around herself, then slowly relaxed them. Images of Alek raced through her mind. Fear for him and a feeling that she was falling were pulling at her, sucking her down into a hole of terror and anxiety.

She felt as if she was going mad with it. There was too much going on for her to take it all in.

She shook her head. She had to stay sane. Stay focused. She had to. For Alek's sake. And Sean's.

She opened her eyes. Pilman and Vaughann were talking at the far end of the room. There was something black poking out from under the sofa Pilman had been sitting on. It was a briefcase. She stared at it, walked in slow motion towards it. Was that Sean's briefcase?

She bent down.

Yes, it was.

A sense of recognition and surprise came over her.

She reached down, slid the briefcase out and took it to the marble coffee table.

'Your husband was up here first thing this morning,' said Pilman, as he came towards here. 'I think that may be his.'

She was sure it was Sean's. They'd bought it in Harrods the previous Christmas. It had been her present to him. It had brass locks, a thick leather handle and some new shock absorbent padding inside for a slim laptop. Modern traditional they'd called it.

'It is. I gave it to him,' she said. She zipped it open.

Inside was Sean's usual collection of items he needed for meetings. There was a navy-blue notebook, a selection of pens, a white cable for recharging his phone, earphones, business cards, some airline face wipes, some BXH documents in a folder, his Sony laptop.

His laptop was upside down and the cables were strewn over it. That wasn't like him. She heard a cough behind her, someone moving. She didn't look around.

She pulled the laptop out quickly.

'I don't think you should be starting that up,' said Pilman. He was standing over her.

'This belongs to my husband,' she said, angrily. 'I have every right to do this.' Alek was missing and he wanted to stop her accessing Sean's laptop?

'I'd prefer if you didn't start that up. Please don't make this unpleasant.'

Fuck him.

Could she remember Sean's password, that was the next question? God, she was tired. She closed her eyes. Images of Alek being held somewhere, as she had been in Jerusalem, filled her mind.

My God, who would take a child? She shuddered.

Yes, she remembered the password. It was the same as the one she'd used in London.

Would he have changed it without telling her?

She tried it.

Vaughann was standing over her as well now. 'That's BXH's property.' He was bending down towards her.

'No, it's not. It's my husband's property.' She looked up at him. She had to keep him away, just for a few minutes.

'Don't touch it or me. Unless you want to be accused of sexual assault, Mr Vaughann.'

He snorted. 'No one's going to believe you, take your word over mine.' He reached down towards the laptop. 'Move away, now.'

Isabel raised her hand, as if she was going to slap him. He made an exasperated noise, straightened up, headed quickly for the main door of the room. She wouldn't have that much time.

'What do you expect to find?' said Pilman.

She didn't want to tell him that she had no idea, but that she knew where to look if there was anything of interest on any computer.

She opened the Windows recycle bin. There was nothing there. Then she used a utility to open up files that had been deleted recently and hadn't been overwritten yet.

One of them was a document called The Likely Impact of Superfast Facial Recognition on Crime, Tax Evasion and Political Corruption. Another was an exciting memo about the Institute Christmas party.

Was there anything else? Was there anything that might help her find Alek?

She scanned the temporary file list.

Pilman coughed.

'Why don't you take the compensation, Mrs Ryan? Things might get very difficult if your husband isn't the family breadwinner any more. You should consider your future.'

Outlook folders. That was the next place to look.

She looked in the inbox, the deleted box and even in Sean's personal email box. She scanned the emails that had come in on Thursday and Friday or had been deleted on either day. It was all routine stuff.

What next? Come on.

Browsing history.

She looked for the history file. It had been deleted.

But there was another way to find a record of the websites Sean had recently visited.

Vaughann was standing right on top of her again. She could see his shoes, feel his presence. She kept looking at the screen. Her muscles tensed. If he tried to take the laptop, she would have to hit him, again. Harder this time.

'I've spoken to Gus Reilly. He's asked me to confiscate any computer equipment up here.' He reached down. 'He will be here any minute.' He had his hand near the laptop's lid.

His superior tone was irritating.

She slapped at him. He pulled his arm away, but too late. She connected with the back of his hand.

'I told you to stay away from me. I will scream rape. And I will press charges.' She didn't look up. Her heart was pounding. Her tone was fierce.

He stepped back.

'You'll regret this,' he said.

She could feel the animosity coming off him. She kept staring at the screen. The third website on the list sent her head into a deep tailspin. It was the website for the strip club in London. Sean had viewed two pages on the site.

It could have been just curiosity or was she still being stupid? The next website was the *Optical Science Journal*'s news section. Then he'd gone to the website for some obscure hedge fund she'd never heard of. She clicked through to the site. They had a webpage that said almost nothing.

Another site he'd gone to was a history of Grand Central station. Had he visited it because he was coming here for the weekend? She clicked the link.

The page he'd been looking at was about a depression-era

private train platform connected to the station. The page featured plans of tunnels connecting the platform to Grand Central and the old post office building next door to BXH, and an explanation of how important the post office had been to the war effort.

What the hell had that got to do with anything?

After that on the list there were a few sites about Paris. One was for a lingerie shop. Another had the opening times of the Louvre. Her heart lifted. He'd been thinking about their trip.

Then there were some pages from the SEC's website about various regulations. One was a page about money laundering and ID checks. That was as far as she got.

'Hey,' a voice called out, in a tone sharp enough to cut the head of a chicken. 'Get away from that laptop.'

She had to keep looking.

She could hear footsteps. She tapped at the keyboard. A second later it started closing.

'What are you doing, tampering with evidence?'

She looked up.

Gus Reilly was closing the keyboard. Her fingers were a second away from being trapped. She pulled them back and smiled up at him. She wasn't going to snap at someone who worked for the New York District Attorney's Office. She wasn't that stupid.

He closed the laptop, picked it up, pulled the plug out, put the laptop under his arm.

'This is evidence in an investigation. I sure hope you haven't deleted anything.'

She pushed herself to her feet. She had pins and needles in both calves. Her head was still pounding and her stomach felt as if she'd eaten something bad.

'Why would I do that? I haven't done anything wrong.'

He made a balloon-exploding noise. 'Paaaah. Yeah, right.

What about trespassing? That's what the NYPD are talking about charging you with for starters. We can lock you up any time.' His face was red, his cheeks bulging.

'I'm trying to find my husband.' Her voice was raised.

'Right, and what you are gonna do now is come downstairs, and make a statement.' He reached towards her, as if he was going to grab her.

She put both hands up. 'Okay, I'm coming. You don't have to manhandle me.'

He looked at Pilman, then at Vaughann. 'You gentlemen all right?'

'Thank you, Mr Reilly. The District Attorney's office is doing a great job,' said Pilman.

Gus motioned for her to come with him.

She didn't look back. In the corridor she said, 'How come they're not under investigation?'

'One thing at a time, Mrs Ryan. Let's deal with your statement first.'

He led her to the main elevators, not to the service elevator she'd come up in.

'Don't think I don't know what you're up to,' he said, as the elevator doors opened.

'What am I up to?' The doors closed behind them.

'Covering up for your husband. And you better understand this, if you've deleted anything at all on his laptop I'm gonna know about it. And on another matter, what were you doing down in the basement?'

'I was looking for Sean. I found Detective Grainger's body.'

'I hope you're not involved in that. That is monstrous what happened to her.' He stared at her, as if watching for her reactions.

'It makes me sick too.'

He looked at the light indicating the floors they were passing.

Isabel had to look down. She felt dizzy. Was Alek okay? Could she do anything to help him?

The elevator stopped on the forty-ninth floor.

Reilly said nothing else until they were in a large meeting room. It had been taken over by a swarm of uniformed police officers, security guards, men and women with badges she didn't recognise.

She was glimpsing the reality of what happens when a police officer is shot. She heard Sean's name three times in less than a minute in that room, and she couldn't even make out what the rest of those conversations were about. It was all a jumble.

She tightened her arms around herself.

'What is the DA's office investigating at BXH?' she said, as Gus Reilly sat down at the head of the shiny black conference table, which dominated the long thickly carpeted meeting room.

'That's all confidential,' he said. 'Sit down, Mrs Ryan. I've got some questions that need answers. And there's a couple of other officers who want a word with you too.'

She sat on the steel and black leather chair beside him and leaned on its armrest.

Nobody was paying any attention to them.

Two young officers, a blonde girl and a tall black officer with gold epaulettes were poring over a set of layout diagrams at the far end of the table. Other people were talking into walkie-talkies or in huddles with colleagues. There must have been fifteen people in the room.

A side table with an antique silver coffee pot and a teapot on a silver tray stood nearby. They looked like items you'd find at Tiffany's.

'Have you been read your rights, Mrs Ryan?'

'Yes,' she replied.

'Have you seen your husband since I saw you last, Mrs Ryan?' Reilly spoke fast, as if he had a lot to do.

'No.'

'What were you looking for on his laptop?'

'A clue for where I might find him.'

'Did you find anything?'

'No.' She stared into his eyes.

His narrowed. 'Are you aware of the investigations the DA's office has been carrying out into BXH?'

She shook her head and leaned forward. 'Is it something to do with the facial recognition software?'

He hitched his trousers up at the side, gave her a knowing look and answered her with a question. 'Did your husband say anything at all about investigations into BXH?'

'No. He's based in London, anyway. Are you investigating the bank there?'

His eyes darted around the room. 'You want some advice, Mrs Ryan?' He turned back to her.

She didn't answer.

'Now I'm only going to say this once.' He sat back, spreading himself onto the armrests of his chair.

'It's as clear as day to me that your husband is guilty as hell, and that he's a murderer.'

She blinked and stared into his watery-blue eyes. It was a weird sensation, hearing someone say that your husband was a murderer, as if he was talking about a parking offence.

'It's not going to be easy to accept that, Mr Reilly.' Her voice sounded as if it was coming from someone far away.

'Sure, I know you don't want to think bad of the guy you married, but you gotta wake up, smell the coffee.'

He was shaking his head slowly. 'You know we got the Metropolitan Police from London sending us over an international arrest warrant and an extradition request any second now.' He paused for effect.

'And I got NYPD officers over there,' he jerked his thumb

towards the other end of the table, 'who are a thousand per cent convinced your husband murdered their colleague.' He leaned forward. 'And mine.'

She could smell his sweat, and a hint of beer. He'd probably been watching a game when he'd been interrupted to come in to BXH.

A wiry, black-haired, uniformed police officer came over to them. He put his hands on his hips and looked down at her. The label under the badge on his left breast read GONZALES.

'You Sean Ryan's wife?'

She nodded.

He raised his eyebrows and turned to Reilly.

'Sergeant wants to know if we can take over.'

Gus Reilly looked at his watch and shook his head.

'I got five more minutes. Your Sergeant agreed to that.'

Officer Gonzales stared at Reilly, as if he wanted him to melt under his gaze. When he didn't, Gonzales turned, went away.

'I don't even know all the people your husband has pissed off.' Reilly leaned towards her. 'And I don't want to know, but if I were you I'd answer each question those officers ask you with the maximum cooperation.' He looked over his shoulder at the retreating officer.

Then he moved his chair closer to her. 'You ain't been in a holding cell with prostitutes and murderers before, have you?'

Isabel leaned towards him. 'My son is missing, Mr Reilly. And my husband is wanted for murder. I honestly don't think anything will shock me any more. But I will fight back if anyone tries to lock me up for no good reason. No one with an ounce of humanity would do that.'

75

The windows of Lord Bidoner's apartment reflected the light from the black candle on the long coffee table. The flame twisted in each section of glass, as if a row of candles had been lit. Outside, the snow was rushing into the windows high above Fifth Avenue, as if it might find a purchase on itself and build a wall against the skyscraper.

'We will not talk again, Doctor Lomas. My colleague will drop the DNA sample into your offices on Monday. The cloning process will be entirely in your hands. I have been told your laboratory is equipped and capable. The final payment will be sent to your Swiss bank account when you have confirmed the identity of the individual inseminated.'

Lord Bidoner turned his swivelling leather chair away from the wall of glass and held the phone closer to his ear.

The doctor's voice came through a little crackled, thanks to the voice encryption app he was using, but it was still clear.

'There will be no contact from anyone else? That's it?' said the doctor.

'We will require a DNA sample once the child is born,'

said Bidoner. He sighed. 'And we will find you if it doesn't match the sample we provide. Do I make myself clear?'

'Crystal,' said the doctor. Then he coughed. 'Is it your DNA we will be cloning, sir?'

Lord Bidoner stared at the candle in front of him. He moved the palm of his hand over it, tasted the pain, let his skin linger on it.

'I cannot answer that question. I was told that you could do this and that a ten-million-dollar donation would ensure your permanent silence. Do you have a problem sticking to this agreement?'

'No, sir.'

'Good. The DNA sample should be treated with great care, doctor, as if your life depended on it.'

He closed the line and stared at the falling snow. He was being optimistic, he knew, that he would find the DNA sample in the BXH building, but it was an optimism born of verifiable evidence. The artefact they were looking for, and its secret chamber, were mentioned on the Nestorian Stele, the first record of Christianity in China, from the year AD 781.

A later manuscript described what the secret chamber contained; a much-sought relic, with visible traces of the blood of Iisus Hristos 伊伊穌斯·合利斯托斯.

Chinese monks had hidden the documents for centuries and the Communists had tried to find them and destroy them, but they hadn't succeeded. And after paying for access to them he had gone to extraordinary lengths to verify the truth of what these records showed.

The search for a true relic of Christ, his blood or a lock of his hair, had been a matter of religious faith up until the latest DNA cloning techniques had been developed.

But now it would be the story of how science brought about the second coming. And this time He would come as a man of power. And He would rule the world as it should be ruled, with a clenched fist, as He would be trained to do.

The change was coming. And with a leader people could have total faith in no one would dare resist. Every religion that had accepted Jesus as a prophet or a Messiah would have to bow before the new order. Popes and imams would kneel before them with their flocks coming in behind them.

And around the Second Christ, Lord Bidoner and his friends would plan the future of humanity.

He turned away from the window and smiled. The destiny of all who lived and all who were to come would be determined in the next few hours. And he would be at the centre of it.

Xena was sitting on the long sofa. She was watching something on a tablet. Her hand was moving fast across the screen.

His investment in her had been the best move he had made in a long time. Her willingness to kill without remorse was a quality few possessed.

Not many had the courage to act upon that most true of sayings, *the end justifies the means*.

There was a thin knife on the leather seat beside her. It was small enough for her to hide almost anywhere, yet big enough to kill with precision.

'It is time,' he said.

Xena didn't smile. She simply picked up the knife and stood.

They headed for the panic room.

76

'I didn't know your son was missing. What happened?' said Reilly.

Isabel told him what Henry Mowlam had told her.

He whistled. 'He thinks it's got something to do with your husband's disappearance?'

She nodded. 'I'm scared, Mr Reilly, but not of my husband.'

'What d'ya mean?'

She leaned towards him. 'I saw a guy who was following me earlier. He was in the basement here at BXH an hour ago. He ran at me as if he wanted to kill me. He was dressed like a security guard.'

'Can you describe him?'

'Tall, bald, I'd know him if I saw him again. Please think about it, Mr Reilly. That video confession is too convenient.'

He stared at her, his eyelids drooping.

'We have ID details of all the guards in the building. I'll get someone to run photos by you.'

She shook her head. She put a hand out to him.

'Can I go back to my hotel? I need to book an earlier flight back to London. I have to be there. Alek is missing. Do you have children, Mr Reilly?'

He stared at her. 'The NYPD want you for questioning.'

She sat up straight and nodded. Then she looked away. A wave of emotion was rising inside her after talking about Alek. She sniffed, held it back.

An older woman, a heavyset New York bleached blonde, with girder-like shoulders, came over to Reilly, and tapped his shoulder.

He didn't turn around. 'Whad'a ya want?'

'I got a problem, sir.' She had no badge on her pinstriped suit.

He shrugged. 'What's up?'

She came around and stood at his side. She was eyeing Isabel as if she might be dangerous.

Then she looked at Gus, an exaggerated questioning expression on her face.

He nodded, almost imperceptibly. 'Go ahead,' he said.

She bent down and whispered loudly, 'I'm getting zero cooperation. Just some bullshit stories about us needing a court order.' Her gaze flickered towards the other end of the room.

Dick Owen was down there, in a huddle with two other tall, thin men in suits. They looked exactly how you'd imagine Securities and Exchange Commission people to look like; serious nerds.

As she watched, Owen moved away from his colleagues, walked towards the double doors at the far end of the room and stood there as if he was talking to someone. She had to lean sideways to get a glimpse of who it was.

Reilly said something. She didn't catch it.

Mrs Vaughann was standing in the doorway.

She was looking at Owen. He was waving his hands, as if explaining something.

She felt a heady rush. Mrs Vaughann might be able to help her, explain to the NYPD how she'd been looking for Sean since yesterday.

She might help her get away from them.

Mrs Vaughann looked in her direction. So did Owen. Isabel waved at her. Mrs Vaughann's hand came up, in a half wave. Then Owen said something to her. She turned on her heel, disappeared. Isabel thought about shouting her name, but Mrs Vaughann was gone.

'I need to see the lady who was just over there,' she said. She pointed at the far end of the room.

'You can see whoever you like when we're finished with you,' said Reilly, without turning to see who she was pointing at.

She gripped her arms tighter around herself and bit into her lip. How long was all this going to take? There was a laptop screen further up the table. It was half turned towards her. There were two images side by side on the screen.

It took at least two seconds for her to recognise the close-up picture of Detective Grainger's face and, beside that, the face of what must have been that poor dancer from that stupid club in London.

Both of them had bloodsplatters on their faces. Both had their eyes open and were staring as if shocked by their own death.

A pounding in her chest was affecting her throat, tightening it. Then a tingling in her fingers made her rub her hands together. She rocked in her chair. Whoever had done that had to be capable of doing the same thing to anyone else. To Alek. There was a creeping cold moving inside her.

'Mrs Ryan.' Gus Reilly had a hand on her arm.

He was looking around, as if trying to work out what she'd been staring at. Then his hand gripped her arm tighter. She felt the veins in her arm throbbing under his grip.

'Do you know if your husband reported BXH for breaking

UK money laundering regulations earlier this year?' His tone was soft. He let go of her.

'I have no idea.'

'Has he ever reported them for anything?'

'Not that I know.'

'Have you ever known him to be violent?'

'No.' She felt a flush on her cheeks. Was she being honest? What about that episode when he'd held her shoulder? She clamped her lips together.

Reilly rubbed his chin. He looked troubled.

'My son is missing,' she said, softly. Her voice broke, catching in her throat. 'I need to get this over with.'

He looked at her, as if he was examining an unusual specimen. 'Why don't you just give up on your husband?'

'I believe in him.' Loyalty had been drummed into her as a child. It was impossible to give up. 'Please, let me go. I have to book a new flight.'

Reilly let out his breath in an exasperated stream.

'Okay, you just hold on. I'll see what I can do.' He stood, headed towards the other end of the room without a backwards glance.

She looked around.

No one was looking at her.

The door at that end of the room was only ten feet away.

This was her chance. It had to be.

A vein in her chest, under her arm, started beating. She didn't turn her head. She stood, headed for the door. This was not what Reilly meant by holding on, she was reasonably sure of that, but it was what she had to do.

A voice in her head was shouting, *don't do it*.

But she wasn't going to listen.

There were uniformed officers in the hall. One was leaning against the wall. He was talking to a shorter officer who was shaking his head. The shorter one stared at her as she passed. Isabel was sure he was going to say something to her.

'It's gotta be three feet thick at least, the concrete down there,' said the officer with his hand on the wall. His accent was a thick New York growl, like something from an old movie.

She didn't hear any more.

And she didn't stop.

Her feet were moving her automatically. She had to tell them not to run. They wanted to. She was sure everyone would spot her guilty face, notice that her veins were throbbing.

But no one did.

So she kept walking. Where was Mrs Vaughann? What had those officers been talking about? Were they looking for Sean?

The elevator wasn't far away. All she had to do was pass the other open door of the conference room.

She heard a shout and nearly jumped out of her skin. But it wasn't her name that had been shouted. And she was near the elevators.

There were two uniformed NYPD officers standing in front of the elevator doors. They were talking to two women waiting there, tapping away at handheld screens at the same time. Were they logging people in and out of the floor?

What about the other corridor? The one that led to that service elevator. She headed across the lobby area in front of the elevators and went straight towards the other corridor, as if that was where she was going all along.

There were three NYPD officers near the service elevator. They looked as if they were waiting for it to arrive. They all had their backs to her, but they would definitely all turn as soon as they heard her coming up behind them.

Was she crazy even thinking she could move around this building, avoiding all these police officers? And any second now a shout would go up behind her from Gus Reilly. The throbbing in her chest was pounding faster now. And her scalp was tingling.

You're totally crazy, Isabel.

And then she saw the words FIRE ESCAPE on a door. The letters were almost the same colour as the door. She'd nearly missed them.

And then one of the officers turned. He was tall, black-haired, like a young Clint Eastwood. He gave her a wide smile. She smiled back at him. They were ten feet apart.

She reached the fire exit door, pushed at it. It opened.

She let it close behind her and stood waiting, her breathing way too fast.

But the door didn't open behind her. No one came after her. Again, she felt as if a truck had passed her by within inches.

The stairs were laid with black tiles, like an expensive bathroom. The roof and walls were painted black up here too. And the lighting was thin LED strips. She headed down.

As she reached the next landing she heard voices far below. She peeked over the edge of the stairs. People were coming up. The vein in her chest went into double time.

She had to get off the stairs.

She pushed the door on the landing open, closing it gently behind her. The spill of light from the door had been enough for her to see the corridor and an elevator door further along. Each floor had a similar layout, though it would have been a lot better if this one had had its lights on, like the floor above.

She stood in the darkness, listening. All she could hear was a faint hissing. And for one sickening moment she imagined some animal lying in wait, until she convinced herself that it had to be the noise of a Xerox machine or some other piece of equipment that hadn't been switched off.

She felt along the wall for a light switch. There had to be one.

The darkness was almost complete now. A thin strip of light under the door to the fire exit was the only illumination she could see. This floor felt way colder than the one above too. It wasn't freezing, but it wasn't far off. There was a slight chemical smell in the air as well, as if the carpets had been cleaned recently.

She got a sudden flashback to the time she'd spent in that cave in Israel. There had been insects there. She could almost feel the scorpions walking over her again, see their red eyes in the darkness.

She pressed her fist to her forehead. There weren't any scorpions in New York.

Suddenly, she felt an urge to go back, to throw herself at the mercies of the NYPD.

At least she'd be safe.

She held her fist in front of her, ready to hit out.

She felt a slight breeze on her fingers, then on her face. Her skin tightened. She stopped, waited, waited some more, then took a small step forward.

This was one of the empty floors Sean had told her all about, the result of all those thousands of people who'd been laid off over the past few years, after the financial crisis.

Every office and division had ended up like a war zone, he'd said, with their own casualty stories about people who'd never made it back from meetings with senior managers.

Then she saw the faint gleam of the elevator doors and heard a rattle as it passed. It didn't stop. She reached around for the elevator button, feeling the wall in giant circles. She found it. It lit up when she pressed it.

77

Gus Reilly's cell phone was warbling. He was on his way back to see Isabel Ryan. He'd spoken to the sergeant who wanted to interview her. The man was in no mood for compromise.

'Reilly here,' he said, into the phone.

'You gotta get back down here, now,' said a voice. 'And bring every officer up there with you. We got a full scale riot going down. If we're not careful we're gonna lose this goddamned building!'

It was the desk sergeant he'd just been with in the foyer.

'What about your officers outside?'

'Some idiot called them away.'

He could hear shouts in the background. The sound of glass breaking.

'What the fuck happened?'

'Someone turned the goddamned BXH ATM machines off!'

A uniformed officer rushed past him, heading for the elevator. Reilly followed him.

Isabel Ryan would have to wait.

78

The elevator lurched. The sick feeling in her stomach was settling in deeper with each floor she went down. An image of Detective Grainger and the cockroaches had come into her mind. She coughed, bent over and dry retched. The acid lingered in her throat. It felt as if she was descending into some haunted basement.

With a ping, the elevator stopped.

The doors slid open.

There was no one in the well-lit corridor in front of her. No murderer. No welcoming committee of policemen. That had to mean the NYPD were breaking through concrete somewhere else, on one of the unused floors.

She stepped out into the corridor. There was a plaque on the wall high up to her left. It was wooden, faded. It looked as if it had been there since the building had been constructed.

It read: PRESIDENT GEORGE WASHINGTON SPENT THE NIGHT BEFORE HIS INAUGURATION, APRIL 29 1789, AT THE FREE MASONS ARMS ON THIS SITE. THE FOUNDATION WALL BENEATH THIS PLAQUE WAS PART OF THAT BUILDING. *APRIL 29 1933. GOD BLESS AMERICA.*

A low grinding noise filled the air. It sounded as if it was coming from the walls. She moved forward, past a double-width doorway. A sign on it read DRAINAGE PLANT.

She kept walking. The next door had the words GENERAL POST on it. It was locked. The corridor was way longer than any of the corridors she'd seen up above.

The light was different down here too, more yellowy. And it flickered occasionally, sending shadows shimmying across the walls, trembling in time to the grinding from the drainage plant room.

And the lights here were on the wall, not on the roof. They were old gas-lamp-style bulbs, which looked as if they had only recently been converted to electricity.

There were boxes at the end of the corridor.

But someone had left just enough room between the boxes and the wall on the right to squeeze past them. She peered beyond the boxes. There was a red steel door back there.

That meant she was right.

It was exactly what she was looking for. The article Sean had been reading on that website had shown the tunnels connecting the old Grand Central Post Office that originally stood next door, to the underground tracks connecting into Grand Central.

When she'd seen the page on his laptop in the penthouse she'd wondered why he was looking at it. And then it had dawned on her. If you want to find Sean, go wherever he's been interested in.

She squeezed into the gap. She could smell damp paper, and something less pleasant, as if an animal had been peeing down here. It wouldn't be easy to get away if she had to get out of here fast.

But she had to see if the door would open.

There was a foot-wide gap between it and the last of the boxes. She touched the door handle. The door was locked, the handle chillingly cold. For a second she thought her fingers might stick to the steel handle, but they didn't.

Then she saw it. A small round wooden box hanging on the wall. It was surrounded by cobwebs. But inside it there was a brass key.

This was still an emergency exit. She took the key, put it in the lock, turned it and pulled the door towards her.

That was when she heard Mrs Vaughann's voice.

'Isabel!'

She looked back along the corridor. Mrs Vaughann was walking towards her. She had almost reached the boxes. Behind her was the bald security guard. And he looked angry.

Meeting him down here felt all wrong. Tentacles of fear reached around her.

'We need to speak to you, Isabel,' said Mrs Vaughann, sharply.

'Sure,' she said as calmly as she could.

She looked at the key in her hand. Would she ever be able to test her theory if she went back?

They were still coming towards her.

'You know you shouldn't be down here, Isabel,' said Mrs Vaughann. There was amusement in her tone. 'And you shouldn't keep running away from my friend Adar. He's the new head of security at BXH.'

Mrs Vaughann was smiling. It was a fixed smile. The smile you might see on a mannequin. The man's gaze, Adar's gaze, was fixed too. On Isabel.

There was a wide-eyed intensity to it. Just like the way he'd been when he'd tried to stop her getting away in the elevator.

Then they reached the boxes.

She looked at them, expecting them to stop, but Adar manoeuvred himself sideways into the gap quickly, as if he didn't want to waste a second. And now she couldn't see Mrs Vaughann any more.

But Adar had something in his hand. It was a six-inch-long black-handled knife.

It's blade sparkled in the yellowy light. And there was a wild intensity to his progress that was unsettling, as if nothing was going to stop him from reaching her. She turned and put the key in the lock.

Her hand didn't even shake.

He'd be here any moment.

And with that weapon he could kill her with one slash.

The door had to open.

She turned the key. It turned only halfway.

She tried the handle. It wouldn't open.

'Stop!' he said.

She could smell him. It was the same sickly-lemony after-shave smell from her dream back in London.

She turned the key the other way and yanked at the handle.

The door opened.

She slipped through, banged it closed behind her, jammed the key in and turned it.

The handle jerked out of her hand.

Her head almost exploded with the pressure flowing through the veins in her neck. The handle moved again and again. The door shook. But it held.

Relief, like a cool breeze, ran through her as she realised he wasn't going to get through.

What the hell did this mean? That Mrs Vaughann was in league with some crazed murderer? Or was she getting it all wrong? Was he carrying that thing for some other reason?

No. That couldn't be right. She bit the edge of her fist. Her hand was trembling. This guy, Adar, was the murderer. And Mrs Vaughann was involved!

Which meant that he was going to kill her if she didn't get away.

Then, strangely, her hand stopped trembling. It was as if the part of her that couldn't believe any of this, that had almost given up on Sean, had found a new way of looking at things. A way that set things right.

Her breathing calmed. Her heart too. She couldn't hear any noises on the other side of the door any more.

She turned. She was in an arched brick tunnel. It looked like a place out of New York in the nineteenth century. It was narrow, barely wide enough for two people to pass, and the brick roof was only two inches from the top of her head. The only light was from the far end, fifty feet away.

The air was dead down here. All around there were shadows. They made the bricks in the wall blend into each other. She could feel cobblestones under her shoes. They were curved, as if they'd been laid directly on the backbone of Manhattan Island.

Suddenly a squeal echoed around her.

The noise was rushing towards her, like some enormous machine filling the tunnel. She leaned towards the wall and saw a flash of lights flicker past the end of the tunnel.

It was a train. The brick passage she was in led into one of the tunnels serving Grand Central.

She looked at her watch. She could barely read it. It was 12:25 a.m. That had to be one of the last trains out of the station. She walked fast towards the light.

A musty smell hit her nostrils. There were cobwebs all around. She could feel them touching her hair.

Then an air-vibrating bang rang out behind her. She turned. Another bang came. They were trying to break through the door.

She stumbled. Her legs felt heavy as if they didn't want to move. Two sets of shiny train tracks stood between her and the far wall. It looked as if it had been painted red a long time ago. Far off to her left there was a low-ceilinged platform with a strip of white light above it. She didn't think. She ran, heading to her left. Her feet were inches from the tracks.

Any second now she could be dead. She heard so many scuttling noises she imagined an army of rats moving out of her path, but she didn't care. Her legs moved. Brick flashed past.

The yellow light on the siding came closer. The dry air was burning her lungs. She could taste a sooty cinnamon grit in her mouth. It was itching her eyes too.

But she wasn't going to stop.

Her gaze was locked on the yellow light. There had to be a way out there. That was why there was a light. Keep going.

Faster.

Each step was like running on chunks of broken glass. The stones underfoot were sharp, almost cutting through the soles of her shoes.

Snake-like cables lined the walls.

She was at the siding. As she turned into it, a shout split the air.

'Stop, Isabel!' It was Mrs Vaughann. They had broken through the door.

A surge of energy poured through her. She ran faster as she entered the siding.

Ahead there was a wide platform, scaffolding reaching to a low roof with round fifties-style light fittings that gave off a dismal glow.

Where was the way out?

There. About halfway along there was a door and, further along, elevator doors.

Thank God!

She pulled herself up onto the platform and raced for the doors. Above her there were modern security cameras.

She reached the door, her heart beating fast. The door was a faded green. She gripped the handle, as her breath came in ragged gasps. She would run up to the street, be gone in a minute. Please open.

The door was locked.

She glanced back along the platform. Adar was at the entrance to the siding. He was walking towards her.

She ran for the elevator, praying it would open. Dread was taking over, filling her mind. Her nostrils were flaring. Her throat felt as if there was a rag in it. Instead of a button the elevator had a small silver keyhole. She wasn't going to be able to call it. In a last despairing act she tried to push the doors of the elevator apart.

'This time you don't get away.'

She turned.

Standing on the track below her was Adar. In his hand he now held a chunky black pistol. He was pointing it at her chest.

'You shouldn't run from me,' he said. He was panting a little. Mrs Vaughann was sauntering towards them, stones crunching under her feet. Isabel could see triumph in her smile.

'Don't upset yourself, Isabel,' she said. 'I told you there was no way out.'

'What the hell's going on?' she said, as defiantly as she could.

'You're trespassing. That's what's going on.'

'I'm looking for my husband.'

'So you say, Isabel.' Mrs Vaughann was being lifted onto the platform by Adar. Then she heard a distant grinding behind her. She knew at once what it meant. The elevator was coming.

A guard, maybe a member of the NYPD with his gun drawn.

Please have your gun drawn. The elevator door pinged.

Isabel, her voice shaking, shouted, 'He's got a gun,' as it opened.

And then she saw who was in the elevator and her mouth opened.

79

Mr Li looked at the expanse of white tablecloth in front of him. He hated being disturbed while he was eating. And he hadn't even been served any food yet. He looked up at his driver. The boy was holding a phone out in front of him. He had an apologetic look on his face. Li reached out and took the phone.

The owner of the Red Dragon restaurant was standing near the door out to 54th Street. He was half bowing in the direction of Li. In the kitchens, the restaurant's two chefs were vying to produce the dishes Li had ordered.

Li listened, then asked a question. 'The woman is there, yes?'

'Yes,' said the voice in his ear.

'She found the passage?'

'Yes.'

Li handed the phone back to the driver. 'We are going,' he said. His tone betrayed nothing, even though he had been looking forward to eating.

His plans would have to change now. He didn't like that. But maybe it would be worth it. He could tie up all the loose strings in one go. There could be no mistakes. Too much was at stake.

The owner of the Red Dragon bowed as Li passed him. The tiny smile on the owner's face could not be seen. Mr Li leaving was good news. His chefs could relax. He could relax. They weren't going to be subjected to one of Li's outbursts. He exhaled deeply.

80

'Sean!' She staggered back. 'Sean.' The second time she said it, it came out quiet.

Behind him was a young Chinese man in a black suit. Sean looked haggard. His face was pale. His eyes sunken. He looked so very different from the Sean who'd left their house a few days before.

A wave of anger, mixed with shock, sent blood rushing to her face. Her mouth opened, but nothing more came out. He came towards her.

She blinked. Her vision blurred. Had she conjured him up?

She wanted to be pleased to see him, but her anger grew as her shock subsided.

He spoke. 'What in God's name are you doing here?' He was angry too.

She pointed over her shoulder with her thumb.

'This pair are about to kill me!' Her words came out in a breathless gasp. She didn't look around. He reached towards her.

'No, they won't,' he said.

What did he mean?

He was inches away from her. She could smell a familiar warmth.

'That bastard behind me probably killed a detective.'

'I'm so glad you're okay.' His voice was soft, soothing.

He held her. And in one world-obliterating second she got it.

She was wrong.

This wasn't the Sean she knew. He was with them.

'You don't have to worry. I have her,' he said, loudly, matter-of-factly.

She turned.

'Don't touch her,' he said. 'You'll get what you want.' He released his grip on her. She stumbled back.

'Well done,' said Adar.

The trap had closed.

She stared at Sean, her breathing coming fast, trying to take everything in, work out what to do.

'You should have stayed at home,' he said.

She kicked at his ankle. 'I came to find you.'

He shook his head. 'Everything gets difficult, now you're involved.' He reached his hand for her.

'They have Alek. And Rose. They'll kill them both if we don't cooperate. We have to be careful, Isabel.'

'What do you mean they'll kill them, why?' Her brain had heard Sean's words, but she couldn't believe what he was saying.

Someone was going to kill Alek?

Sean's shoulders stiffened. He looked away. He seemed resigned. 'They want something from me. I was trying to find a way through this. I was trying to protect you both.'

All she could see was his face, and in it an echo of Alek's. Anxiety was blooming inside her. She shook her head. She wanted it to be a lie.

'Why don't you show Isabel some photos, Adar?' said Mrs Vaughann.

Adar put a hand in his pocket, took out a phone, pressed at the screen and turned it to face her. She wanted to scream. Everything she held dear was being threatened.

Someone had taken a picture in their home. She'd have recognised the yellow wallpaper in Alek's room anywhere.

The picture was of her son, sleeping with his duvet tucked up to his chin. The truly disturbing thing was the shaft of a short-bladed knife that whoever was working the camera was holding within an inch of Alek's right eye.

It was a similar knife to the one she'd seen in Adar's hand.

One good push and Alek would die in the most horrific manner. That was the message from the picture. But there was another message too.

She swallowed as it sank in.

Sean had every reason to do what he'd done. She glanced at Sean. Their eyes met for a moment. Again her world had turned. But what did this mean for Alek and Rose? For them all?

'Do show her the other ones,' said Mrs Vaughann.

Adar dabbed at the screen and turned it to face her again.

The pictures, which scrolled by, sent more tremors through her. A prickling at her eyes and in her cheeks sent messages to her hands to form fists, as if her body had taken over and a defensive mechanism had started up.

The first picture one was of her, sleeping in their bed, alone at home. Her arm was bare. It could have been taken any night Sean wasn't there.

But she knew what night it had been taken with a terrible certainty. Last Thursday night, when she'd had that awful dream, when Sean hadn't come home. When she'd smelled that lemony odour.

If she'd woken right then, would he have killed her? Was that what they planned to do now? Her mouth was dry. But her mind was clearing.

'I'm sorry,' said Sean. He stepped back.

'I had to do what they wanted. No matter what it meant for me, or for us. I didn't tell you anything, because I didn't want you to come after me.' He was angry again.

She looked at Mrs Vaughann.

'Why are you doing all this?'

Mrs Vaughann laughed, as if Isabel had just told a spectacularly funny joke. Her head went back. Then she smiled warmly, as if it was all nothing to her.

'They want something,' said Sean.

He took a step forward. 'Let her go, for God's sake,' he said. There was desperation in his voice. 'She can't prove anything. It'll be her word against yours. She'll be the wronged wife of a murderer.'

'It's too late for that,' said Mrs Vaughann.

Sean's eyes widened. 'Don't harm her. You still need me.'

Mrs Vaughann showed them her smile again. 'Maybe, let's find out. Get back in the elevator, Sean. Let's visit our friends.'

It was a tight squeeze. Isabel was beside Sean at the back. He smiled at her, but it was a broken smile. Adar, Mrs Vaughann and the Chinese guy were all staring at them.

Sean gripped her hand. She gripped back. It was good to hold him. His warmth ran up her arm.

The elevator kept going up for a long time. When it opened they were looking into a spectacular glass-walled reception area. It was poorly lit, only a few recessed lights in the ceiling were on. A grey square symbol was etched into the glass wall separating the elevators from the reception.

'Go inside,' said Adar. He put a card against a screen attached to the wall. It lit up briefly in blue, then a click sounded and a glass door slid open to the right.

'Sure,' said Sean. He sounded confident again. She wanted to scream at them all, demand that they let her son and friend go, but a voice inside kept telling her to wait for the right moment.

A minute later they were in a modern meeting room with silver chairs strewn around as if a meeting had broken up in disarray. There was a podium with a blue microphone at the far end. Behind the podium was a big LCD screen.

One wall of the conference room was all windows. Isabel had no idea what was beyond them, because the grey vertical blinds in front of each window were pulled closed. The light in the room was painfully bright.

She hugged Sean as if that might stop him leaving her ever again. Then she pushed him away.

Adar was standing by the door like some military policeman guarding them. Mrs Vaughann and her Chinese friend had disappeared.

'What's the plan?' said Isabel, in a low voice as they walked down the room towards the podium.

He gripped her arm. 'They think they need me,' he said. 'I know this seems crazy, but the whole takeover thing is a cover for something else. They won't harm any of us. I won't cooperate if they touch one hair on your body.' He was trying to reassure her. It wasn't working.

Surely, when he'd done what they wanted him to do they would dispose of them both. Of them all.

'What do they want from you?'

Before he had a chance to answer, the door of the room opened and in came an older Chinese man with Mrs Vaughann.

The Chinese man took a seat and rested his hands on his knees. He looked like someone's grandfather, though his hair was still black. His skin was hanging on his face as if he'd recovered from an illness.

'Are you going to introduce us?' she said.

The Chinese man's eyebrows went up. It was clear from Mrs Vaughann's expression that he was the guy in charge.

He spoke.

‘My name is Li,’ said the Chinese man.

His willingness to share his name sent a shiver through her. He had to be planning to dispose of them.

He turned to Sean. ‘Now that your wife is here, Mr Ryan, there is no reason for you not to finish your job for me.’ His tone was firm. He seemed the kind of a man who would sit and watch, without wincing, as thousands died in front of him.

‘And you will end up paying half the price you originally offered for BXH.’

‘You are wrong, Mr Ryan.’ Li paused. He smiled. ‘We will pay less than that.’

‘I’ll do what you want,’ said Sean. ‘Everything you want.’

Li’s face was expressionless.

What was Sean doing?

‘If you release my wife,’ Sean pointed at her. ‘And my son Alek, and the woman who was with him.’

Li looked at Sean, as if he was examining a specimen of stupidity. ‘You Westerners, you are all such optimists, aren’t you?’

‘Are you going to release them or not? I thought you wanted a big payday.’

‘Aaah, you people think it’s all about money.’

‘For me this is about my family,’ said Sean. ‘I don’t care about anything else.’

‘Come then,’ said Li. He waved at Sean, turned and headed for the door. It was clear he expected Sean to follow.

‘Hold on a minute,’ said Isabel. ‘How do you know he will do what you want? You need to bring me too.’

Li looked at her. There was disdain in his eyes. He took his phone out of his pocket.

‘You want to watch what will happen to your boy if your husband doesn’t cooperate?’ He tapped his pocket.

She walked towards him, anger bubbling inside her. He was standing between her and Adar.

He stepped back as she came near him.

'Let my son go, you bastard. You'll get what you want.' She jabbed her finger towards his chest. He stepped back. He was near Adar now. She followed him.

'My husband isn't going to tell you anything until you release my son. Do you understand?'

Li's hand came up quickly. He gripped her wrist. In a second her arm was twisting and she was falling to her right.

'Never come near me, stupid woman. Maybe I kill you all for that. You and your stupid family. You are nothing to me.'

She was down on one knee, fear seizing up every cell in her body. Her eyes squeezed tight as tears of frustration made her vision swim.

81

Henry Mowlam was still at his desk. He hadn't pulled an all-night shift in six months, but there was no way he was going home now.

'Have they broken into the building?' he shouted.

'Yes,' Major Finch replied.

She was at the console beside his. She was watching the TV signal from New York. It was showing a live CNN feed from outside BXH. Someone had started throwing cans at the doors of the BXH building thirty minutes before and the security guards had retreated inside. One of the glass doors had shattered. Then the other.

The make-up of the crowd outside the bank had changed in the past few hours. There were down and outs and people with ski masks, with more arriving. One older vagrant with his fist in the air was urging people on.

Henry wasn't able to watch the scene from outside BXH because he was finally watching what was going on inside, and he was also looking up the owners of a building nearby, where Isabel Ryan's mobile had been traced to.

The BXH feed, from a camera on the basement stairs,

showed a team with a concrete drill attempting to break through a brick wall leading off an underground stairwell.

The NYPD had figured out that there were levels in the basement of BXH that they were unable to access via the elevators and they'd decided to take the brute force way to open them up.

The only feedback he'd received about what was going on was when his FBI contact had emailed him details of how to watch events. He'd indicated that the NYPD were determined to catch whoever had murdered their colleague and they weren't going to leave any level in the BXH building unsearched in their hunt for Sean Ryan.

On his other screen he was flicking through the floor maps of the building Isabel was in, trying to see which floor she might be on.

But so far he had come up with nothing,

'They've broken through,' he said, softly.

Major Finch stood and came behind him. They both watched as a section of brick wall collapsed and two NYPD officers shone torches into the space beyond.

82

'Let go of her,' shouted Sean. She could hear him storming towards them. Li took his eye off her.

Adar shouted. 'Stay where you are.'

An explosion ripped through the air. A ripple-like shock-wave passed by her. Adar had fired his gun. She could smell the cordite.

'The next one kills your wife,' shouted Adar.

She looked around. Sean was standing two feet behind her. His hands were up. Thank God the bullet hadn't touched either of them. Or had it? She looked down at her body expecting to see blood somewhere. But there wasn't. She heard a faint whistling sound and a clacking. One of the window blinds was vibrating. It had a small hole in it near one edge.

'We have no more time,' said Li. 'You come now, Mr Ryan, or you watch your wife die.'

'Okay,' said Sean. He was beside Isabel helping her up.

'Nice try. Stay here. I'll be back for you.' He leaned close to her ear. 'If you get a chance, take it.'

She shook her head.

'No whispering,' said Adar. He pointed the gun at Sean.

Sean shrugged. As he left the room he turned and looked at her. It was a look that said *I may never see you again.*

'Give me your phone,' said Adar before he left the room.

She handed it to him.

'Turn out your pockets.'

She did. She had a few dollars and her credit cards in a small wallet, nothing else. Then she was alone. The door was locked. She checked the room for a phone. There was none. Nor was there anything she could use as a weapon, unless she could swing a chair at him when he came back in.

Seeing Sean had given her hope, but finding out that these people were holding Alek and Rose had sent her mind spinning and anxiety churning inside her.

She went to the window that had been broken by the bullet and pulled back the shivering blinds. There was a crack in the glass, a hole the size of a finger. The crack went from a corner of the window to the hole and then on. He'd been lucky the whole thing hadn't shattered.

She pulled up the blinds.

Outside, snow was piling into the glass. A few flakes came in through the bullet hole along with icy air.

She put her hand near the hole, felt cold air rushing in.

Maybe this was their chance. If she could attract the attention of someone below, maybe they'd come up to see what was going on.

She couldn't let this play out. She had to do something.

She picked up one of the plastic chairs, carried it over and threw it at the window. It bounced off the glass.

She examined the glass again. The crack was still there. Nothing had changed. There was a glass water pitcher at the podium. She launched it at the bullet hole. It smashed into pieces.

For a moment she thought it had done the job, but then

she saw it hadn't. And then she heard a shout from outside the door. Adar would be back any second.

And God only knew how he'd react to what she'd been doing.

She picked up a chair, aimed one of the legs at the bullet hole and ran for the window. She assumed she would be able to stop herself if it broke, and swerve to the window frame on the right.

She was wrong.

Behind her came a shout.

Then the chair hit the glass and it shattered. She fell down onto the carpet near the window. The air around her and the glass from the window were being sucked out in front her. A vortex of wind was pulling her towards a jagged hole of glass and blackness.

She couldn't stop.

And then the floor swayed, as if the loss of the window had affected it.

She spread her hands on the carpet, trying to dig her nails in. A roaring wind filled her ears. She was looking into the mouth of a freezing hell.

That was when she realised that the BXH building was straight across from her. And lights were on all over it. She could see people working in offices. But not one of them was looking at her.

'Fool,' shouted Adar behind her.

A hurricane wind was sucking her inexorably towards the now six-foot-wide jagged hole in the glass. In another second or two she'd be falling towards the concrete of 45th Street.

She did the only thing she could. She reached towards the jagged edge, and let the sucking momentum take her towards the lip of steel that extended all along the bottom edge of the window.

As she did, she heard a howling noise and felt something

whistling past her head. Another object flew past her. She glanced behind her. Adar was standing still, as if nothing could affect him, but the partition behind him, separating the room from the hall, had a big crack in it.

Then a section of the partition peeled away under the force of the sucking vortex as the wind outside shifted. And Adar turned just as it hit him. He went down like a felled boxer.

An alarm was ringing. Then another. She could see down the corridor outside the room. Her hair whipped across her face. The wind was icy. There were swarms of stinging snowflakes in it. The Chinese man, Li, was looking out from a door along the corridor.

He had a shocked look on his face. She pushed herself back along the carpet, her body tight to it, the wind swirling and sucking, as she crawled towards the corridor. She saw Sean coming towards her. He was bending down, half crouching.

She reached out for him. Time had slowed. She tried to rise from the carpet, but she was pulled backwards if she did.

But then the thought of the danger Alek was in made a burst of energy rise up from deep inside her. She pushed herself forward. Sean grabbed her as a great crack sounded around them. She didn't want to look around, but she couldn't stop herself. Two sections of the windows, including a large undamaged plate of glass, were being sucked out into the storm. Then a violent swirl of snow, like the maw of a white bear, rushed in.

They were in the corridor now and the power of the wind had lessened. In front of them the elevator doors opened. Li walked into it, calmly, as if nothing was going on. She felt something in her back. The young Chinese man was behind them.

‘Get into the elevator,’ he said. His expression gave nothing away.

And then her, Li, Sean and the young Chinese man were all inside and the elevator doors were closing, just as some papers flew by heading towards the rip in the wall of the corridor.

It felt like closing the door on a nightmare.

She glanced behind her. The young Chinese man’s gun was black, small and deadly looking.

‘Maybe it is better if your lovely wife comes with us,’ said Li. ‘I think she might make too much trouble back there.’

Then the elevator went dark. She reached forward, hoping to take the gun from the Chinese man. She’d been taught how to do it, how to bend a barrel upwards and to the side quickly and force someone to loosen their grip as their fingers bent painfully. But her fingers touched skin, then clutched at thin air.

And she knew what was going to happen next.

She pushed her hand out to the left, pushing Sean away from her, while at the same time twisting her own body away to the right.

The explosion from the gun barrel filled the confined space with a wave of noise and light. She heard Sean grunt. Dread filled her.

But she had seen him. He was in the corner in front of her. As darkness engulfed them again and the wave of noise echoed, she reached out with her hand and felt it connect. She had a hold on the deadly end. The barrel. It was hot, burning her fingers. But she knew what she had to do.

She jerked it up and to the right. The man screamed as his fingers were squeezed as if in a vice. That was when she registered the noise beside her. Sean was struggling with Li.

‘Stop struggling or I kill your husband,’ said Li.

A second later the doors of the elevator pinged and opened. She let go of the gun, then stepped back.

'If you do that again I will put holes in both of you,' Li shouted. He had a similar gun to the other man.

'Come on, let's go,' he said.

'Where?' said Sean.

Li sighted along the barrel of the gun.

'You will want to come, when you see what we have waiting for you.' First he pointed it at Sean's head, then at his chest. He took another few steps back, sighting along the barrel.

Then the four of them were together on the cold basement platform. There was no evidence of the destruction that was being wrought above them by the hole in the side of the building.

Sean gripped her shoulder.

'We have to go with him,' he said.

'What the hell is this all about?' she said. She kept her eyes on Li.

'All I want to do is find a way to get Alek released,' said Sean.

'Don't make trouble, Mrs Ryan,' said Li. 'It will be worse for your son if you do. I promise you that. Much worse.'

83

Henry Mowlam watched as the blinking light on the street grid of Manhattan disappeared.

'She's not moving.'

'No kidding, Sherlock.' Major Finch was standing behind him.

'Do you have the original plans of the BXH building?'

Finch dropped the print-out onto his desk. 'I'm sure it's online somewhere,' she said.

'No time.' He peered down at the illustration. 'These are tunnels that connect the bank to all the nearby buildings.' He looked at an elevation drawing of the BXH building.

'There are more levels here than the NYPD have been searching.' The wall they had broken through had led to an empty floor.

He pointed at the lower levels of the line drawing showing a side-on view of the BXH building.

'This old elevation goes a lot deeper than the new ones. Haven't they figured out how to get into them yet? I bet Sean Ryan has. That's exactly the sort of place he'd be hiding out. In secret vaults.'

'Have those rioters given up yet?' he asked, looking up at Finch.

'The National Guard are there now,' she said. 'There's chatter about them opening fire . . .'

84

Isabel followed Sean and Li back along the platform, along the tunnel and into the BXH building. She stumbled a few times, her head pounding with worry about Alek.

The grinding noise of a slow-moving train echoed as they made their way back into the post room corridor of the BXH building.

'Where the hell are we going?' she said, as they waited at the elevators. It seemed a long time since she'd come this way, but it was only a little over forty minutes.

She was relieved that she'd found Sean, that he was innocent of the murders, but the knowledge that Alek was in danger had undermined everything.

There were three elevator doors in the small ill-lit corridor. The centre one had a gold painted surround. The other two were silver.

'You can at least tell us which way we're going,' she said. 'Up or down? We'll find out soon enough.'

'Down,' said Li. 'When they built the BXH building it was the last great American extravagance before the Wall Street crash. The vaults are truly unbelievable.' He turned to Sean. 'Did you know that?'

'You will pay if our son is harmed,' said Sean. 'I promise you that.'

Li smiled.

Isabel was looking at the call plate for the gold elevator. It was this button Li had pressed. It had the BXH logo on it. The letters had a square around them and an arrow above them.

'If you cooperate,' said Li. 'And if I get what I want, I will save your son, Mr Ryan.'

The golden elevator doors opened and Li led the way in. He kept the gun pointing at them. His assistant pushed his gun into Sean's side.

Then Li tapped a code into a keypad beneath the plate indicting the floors. She saw him press the # and * buttons and some numbers near it. She looked at the buttons indicating the floors.

There were seven basement levels. Three of them weren't lit up, as if they were unused, until he tapped in the code, then they lit up like the other round yellow buttons.

Li pressed the bottom button of these three. Then he pressed the two buttons above the bottom one.

'I want you to see what's on these floors too,' he said. The elevator went down for a long time. It took almost as long as it had taken to ride up to the executive floor. Could the basement really be this deep?

Then there was a rattling, as if it was passing a choke point. The lights flickered. Isabel's nose wrinkled. A damp smell had seeped into the elevator. There was a sudden grinding noise, as if they were rubbing up against something and were vulnerable to being squeezed.

Then the elevator stopped and the doors pinged open. What greeted Isabel was the exact opposite of what she'd expected.

It was the wall of a coal mine, black, cracked with

protrusions pushing forward. There was a narrow ledge at the level of the elevator. It looked as if the floor of a passage had fallen away. The roof above was curved, cracked.

A strong smell came into the elevator. It was the smell of sewers.

Li pressed the button to close the doors. 'We explored that yesterday,' he said. 'There is no way out. It would be easy to die there, if no one came to rescue you. Maybe we leave you there if you cause trouble, either of you.' He pressed the close door button.

The wait was short this time, and there was more grinding. When the doors opened Isabel's head was pounding. She could feel the distance they had travelled down and she didn't like it.

The smell was the first thing that hit her, physically. Isabel had to cover her nose. The spill of light from the elevator showed an expanse of sand, dotted with dark patches. There was a rock wall to the left again. It was similar, but smoother than the one on the floor above.

A rustling sound came to her as the noise of the elevator died away.

There were spots of red in the distance, in the shadows.

They seemed to be coming towards them. Li pressed the button to close the doors.

'Every time they come quicker,' he said. 'They must be hungry.'

The doors seemed to take a long time to shut. In the seconds that it took she saw giant white rats racing towards them.

They were albinos. She'd never seen anything like it. Her mouth opened.

They covered the sand like a shifting carpet. And they were scrambling over each other. They were racing towards them, their thin legs jumping forward and their scrawny faces intent.

Isabel was gripped by revulsion. Her muscles tightened. Every single one. She lifted her hands to ward them off.

Sean and Li were pushing the doors closed.

And then she heard the squealing.

'Push, Mr Ryan,' said Li. 'They are very quick.'

'What the hell was that?' shouted Isabel, as the doors closed. An explosion of scratching echoed in the elevator as it went down again. There was a ferociousness to it that she'd never heard before.

'I saw animals just like that in Vietnam,' said Li. 'Rats that live without ever seeing the sun, and they all eat each other. And anything else they can find.' He widened his eyes. Then he laughed.

'Cannibal rats,' said Isabel. The thought of the rats sent her shifting from one leg to the other as the elevator continued on down. There was another gap before the doors opened again.

Isabel gripped Sean's shoulder.

What the hell else could be down here?

She was near the front of the elevator, ready to push them closed again if more rats appeared. But this time the space they were looking into was lit by a tripod of floodlights near the elevator and another tripod of lights at the far end of a high cavern.

A thick orange cable ran from the elevator to the floodlights. But even with the lights, part of the cave was in shadow.

'We have seen no rats on this level, Mrs Ryan. It is a sealed cavern,' said Li.

'I read about this,' said Sean. 'Apparently the builders came across a shaft into the gneiss bedrock of Manhattan when they were digging the basement levels of the bank out.' The two of them stood still in the elevator, watching, taking the space in.

'There were rumours of huge caverns going around for decades. They were always denied.'

Isabel wasn't sure about getting out. The cavern looked empty of those vile creatures, but the thought of them was still sending shivers across her skin.

Li walked out of the elevator, turned and beckoned Isabel and Sean out onto the grey, slate-like rock floor of the cavern. Isabel stepped forward. Sean followed her. The roof curved, but was natural looking, with darker rocks jutting out against the grey background. It was fifty feet above their heads. And it was pitted with cracks and folds. The walls, a hundred feet away on each side, were similarly cracked and uneven.

'There are Indian markings on the walls,' said Li. 'And there are bones somewhere over there.' He pointed at the far end of the cavern.

That was when Isabel saw the four tombs. They were square, squat, and looked to be made of the same rock as was all around. 'This way,' said Li.

Sean and Isabel followed him. The cavern was a sight that made her head go back and turn as she walked forward to take it in. It was a natural underground hall. She was shocked at the size of it.

As she turned, she saw that around the elevator door there was an arch of yellow bricks in an art deco style. Someone had gone to a lot of trouble down here.

There was no noise in the cavern, just an echo of their footsteps. There was no smell either, which reassured her. No smell meant no horrible animals eating each other down here.

As they came up to the tombs Isabel saw that they were bigger than they'd looked from the far side of the cavern. They were ten feet high, flat-roofed and laid out as if at the points of a compass.

They reached the bottom of the compass first. Sean walked around it quickly.

'This is not the interesting tomb,' said Li.

When Isabel walked past it she saw that it had a gate made of iron bars. The gate was open. She walked near it. Inside there was a stone sarcophagus with the lid pushed aside at the far end of a large chamber.

'There are only bones in there,' said Li, pointing at the tomb Isabel was looking into.

'This is the one that will interest you, as you are looking for your son.' He pointed at the tomb at the north point of the compass. It was far bigger than the others, though it had the same flat-roofed style and was made from the same black rock, rough cut into large blocks.

Each tomb had a ridge jutting out from the roof about ten feet from the ground. The roof had been made to extend over the walls.

'Who the hell is buried down here?' said Isabel.

'Past presidents of BXH,' said Sean. 'This is a company mausoleum.'

'Yes. Come on.' Li looked back towards the elevator. Then he looked at his watch.

Sean came up beside Isabel as they walked behind Li. 'I honestly thought I could sort this all out myself,' said Sean.

She squeezed his arm and looked back at the elevator. It seemed a long way off. 'I hope to God we save Alek. I hope they haven't done anything to him.'

As they got closer they saw that the gate in front of the last tomb was open too. This gate was double height and width, and made of pitted iron bars, like the first one they'd passed.

'Go inside,' said Li.

The chamber was far larger than in the other one and had an altar at the far end, as if it had been used as a chapel. Isabel felt uneasy as soon as she went in. The light was poor, coming from slits in the walls. But what set her most on edge was what was on the side wall to their left.

There was a carving of the square and arrow symbol in a large piece of black rock embedded in the other, smaller pieces that made up the wall.

And in front of the altar was one heavy wooden pew, where people could kneel.

Li's assistant had pushed them forward while they were walking here, and now he stood at the door, his gun pointing towards them.

'Kneel,' said Li.

'This is total bullshit,' said Sean. 'We're not playing some stupid game for you.'

'This is no stupid game,' said Li. 'You will do what I say or you will not see your son again. It is not my fault your wife joined us, Mr Ryan. It was bad timing for her and you, that is all.' He looked at his watch again.

'Come on, kneel or my friend will put a bullet in your thighs and you will certainly kneel then. But very painfully.'

Sean and Isabel went to the wooden pew and knelt. The pew had a front piece where you could rest your arms. It also had holes in it, where you could put your arms through. There were spaces for five people to kneel.

Isabel didn't like the look of it. Then, after peering over the front edge, she noticed the manacles on the far side. They were iron. She liked that even less.

'What the fuck is this?' said Sean. He went to stand up.

Isabel turned just in time to see Li pressing a gun hard into his back. Then she felt something hard and cold pressing into her backbone.

'My friend will shoot your wife and you can watch her bleed to death or you can do what I say and you will see your son,' Li shouted.

'Sean, kneel,' said Isabel. They had to wait for the right moment before doing anything.

Sean grunted angrily, but he knelt.

'Both of you put your hands through the holes.'

Isabel had been debating with herself at what point to try to get away, but with a gun pressing hard into her back this was not the moment for heroics.

'Is Alek here?' she cried out. 'I want to see him.' She pushed her arms through the holes.

'You will have your wish.' Li went around and lifted the manacles that had been dangling in front of the pew. They fitted perfectly over their wrists and when they were closed, with only a simple thumb-sized piece of iron through a hole, they were trapped. You could release the manacles just by pulling the piece of iron out, but without a hand to reach it, you were imprisoned.

'Where the fuck did you get all this?' said Sean.

'It was here. I imagine they used it to punish people.'

They were kneeling on a rough wooden board and facing the altar.

Li looked at his watch again.

'Are you expecting someone?' said Isabel.

A voice answered from behind them.

'You brought the two of them, Li. We are in luck.'

Isabel turned. Two people had entered the chapel. One of them was carrying her son. She let out a strangled shout and tried to get up, yanking hard at the pew. The manacles prevented her. They cut deep into her skin. She didn't care. She pushed more against them. She twisted her body around following the man who was carrying him, her eyes wide, her muscles straining.

'You sick bastard, let him go. How did he get here?' She pulled her hands back, trying to free them. The iron cut into her skin. A rush of fear for Alek sent her body rocking backwards and forwards.

Whoever the man was, he was cruel looking. He was tall, hard-faced and dressed in a black suit and shirt. His grey hair was slicked back. He had half-sunken eyes and pale skin.

'Stay quiet,' shouted the man. He walked past her. 'You are here for a reason.'

Sean shouted. 'What the hell are you doing here, Xena? You were Mark's friend.'

Behind the man carrying Alek was an Ethiopian woman. Isabel looked at her, then peered closer. Xena had been with Mark in Cairo. She'd been injured during their rescue in the Judean Hills.

She must have been a traitor all along. Was she why Mark had died?

'We learned a lot in Israel,' said the man, as he headed for the altar.

'And I am not yours to judge,' said Xena. She stood behind them.

The man carrying Alek laid their son on the altar. Whether he was sleeping or dead they had no way of knowing.

Isabel tried to move the pews forward now, but they were too heavy. She strained upwards to see Alek's face, but all she could see was his cheek. She let out a protracted groan. Her hands were in fists.

'What have you done?' she shouted.

'Your son is still alive,' said Xena.

'What the hell do you want him for? He's a child!' Her voice shook with desperation.

'Do you remember Robert Maximilian Kaiser?' said the man now standing over Alek on the far side of the altar. He had placed Alek lying face-up on the stone.

'Yes, we do,' said Sean. 'Somebody burnt him to death.'

'Well, before he died he told us that you were probably the only people who knew the truth about the symbol and the book, because you knew where it had been found.'

Isabel was leaning up as high as she could go, staring at

Alek. He had a black silk band tied around his forehead. Was he injured? Please, no.

'What have you done to him?'

'He is sedated, but he will meet a fate worse than Kaiser's, if you do not cooperate.'

'What the hell do you want from us? What the hell is this?' Isabel screamed.

'You will see,' said the man.

He bent down and then stood straight. In his hand was a knife. He raised it in the air above his head and began mumbling something over and over.

'*Quarto quattuor invocare unum.*' After he had repeated it four times, louder each time, he moved the knife slowly downwards, towards Alek.

Isabel shrieked, 'No.'

She looked around. Would anyone help them, help Alek? All eyes were on the altar.

'Someone stop this!' she shouted.

No one moved.

'You'll pay for this!' shouted Sean.

The room reverberated with echoes of their panicked shouts.

'Innocent blood is the most powerful,' said the man, softly, as if he hadn't heard them.

'You bastard. What are you doing! Alek!' Isabel's scream ripped the air.

Xena was at the altar. She'd lit a black candle. She was holding something into the flame. It smouldered thickly and filled the air with a pungent, sickly odour, the odour of death.

85

Henry looked at his screen. It showed an image of a broken brick wall and NYPD officers standing around.

'They still haven't found the other floors,' he said. There was frustration and tiredness in his voice.

'Are they still planning to drill through the bottom level?' said Finch.

'There's some issue about the sewers in the area,' said Henry. 'Apparently there's all sorts of strange underground vermin in that part of Manhattan. They're bringing in pest control specialists before they go down any further.'

He put his head in his hands.

'I really don't think they have time for that.'

'What the hell was in that book that's so particularly disturbing you?' said Finch.

Henry looked up at her. 'Every drop of blood is drained from a child's body, while human skin is burnt as incense.'

Finch let out her breath in a slow whistle.

'You don't want that on your conscience.'

86

Isabel screamed again. She hadn't seen the first cut being made, but she had seen the knife with blood dripping from its edge being raised afterwards.

She roared louder, her throat straining, as the knife was lowered again. This time the man sliced at Alek's bare leg; he only had his underwear on.

A trickle of blood flowed.

Isabel let out a muffled, heart-rending, moan.

Alek groaned softly, as if in reply. Then the knife went up in the air again.

'The next cut will be deeper,' he said.

'You bastard! You sick bastard. Why are you doing this?' screamed Isabel. She could almost feel the blade on her own skin. She was pulling at the manacles rhythmically now, hoping they might break from the repeated strain.

But they didn't.

Then Alek groaned again.

Sean was shouting. 'Leave him, take me! Kill me, please!'

'It's not your blood we want,' said the man.

He raised the knife again.

'What are you doing this for?' shouted Isabel.

The man lowered the knife.

'Your son will die if I go on.' He paused, looking from Isabel to Sean. 'But I will stop, if you succeed where we have failed.'

'Succeed? How?' Xena had been holding the edge of a square piece of what looked liked dried parchment in the candle flame. As the man spoke she took it out of the flame and laid it on the altar near Alek's feet.

He pointed at the wall on their left. 'You will solve this puzzle. That block of stone has holes in it. I believe it can be opened by someone who knows the secret of that symbol.'

Sean and Isabel turned to the symbol on the wall. It did have small holes where the lines intersected.

'Only this will save your son.'

'What? Are you crazy?' said Isabel.

'No, far from it.'

'This is totally sick.' Sean pulled at the manacles, trying to free himself.

Xena came forward and watched. The skin on his wrists looked raw.

'You will help me with this symbol. Then I will not need to finish this ritual. Otherwise . . .' he reached down and picked up the knife. He swiped it through the air.

'The ritual will be completed and quickly.'

Isabel jerked again at the manacles.

'You are all mad.'

'No, we're not,' said Li. 'There is something hidden down here, and I believe my friend is providing a good incentive for you to help us.'

'What kind of a sick ritual cuts a child?' said Sean.

'An ancient and sacred Byzantine ritual,' said the man. 'Once their Empire was as powerful as the US is now. They were the only people who could ever turn base metal into gold, until now. The symbol hides an ancient secret. A puzzle you will help us solve.' He pointed at the wall.

'I don't have the answer,' said Sean. 'You can't do this to us.'

'The ritual will be finished with your son if this puzzle isn't solved.' He sounded very sure of himself.

'Set me free. I will open it for you,' said Isabel.

She was watching the altar. She knew she couldn't trust any of them, even if she gave them what they wanted, but she also knew she had to take her chance.

'How did you find this place?' she said. She was trying to sound normal, though the thought of Alek bleeding was making her shake.

'A friend. He heard about this place two years ago. He explained about what was down here, about this symbol, and I knew we had to buy this bank, to get access. It fitted with every piece of research we had done. But we had to move slowly. I encouraged him to employ you, Sean. I wanted you close at hand if we needed you. And now we are ready for the end game. You must open this up.'

Alek let out a groan on the altar and shifted. He was alive.

'Undo these,' said Isabel.

'Set her free,' said the man.

Li came forward and undid Isabel's manacles.

Sean turned to Xena. 'You tried to help me in Jerusalem, why?'

Xena shook her head, as if she pitied him.

'My friend, Arap, went too far in Jerusalem,' said the man. 'We wanted you to find your wife. We thought you might be useful to us. We will see. You should help your wife solve this.'

Isabel remembered what Sean had told her about Xena. There had been a lot of things that hadn't made sense, like the fire at the villa she'd been held in. Had Xena started that to cover up evidence?

She walked quickly to the altar, hugged Alek and listened to his breathing. She checked his wounds. There was a cut on his forearm and another on his calf. Both were bleeding slowly. She pressed his arm into his side. She tried to tear a strip off her shirt to stem the bleeding, but the man intervened, pushed her to the side.

'There will be time for that later.'

She didn't believe a word. She wanted to grab Alek, run out and back to the elevator, but there were too many people to get past. She needed a distraction. And she needed it quickly.

She went to the symbol.

The square and arrow symbol was carved into the rock. The small holes were square. Narrow recessed grooves marked out all the lines.

'Do you have a key?' She put her finger into the bottom hole.

'No. And we tried pressing every hole, in every combination,' replied the man.

'These holes are here for a reason,' said Isabel. She tapped the stone. There was no echo.

'What was that riddle we found with the symbol in Istanbul, Sean?' said Isabel, quickly.

'What new path must you take if you go from famine to death, yet wish to take each path, and each once only.'

Isabel went close to the stone and looked inside the holes. 'You know there's a colour in there. It looks white.' She put her hand to her forehead. 'White is for purity, right? That's what a white wedding dress is about.'

'And black is for death,' said Sean.

'So what's green for?' Isabel asked.

'Bile, sickness, famine?' said Sean.

She looked in the hole on the left.

'There should be green in this hole, if it's following the pattern from the symbol.'

She bent down. She had to figure this out.

She put her eye near a hole. There was a faint greyness at the back. Was that green? She couldn't see.

'Let me look,' said Li, who was standing near her now. He bent down.

'There is a little green dot at the back.'

'If we follow the riddle, follow a path around the symbol from famine to death, from green to black and press in the holes on the path around the symbol that will open this up.'

She was talking and also looking for a way to get hold of Li's gun. It was in his waistband now. Then they might really have a chance. She was far from sure she could solve the puzzle.

But she tried it, pressing the back of each hole in turn, then running her finger along the connecting grooves to the next hole. But each time she found that one of the paths or grooves hadn't been passed along. You couldn't travel along all the lines without going over one of them twice. The riddle wasn't solvable.

Li came closer to her.

'We got as far as you.'

'You have to go along each line only once,' said Sean.

'You have a few minutes left, that is all,' said the man.

She wanted to run at him, hit him, but she held herself back. She needed a weapon.

How could this puzzle be solved?

What did she know about puzzles?

A memory of a puzzle book came to her. She'd bought Mark, her ex, an illustrated one when they'd been together. She'd partly bought it for herself too. Some of the puzzles had been listed as unsolvable. It was supposed to keep him entertained when they'd been working together in Istanbul. It hadn't succeeded. But one of the puzzles had been German, about bridges you had to cross. It had had lines in it.

What was it? She saw the book in her mind. Then she saw the page again. Each bridge had been a different colour. The bridges of Königsberg. That was it. She hadn't thought about it in years. But what had been the solution?

'Wait,' said Isabel. She traced a finger around the square again. A tingle of anticipation ran through her. What had someone said about a new piece?

'If we create a new path, from white to red, that would fit the riddle. We'd have a way to get from green to black and go along each path only once.' She pressed into the holes in sequence, ending up at white, then pressed red, then the black hole.

When she pressed into the final hole nothing happened.

She banged her fist against the stone in frustration. Was she going to lose everything because of a stupid rock, a stupid puzzle she'd got wrong?

She banged the rock again, even harder.

She heard a hissing sound.

It seemed to be coming from the wall. As she watched, a six-foot-wide square hole in the wall opened as the rock slid back and down with a grinding noise from where the symbol had been.

'Look,' she shouted, elation rising fast inside her.

It had worked. She'd been right!

A glimpse of light had appeared in her tunnel of desperation.

She touched the wall where the square had opened. Inside it, beyond a two-foot-thick lip of rock, was a smaller, darker room. It was bare except for a foot-high urn made from grey sparkling rock in the centre. On top of the urn there was a green statue. There was a thin layer of dust everywhere, and a few small cobwebs in the corners of the low grey roof.

She bent forward.

Li slapped her back. 'Your wife did it, Mr Ryan! We should

have invited her, not you to come to New York.' He slid over the lip of the hole.

'Well done,' said Sean.

'Don't touch anything,' said the man who'd been standing over Alek. He went past Isabel and followed Li.

Isabel went to Alek, cradled his head, lifted him up and held him in her arms.

She shouted. 'You've got what you want. Let us go now.'

'Do not attempt to leave,' said the man. 'We will shoot you all down if you do.'

Isabel stood there holding Alek. She was looking sideways at Li's assistant. Overpowering him was their best bet now. But they had to take their chance soon. She moved towards the opening in the wall, hoping the assistant would join her out of curiosity.

'That's made of felsic, Lord Bidoner,' said Li. He was peering at the foot-high urn.

Lord Bidoner, thought Isabel. Now we know who this bastard is. But it also meant they were even less likely to let them go.

'Felsic?' said Bidoner.

'It's a quartz. It can be fragile.'

'I am more interested in what is inside this,' said Bidoner. There was a hum of excitement in his voice, as if he was aroused. 'The destiny of humanity.'

Li was waving his phone around, using the light from the screen to illuminate the glistening felsic urn and what stood on top of it.

Isabel peered at the green standing figure statue, which sat on top of the urn. It glistened in the dim light. The foot-high figure was of a thin man with a long beard and ringlets of hair coming down past each ear.

'What the hell?' she said, leaning closer. Li's assistant was near now. Only two feet away. He was watching what was going on. She held Alek tighter in her arms, then took another step closer to the wall and peered into the room beyond the window-like opening.

Bidoner put a hand on Li's arm. 'We have all waited a long time for this,' he said. His voice was low, reverential.

Li put a hand out and stroked the head of the statue, as if it was a child's.

Sean and Isabel looked at each other. He moved his head, indicating that she should come to him. She moved a foot in his direction. Nobody noticed.

Li spoke quietly.

'This is also the pride of the Chinese people.'

'You have kept it in your care,' said Bidoner.

Isabel raised her eyes. What were they on about?

'Do not try to release your husband, Mrs Ryan.' Li glared at her.

'What the hell is that statue and what's in it?' she said. She had to keep them talking. There was no way they were going to let her, Sean and Alek go. She had solved their puzzle, but that didn't mean they were going to stop their sick ritual.

'The first Emperor of the Chinese, Qin Shi Huang, the man who brought us together, had this commissioned as the symbol of a unified China. It contains a mythical power – so the ancient stories say. See the wavy lines on it?' Li didn't wait for a reply.

'These symbolise the three unruly dragons being unified. For as long as this was in China we were the most powerful nation in the world. And now I will take it back. And all will come and bow before us again.'

He stroked the head. He was smiling, as if he had been reborn.

'So what's it doing buried down here?' said Isabel. It was hard to believe that the statue held such significance. It needed a polish. She could imagine it in a museum, but the symbol of China? And what did Bidoner mean about something being inside it?

'This was stolen from the Summer Palace in Beijing when it was looted in the Second Opium War,' said Li. 'The Qing Emperor said that losing this was worse than the burning of a thousand acres of his palaces.'

'So how did it end up here?'

'It was taken to Hong Kong by British mercenaries,' said Bidoner. He seemed captivated by the statue. 'The bank it was lodged in was taken over by BXH a hundred years ago, in an arranged financial crisis in the colony.'

Li stroked it again. 'We guessed it might be secreted somewhere in this building,' he said.

'Which one of you gets it?' said Isabel.

'Now we are part of the takeover of BXH the statue is ours, again.' Li looked at Bidoner. 'And what's inside it will be shared.'

Lord Bidoner smiled.

'They thought there was nothing of value down here,' said Li. 'Just a long-lost mausoleum to past presidents. They know nothing about real value. The value of what people believe in. This will change everything.' He reached forward with both hands and grabbed the statue.

Bidoner put his out to steady the urn, but it was too late.

As Li lifted the statue, a crack sounded. When he released it with a swift upward motion the sides of the urn fell outwards and smashed into fragments with a noise that filled the two rooms with a roll of sound.

Isabel went closer to the wall again and looked into the chamber with the urn. In the place of the urn there was a jagged-edged hole a foot across. There was a dark space below where the urn had been, a deep hole.

And then she heard something. A far away rustling, like leaves on a path being scrunched by walkers.

An ominous feeling swept over her, making her jerk away from the wall. Li was clutching the jade statue to his chest, as if it was a baby. That was when Isabel heard the rustling noise again, only louder.

'No!' Bidoner shouted.

He stepped back from the hole, as if he'd seen something horrible. Then he turned to Isabel. She saw wide-eyed fear in his face.

'Run!' he yelled.

Li was scrambling over the low wall that separated them from the main room.

The sight she saw next sent a shout to her lips.

'Sean!'

Pale rats, giant rats, were streaming out of the hole in the ground where the urn had been. They were leaping in the air and even from twenty feet away, she knew what they had to do.

'We have to go,' she screamed.

Li glanced back, letting out an odd high-pitched yelp.

The rats were like the ones they'd seen up above. And within a few seconds a group of them had attacked Bidoner, who was only then reaching for the wall that Li had just scrambled over.

He screamed. It was a chilling scream of terror. Isabel felt pleased and shocked at the same time. Li didn't make any effort to go back for Bidoner. He was almost at the gate out of the chapel already. His assistant, looking terrified, was with him.

There was no one guarding them. Isabel put Alek down by Sean and went to undo Sean's manacles. They came free after a few of the longest seconds she'd ever experienced.

'Take Alek, Sean. Run as fast as you can. Don't worry about me. Get him out of here.'

Xena was the only one who tried to do something about the rats. Bidoner screamed as about five of them, like small dogs, bit into him as he tried to exit the inner chamber. Two were on his arm, one was on the other arm and one was near his neck.

Xena had a knife in her hand and she lashed out at the rats as they swarmed, sending two, then a third, into the air, blood flowing. But there were too many and as she flailed with them, Sean took hold of Alek.

Then Isabel saw the gun in Bidoner's hand. It was facing the rats coming out of the hole. It went off, with an echoing thud as he shouted a curse she didn't understand. Then, as his arm flailed, the gun fell and slid across the floor. Xena hadn't seen it fall. She was trying to pick rats off Bidoner. Isabel picked up the gun and went after Sean and Alek.

She turned as she passed through the gate and saw more rats jumping on Bidoner. There were more and more of them piling their teeth into him. Then she heard a gnawing sound and saw Xena stepping back from the rats at their feasting. She had a squirming rat in each hand. She threw them at the wall.

Isabel raced on. She never saw Bidoner again.

Sean, with Alek in his arms, and Li and his colleague were all running back to the elevator.

Sean was behind the others, but gaining on them.

As she raced after them Isabel stumbled, almost fell. She looked back. Xena was not far behind. Then she was coming up on Li. Sean was ahead, even though he was carrying Alek. Li was weighed down with the statue. The elevator was still a hundred feet away. Isabel looked over her shoulder again, fear filling her mind. Were the rats coming?

They were!

They had been delayed by their feasting in the chapel, but there must have been more rats who were still hungry.

And now there was a pack running after them.

Her heart pounded. She thought about using the gun on Sean and Alek if the rats caught them.

Li shouted and his colleague, who had been running near him, responded. Isabel turned just in time to see the man holding his gun out to Li, passing it to him. Isabel looked forward again.

Then she heard a shot.

Had the rats reached Li already?

She turned, but only Li was following her. And there was a hand behind him, near the ground, waving in the air. Then she realised. He had shot his assistant.

She turned her head and kept running, determination and fear pushing her on.

Every muscle was straining now. Her feet were pounding rhythmically on the stone. The hairs on her arms and on her back were standing up. She was running as fast as she'd ever run. Her breath was coming in thick gulps. Her thigh muscles were aching. Then she turned. The rats were on Li's assistant. She glimpsed white fangs and claws.

Li was wheezing, and still behind. 'Drop the statue!' she shouted.

He shook his head furiously. Xena was off to the left, far enough away that she couldn't be shot easily by Li.

The squealing behind them was getting louder again.

'Come on, Isabel,' Sean shouted. He was waving her forward.

Her legs were aching, her lungs burning. She turned her head and gasped.

Li had fallen. The rats were on him. He was screaming. They formed a little hill and were swarming all over him. His hand was raised high and lashing about. She slowed, Sean shouted at her.

She glanced back again. A large rat had jumped up to bite

Li's hand. It held on tight as he swung it around in a despairing movement.

A strangled shout twisted in her throat. Fear and revulsion gripped her.

And then, as she watched, she saw Xena heading for Li. She slowed, kept watching. There was no doubting Xena's courage. But she didn't engage with the rats this time, she bent and picked the statue up, which was behind Li, and ran off, fast, towards the wall of the cavern on the right. Was there another way out?

'Come on,' shouted Sean. The rats had been distracted, but who knew for how long.

They reached the elevator.

Sean pressed the button, banged on the elevator doors. Then he tried to pull the doors open. They wouldn't budge.

They turned to watch the final act of Li being eaten. Alek was resting on Sean's shoulder, still knocked out, oblivious. There was blood all down Alek's arms and legs. It was all over Sean's shirt now and on his trousers too.

Li's body jerked and the whole hill of rats moved as blood fired a few feet up into the air, then sprayed the white rats in a mist that died quickly. Sean banged on the doors again.

It wouldn't be long before the rats realised there was more to eat than Li and his colleague.

And then the elevator doors pinged.

Isabel felt a great rising wave of relief.

But inside was Adar and her relief fled. He had a purple bruise on the side of his face and a sour expression. He had a black gun too. It was pointing at them.

He stepped out of the elevator and waved his gun at Sean and Isabel. 'You two. What happened to the others?' He glanced across the cavern and his mouth opened. His eyes widened.

Isabel turned away from Adar and pulled the gun from

her waistband, slowly. She would get only one shot. But she wasn't afraid. She'd been top of her class in pistol drill in the Foreign Office the year she'd joined. She swung the gun up. She took a deep breath and shifted fast down onto one knee.

Adar was moving too, turning. The barrel of his gun was coming around. Everything slowed as she watched it coming to face her.

He was too fast.

She heard an echoing crack. Something punched her shoulder, swinging her around. She'd been hit!

She fell. Sean shouted.

But her arm was still in front of her and she was still holding the gun. She sighted along the barrel, and pulled the trigger. The force of the shot sent her shoulder back with an agonising jerk.

And then Sean was pulling her up.

'We gotta go!' He shouted.

She could hear the rats squealing again as she passed Adar. The sound they made was the growl of a hungry pack. She saw a pulsing red hole in Adar's chest as they passed him. He was twitching, his eyes blinking, as if he was trying to get up, but the flow of blood made it clear that he had no chance.

The last thing she saw as the elevator doors closed were the rats jumping high as they reached Adar. He was still alive as they began their meal. His arms flailed and then they were all over him, covering him in a seething whiteness.

The elevator doors closed.

But something was in it with them. She heard Sean screaming. She was leaning against the back wall, dizzy. Then she heard a thud and the squealing stopped.

'What's the code start with?' shouted Sean.

'A hash . . . a . . .' Her voice trailed off.

She could hear him tapping at the keys. He tapped twice. Then they were moving.

The elevator creaked a few times, but she didn't care. Sean had his shirt off. He was tearing it into strips. There was a horrible bone-deep thumping coming from her shoulder.

'Is Alek okay?' she said.

'Sit down,' he shouted at her.

She sat on the wooden floor. There was something warm dripping down the side of her body. Was she under a leak? Then her head was emptying, swirling. It had become light.

There was a voice calling. It was far away.

'Is Alek okay?' she was saying, again and again.

Then there was a buzzing, voices.

But she couldn't understand the words. And everything was dark.

EPILOGUE

It was a month before Henry Mowlam finished his report on what had happened at BXH.

No redundancies had been announced yet at the bank. BXH, and its regulators, were still assessing the damage. The riot that had occurred outside the BXH building in Manhattan had evaporated after the National Guard had turned up, but the shockwaves had taken days to pass in the US.

What happened in the secret mausoleums under the bank didn't come out in anything even approximating the truth. One newspaper claimed the bones discovered in the underground cave had been there for centuries. Another tried to start a panic about commuters being at risk from rats. Then it was revealed that thousands of rats had been killed by a team of specialists in the hours after the cavern was opened up.

The SEC suspended the takeover and BXH's shares as an investigation was carried out into all matters surrounding the events at the bank.

It was unlikely, but not impossible, that the takeover would still go ahead. The other members of the board of the Ebony Dragon hedge fund had disowned Lord Bidoner.

And the Chinese authorities had made clear they had no part in any murders or illegal activity. They denied all knowledge of what Li and his assistant had been up to.

The Vaughanns were charged with a series of offences within days.

Sean, during an interview back in London, blamed himself for what had happened to his family.

Sean had proved that he was waiting at City Airport in the east end of London while the BXH jet was readied for departure, when the dancer was murdered in Soho. Security camera evidence had backed him up.

'You should have gone straight to the police when you discovered Alek was being threatened,' said Henry, softly.

'I know,' said Sean.

'Are you still at BXH?' said Henry.

'No, they terminated the facial recognition project.'

'How's Alek these days,' said Henry.

'He's okay. It's amazing, considering what happened.'

'Kids are very resilient,' said Henry.

'He still has nightmares, though.'

'And Rose Suchard is all right?'

'She's still a bit shaky, but she's very grateful to the Metropolitan police. She says the officers who traced her phone call deserve a medal from the Queen.'

Henry smiled. 'The NYPD released you quickly.' He looked at his notes.

'Not that quickly. They questioned me for twelve hours. I had to repeat the whole thing three times. Lord Bidoner's body led them to an apartment that he had a pass key for. They found Alek's jacket there. The fact that Adar was found to have a knife on him and I was on the security camera tapes in that other building when Grainger was killed was enough to convince them that I was telling the truth.'

'They found other things in Lord Bidoner's apartment too.'

'What things?'

'Pieces of skin in a fridge. That backed up what you said about him burning something weird in a candle.'

'I didn't know that was human skin.'

'It links him to a number of murders. If you ever hear anything about Xena again you must inform us immediately.'

'There wasn't anything about him being a murderer in the newspapers.'

'No, thankfully. He's one psycho the world doesn't need to know about.' He rubbed the table between them, as if rubbing away a stain.

'Has anyone found any trace of Xena or the statue?' said Sean.

'No, she's disappeared into thin air. They found a tunnel, which connects that cave to an abandoned subway station. It was used by whoever built those mausoleums.'

'What do you think was in that statue that Lord Bidoner wanted so badly?'

Henry shrugged.

'I hope I never see it again.' Sean sounded angry for the first time during the two hour interview.

'I can understand that, given everything that happened.' Henry paused. 'I think we can let you go now.'

Isabel opened the door quickly when Sean got home that night.

Her shoulder still had a bandage around it.

They hugged, Sean unwilling to let go. Isabel pulled away.

'It is definitely all over now, isn't it?' she said. 'All that stupid symbol stuff is finished.'

'Yes,' said Sean. He hugged her again.

'Thank God. I never want to hear about any of it again.' She held him tight.

'Do they accept everything you told them?'

'Yes. Everything. He even apologised for doubting me.'

She didn't reply this time. She just hugged him. Hard. He could feel her heart beating, smell her warmth. He breathed it in. He'd been worried about her. She'd been different since the hospital had released her in Manhattan, and it wasn't just because she'd lost a lot of blood and suffered a flesh wound. It seemed she was relishing being alive.

'We've been very lucky,' she whispered. 'Everything's back the way it should be. Now I just want a normal boring life again. No more adventures. Please. And I never want to hear about that Xena bitch ever again.'

'You won't.' He breathed deep. It was all over.

And he hoped he was right about Xena.

Then he pulled away. He'd heard Alek coming down the stairs. He bent down and opened his arms. It was time for them to be a family again.

The Manhattan that I Love

Manhattan, the island that is most of what I know of New York, is a city of the imagination. I dreamed of going there for decades, before I finally arrived on a Greyhound bus from Toronto in 1988. I loved every part of it then. And I still do.

It teems with people. And it's full of wonders. I have been back many times since and every time it shows a different side to me. I have wandered the streets at dawn, when it's almost quiet, and crossed Times Square on a Saturday night when it's jammed full of people, and always it is gorgeous and full of surprises.

I imagine Manhattan as a city in a snow globe, captured for ever in its twentieth-century magnificence, its skyscrapers reaching high and its lights twinkling below.

Here are some of the places I love visiting when I am there:

The Empire State Building is, for me, the iconic New York skyscraper. Located on Fifth Avenue, this building, with its 102 floors, is hard to miss. It is 1,250 feet high and has an antenna at the top that extends by another 204 feet.

It was the tallest building in the world after it was completed in 1931. And it remained the tallest building for forty years afterwards. An art deco masterpiece, it is simply one of the wonders of the modern world. And it was built in just fifteen months. The observation deck, which has seen over one hundred million visitors, took in more than the rent for the whole building during its first year of operation.

The second place I like visiting is also an icon, but this time it is a shop; Macy's. There's something about a huge department store, with great offers on every floor, that says a lot about New York to me. I love a bargain and I love quality. Macy's represents all that.

Apparently there are 798 Macy's stores across America, but it's the iconic store in Herald Square in Midtown Manhattan that I love to visit. Macy's features, in my mind at least, in many classic movies about New York, but the only one it is central to, that I am aware of, is *Miracle on 34th Street*, the 1947 Christmas time movie, which we used to watch repeats of on TV when I was young.

The next place I urge you to visit in Manhattan is a traditional New York diner. They are fast, friendly and the food fills you up.

If you want the classic American hamburger experience a good diner in Manhattan is the way to do it. And if you want something a bit modern, something organic and green, you can get that too in the huge array of diner-type restaurants at street level all over Manhattan. If you're on a budget a Manhattan diner is a great way to see how real New Yorker's live, without maxing the credit card.

After you've had lunch I recommend a visit to Grand Central Terminal. The picture opposite is one I took of a platform deep underground. The distant lights would be approximately where the long-lost platform actually exists connecting the Waldorf Astoria to a siding near Grand Central. I was almost arrested the time I took this picture! Grand Central is still the largest train station in the world, because of its forty-four platforms and sixty-seven tracks. It was largely completed in 1913 although the construction took ten years as the railroad

companies needed to keep the tracks running. And new underground levels are still being built!

One of the innovations of the new terminal, when it was built, was the dual level underground platforms, which are still in use. And this is disregarding the subway system that now connects into Grand Central.

Grand Central is most famous for its huge main concourse, 275 feet long, 120 feet wide and 125 feet high. It features in iconic American movies such as *North by Northwest*, *The Fisher King* and *Superman: The Movie*.

I spent hours in Grand Central the last time I was in Manhattan. It has a pulsing energy and to my mind, a cinnamony smell that is unique. It's a commuter station now, despite its size, so you don't get as many passengers with piles of luggage, but it's still the most romantic of places. You can meet your lover at the information booth in the centre of the main concourse, then head to the Oyster Bar or to one of the other numerous restaurants in the dining concourse.

Grand Central has a whispering gallery too, a low ceramic arch near the Oyster Bar, where a whisper can seem like a shout. It's a popular place for marriage proposals, apparently.

The next place I like to visit in Manhattan is Times Square. The first time I visited the city I listened to a preacher on a soap box at a corner criticising the racial divide in America. The atmosphere was electric. People were hurrying by. The next time I visited in the '90s the atmosphere was totally different. It was more family friendly. And it's stayed that way.

Times Square, also in Midtown Manhattan, is at the intersection of Broadway and Seventh Avenue and stretches from 42nd to 47th Street. It's been called the Crossroads of the World and the Great White Way. The theatres of Broadway are close by and the pull of this whole area sees over 300,000 visitors pass through Times Square every day. It is believed to be the most popular tourist destination in the world with thirty-nine million visitors annually, increasing each year on New Year's Eve when the New Year is ushered in in America with a Waterford crystal ball being lowered at midnight, while a million people watch from the streets all around. Times Square is named after *The New York Times*, which moved to a building in the area in 1904. Soon after the first electrified advertisement sign appeared on another building nearby. From the 1920s until the 1990s the area developed a reputation for sleaze and gangsterism, but that has now been dispelled.

Manhattan has many beautiful sight, its museums, art galleries, restaurants and parks are renowned all over the world. Its sombre memorials are also well worth visiting, but the above are the places in the city that captivated me.

Finally, I would like to thank all the inhabitants of Manhattan and everyone who works to keep the city functioning, for keeping my fantasy city alive while I am not there. Thank you all.